CHIMERASCOPE

DOUGLAS SMITH

D0595675

ChiZine Publications

FIRST EDITION

Chimerascope © 2010 by Douglas Smith
"Introduction" © 2010 by Julie Czerneda
Jacket design © 2009 by Erik Mohr
All Rights Reserved.

LIBRARY AND ARCHIVES CANADA CATALOGUING IN PUBLICATION

Smith, Douglas, 1952 June 2-
    Chimerascope / Douglas Smith ; introduction, Julie Czerneda.

ISBN 978-0-9812978-5-9

    I. Title.

PS8637.M5657C55 2010   C813'.6   C2009-907158-4

CHIZINE PUBLICATIONS
Toronto, Canada
www.chizinepub.com
info@chizinepub.com

Edited, copyedited, and proofread by Sandra Kasturi, Helen Marshall, and Brett Alexander Savory

Printed in Canada

CHIMERASCOPE

To my writer friends in the *Ink*Specs*, who provided much needed critique and support for each of the creatures contained herein: Mici Gold, Lorraine Pooley, Isaac Szpindel, Alex von Thorn, Sue Witts, and the late Ken Basarke

To the many editors who gave these creatures a home, but most especially to Julie Czerneda, Robert J. Sawyer, Tracy Schoenle at *Cicada*, Andy Cox at *TTA*, and everyone at *On Spec*

And finally, with love, to my wife, Susan, and my sons, Mike and Chris, for the love they have always given to the creature who wrote this

Table of Contents

INTRODUCTION
BY JULIE CZERNEDA

. . . I will wear my heart upon my sleeve . . .
—*Othello*, Act One, Scene One, Shakespeare (1604)

To wear your heart upon your sleeve is to expose your innermost emotions to the world. Writers do that. They expose their most private feelings to total strangers. Not once, not by accident, but deliberately and, to all extents and purposes, permanently. Yet writers are not, as a rule, extroverts. We work alone, imagining our worlds and populating them, moving characters through their lives, adding laughter, tears, horror, joy, or simple curiosity at whim. As we work, do we think ourselves safe from discovery? Puppet masters in the dark?

We're not and we know it. The moment our words are read by someone else, we're revealed for who we are, what we feel, how we believe. It's in that moment a writer's honesty and courage must triumph. Heart on a sleeve, where anyone can see it, because anything less is a cheat. The writer who flinches at exposure, who dares not show the depths of his fears and loves or show what truly matters above all else to him as a real person, will fail to capture any reader's head or heart. Worst of all, that writer will fail the story.

Douglas Smith is a quiet man. (He's also charming, handsome, and lights up a room, but I didn't tell you that.) He doesn't talk about himself. He doesn't casually express passionate opinions (except about *Buffy*, but I didn't tell you that, either). He's the classic nice Canuck who hangs back in a crowd, happy to have his friends and family in the spotlight, always there if you need him.

When he writes? Oh, when he writes. That's when Doug takes out his heart, pins it to his sleeve, and shows the world exactly who he is and what he cares about. His stories brim with his love for humanity, warts and all. His characters are regular folks. They make bad choices or face terrifying evil. Some succeed. Others succumb. Many struggle against hopeless odds. But even the most desperate, wrenching tragedies contain the seeds of redemption and love.

I believe you'll know Doug, by the time you've read this collection. Not the details of his life, but what really matters. The details of his heart. The fine workings of a man who believes in family, in love, and in people, despite the overwhelming hardships that can afflict a life. Who knows how marvellous it is when honesty and courage find a way.

Welcome to *Chimerascope*.

Julie Czerneda

AUTHOR'S INTRODUCTION

One of those natures that the ancient fables tell of, as that of the Chimera or Skylla or Kerberos, and the numerous other examples that are told of many forms grown together in one.
—Plato, *Republic* 588c (trans. Shorey)

Chi·mer·a (ki-meer-uh, kahy-meer-uh) *noun*

1. A fire-breathing monster of Greek mythology, commonly represented with a lion's head, a she-goat's body, and a serpent's tail. The Chimera ravaged Lycia before being killed by Bellerophon with the aid of Pegasus.
2. Any imaginary creature made up of grotesquely disparate parts.
3. An impossible or foolish fantasy.

-scope (skohp) *suffix*
1. An instrument used for viewing or examination.

Chi·mer·a·scope (ki-meer-uh-skohp) *noun*
1. An instrument, in book form, used for viewing a disparate (but hopefully, not grotesquely so) collection of impossible (but hopefully not foolish) fantasies.
2. Or not . . .

The book you are holding doesn't breathe fire, nor does it harbour (to the best of my knowledge) any plans to ravage Lycia. Yet assembling this book, my first "full" collection of short fiction, made me feel like I was building a chimera.

Now, writers are used to building fantastic creatures. We call them stories. We construct them from the pieces of ourselves that make us who we are—all the accumulated detritus of a lifetime of experiences, good and bad, happy and sad, remembered and imagined.

These story creatures remain caged inside our heads and our souls, until we write them into freedom, releasing them into the world, unleashing them on an unsuspecting humanity. And then we do it again. Another story. Another metaphorical monster ready to ravage some symbolic Lycia.

The problem comes when we try to recapture these beasts and squoosh them into a larger creature of the imagination called a story collection. The resulting creation often consists of, as per definition #2, "grotesquely disparate parts."

But maybe they do fit. Maybe you can't see the stitches where I've sewn these tales together, one after another, back to back, in some supposed order, to build the bigger beast. Or worse (from the writer's perspective), the larger creature may be only too coherent.

I'm sure that I have themes that I deal with repeatedly in my writing. Perhaps the creations that are my stories, assembled together here in this chimera that you hold, will reveal that larger creature, a thing built from loves and hates, dreams and fears, prejudices and paranoias. I just can't say that this larger creature appears clearly to me.

I know that I write about characters that I care about and like to spend time with. I know I write about love—lost, found, and lost again. I know that my preferred ending is bittersweet, because that's how I see life. I write about myths, because they have endured for a reason. I write about people with things inside them, because we all have things inside us.

In short, I write about a lot of things, which makes this book the chimera that it is.

When I was assembling this collection, I found, to my surprise, that I couldn't include all the stories that I wanted to. So some stories will have to wait for the next collection, if there is one. What I've included here are my own favourites and favourites of fans who have been kind enough over the years to tell me so. All of the stories, save one new one that appears here for the first time, have appeared in professional magazines and anthologies. This collection includes early stories through to more recent ones, and spans just over a decade of my writing. It includes a mix of SF, fantasy, horror, and surreal, sometimes in the same story. And, in case you believe that awards are any indication of merit, it includes one Aurora Award winner (a Canadian thingy), nine Aurora finalists, a Best New Horror selection, and three Year's Best Fantasy & Horror honourable mentions.

I struggled with how to arrange the stories. By genre? Mood? Style? Date written? Date published? In the end, does it matter? I mean, you're going to read them all, right? *Right?*

Well, in the end, I had to put them in some order. So, since this collection is an assemblage of disparate parts, I went with a disparate ordering as well. I've arranged them more or less chronologically, with most of the older stories in the first half, but I've tried to alternate stories in terms of genre, mood, and length. So as much as possible, the stories will move from fantasy to SF to horror and back again, from sad to upbeat, from dystopic futures to hopeful ones, from love lost to happily ever after.

And hopefully, assembled as they are, these many forms will grow together into one.

Enjoy.

Douglas Smith
2009

Ever since my oldest son was about five and until my youngest son decided it was no longer cool, we'd go to a circus that toured Toronto each summer. The circus would just set up in the parking lot of a big suburban shopping mall, charge way too much for popcorn and candyfloss, and put on a fair to middling show. It was no Cirque du Soleil, but it was for a good cause and we had fun. My youngest son is physically handicapped, so when he started going, we'd always sit in the area reserved for wheelchairs right at ringside. Being that close let me notice something I'd missed from farther back. All of the performers did double or triple duty as circus hands, setting up equipment, acting as safety catchers, or even shovelling up after the horses and elephants. Seeing the trapeze artist, who had just dazzled the crowd in a spiffy sequin outfit, show up in coveralls to clean up elephant poop gave me the idea of a down-and-out circus of aliens, just scraping by. I coupled it with another idea about a drug I ended up calling Scream, made the big act a pair of bird-like aliens, and wrapped it around a character called Trelayne. "Scream Angel" won the Canadian Aurora Award in 2004 for best short story and received an honourable mention in The Year's Best Fantasy & Horror.

They stopped beating Trelayne when they saw that he enjoyed it. The thugs that passed as cops in that town on Long Shot backed away from where he lay curled on the dirt floor, as if he was something dead or dangerous. He watched them lock the door of his cold little cell again. Disgust and something like fear showed in their eyes. The taste of their contempt for him mixed with the sharpness of his own blood in his mouth. And the *Scream* in that blood shot another stab of pleasure through him.

He expected their reaction. The Merged Corporate Entity guarded its secrets well, and Scream was its most precious. Long Shot lay far from any Entity project world and well off the jump route linking Earth and the frontier. No one on this backwater planet would know of the drug, let alone have encountered a Screamer or an Angel. That was why he had picked it.

Their footsteps receded, and the outer door of the plasteel storage hut that served as the town jail clanged shut. Alone, he rolled onto his side on the floor, relishing the agony the movement brought. He tried to recall how he came to be there, but the Scream in him turned each attempt into an emotional sideshow. Finally he remembered something burning, something . . .

. . . *falling.*

It had been one of their better shows.

He remembered now. Remembered last night, standing in the ring of their makeshift circus dome, announcing the performers to an uncaring crowd, crying out the names of the damned, the conquered. Each member of his refugee band emerged from behind torn red curtains and propelled themselves in the manner of their species into or above the ring, depending on their chosen act.

He knew the acts meant little. The crowd came not to see feats of acrobatics or strength, but to gawk at otherworldly strangeness, to watch aliens bow in submission before the mighty human. Trelayne's circus consisted of the remnants of the subjugated races of a score of worlds, victims to the Entity's resource extraction or terraforming projects: the Stone Puppies, lumbering silica beasts of slate-sided bulk—Guppert the Strong, squat bulbous-limbed refugee from the crushing gravity and equally crushing mining of Mendlos II—Feran the fox-child, his people hunted down like animals on Fandor IV.

And the Angels. Always the Angels.

But curled in the dirt in the cold cell, recalling last night, Trelayne pushed away any thoughts of the Angels. And of *her*.

Yes, it had been a fine show. Until the Ta'lona died, exploding in blood and brilliance high above the ring, after floating too near a torch. Trelayne had bought the gas bag creature's freedom a week before from an *ip* slaver, knowing that its species had been nearly wiped out.

As pieces of the fat alien had fallen flaming into the crowd, Trelayne's grip on reality had shattered like a funhouse mirror struck by a hammer. He could now recall only flashes of what had followed last night: people burning—screaming—panic—a stampede to the exits—his arrest.

Nor could he remember doing any Scream. He usually stayed clean before a show. But he knew what he felt now lying in the cell—the joy of the beating, the ecstasy of humiliation. He must have done a hit when the chaos began and the smell of burnt flesh reached him. To escape the horror.

Or to enter it. For with Scream, horror opened a door to heaven.

Someone cleared their throat in the cell. Trelayne jumped, then shivered at the thrill of surprise. Moaning, he rolled onto his back on the floor and opened his eyes, struggling to orient himself again.

A man now sat on the cot in the cell. A man with a lean face and eyes that reminded Trelayne of his own. He wore a long grey cloak with a major's rank and a small insignia on which a red "RIP" hovered over a green planet split by a lightning bolt.

The uniform of RIP Force. A uniform that Trelayne had worn a lifetime ago. Grey meant Special Services: this man was RIP, but not a Screamer. RIP kept senior officers and the SS clean.

The man studied a PerComm unit held in a black-gloved hand, then looked down at Trelayne and smiled. "Hello, Captain Trelayne," he said softly, as if he were addressing a child.

Trelayne swallowed. He was shaking and realized he had been since he had recognized the uniform. "My name is not Trelayne."

"I am Weitz," the man said. The PerComm disappeared inside his cloak. "And the blood sample I took from you confirms that you are Jason Lewiston Trelayne, former captain and wing commander in the Entity's Forces for the Relocation of Indigenous Peoples, commonly known as RIP Force. Convicted of treason in absentia three years ago, 2056-12-05 AD. Presumed dead in the MCE raid on the rebel base on Darcon III in 2057-08-26."

Trelayne licked his lips, savouring the flavour of his fear.

"You're a wanted man, Trelayne." Weitz's voice was soft. "Or would be, if the Entity knew you were still alive."

The Scream in Trelayne turned the threat in those words into a thrilling chill up his spine. He giggled.

Weitz sighed. "I've never seen a Screamer alive three years after RIP. Dead by their own hand inside a month more likely. But then, most don't have their own source, do they?"

The implication of those words broke through the walls of Scream in Trelayne's mind. Weitz represented real danger—to him, to those in the circus that depended on him. To *her*. Trelayne struggled to focus on the man's words.

". . . good choice," Weitz was saying. "Not a spot the Entity has any interest in now. You'd never see Rippers here—" Weitz smiled. "—unless they had ship trouble. I was in the next town waiting for repairs when I heard of a riot at a circus of ips."

Ips—IPs—Indigenous Peoples. A Ripper slur for aliens.

Weitz stood up. "You have an Angel breeding pair, Captain, and I need them." He pushed open the cell door and walked out, leaving the door open. "I've arranged for your release. You're free to go. Not that you can go far. We'll talk again soon." Looking back to where Trelayne lay shivering, Weitz shook his head. "Jeezus, Trelayne. You used to be my hero."

Trelayne slumped back down on the floor, smiling as the smell of dirt and stale urine stung his throat. "I used to be a lot of things," he said, as much to himself as to Weitz.

Weitz shook his head again. "We'll talk soon, Captain." He turned and left the hut.

Think of human emotional response as a sine wave function. Peaks and valleys. The peaks represent pleasure, and the valleys pain. The greater your joy, the higher the peak; the greater your pain, the deeper the valley.

Imagine a drug that takes the valleys and flips them, makes them peaks, too. You react now to an event based not on the pleasure or pain inherent in it, but solely on the intensity of the emotion created. Pain brings pleasure, grief gives joy, horror renders ecstasy.

Now give this drug to one who must perform an unpleasant task. No. Worse than that. An immoral deed. Still worse. A nightmare act of chilling terminal brutality. Give it to a soldier. Tell them to kill. Not in the historically acceptable murder we call war, but in a systematic corporate strategy—planned, scheduled, and budgeted—of xenocide.

They will kill. And they will revel in it.

Welcome to the world of Scream.

—Extract from propaganda data bomb launched on Fandor IV CommCon by rebel forces, 2056-10-05 AD. Attributed to Capt. Jason L. Trelayne during his subsequent trial in absentia for treason.

Feran thought tonight's show was their finest since the marvellous Ta'lona had died, now a five-day ago. From behind the red curtains that hid the performers' entrance, the young kit watched the two Angels, Philomela and Procne, plummet from the top of the dome to swoop over the man-people crowd. Remembering how wonderfully the fat alien had burnt, Feran also recalled the Captain explaining to him how that night had been bad. The Captain had been forced to give much power-stuff for the burnt man-people and other things that Feran did not understand.

The Angels completed a complicated spiral dive, interweaving their descents. Linking arms just above the main ring, they finished with a dizzying spin like the top the Captain had made him. They bowed to the applauding crowd, folding and unfolding diaphanous wings so the spotlights sparkled on the colours.

Feran clapped his furred hands together as Mojo had taught him, closing his ear folds to shut out the painful noise of the man-people. As the performers filed out for the closing procession around the centre ring, Feran ran to take his spot behind the Stone Puppies. Guppert the Strong lifted Feran gently to place him on the slate-grey back of the nearest silica beast.

"Good show, little friend!" Guppert cried. His squat form waddled beside Feran. Guppert liked Long Shot because it did not hold him to the ground as did his home of Mendlos. "Of course, Guppert never go home now," he had told Feran once, his skin colour darkening to show sadness. "Off-planet too long. Mendlos crush Guppert, as if Stone Puppy step on Feran. But with Earth soldiers there in mecha-suits, now Mendlos not home anyway."

Waving to the crowd, the performers disappeared one by one through the red curtains. Feran leapt from the Stone Puppy, shouted a goodbye to Guppert, and scurried off to search for Philomela. Outside the show dome, he sniffed the cool night air for her scent, found it, then turned and ran into the Cutter.

"Whoa, Red! What's the rush?" The tall thin man scowled down at Feran like an angry mantis. The Cutter was the healer for the circus. "Helpin' us die in easy stages, s'more like it," was how the Cutter had introduced himself when Feran had arrived.

"I seek the Bird Queen, Cutter," Feran replied.

Sighing, the Cutter jerked a thumb toward a cluster of small dome pods where the performers lived. Feran thought of it as the den area. "Don't let him take too much, you hear?"

Feran nodded and ran off again, until a voice like wind in crystal trees halted him. "You did well tonight, sharp ears."

Feran turned. Philomela smiled down at him, white hair and pale skin, tall and thin like an earth woman stretched to something alien in a trick mirror. Even walking, she made Feran think of birds in flight. Philomela was beautiful. The Captain had told him so many times. He would likely tell Feran again tonight, once he had breathed her dust that Feran brought him.

"Thank you, Bird Queen," Feran replied, bowing low with a sweep of his hand as the Captain had taught him. Philomela laughed, and Feran bared his teeth in joy. He had made the beautiful bird lady laugh. The Captain would be pleased.

Procne came to stand behind Philomela, his spider-fingered hand circling her slim waist. "Where do you go now, Feran? Does Mojo still have chores for you?" He looked much like her, taller, heavier, but features still delicate, almost feminine. His stomach pouch skin rippled where the brood moved inside him.

"He goes to the Captain's pod," Philomela said. "They talk—about the times when the Captain flew in the ships. Don't you?"

Feran nodded. Procne's eyelids slid in from each side, leaving only a vertical slit. "The times when those ships flew over our homes, you mean? Your home, too, Feran." Procne spun and stalked away, his wings pulled tight against his back.

Feran stared after him, then up at Philomela. "Did I do wrong, Bird Queen?"

Philomela folded and unfolded her wings. "No, little one, no. My mate remembers too much, yet forgets much, too." She paused. "As does the Captain." She stroked Feran's fur where it lay red and soft between his large ears, then handed him a small pouch. "Feran, tonight don't let the Captain breathe too much of my dust. Get him to sleep early. He looks so . . . tired."

Feran took the pouch and nodded. He decided he would not tell the Captain of Philomela's face as she walked away.

>>>>>>>>>>>>>> **Merged Corporate Entity, Inc.** >>>>>>>>>>>>>
Project Search Request

Search Date: 2059-06-02

Requestor: *Weitz, David R., Major, RIP Special Services*

Search Criteria:

Project World: *All*   Division: *PharmaCorps*

Product: *Scream*   Context: *Field Ops / Post-Imp*

Clearance Required: AAA   Your Clearance: AAA

>>>>>>>>>>> **Access Granted. Search results follow.** >>>>>>>>>>

Scream mimics several classes of psychotropics, including psychomotor stimulants, antidepressants, and narcotic analgesics. It acts on both stimulatory *and* inhibitory neurotransmitters, but avoids hallucinogenic effects by maintaining neurotransmitter balance. It enhances sensory ability, speeds muscular reaction, and lessens nerve response to pain. It affects all three opiate receptors, inducing intense euphoria without narcotic drowsiness.

Physical addiction is achieved by four to six ingestions at dosage prescribed in Field Ops release 2.21.7.1. Treated personnel exhibit significantly lowered resistance to violence. Secondary benefits for field operations include decreased fatigue, delayed sleep on-set, and enhanced mental capacity.

Negative side effects include uncontrolled masochistic or sadistic tendencies, such as self-mutilation or attacks on fellow soldiers. Scream is therefore not administered until military discipline and obedience programming is completed in boot camp. Long-term complications include paranoid psychoses and suicidal depression. Withdrawal is characterized by hallucinations, delirium, and seizures, terminating with strokes or heart attacks.

Attempts to synthesize continue, but at present our sole source remains extraction from females of the dominant humanoids on Lania II, *Xeno sapiens lania var. angelus* (colloq.: Scream Angel). The liquid produced crystallizes into powder form. Since the drug is tied to reproduction (see Xenobiology: Lania: Life Forms: 1275), ensuring supply requires an inventory of breeding pairs with brood delivery dates spread evenly over—

*** *File Transfer Request Acknowledged* ***
Xenobiology File: Lania: Life Forms: 1275

The adult female produces the drug from mammary glands at all times but at higher levels in the reproductive cycle. Sexual coupling occurs at both the start and end of the cycle. The first act impregnates the female. The brood develops in her until delivery after thirty weeks in what the original Teplosky journal called the "larval form," transferring then to the male's pouch via orifices in his abdominal wall. For the next nineteen weeks, they feed from the male, who ingests large quantities of Scream from the female. The brood's impending release as mature nestlings prompts the male to initiate the final coupling—

Trelayne lay in his sleep pod at the circus waiting for Feran and the hit of Scream that the kit brought each night. The meeting with Weitz had burst a dam of times past, flooding him with memories. He closed his eyes, his face wet with delicious tears. Though all his dreams were nightmares, he did not fear them. Terror was now but another form of pleasure. Sleep at least freed him from the tyranny of decision.

Twenty again. My first action. I remember . . . Remember? I'd give my soul to forget, if my soul remains for me to barter.

Bodies falling against a slate-grey sky . . .

The RIP transports on Fandor IV were huge oblate spheroids, flattened and wider in the middle than at the ends. Trelayne and almost one hundred other Rippers occupied the jump seats that lined the perimeter of the main bay, facing in, officers near the cockpit. Before them, maybe a hundred Fandor natives huddled on the metal floor, eyes downcast but constantly darting around the hold and over their captors. The adults were about five feet tall and humanoid, but their soft red facial hair, pointed snouts and ears gave them a feral look. The children reminded Trelayne of a stuffed toy he had as a child.

Fresh from RIP boot camp, this was to be his first action. These Fandorae came from a village located over rich mineral deposits soon to be an Entity mining operation. They were to be "relocated" to an island off the west coast. He added the quotes in response to a growing suspicion, fed by overheard jokes shared by RIP veterans. He also recalled arriving on Fandor, scanning the ocean on the approach to the RIP base on the west shore.

There were no islands off the coast.

The other Rippers shifted and fidgeted, waiting for their first hit of the day. The life support system of their field suits released Scream directly into their blood, once each suit's computer received the transmitted command from the RIP Force unit leader. If you wanted your Scream, you suited up and followed orders. And god, you wanted your Scream.

His unit had been on Scream since the end of boot camp. Trelayne knew he was addicted. He knew that RIP wanted him and all his unit addicted. He just didn't know why. He had also noticed that no one in his unit had family. No one would miss any of them. Another reason to follow orders.

Twenty minutes out from the coast, a major unbuckled his boost harness and nodded to a captain to his right. Every Ripper watched as the captain hit a button on his wrist pad.

The Scream came like the remembered sting of an old wound, a friend that you hadn't seen in years and once reunited, you wondered why you had missed them.

The captain's voice barked in their headsets, ordering them out of their harnesses. Trelayne rose as one with the other Rippers, StAB rod charged and ready, the Scream in him twisting his growing horror into the anticipation of ecstasy. The Fandorae huddled closer together in the middle of the bay.

The captain punched another button. Trelayne felt the deck

thrumming through his boots as the centre bay doors split open. The Fandorae leapt up, grabbing their young and skittering back from the widening hole, only to face an advancing wall of Rippers with lowered StAB rods.

Some of the Fandorae chose to leap. Some were pushed by their own people in the panic. Others fell on the StAB rods or died huddled over their young.

Trelayne pulled a kit, no more than a year, from under a dead female. He held the child in his arms, waiting his turn as the Rippers in front of him lifted or pushed the remaining bodies through the bay doors. When he reached the edge, Trelayne lifted the kit from his shoulder and held it over the opening. It did not squirm or cry, only stared a mute accusation. Trelayne let go, then knelt to peer over the edge.

A salt wind stung sharp and cold where it crept under his helmet. He watched the kit fall to hit the rough grey sea a hundred feet below. Most of the bodies had already slipped beneath the waves. The kit disappeared to join them.

A nausea that even Scream could not deflect seized Trelayne. Pushing back from the edge, he wrenched his visor up to gasp in air. A Ripper beside him turned to him, and for a brief moment Trelayne caught his own reflection in the man's mirrored visor. The image burned into his memory as he fought to reconcile the horror engulfing him with the grinning mask of his own face . . .

Dreaming still . . . falling still . . . falling in love . . .

Trelayne made captain in a year, as high as Screamers could rise in RIP. He took no pride in it. When the Scream ran low in him, his guilt rose black and bottomless. But his addiction was now complete. Withdrawal for a Screamer meant weeks of agony, without the filter of Scream, then death. The Entity was his only source. He did what he was told.

Rippers burnt out fast on project worlds, so the Entity rotated them off relo work every six months for a four-week tour on a "processed" world. Trelayne's first tour after making captain was on Lania, the Angel home planet, arranging transport of Angel breeding pairs from Lania to project worlds with RIP Force units. The Entity had found that, with Angels on-planet, concerns over Scream delivery could be put aside for that world.

Sex with an Angel, said RIP veterans, was the ultimate high. But upon arrival, Trelayne had found them too alien, too thin and wraith-like. He decided that their reputation was due more to ingesting uncut Scream during sex than to their ethereal beauty.

Then he saw *her*.

She was one of a hundred Angels being herded into a cargo shuttle that would dock with an orbiting jump ship. Angels staggered by Trelayne, their eyes downcast. He started to turn away when he saw her: striding with head held high, glaring at the guards. She turned as she passed him. Their eyes locked.

He ordered her removed from the shipment. That is how he met her. As her captor. Then her liberator. Then her lover.

The Earth name she had taken was Philomela. Her Angel name could not be produced by a human throat. She brought him joy and pain. He was never sure what he brought her. She gave herself willingly, and her pleasure in their lovemaking seemed so sincere that he sometimes let himself believe—believe that she clung to *him* in those moments, not to a desperate hope for freedom. That she did not hate him for what RIP had done to her people.

That she loved him.

But Scream strangled such moments. Though not on combat doses, he still needed it for physical dependency. On low doses, depression clouded life in a grey mist. Could she love him when he doubted his own love for her? Why was he drawn to her? Sex? His private source of Scream? To wash his hands clean by saving one of his victims? And always between them loomed an impassable chasm: they were separate species who could never be truly mated.

The news reached him one rare afternoon as they lay together in his quarters. His PerComm unit, hanging on the wall above them, began to buzz like an angry insect. He pulled it down and read the message from the Cutter, the medic in his unit.

She watched him as he read. "Jase, is something wrong?"

He had come to expect her empathy. Whether she could now read his human expressions or sense his mood, he didn't know. He threw the unit away as if it had stung him and covered his face with a hand. "Mojo. One of my men, a friend. He's *fallen*."

"Is he—"

"He's alive. No serious injuries." As if that mattered.

"Do you think he tried to take his life?"

"No," he said, though the drug in him screamed yes.

"Many do—"

"No! Not Mojo." But he knew she was right. Suicide was common with Screamers, and "joining the Fallen" was a favoured method—a dive that you never came out of. The Entity punished any survivors brutally. Screamers were easily replaced, but one LASh jet could cut the return on a project world by a full point.

"Now comes the judging your people do?" she asked.

"Court martial. Two weeks." If they found Mojo guilty, they would discharge him. No source of Scream. *Better to have died in the crash*, he thought. He got out of bed and began dressing. "I have to leave Lania, return to my base. Try to help him."

"They will judge against him. You will not change that."

"I know. But I have to try. He has no one else."

She turned away. "We have few moments together."

She was shaking, and he realized that she was crying. He misunderstood. "I'll be back soon. It'll be better then."

She shook her head and looked up at him. "I mean that we have few moments *left*. It is my time."

He stood there staring down at her. "What do you mean?

"I must produce a brood." She turned away again.

"You mean you will take a mate. One of your own kind."

"His name is Procne," she said, still not looking at him.

He didn't know what to do or say, so he kept dressing.

She turned to him. "I love you," she said quietly.

28

He stopped. She waited. He said nothing. She lay down, sobbing. He swallowed and formed the thought in his mind, opened his mouth to tell her that he loved her, too, when she spoke again. "What will become of me?" she asked.

All his doubts about her rushed in to drown the words in his mouth. He was but a way of escape to her. She did not love him. She would give herself to one of her own. She was alien. The Angels hated RIP for what they had done. She hated him.

He pulled on his jacket and turned away . . .

The trial. I tried, Mojo—but nothing can save us when we fall, and we were falling the moment they put it in our blood . . .

The day after Mojo's trial, Trelayne entered the RIP barracks pod. The Cutter and two other Rippers sat on drop-bunks watching Mojo stuff his few possessions into a canister pack. Mojo wore his old civvies, now at least a size too small. He still had a Medistim on his arm, and he moved with a limp.

The others jumped to attention when they saw their visitor. Cutter just nodded. Trelayne returned the salutes then motioned toward the door. After a few words and half-hearted slaps on Mojo's back, they filed out, leaving Trelayne and Mojo alone.

Mojo sat down on his bunk. "Thanks, Cap. Hell of a try."

Trelayne sat, forcing a smile. "You forget we lost?"

Mojo shrugged. "Never had a chance. You know that. None of us do. Just a matter of time. If the Scream don't get you, they will. No way out for the likes of us."

Trelayne searched Mojo's broad face. *I have to try*, he thought. *We won't get another chance.* "Maybe there is a way."

Narrowing his eyes, Mojo glanced at the door and back again. He looked grim. "I'm with you, Cap. Whatever, wherever."

Trelayne shook his head. "They'll kill us if we're caught."

"I'm a dead man already. We all are."

Trelayne sighed and started talking . . .

And so the fallen dreamed of rising again, eh Mojo? What fools we were. But we gave them a run for a while, didn't we?

Trelayne returned to Lania. In his absence, Philomela had taken Procne as her mate. She refused to see Trelayne. He added her and Procne to the next cargo of Angels being shipped to the project worlds, with himself as the ship's captain.

He did not see her until after their ship had made the first jump. Philomela was summoned to the captain's cabin, to be told to which planet she and her mate had been consigned.

She stiffened when she entered and saw him. "You."

He nodded and waited.

"Sending us into slavery to be bred and milked like animals, this was not enough? You had to be here to see it happen, did you, Jason?" She looked around. "Where is the captain?"

"I am the captain on this trip."

She looked confused. "But you have never gone on these . . ."

He sighed. "Please sit. I have much to say . . ."

Why did I risk everything to save her? Love? Guilt? As penance? For her Scream? In a desperate hope that one day she would turn to me again? Or as I fell, was I willing to grasp at anything, even if I pulled those I loved down with me?

From the ship's observation deck, Trelayne and Philomela watched a shuttle depart, carrying a "shipment" of twenty pairs of Angels for the project world below.

"Do you know why I chose my Earth name?" she asked.

Her voice was flat, dead, but he heard the pain that each of these worlds brought her as more of her people were torn away, while she remained safe, protected. "No. Tell me," he said.

"In a legend of your planet, Philomela was a girl turned into a nightingale by the gods. That image pleased me, to be chosen by the gods, elevated to the heavens. Only later did I learn that the nightingale is also a symbol of death."

Trelayne bowed his head. "Phi, there's nothing—"

"No, but allow me at least my bitterness. And guilt."

Guilty of being spared. By him. She and Procne spared, only because an addict and xenocide and soon-to-be traitor needed his drug source close. He had stopped trying to examine his motives beyond that. The Scream would mock the small voice in him that spoke of a last remnant of honour and noble intent.

"My sister is on that shuttle," Philomela said quietly.

Trelayne said nothing for there was nothing to say. They watched the tiny ship fall toward the planet below . . .

At each planet on that trip, we gathered to us the castoffs, the unwanted, the remnants of a dozen races, together with the Fallen. And then, suddenly, there was no turning back . . .

Trelayne's first officer, a young lieutenant-commander named Glandis, confronted him on the bridge. She wasn't backing down this time. "Captain, I must again register my concern over continued irregularities in your command of this mission."

Trelayne glanced at the monitor by his chair. Mojo and eleven other ex-Rippers were disembarking from a shuttle in the ship's docking bay. In two minutes, they would be on the bridge. He tapped a command, deactivating all internal communications and alarms. He turned to Glandis. "Irregularities?"

"The ip *cargo* we have acquired at each of our stops."

"Those *people* are to be transported to the Entity's Product R&D centre on Earth," Trelayne responded.

Glandis snorted. "What research could the Entity conduct with—" She read from her PerComm. "—a Mendlos subject?"

"Physiological adaptation to high-grav," Trelayne replied.

"A Fandorae kit? A Fanarucci viper egg?"

"Biotech aural receptor design, and neural poison mutagenics development." *One minute more*, he thought.

Glandis hesitated, some of the confidence leaving her face. "You have also protected one specific breeding pair of Angels for purposes that have yet to be made clear to me."

"They, too, are slated for Entity research." Trelayne rose. *Thirty seconds.* "Synthesization of Scream."

"What about this stop? It was not on our filed flight plan."

"Late orders from RIP Force command." *Fifteen seconds.*

"I was not informed."

"You just were."

Glandis reddened. "And what purpose will a dozen disgraced ex-members of RIP Force serve?"

Now, thought Trelayne. The door to the bridge slid open. Mojo and four other ex-Rippers burst in, Tanzer rifles charged and pointed at Glandis and the bridge crew. Glandis turned to Trelayne with mouth open then froze.

Trelayne had his own weapon levelled at Glandis. "Their purpose, I'm afraid, is to replace the crew of this ship."

And so the Fallen rose again, to scale a precipice from which there was no retreat, and each new height we gained only made the final fall that much farther . . .

After leaving the Bird Queen, Feran ran past the closed tubes of the barkers, the games of chance, and the sleep pods of the performers. The kit moved easily among the ropes, refuse, and equipment, his path clear to him even in the dim light of sputtering torches and an occasional hovering glow-globe.

The show used fewer glow-globes than when Feran had first arrived. The Captain said the globes cost too much now. Feran didn't mind. He needed little light to see, and liked the smell of the torches and the crackle they made.

Turning a corner, Feran froze. Weasel Man stood outside the Captain's pod. The Captain said that the man's name was Weitz, but he reminded Feran of the animals the kit hunted in the woods outside the circus. The door opened. Weasel Man stepped inside.

Feran crept to the open window at the pod's side. He could hear voices. His nose twitched. His ears snapped up and opened wide, adjusting until the sound was the sharpest.

Trelayne lay on his sleep pod bunk, shaking from withdrawal. Feran was late bringing his nightly hit. Weitz lounged in a chair, staring at him. It had been five days since their meeting in the jail. "Where've you been, Weitz?" Trelayne wheezed.

"Had some arrangements to make. Need a hit, don't you?"

"It's coming," Trelayne mumbled. "What do you want?"

Weitz shrugged. "I told you. The Angels."

"But not to hand them back to the Entity, or you'd have done it by now," Trelayne said. But if Weitz wanted the Angels, why didn't he just take them? He had his own men and a ship.

Weitz smiled. "Do you know there are rebels on Fandor IV?"

"Rebels? What are you talking about?" Where was Feran?

"Ex-RIP rebels like you, or rather, like you once were."

"Like me? God, then I pity the rebels on Fandor IV."

Weitz leaned forward in his chair. "I'm one of them."

Trelayne laughed. "You're RIP SS."

"I assist from the *inside*. I supply them with Scream."

Trelayne stared at Weitz. This man was far more dangerous than he had first appeared. "You've managed to surprise me, Major. Why would you risk your life for a bunch of rebels?"

Weitz shrugged. "I said you were my hero. The man who defied an empire. I want to do my part, too."

Trelayne snorted. "Out of the goodness of your heart."

Weitz reddened. "I cover my costs. No more."

I'll bet, Trelayne thought. "Where do you get Scream?"

"I . . . acquired a store doing an SS audit of a RIP warehouse."

"You stole it. A store? Since when can you store Scream?"

Weitz smiled. "A result of intense research prompted by your escape with the Angels. You made the Entity realize the risk of transporting breeding pairs. Angels are now kept in secure facilities on Lania and two other worlds, producing Scream that's shipped to project worlds with RIP forces. Angels live and die without *ever* leaving the facility they were born into."

Trelayne shuddered. Because of him. But the Scream in him ran too low to find any joy in this new horror.

They fell silent. Finally Weitz spoke. "So what happened, Trelayne? To the Great Rebel Leader? To the one man who stood up to the Entity? How'd it all go to hell?"

"Screamers are in hell already. We were trying to get out."

"You got out, in a stolen Entity cruiser. Then what?"

Shivering, Trelayne struggled to sit up. Where was Feran? "We jumped to a system the Entity had already rejected. Only one habitable planet. No resources worth the extraction cost."

"And set up a base for a guerrilla war on the Entity."

"No. A colony. A home for the dispossessed races."

"You attacked Entity project worlds," Weitz said.

"We sent messages. There was never any physical assault."

"Your data bombs flooded Comm systems for entire planets."

"We tried to make people aware of what the Entity was doing. Almost worked." Trelayne fought withdrawal, trying to focus on Weitz. The man was afraid of something. But what?

"I'll say. You cost them trillions hushing it up, flushing systems. But then what? The reports just end."

"The Entity still has a file on us?" That pleased Trelayne.

"On you," Weitz corrected. "You've got your own entire file sequence. Special clearance needed to get at them. Well?"

Trelayne fell silent, remembering the day, remembering his guilt. "I got careless. They tracked us through a jump somehow, found the colony, T-beamed it from orbit."

"An entire planet? My god!" Weitz whispered.

"A few of us escaped." But not Phi's children, her first brood. More guilt, though she had never blamed him.

"In a heavily armed cruiser with a crew of ex-Rippers."

He looked at Weitz. *That* was it. Even through the haze of withdrawal, he knew he had his answer: Weitz thought Trelayne still had a band of ex-Rippers at hand, battle-proven trained killers with super-human reflexes and their own Scream supply. Something like hope tried to fight through the black despair of his withdrawal. Weitz would try to deal first.

"And this?" Weitz took in the circus with a wave of a hand.

"After we lost the base, we had to keep moving. As a cover story to clear immigration on each world, I concocted a circus of aliens. Then I ran out of money, had to do it for real."

"What if someone had recognized you? Or knew about Angels?"

Trelayne struggled to speak. "We avoided anywhere with an Entity presence, stayed off the main jump routes." He started to shiver. "Why do you want Angels if you have a store of Scream?"

"My supply'll run out, and I can't count on stealing more."

Trelayne stared at Weitz. "So what's the deal?"

Weitz smiled. "Why do you think I won't just take them?"

"Against a crew of ex-Rippers pumped on Scream?"

Weitz's smile faded. He studied Trelayne. "Okay. Let's assess your position. One: I gave your ship's beacon signature to Long Shot's space defence. If you run, you'll be caught."

Trelayne said nothing.

"Two: if you're caught, your ip pals get sent back to their home worlds. And you know what that means."

Trelayne stayed silent, but his skin went cold.

"Three: you, Mojo, and the medic get executed for treason."

"Like I said, what's the deal?"

Weitz studied Trelayne again, then finally spoke. "Both Angels for my store of Scream—a lifetime supply for you and your men. I lift the order on your ship and turn my back as you and your band jump. Your life goes on, with Scream but no Angels."

Life goes on, if you called this life. That much Scream was worth a fortune. But nowhere near the value of a breeding pair.

So there it was. Betray his love or die. What choice did he have? Refuse, and Weitz would turn them over to the Entity, and all would die. Run, and be killed or caught by the planetary fleet. Give her up, along with Procne, and at least the others would be free. Besides, she had turned from him, taken one of her own. She had only used him to escape, had always used him. She was an alien and hated him for what he had done to her race.

She had never really loved him.

All that stood against this were the remnants of his love for her, and a phantom memory of the man he once had been.

Outside, Feran waited for the Captain's reply to Weasel Man. He didn't know what the Captain would do but he knew it would be brave and noble. Feran listened for the sound of the Captain leaping to his feet and striking Weasel Man to the floor. But when a sound came, it was only the Captain's voice, small and hoarse. "All right," was all he said.

"You'll do it?" That was Weasel Man. Feran did not hear a reply. "Tomorrow morning." Weasel Man again. The door opened, and Feran scooted under the pod. Weasel Man stepped out smiling. Feran had seen sand babies smile like that on Fandor just before they spit their venom in your eyes.

As he watched the man walk away, fading into the darkness, something inside Feran faded away as well. He stood staring into the shadows for a long time, then turned and entered the pod. The Captain lay in his sleeping place. He seemed not to notice Feran. The kit put the pouch from the Bird Queen on the table, then left without a word. The Captain did not call after him.

How long Feran wandered the grounds, he did not know. Some time later, he found the Cutter and Mojo sitting in front of a fire burning on an old heat shield panel from the ship.

"Seen the Captain, Feran?" asked Mojo. Feran just nodded.

"He's had his bottle? All tucked in for the night?" the Cutter asked. Feran nodded again as Mojo scowled at the Cutter.

They sat silently for a while. "Does it hurt when you lose someone you love?" Feran asked, ashamed of the fear in his voice, the fear that he felt for Philomela.

The Cutter spoke. "Hurts even more to lose 'em slowly. Watch 'em disappear bit by bit 'til nothing's left you remember."

Feran knew the Cutter meant the Captain. "Shut up, Cutter," Mojo growled. "You've never been there. Only a Screamer knows what he lives with." He patted Feran's head. "Never mind, kid."

The Cutter shook his head but spoke no more. Feran rose and

walked slowly away to once again wander the Circus grounds. This time, however, something resolved itself inside his young mind so that when he found himself outside the sleep pod of the Angels he interpreted this as a sign that his plan was pure.

The Bird Queen was alone. She spoke little as he told his tale, a question here or there when the words he chose were poor. She thanked him, then sat in silence, her strange eyes staring out the small round window of the pod.

Feran left the Angel then, not knowing whether he had done good or evil, yet somehow aware that his world was a much different place than it had been an hour before.

*** *Search Results Continued* ***
Xenobiology File: Lania: Life Forms: 1275

The impending release of a brood of mature nestlings prompts the male Angel to initiate final coupling. This act triggers the female's production of higher concentrations of Scream. Scream is the sole nourishment that the young can ingest upon emergence, and also relieves the agony of the male after the brood bursts from him. The female must receive the nestlings within hours of the final coupling, or she will die from the higher Scream level in her blood, which the nestlings cleanse from her system.

The evolutionary advantage of this reproductive approach appears to stem from the increased survival expectations of a brood carried by the stronger male, and the ensured presence of both parents at birth. Although Teplosky drew parallels to the Thendotae on Thendos IV, we feel . . .

Unable to sleep, Feran rose early the next day. A chill mist hung from a grey sky. For an hour, he wandered outside the big dome, worrying how to tell the Captain what he had done and why. He stopped. Toward him strode the Captain, with Mojo at his side. Both wore their old long black cloaks, thrown back to reveal weapons strapped to each leg. The gun metal glinted blue and cold, matching the look in the Captain's eyes.

Feran felt all his fears of the previous night vanish like grass swimmers into the brush. The Captain *was* going to fight. He would beat Weasel Man, and all would be well.

The Cutter stepped out of the dome as the Captain and Mojo stopped beside Feran. The Captain reached down to ruffle the fur on Feran's head, then glanced toward the dome. "Ready?"

The Cutter nodded. "Just get him inside."

A cry made them turn. Procne ran toward them, stumbling with the bulging weight of the brood inside him. "She's gone! She's gone!" he cried. He fell gasping into the Cutter's arms. Feran went cold inside.

The talking box on the Captain's belt beeped. He lifted it to his face. "It's from Phi. Time delayed delivery from last night." They waited as he read. When he spoke, his voice was raspy, like when he took too much dust. "She's given herself to Weitz. She knows that I won't surrender her and Pro, that I'll fight. She doesn't wish me or any of us to die." He dropped the device in the dirt. "She knows me better than I know myself, it would seem," he whispered.

"Our brood—" Procne began.

"She says she would rather her children die than live as slaves, kept only to feed monsters that destroy races."

"No! Our final coupling was last night. The brood comes!" He placed a thin hand on his pouch. "The essence they must feed on is rising in her blood. If she is not here when they emerge, they will die. If they die without cleansing her . . ."

"She will die, too," the Captain finished. "She knew this."

Mojo frowned. "How'd she know about Weitz? You only told me and Cutter, and just this morning." The Captain shook his head. Cutter shrugged.

Feran felt as if he were outside his body watching this scene but not part of it, unable to act. Well, he *had* acted, and this was what had come of it. He heard a voice saying "I told her." It seemed to be coming from somewhere else, and only when they all turned to look at him did he realize he had spoken.

Silence fell. The Captain knelt down before him, and all the words that Feran had tried to find before came pouring out. He turned his head, baring his throat to the Captain, offering his life. Instead, warm arms encircled him and held him tight. Feran knew that this was a "hug" and found it oddly comforting. The Captain whispered "Oh Feran," and Feran began to sob.

"So now what?" the Cutter growled as the Captain stood.

They waited. Then the Captain spoke, his voice as calm as when he told Feran a story. "Same plan, with one change. We need Pro with us." He turned to Procne, and Feran felt a stillness settle, like before two alpha males fought. "You and I, we've never quite got it straight between us. Just knew that she somehow needed us both. You never forgave, never trusted me. Can't say I ever blamed you. Well, I'm asking you to trust me now. If only because you know I wouldn't hurt her."

Procne stared at the Captain for several of Feran's heart beats, then nodded. The Captain turned to the Cutter. "Take Pro inside. Make it look like his hands are tied." He spoke then to all of them. "Nobody moves till I do, and I won't move until I know where he's got Phi. And remember: we need Weitz alive."

Muttering under his breath, the Cutter pulled Feran into the dome. Feran looked back. The Captain and Mojo strode toward the main entrance, their long cloaks closed, hiding their weapons and shutting out the rain that began to fall hard and cold.

Inside, Feran saw Guppert standing beside two Stone Puppies. He scampered over to them, glad to leave the morose Cutter, then stopped. Weapons were strapped to one side of the great silica beasts, the side hidden from the door. The Puppies lay on the ground, and Guppert's shoulder came to the top of their backs.

Guppert grinned and rapped a fat fist on the slate side of the nearest one. "Puppies make good fort, Guppert thinks." He pointed to the ground. "This where you come, little one, with Guppert, when I give word." He waddled around to the other side of the Puppies where water buckets and scrub brushes lay. "Now, we get busy looking not dangerous." He and Feran began scrubbing the Puppies. The Cutter stood with Procne between them and the entrance, Procne's hands bound behind him.

Feran heard them first. "They are here," he whispered.

Cutter nodded. A few seconds later, two men in RIP SS uniforms entered with guns. They looked around, then one called outside. "All clear." Weasel Man came in, then the Captain and Mojo, and more men in SS uniforms. Feran counted, his hope fading as each one entered. Ten, plus the first two, and Weasel Man. Four carried a metal case, their guns slung.

"Thirteen. Damn, I hate thirteen," muttered the Cutter as he left Procne and sauntered toward a Puppy. Still scrubbing, Guppert moved to the hidden side of his beast. Feran followed.

Weasel Man looked around. "Where's the rest of your crew?"

The Captain shrugged. "Dead or deserted."

Weasel Man raised an eyebrow and glanced at his men. The Captain nodded at the case. "That our stuff?" he asked, pulling back a sleeve to reveal a Medistim pack. He hit a button on it. Feran knew that he had just taken a "hit." Mojo did the same.

Weasel Man wrinkled his brow. "It was going to be."

The Captain smiled. "But you've reconsidered."

"We have the female already—" Weasel Man said.

"Her name is Philomela," the Captain said.

"And you're outnumbered—"

The Captain nodded. "Just a bunch of old derelicts."

"—so now I think we'll just take this one, too."

"His name is Procne." The Captain hit the stim pack again. So did Mojo. Feran had never seen the Captain take two hits. "So you'll leave me and Mojo to die in slow agony?"

Weasel Man shifted on his feet. Feran smelt his fear. The man nodded at the case. "That's worth a fortune—"

"And you have to cover your costs, don't you? Where is she?" the Captain said, taking a third hit.

"On my ship, hovering above us waiting for my call." Weasel Man patted his talking device. "Now, why don't—"

Being a predator, Feran was the first other than the Captain to know that the moment had arrived. The killing moment. And in that moment, for the first time, Feran realized something.

The Captain was a predator, too.

Weasel Man was still talking, "—this over with—"

The Captain and Mojo, moving faster than Feran thought men could move, threw back their cloaks and pulled their guns. The Captain shot Weasel Man twice, once through his gun arm and once through his leg. The air sizzled as Mojo fired, killing three before they could even raise their weapons. The Captain shot three more before Weasel Man hit the ground screaming. Feran closed his ear flaps to shut out the screams, his nose stinging from the burnt-air smell. The Cutter and Guppert shot one Ripper each from behind the Puppies. The last four, who had kept their guns slung, died still reaching for their weapons.

As he watched, Feran felt only fear. Not of the killing, for he knew killing, but fear of the look on the Captain's face.

The Captain stepped over the bodies to where Weasel Man lay like a trapped animal, and placed his weapon against the man's head. "Call your ship. Tell them to land outside this dome to pick up the other Angel."

Weasel Man spat blood. "Screw you."

The Captain put his gun against Weasel Man's forehead. The man swallowed, but shook his head. "You wouldn't kill an unarmed man in cold blood, Trelayne. You aren't capable of it."

But for the twitching of one eye, the Captain seemed carved from stone. Then he laughed. He laughed and laughed until Feran felt fear again—fear that he did not really know this man. Suddenly the Captain reached down and with one hand lifted Weasel Man by the throat and held him off the ground. Feran had no words for what he saw in the Captain's eyes as his voice boomed inside the dome. "I HAVE RIPPED BABIES FROM MOTHER'S ARMS. I HAVE KILLED THOUSANDS AND LAUGHED WHILE THEY DIED. I HAVE ENDED RACES. LITTLE MAN, I AM CAPABLE OF THINGS YOU COULD NEVER IMAGINE." The Captain dropped him then and looked down at the man, and Feran heard the sadness in the Captain's voice as he almost whispered, "I am capable of *anything.*"

Weasel Man lay gasping in the dirt. Then he looked up, and Feran knew the Captain had won. Weasel Man was baring his belly and neck, showing submission. He took his talking device with a shaking hand and spoke into it. Feran couldn't hear the words, but the Captain nodded to the others.

Feran relaxed. Guppert and the Cutter were slapping each other on their backs. Mojo sat slumped on the ground, his head between his knees, sobbing but apparently unhurt.

A cry cut the air. Feran spun, teeth bared. High above, Procne hovered, wings beating, head thrown back, face contorted in agony. His pouch bulged, then split as a cloud of bloody winged things burst from him and fell screeching toward them.

The brood had arrived.

Trelayne had not taken combat doses of Scream for over two years. The killing, and the joy it had brought, had shaken him. Now as the brood rained down bloody chaos from above, he felt his tenuous grip on reality slipping away. Knowing that the brood must live or Phi would die, he tried to follow what they were doing, but the Scream kept drawing him to the bloody corpses. He realized then that the brood was also being drawn to them.

Resembling winged toads with humanoid faces, grey and slick, the brood swarmed over the bodies, driving a long tendril that protruded from their abdomen into any open wound. But they stayed only a second at each spot, and with each attempt became more frenzied. *Scream*, he thought, *they need blood with Scream.*

"Trelayne!"

The cry spun Trelayne around. Weitz knelt, Tanzer held in a shaking hand. Blood soaked an arm and leg, and flowed from his forehead. Weitz levelled the gun at Trelayne.

The brood found Weitz before he could fire, swarming him, plunging their tendrils into each wound, into his eyes where the blood had run down from his forehead, probing, searching. Screaming, he clawed at them, then stiffened and fell forward.

The nestlings leapt up from his corpse to form a shrieking, swirling mass above the ring. They were tiring. *They are dying*, Trelayne thought. *Blood with Scream. Blood with Scream.*

He tore open his shirt. Pulling a knife from his belt, he slashed at his chest and upper arms. He dropped the knife and stood with arms outspread, blood streaming down him, waiting for the smell of the Scream in his blood to reach the brood.

They swooped down from above the ring, swarming him like bees on honey, driving their tendrils into his flesh wherever he bled. The pain surpassed even what Scream let him endure. A dark chasm yawned below him, and he felt himself falling.

Trelayne awoke on his back, pale green light illuminating a bulkhead above him. The weight pressing him into the bed and the throb of engines told him he was on a ship under acceleration.

Something was wrong. No. Something was right. Finally he felt right. He felt human. He felt . . .

Pain. Real pain. Pain that hurt. He tried to rise.

"The Captain has returned to us." It was Feran's voice.

"In more ways than one, fox boy, in more ways than one." The Cutter's face appeared above him. "Lie still for chrissakes. You'll open the wounds again."

Trelayne lay back gasping. "What happened?"

"We won. We took Weitz's ship."

"Mojo? Procne? Phi—where's Phi?" he wheezed.

Her voice came from across the room. "All your family is safe. Guppert, the Puppies. All are here with us."

Trelayne twisted his head. She lay on another bunk, Procne asleep beside her. "Didn't know I had a family," he said weakly.

"We knew, Jason Trelayne. All along we were your family."

The Cutter moved aside, and Trelayne could see the brood clinging to her. She smiled. "Yes. You saved my children."

"I haven't seen that smile in a long time, Phi."

"I have not had reason for a long time."

"I feel . . . I feel . . ."

"You feel true pain. And you wonder why." Her gaze dropped to something at his side. Only then did Trelayne realize that one of the brood lay beside him, and that the tiny creature still had its tendril inside him. He tried to move away.

"Lie still, dammit," the Cutter snapped. "This ugly little vacuum cleaner hasn't got you quite cleaned up yet."

"What are you talking about?"

The Cutter checked a monitor on the wall above the bunk. "The brood's feeding's reduced the Scream in your blood to almost nil. The big bonus is zero withdrawal signs. Remember when you tried to kick it when we started the colony?"

Trelayne nodded, shuddering at the memory.

The Cutter rubbed his chin. "These little suckers must leave somethin' behind in the blood, lets the body adjust to lower levels of Scream. Angels'd need the same thing when the brood feeds from 'em." He looked at Trelayne. "You just bought a new life for every Screamer the Entity ever got hooked."

As the implication of that sank in, Mojo's face appeared at the door. One of the brood clung to him as well. "We're nearing the jump insertion point. Where're we headed, Cap?"

Silence fell, and Trelayne could sense them waiting for his answer. He remembered something Weitz had said and smiled through his pain. "I hear there are still rebels on Fandor IV."

Mojo grinned and disappeared toward the bridge with Cutter. Trelayne turned to Feran. The kit moved away. Trelayne's smile faded as he understood. He stared at the kit then spoke very quietly.

"Feran, the Captain Trelayne that you saw in the dome today . . . he died with all those other men. Do you understand?"

An eternity passed. Then Feran ran to him and hugged him far too hard, and it hurt. His wounds hurt. The nestling at his side hurt. God, it all hurt, and it was wonderful to hurt again and to want it to stop.

Later, the ship slowed for the jump, and weightlessness took him. But to Trelayne, the sensation this time was not of falling. Instead, he felt himself rising, rising above something he was finally leaving behind.

As a child, I spent many summers with my family at a cottage on Lake Huron's Georgian Bay. My favourite memories are of early mornings, windy and overcast, walking on the wide sandy beach, alone except for the crashing of waves and the cries of the gulls. Many years later, I took karate with my oldest son. One summer, our club held a weekend camp at Georgian Bay. Much to my surprise, the location was the same collection of cottages from my childhood, and I spent the weekend practising and sparring on that same beach. At the end of the weekend, I walked that beach again, remembering those summer mornings. Somewhere in that stroll, this story was born. "The Red Bird" combines martial arts, a lonely beach, and a very singular bird that is definitely something more than a simple seagull, into a fable set in what might or might not be late fourteenth-century Japan. The story was an Aurora Award finalist in 2002.

THE RED BIRD

Asai first saw the Red Bird the night the soldiers burnt his village. Fleeing in terror through rain and flames and killing, his parents dead in the mud behind him, the boy heard his name called above the screams of the dying. Called from on high.

He looked up. Aflame against the black sky, a hawk of burning plumage hovered over the forest entrance. A voice cried in his mind. *Asai! To me, to me, Asai!*

Asai ran toward the trees. A mounted rider, gleaming katana raised, burst from a smoking house to block his path. A ruby light flashed from the hawk, striking the sword and swordsman. Exploding into flames, the soldier fell screaming to the ground. Oblivious, the man's horse bent a leg for the child to mount.

Ride, Asai! Fly with me! the hawk called.

Once in the saddle, the boy clung with bleeding fingers as the horse thundered through the streets past soldiers and the dead. At the forest edge, Asai dared a last look back. The village priest stood before the burning shrine. A rider bore down on him, spear lowered. Hands crossed on his chest, the priest closed his eyes. The look of peace on his face burnt into Asai's memory. The boy turned away, blinded by tears.

They rode on through black woods lit only by the hawk's bloody glow. Trees surrendered to scrub grass then to sand and crashing surf. Just as Asai felt he would fall from the saddle, the horse stopped before the Temple of the Hidden Light.

At the base of steps rising into the darkness of the sea cliff waited the Warrior of the Red Bird. His gaze from beneath his visor was both warm and chill. His armour began to glow with a ruby light from above. A flutter of wings came, and the Red Bird settled with the grace of beasts onto his shoulder.

The Warrior spoke to the hawk. "Is this the one, Master?"

Yes, Ikada.

The Warrior lifted the child from the horse as easily as a bird carrying a leaf and bore him into the Temple. Servants tended his wounds, then bathed and fed him. That night, alone on silken sheets and feathered bed, Asai dreamt of the Red Bird and the look on the face of the priest.

The next day, Ikada, Warrior of the Red Bird, Defender of the Temple of the Hidden Light, began to teach Asai the *bushido*, the Way of the Warrior, and of the Hundred Deaths.

Each day, as the sun first set fire to the cliffs above the white Temple walls, the man and boy would rise and enter the Chamber of the Silver Blade. There, sitting on cushions of carmine silk on a floor whose mosaic tiles told of generations of Warriors, Ikada taught Asai. In those first mornings, Asai had many questions.

"Who is the Red Bird?"

Ikada looked around before answering. "The scarlet hawk is the spirit of this place. It is He that we serve."

"What is this place?"

"The Temple of the Hidden Light." Ikada spoke the words as if they might frighten something away.

"What is the Hidden Light?"

Ikada looked away. "That which we defend."

"But what is it?" the boy persisted.

Ikada turned back. Asai first saw the sadness that he would come to realize lived in Ikada always. "I do not know," he said.

When the sun was high, they sparred on the Thousand Steps, where each stone riser but the two topmost bore a Warrior's name.

"Are there other warriors of the Red Bird?" Asai asked, avoiding a foot sweep as he had learned just that morning.

Ikada paused a step below Asai, leaning on his sword. His long braids danced as he shook his head. "The Red One's warriors have been many, but at any time only one wears the name."

"How many have there been?"

"You, Asai, will be the thousandth defender of the Temple." Ikada looked at Asai, a sad light in his eyes. "And the last."

"Why must there be a last?"

With a solemn expression, Ikada leaned very close to Asai. "We've run out of steps," he whispered.

Asai stared back dumbly until Ikada threw back his head, roaring with laughter. "A small joke on my small hawk," he said when he could control his merriment. The tears streamed from his eyes, but Asai could still see the sadness.

"But why?" the boy asked again.

Ikada shook his head. "One day, but not yet."

As the sun kissed the sea at dusk, they sparred on the sand, weaving their *kumite* among rusted weapons and bleached bones.

"Who were these men?" Asai asked as he moved back from an attack, stepping over a gleaming rib cage poking from the sand.

"Soldiers of warlords who thought to plunder the Temple." Ikada lifted a skull, a tarnished circlet still on its brow. "And some warlords themselves. Eh, Kiyomori?" He grinned. "You came to kill Ikada, didn't you, Shogun? Well, many have come." He dropped the skull. "And many have died."

"Why do you serve the Temple?" Asai asked.

Ikada blinked. "Why, because I was chosen. There is but one chosen in each generation. The honour is great."

"How are the Warriors chosen? How were you chosen?"

Ikada smiled down at the boy, the wind off the sea whipping his braids behind him. "As you were. By the Red Bird."

"But why was *I* chosen?" Asai now had a home, and Ikada was like a father, yet Asai felt a fear he could not explain.

Ikada again shook his head. "Only the Red Bird knows."

Somehow, the answer disturbed Asai more than the question.

Asai looked forward to the evenings, when he put aside martial arts for other studies. The temple library was a huge domed room tiled in blue ceramics. Towering wooden racks jammed with parchment scrolls lined the walls. Asai would sit at a low table while Ikada read or taught from diagrams and maps.

Once Asai learned to read, he devoured every text he could find. He spent every spare hour in the library and had servants bring scrolls to his room to read before sleeping.

Ikada worried at this. "Asai, you have fought hard today and studied long. Take time to relax, to dream."

Asai smiled. "For me, to read is to relax, and these," he said, sweeping his arm past the scrolls, "these feed my dreams."

Not all days were so. On some, the temple bell thundered its call through the halls and down the steps. Then Ikada stopped whatever he was doing and called, "Asai! The Blade!"

Asai would run to the Chamber of the Silver Blade to take down the weapon from the wall. Made by a sword master to the first Shogun Yoritomo, its steel was folded a hundred times, polished to a silvery sheen. When Asai returned, Ikada would be dressed in his battle armour, a red sash around his waist.

Ikada would sheathe the blade on his back and stride to the crest of the Thousand Steps to survey the sand below. Most days brought but a solitary challenger or a small band.

On this day, Asai stood beside Ikada, staring down at rank after rank of soldiers arrayed on the beach. Asai had never seen so many people. Ikada grinned. "Shugon Antoku seeks to impress us." He descended the steps, humming a tune, Asai at his side.

"What is happening, Sensei?" the child asked. Shugons were local warlords, servants to the Shogun.

"Antoku seeks entrance, but the Red Bird finds him unworthy. This Shugon is famed for his cruelty. I will fight his champion, Harata, the tall one in front—a great swordsman."

"What of the army? Why does Antoku not just attack?"

Ikada just smiled and looked up to where the Red Bird circled the beach. No other answer came, and Asai fell silent. They reached the bottom step, and Ikada walked out to Harata.

The two warriors bowed and stepped back, drawing their blades. Harata lunged. Holding his stance, Ikada raised the Silver Blade, handle high and point angled low, as Harata's sword stabbed at his throat. Harata's blade slid off Ikada's, missing its mark. Ikada thrust, and the Silver Blade's point pierced Harata's chest armour. Before the man's body hit the sand, Ikada had turned to walk back to the steps, his sword sheathed again.

A gasp escaped the ranks of men. Mounted on a grey mare, Shugon Antoku raised his sword, screaming "Attack!" Twenty cavalry broke from the larger body. Asai cried a warning, but Ikada just smiled and kept walking. As the riders neared Ikada, the beach erupted in fire, and Asai choked on smoke and heated air. When his dazzled eyes could see again, Asai gazed out on the charred bodies of twenty men and horses. Overhead, the Red Bird circled, its outline still glowing against the sky.

"Only one may challenge," Ikada said as they climbed back.

"What if another wishes to fight you now?"

Ikada looked hurt. "Asai! Even Ikada needs his rest. One challenge a day is all the Red Bird allows."

They were not alone in the Temple. Ikada granted access to the library to visiting Jodo Shin priests. In return, the holy men gave the dharma or recited sutras for the dead. The Temple also housed servants who tended to chores and the two warriors' needs. As Asai grew, he became aware of a new need of his own.

The Temple servants included the Warrior's concubines. Although his father had told Asai of the ways of the flesh, knowing of it was far removed from feeling it. Ikada was not blind to the change. On the night Asai turned fourteen, Ikada sent his favourite concubine to the boy's bedchamber.

Neither spoke of it the next morning, but a smirk played on Ikada's face throughout the day. After that, Asai took a woman most nights, sometimes just to avoid being alone. Other nights he did not, just to be alone. The boy was tender and gentle, much loved by many of the women, but he never chose a favourite. Nor did he talk with them of much beyond his studies and Temple life. He knew this bothered Ikada, but the Warrior said nothing.

So through all the days of all the years, Ikada would teach and Asai would learn. The orphan learnt well. Asai turned eighteen as Master of the Hundred Deaths, save one.

One day as they sparred on the sand, Ikada stepped back, calling "Yamat!" sharply. Asai lowered his sword, glad for a break. The sky swirled in grey humour, and a wind off the waves stung his eyes. Ikada stared past him up the Thousand Steps.

Above the cliffs, brilliant against the bleak sky, circled the Red Bird. Asai felt a strange dread as the hawk spiralled lower. A ruby beam burst from the bird to dance on the top steps for two breaths. Rising, the Red Bird vanished into the clouds.

Asai turned to speak, but Ikada's face choked off the words in Asai's throat. Ikada walked past him, never taking his eyes from the summit. Reaching the steps, he climbed with the gait of a man going to his own execution. Asai followed in silence.

Near the summit, Ikada stopped. Asai came to stand beside him, staring at the next to last step of the Thousand. The name *Ikada* was burnt now in Kana symbols into the stone.

"Sensei," Asai began, but Ikada raised his hand. Turning his back on the step, Ikada gazed at the sand below. Asai looked down, too. A sole rider sped along the surf's edge, black armour, weapons and saddlery, a dragon's tail of sand in his wake. Ikada watched for a breath then began his descent. Asai followed, unable to speak of the fear in his breast.

At the bottom, Ikada drew the Silver Blade from the sheath on his back. He raised it to his lips then laid it on the bottom step. "Asai, give me your sword," he said quietly.

Asai glanced at the Silver Blade but said nothing. He handed Ikada his katana, a true but unremarkable weapon.

Ikada sheathed it. The black samurai now stood waiting. Ikada's voice was soft. "Asai, today the Red Bird will know how well Ikada has taught you." Grasping Asai's shoulders in both hands, he smiled. "You have been a fine student and a better friend. I love you as I would my own son. Good-bye, Asai."

Without another word, Ikada strode across the sand to his challenger. Both bowed and in an eye blink drew their blades and stepped back into fighting stance, swords vertical in a two-handed grip. The samurai moved in at once, feinting a head cut but shifting to slash across the ribs. Parrying, Ikada slid his blade along the other's, nicking the samurai's neck. The man retreated, but Ikada closed again, pressing his attack.

Many times, Ikada came within a hair's breadth of ending the battle but could not deliver a death cut. Bleeding from a dozen places, the black samurai now fought with his blade in his left hand, right arm hanging limp at his side.

Then Ikada, blocked on a vicious downward cut, dropped into a crouch to execute a perfect reverse spin. His blade slashed under the man's guard, slicing a thigh. Grunting, the samurai fell to a knee. Ikada closed, sword raised for the final blow.

And slipped—on something in the sand. Something round and white. His blade swung wide from its *kamai* position. Still kneeling, the black samurai thrust upwards. As the point entered Ikada's throat, Asai's own throat gave his scream life.

Asai ran onto the sand, Silver Blade over his head. The samurai stood and grinned, no doubt at the sight of a man-child warrior. The two engaged, and the grin vanished. Asai attacked with such fury that the samurai could only parry and retreat. The black warrior stumbled. Asai beat away a feeble slash, and the man's sword flew from him.

"I beg mercy!" the samurai cried, on his knees before Asai.

"Beg to the demons!" Asai spat. His sword sang across the neck of his foe. The helmeted head spun lazily in the air, drops of blood shining in the evening sun, to land in the sand.

Asai stared at the Silver Blade in his hand, unable to remember picking it up. He stumbled to Ikada, feeling for a pulse that he knew he would not find. Tears streaking his face, he picked up the object that had tripped the Warrior. A skull, a circlet of metal still attached, grinned back at him.

From above came the beat of wings. The Red Bird settled on Ikada's chest. Lowering its head into the liquid pooling at the wound, it then touched its dripping beak to its feathers, repeating this until it glistened with blood. The hawk began to glow in the dim light. The glow died, and the bird's plumage grew a deeper shade of red. The bird leapt into the air again.

"Is this how you honour one that served you?" Asai shouted at the hawk circling above, the pain inside him overcoming his fear.

Such is the final test for each of my Warriors. Asai felt the misery in those words, a black pool of infinite depth. He looked into that pool and drew back in fear from its edge. Drew back from something he was not yet ready to face.

Asai watched the Red Bird disappear into the darkening sky. He then carried Ikada up the Thousand Steps. In the Vault of Heroes, he prepared the body. He opened the next-to-last sepulchre and laid Ikada on the bier. After reading from the bushido, he closed the sepulchre, snuffing out all candles but one. He left the vault, the Silver Blade on his back.

That night, Asai lay awake thinking of things left unsaid.

The Red Bird came the next day as Asai did kata before the waves. The sky was grey and the wind chill. The hawk landed on a skeletal hand grasping at the sky from the sand.

Ikada is dead. You are the Warrior now.

Asai felt anger again. "You could have saved him, bird."

I could not.

"Why?"

It is not the way.

Fury erupted in Asai. "What is the way? Why must we die to serve you?" He flung the Silver Blade to stick in the still-red sand where Ikada had fallen. "Why am I here, you bloody crow?"

The Red Bird was silent, and fear tempered Asai's anger. Then the hawk spoke. *You must seek the Hidden Light. You are the last. The last hope for your people.*

"Why am I the last?"

The sands run out.

"Where is the Hidden Light?"

The bird looked at him. *It is here.*

"But what is it?"

That which you must seek.

Asai's anger built again. "And what if I fail, crow?"

A thousand years of misery for your kind.

His fear returned. "Why?"

War dogs gather. The light dims. You must pass the test.

A thought flew to him. "Who must? I or my people?"

Something in the hawk's gaze recalled the look Ikada would wear when Asai had mastered a new Death.

Wisdom begins. Opening its wings, the bird leapt into the face of the sea breeze. Asai watched it vanish in the clouds.

She came to him on the anniversary of Ikada's death. As the temple bell rang, Asai descended the steps to face a small figure clad in what seemed the castoff armour of a dozen warriors. A slim hand removed an ill-fitting helmet, and he first looked on her face. "My name is Sawako," she said.

"I do not wish to kill you," Asai replied, staring at her.

"Then we begin well for I do not wish to be killed." Taking off the rest of her armour and untying a sash at her waist, she pulled her dress off over her head to stand naked before him.

Asai stood transfixed for several breaths. Then sheathing the Silver Blade, he walked to her and pulled her to him in a long kiss. After what seemed a lifetime, he broke off the kiss, scooped her into his arms and carried her up the steps into the Temple. Overhead, the Red Bird cried unheeded.

That night after their lovemaking, Sawako told her story. "My village lies two days to the east. When news of Ikada-san's death reached us, Antoku, the local Shugon, promised to bring the Shogun the Temple's secret. Two moons ago, he chose a swordsman of my village to challenge the Warrior. To challenge you."

She looked away. "The man did not return. In his wrath, Antoku sentenced each first son in the village to die. I begged that we be given another chance to do Antoku honour, that I would bring him the secret. He laughed and was going to give me to his men. Then a Jodo Shin priest told him of my birth."

"What of your birth?"

"The priest said that on the night I was born, an omen appeared in the sky above our village."

Asai felt a coldness grip his belly. "What was this omen?"

Sawako turned back to him, snuggling her head into his chest. "A great red hawk, whose plumage glowed as if on fire."

The next morning, Asai showed Sawako the Temple. As they walked, she told more of her bargain with Antoku. "I did not promise to defeat you, only to find the secret. Antoku has given me one year. If I fail, he will execute my entire village." She laid a hand on the silken arm of his robe. "Show me the Light. You need not surrender the Temple but you will save my people."

Asai looked into her eyes. "Sawako, I cannot. I defend what I do not know. No Warrior has ever discovered the Hidden Light, and I am the last." He told her of the prophecy, and Sawako seemed to fall into deep thought. They walked in silence.

Later they sparred on the beach with wooden *bokken*. The village samurai had taught her well. She was quick with fine form, but he had the reach, strength, and years of daily study.

Resting on the beach after, she spoke again of the Light. "You must find it or misery will befall our land. I must learn of it or my people die." She turned to him. "Let me help you."

Asai laughed, leaning on an elbow beside her. "So a woman-child will succeed where a thousand Warriors have failed?"

Sawako shrugged slim shoulders. "I can hardly do worse."

Asai scowled. "How could you help me?"

"The priests taught me to read and write." She pulled him close, and he felt her warm breath, smelled its sweetness. "And I can help you as I did last night. You are far too serious."

Asai felt his face grow hot. "What if we fail? What if a year comes, and the Light remains hidden? What then?"

She stood with her bokken. "Then to me, you will again become the Warrior." She turned away. "And I must kill you."

Sawako stayed, and their lust grew to love. Each morning, they sat close together in the library, reading and discussing the great philosophers. Their hunger for the secret that remained hidden lived with them each minute.

Sometimes, Asai felt he had found a great truth and sought out the Red Bird. The hawk always knew of his need and came. Explaining what he had learned, Asai would wait for a reply.

When it came, it was always the same. *You grow wise.*

"Is this the Light?"

No.

One such morning, when Sawako had been with him for about two months, Asai stood on the cliff edge, the hawk beside him. After receiving this answer again, Asai exploded in fury. "Why do you play this game? Where is the light?"

You grow close. Closer than any other.

Asai hesitated. "You never speak of Sawako, never asked me of her. Did I do wrong? Have I violated my duty?"

You alone can judge that.

"What of her birth omen? Was that you, Red Bird?"

Spreading its wings, the hawk leapt off the cliff. Asai called after it, but the only answer was the cold wind. That night, Sawako told Asai she carried his child. The next day, he took her as his wife.

She named the boy Shirotori. It meant "White Bird." When Asai asked her of it, she said "This world has seen enough of red. White is the colour of peace."

And the shrouds of the dead, Asai thought but said nothing.

Asai had never known the joy he felt with his wife and child. Yet, as the year wore on and the light stayed hidden, he felt the sands of happiness slipping through his hands. On the first day of the twelfth month since Sawako had come, Asai found her dressed again in her armour, doing kata by the sea.

"Why do you do this?" he asked, his voice breaking.

"Because I must," she said. Her face was wet—with tears or sea spray, he knew not which. She turned back to her kata, and he turned his back on her.

On the eve of the anniversary of Sawako's arrival, Asai stood on the topmost Temple step, dripping with sweat, Silver Blade in his hand. The hawk settled onto a dragon statue beside him, glowing blood red in the night. *You train hard.*

"To kill the woman I love, the mother of my son." No reply came. Asai turned to the hawk. "Why must she die, crow? What does it serve?" No answer. "Over two hundred in her village will die with her. Why? What good is in this?" His rage built. "Is it the blood you need, death bird?" Still no answer came, and Asai could hold his fury no longer. "Then I give you blood!"

He swung the sword, and the hawk sprang into the air. The bird was too fast, but the Silver Blade clipped a tail feather. As the hawk vanished into the dark sky, the feather floated to land on the top step, where it seemed to melt. Touching the sticky puddle, Asai drew his finger back. It dripped blood.

He drew a line on his forehead with the blood. "Is it not fitting that I wear this mark?" he asked the night. He slumped to the steps. "If I win, she dies and two hundred more. And with her dies my love, my reason for life. No, our son would live but with no mother. What do I know of raising a child?" He stood to gaze at where the moon silvered the surf below. "But if I die, no other dies. Only Asai. What loss is that?"

The wind whispered his name. He smiled sadly. "Asai, just Asai. No loss in that." Turning from the sea, he entered the temple. That night he made love to Sawako for the last time.

They rose early and in silence. He watched her dress then walk to where he sat on the window ledge. She kissed him long and deeply. Then picking up a scroll from her table, she left not looking back. He watched her go, her tears cool on his face.

Asai stayed at the window until he saw her descend the Steps. Then he dressed and broke fast lightly. He visited each servant, saying his good-byes without saying so. In the nursery, he held his son for a long time, singing in a low soft voice a song that Sawako sang to Shirotori each night. He left special instructions with the servant who cared for the child.

In the Chamber of the Silver Blade, Asai knelt at the low table where Ikada had taught him the Way. On it stood a vial of green liquid. His studies had brought knowledge of herbs and potions. Sawako was a fine swordswoman, but Asai knew she was no match for a Warrior. His reactions were too instinctive to trust the outcome to his intent alone. The poison would work slowly, at first to impede his movements, finally to stop his heart if her blade had not done so.

He raised the vial and drank.

He stared at the top step, still blank above Ikada's name, and called to the hawk circling overhead. "Why is my name not written here, crow? You knew Ikada would die! Do you not know that I die today?" The hawk continued to circle. "So be it," Asai cried and slashed at the stone with the Silver Blade. Again and again he swung, until his name stood carved above Ikada's. With a last glance skyward, he descended the steps.

She knelt on the sand facing the sea and did not answer when he called her name. He stumbled over shifting sand, the poison burning in his muscles. He was about to call her name again when he saw the blood and the blade point protruding from her back.

His throat choked a cry that tore his heart as he ran to her. He wrenched the sword from where she had thrust it in her breast. Her face was cold as he took it in his hands. "Why?" he cried to the wind, knowing the answer even before he saw the scroll beside her, before he read the words she had written.

Dearest love, I will say do not grieve, yet I know you will. Know that I loved you and was sure of your love. I saw no other way. The Light stays hidden. I failed my people and cannot live while they die. I could never harm you but feared you would work your death to save me. This is my answer to the question we lived with this joyous year. Raise our son with the love you gave me. Forever, your Sawako.

His sobs became spasms as he lay her on the sand. "We die for nothing, my love," he cried. *No*, he thought, *I can still save her people.* Lifting her sword, he turned its point to his breast. "If I die by your sword, Sawako, you have won the Temple." He threw himself on her blade, falling beside her. As he lay dying, her face recalled to him the doomed priest's look of peace the night the Red Bird first came to him.

The Red Bird settled on the fallen Warrior's chest and dipped its beak into the wound around the blade. Painting itself in the man's blood, it hopped then to the woman's body that lay beside him, adding her blood to its red sheen.

A glow touched its feathers, then burst into brilliance as the hawk leapt into the air aflame. Fire burned away the scarlet coat, and from the centre of a winged sun emerged a great eagle, with feathers of burnished gold. The eagle spread its wings.

From each wing, a feather fell to land on the two lovers. The feathers became white flames, and fire consumed the bodies. From the smoke flew two white doves who circled first each other and then the eagle as all three disappeared into the sky.

Shugon Antoku and his army arrived at Sawako's village to find it deserted. Travelling monks told of two white doves who led a band of people eastward. When Antoku reached the Temple of the Hidden Light, Sawako's people were encamped on the sand. A shimmering wall of white light separated them and the Temple from Antoku and his men. Antoku ordered the villagers slain.

As the first soldiers touched the white wall, their bodies burst into flames and blew away, ashes on the wind. Those behind fled in terror, screaming of demons. Antoku cursed them as cowards but was left alone on the sand, his promise to the Shogun unfulfilled. He regarded the white wall for a long time, then drew and fell on his sword.

When he turned eighteen, Shirotori, son of Asai, son of Sawako, began to preach the Way of the Hidden Light. Villages fell under his protection and his teaching. His followers grew and the Way spread. Armies deserted any Shugon who raised arms against him. Soon his reach extended to the Shogun's palace.

On the anniversary of his parents' deaths, Shirotori stood on the steps of that palace as the Shogun broke his sword and bent his knee to the boy.

Shirotori's rule was just and kind. The people said that truth and love rode with him always, in the form of two white doves on each shoulder. He was known by many names. The Prophet. The Truth. The Loved.

But most called him *Kashoku*, which meant Bright Light.

This was the first pure horror story I ever wrote. It was an Aurora finalist and was selected for The Mammoth Book of Best New Horror #13. A movie adaptation of the story from TinyCore Pictures will be touring film festivals and will be available on DVD in 2010. More on this one later.

BY HER HAND, SHE DRAWS YOU DOWN

By her hand, she draws you down.
With her mouth, she breathes you in.
Hope and dreams and soul devoured.
Lost to you, what might have been.

By her hand, she draws you down . . .

Joe swore when he saw Cath doing a kid. He had left her for just a minute, to get a beer from the booth on the pier before it closed for the night. Walking back now, he could see Cath on her stool, sketchpad on a knee, ocean breeze blowing her pale hair. A small girl sat on another stool facing her, a man and a woman, parents he guessed, beside the child.

Kid's not more than seven, he thought. *Cath promised me no kids. She promised.*

The sun was long set, and the air had turned cool, but people still filled the boardwalk. Joe wove through the crowd as fast as he could without attracting attention. Cath had set up farther from the beach tonight, at the bottom of a grassy slope that ran up to the highway where their old grey Ford waited.

"Last night tonight," Cath had said when they had parked the car earlier. "*It* wants to move on. I can feel the change."

Joe had swallowed and turned off the ignition. He was never comfortable talking about it. "Where's it headed?"

Cath had just shaken her head, grinning. "Dunno. That's part of the fun, isn't it? Not knowing where we're going next? That's fun, isn't it, Joe?"

Yeah, loads of fun, he thought now as he approached Cath and her customers. It *had* been fun once, when they'd met, before he learned what Cath did, what she had to do. When his love for her wasn't all mixed up with fear of what she would do to someone.

Or to him.

The child's parents looked up as Joe came to stand beside Cath. The father frowned. Joe smiled, trying to hide the dread digging like cold fingers into his gut. Turning his back to them, he bent to whisper in Cath's ear. That flowery scent she had switched to recently rose warm and sweet in his face. *Funeral parlours*, he thought. *She smells like a goddam funeral parlour.*

"Cath, she's just a kid," he rasped in her ear.

Cath shook her head. Her eyes flitted from the girl to her pad. "Bad night. I'm hungry," she muttered, ignoring Joe.

Joe looked at the drawing. It was good. But they were always good. Cath had real talent, more than Joe ever had. She would set up each night where people strolled, her sketches beside her like trophies from a hunt. People would stop to look, sometimes moving on, sometimes sitting for a portrait.

Eventually Joe and Cath would move on, too. When the town was empty, Cath said. When the thing inside her wanted to move on. They had spent this week at a little New England vacation spot. At least they were heading south lately. Summer was dying, and Joe longed to winter in the sun. Sleep for Joe was rare enough since he'd met Cath. Winters up north meant long nights in bars. Things closed in then, closed in around him. On those nights, he would lie awake in their motel bed, feeling Cath's eyes on him, feeling her hunger.

He looked at the sketch, at the child captured there, perfect except for the emptiness that spoke from the eyes, from any eyes that Cath drew. And the mouth.

Where the mouth should have been, empty paper gaped. Cath left the mouth until the end. The portraits always bothered Joe when they looked like that. To him, the pictures weren't waiting to be completed, waiting for a last piece to be added. To Joe, something vital had been ripped from what had once been whole, leaving behind a void that threatened to suck in the world around it. An empty thing but insatiable. Waiting to suck him in, too.

"Cath," he whispered. "You promised."

She ignored him again. Joe wrapped his fingers around the thin wrist of her hand that held the sketchpad. "You promised."

Cath snapped her head around to glare up at him. Joe caught his breath as anger met hunger in her grey eyes, becoming something alive, something that leapt for him.

The father cleared his throat, and the thing in Cath's eyes retreated. Cath turned to the parents. "Sorry, can't get her right. You can have this." Tearing the sketch from her pad, she shoved it at the mother. "We gotta go." Cath stood and folded her stool as the child ran to peek from behind the father's legs. Joe grabbed the other stool and the canvas bag that held Cath's supplies. He put an arm around Cath's waist, leading her away.

The father started to protest. "But you're almost done. You just need to draw in the mouth."

Cath stopped, and Joe swore. He just wanted to get her out of there. She walked back to the man who exchanged glances with his wife. Cath touched a finger to her lips. "Mouths are the hardest part. The most important part," she said. "Everyone—they say 'the eyes are the windows of the soul.' They say 'Oh, you got the eyes just right.' They don't know. They don't know it's the mouth you gotta get just right. That's what makes a picture come alive. Like it's gonna just start . . . breathing."

The father cleared his throat, but the mother tugged at his shirt. Joe grabbed Cath's arm and pulled her away. The man muttered something, but Joe didn't care.

He led Cath to a gravel path that switched back and forth up the steep hill to the highway above. Halfway up, an observation area looked down on the pier and the beach and the boardwalk. Cath twisted away from him there. A low stone wall ran around the area's edge, and two lampposts stood at either end. Putting her stool down under the nearest light, she began setting out her sketches against the wall.

Joe dropped the other stool and sat down. The fatigue that lived with him always now rose to engulf him. He felt dead inside, all used up, like the way Cath's pictures made him feel, waiting to be sucked into the void. "We had a deal," he said.

Cath sat, looking up and down the path. "I'm hungry."

"No kids, remember?" Joe said. "And nobody with a family depending on them." He tried to make his voice sound strong, but his hands were shaking.

She opened her pad. "Kind of cuts down the field, Joe."

"Use one of the sketches you've got put away."

Cath laughed. A bitter, empty sound. Joe imagined the mouths she drew making that kind of sound. Cath looked at him finally. "All gone. Used 'em all."

Joe felt the emptiness again, a void gaping below, drawing him down. He leaned forward, head between his hands, fingers pressing hard on his temples, trying to make his fear go away. "Jeez, Cath. All of them?" He searched her face for some hope.

Cath shrugged. "Girl's gotta eat." She stared past him, and he heard gravel crunching underfoot. Joe turned, his hand slipping by reflex to touch the switchblade inside his boot top.

A fat man in black pants, white shirt, and paisley tie loosened at the neck was struggling down the steep path from the highway, a beach chair in each arm. He walked over to the stone wall and put down the chairs to rest. Nodding at Joe and Cath, he glanced at her sketches. He began to turn away but then looked back. His eyes ran over the portraits lined against the low wall like prisoners before a firing squad. The man whistled.

Joe sighed, from regret and relief. Cath would eat tonight.

With her mouth, she breathes you in . . .

The man's name was Harry. He haggled with Cath over the price then he sat down, and Cath started sketching. Joe glanced at the two chairs that Harry had carried, but he couldn't see a wedding ring, so he kept silent.

Cath worked quickly, her hand slashing at the page, pausing only to switch the colour of her pencil. When only the mouth remained unfinished, she put the pad down on her lap.

Harry looked down at the sketch. "There's no mouth."

"Mouths are special, Har," Cath said. She puckered at him, and Harry laughed, a nervous squeaky sound. Cath touched a finger of her drawing hand to Harry's lips. He gave that little laugh again but didn't pull away. Cath ran her fingertips slowly over his lips, tracing each curve and contour. Sitting on the stone wall, Joe thought of her fingers on his own skin at night in bed, tracing the lines of his body. Love and fear and lust—with Cath, they all mixed together, colours in a picture flowing into each other, until you couldn't separate one from another.

She lowered her hand to the paper, her eyes still on Harry's mouth. Picking up a red pencil and dropping her eyes, her hand began to stab at the paper in short urgent strokes. The mouth grew under her fingers as Joe watched. She finished in seconds. Removing the sketch sheet, Cath handed it to Harry. He regarded it for a moment, grunted his approval and paid her. Portrait under his arm, he picked up his chairs and nodded a good-bye.

After watching Harry labour down the path toward the boardwalk below, Joe walked to where Cath sat cross-legged on the ground, her sketch pad on her lap. She carefully lifted a sheet of carbon paper from the top of the pad. A copy of the sketch she had just rendered of Harry stared up at Joe in black and white. *No colour,* thought Joe. *As if all the life's been sucked out of it. No,* he thought. *Not all of it. Not yet.*

From her canvas bag, Cath removed a small rosewood box, its hinged cover carved with letters in a script Joe thought was Arabic. He'd never checked, wanting to know as little as possible about the thing. Cath opened the lid and withdrew what looked like a child's crayon but without any paper covering.

The crayon was as long as Joe's middle finger but thicker, and a red so dark it was almost black. Joe remembered drawing as a kid, the crayons, the names of the colours. Midnight blue, leaf green, sunshine yellow. He knew the name that this one would have carried: blood red. It glinted in the overhead light as if it would be sticky to the touch, but Joe had never touched it, so he didn't know for sure. He didn't want to know.

Hunched over the portrait copy, Cath began to retrace the lines of the mouth with the red crayon, adding colour and shading. She worked with almost painful slowness. Joe remembered how once she had made a mistake at this stage, how the fury had burst from her like a wild thing caged too long.

At last, Cath straightened. She gave the mouth one last appraising look then returned the crayon to the rosewood box. Joe walked back to the low stone wall. He knew he would turn back to watch her. He always did.

Below, Harry had reached the boardwalk. The big man put down one chair to wave to someone on the beach. Joe's stomach tightened. A woman waved back at Harry, and a small boy and girl ran to hug him. *Jesus, no*, thought Joe.

He turned back. Cath sat hunched over the portrait of Harry on her lap. Joe rushed to her, praying that it wasn't too late, a prayer that died when he saw the picture. It had started.

The portrait's mouth was moving, fat lips squirming like slick red worms on the paper. A pale vapour rose thin and wispy from those lips. Cath bent her head over the mouth and sucked in that misty thing that Joe never wanted to name.

A scream rose from the beach. A woman's cry, a thing of pain and fear. Between her sobs, Joe could hear children crying.

He walked back to the low stone wall and looked down at the crowd gathered where Harry had fallen. Joe stood there, eyes locked on Harry's still form, feeling the void opening below him again. "Cath, we have to get out of here."

Cath didn't answer him. Joe tore his eyes from the scene below and turned back to her. She was standing now, looking south, down the coastline. "It wants to move on," she said.

Hope and dreams and soul devoured . . .

Joe drove staring at the white lane markers slicing the dark two-lane one after another, like brush strokes by God on a long black canvas. White on black. The negative image of Cath's secret portraits. Black on white, white on black. Just the red missing. Just that blood red.

How long before some cop put it together? A string of deaths, all the victims drawn by a young woman with a male companion. Christ, Harry died with a sketch in his hand.

Cath stirred beside him, and then he felt her eyes on him. He could always feel her gaze, like a physical touch, like a brush dipping into him, drawing something from him. *Is that how you do it, Cath? How you take the thing you take? Capture it in your eyes, then cage it through your fingers onto the page? Have you been feeding on me, too?*

"I'm still hungry," Cath said. Her voice was small, almost child-like in the dark.

He knew what she meant. "We'll hit town soon," he said. But it would be three in the morning when they arrived. No one around. No one to draw. And she had no pictures left. Cath said nothing but looked away. After a while, he figured she was asleep. Then he felt her eyes again.

"I don't *want* to hurt people, Joe."

He swallowed. This was new. She never talked about it, even when he did. He should say something now, something smart, something that would lead them out of this. He should, but he had nothing left to say. He could only nod. "I know, babe."

"It just gets so hungry. I get so hungry."

"I know."

"I can't stop it. It keeps pulling me, making me . . ."

He could feel her pain in those words. And his fear.

"I'm tired," she said. "So tired I wish I could just go to sleep and never wake up. Ever been that tired, Joe?"

He swallowed again. *All the time*, he thought, but he just nodded. Cath looked away, and he took a breath as if he was coming up for air.

"I'm hungry," she said again.

"I know."

Her eyes settled on him again like a beast on his chest.

"I could draw *you*, Joe."

His hands tightened on the wheel. Cath had said it the way a kid told you she could ride a bike or tie her shoe. The lines flashed by in the headlights. White on black, no red.

"Don't even need to see you," she said. "Know you so well."

Joe stared at the road. *Don't look*, he thought.

"Know your face like I know my own," she said.

The burden of her gaze lifted. He looked at her.

Her eyes were shut, and her hand moved in her lap, mimicking drawing motions. "Don't even need light. Could draw you with my eyes closed." Her hand stopped, and she leaned her head back. A few minutes later, Joe could hear her breathing slow and deepen.

So there it was. He always knew it would come to this. This was why he had stayed, even after he learned what Cath did, what she was. Afraid that when he left, when Cath no longer needed him, she would draw him down. Draw him down onto the page from memory, then drink him in like all the others.

The road lines flew at him like white knives out of the night. White knives and blackness. Just the blood red missing. Taking a hand from the wheel, he felt inside the top of his boot, running his fingers over the bone handle of his switchblade.

A few miles down the road, he found a wide shoulder and pulled over, turning off the engine and the lights.

Cath still slept. Hands shaking, Joe pulled the knife from his boot. *It's self-defence*, he thought. But he just sat holding the knife. It was for the best. How many more would she kill? But he still loved her. Could he do it? He was tired, so tired. He leaned back. He only slept now when Cath did, when he didn't feel her eyes. He closed his eyes. Her breathing brushed his ears, soft and deep, soft and deep, soft . . .

He awoke to the sound of scratching on paper. He looked over. Framed against the moonlight, Cath sat hunched over her sketchpad, her hand moving in short, sure strokes.

"Kind of late for drawing, isn't it, Cath?" Joe asked. His throat was dry. He fumbled in his lap for the knife.

"Hungry," she said, her voice barely audible.

"Dark, too," he said, blood pounding in his ears.

"Don't need light. Drawin' from memory," she whispered.

Drawing from memory. Drawing him. He knew she was drawing him. "Don't, Cath." His thumb found the blade's button.

"Tired of being hungry." She sat back, eyes on the sketch.

He couldn't see the picture, but he saw the red crayon in her hand. She'd finished the mouth. "Please, don't do it," he said. His cheeks felt cool and wet. He realized he was crying.

Cath lifted the paper to her face. She was crying, too.

"Don't!" Joe screamed. The knife blade clicked open.

"Bye, Joe. Sorry." Cath breathed in through her lips.

Joe saw a pale wisp rise from the paper and move toward her mouth. Saw his hand gripping the knife flash forward. Saw the blade slice her white T-shirt and slide between her ribs.

Saw the red, the blood red, flow over the white of her shirt to blend with the black of the night and the shadows.

Cath spasmed and fell sideways onto him. Surprise mixed with peace in her face. "Thanks . . . Joe," she whispered. Her eyes closed and her head slumped back. A wisp of mist escaped her lips.

That's me, Joe thought. Sobbing, he pressed his lips to hers, sucking in the breath and the grey mist from her mouth.

Bitter and sour, the thing burned his throat as he breathed it in. Something was wrong. Joe felt a presence of something dark, something . . . *hungry*.

His head spinning, Joe flicked on the dome light. Blood soaked into his shirt where Cath slumped against him, the picture still clenched in her hand. Joe stared at the sketch, a scream forming in his mind.

A familiar face stared back at him from the page, a face that Cath knew from memory. The face she knew best of all.

Not Joe's face.

It was Cath.

She hadn't been drawing him. She'd been feeding herself to the thing that had lived in her. Cath had been killing herself.

The emptiness that was the mouth in Cath's pictures gaped beneath him, and Joe felt himself being drawn down.

Lost to you, what might have been . . .

A February evening, St. Pete's Beach. Joe sat on his stool, his back to the beauty of a Gulf sunset. His portraits lay strewn on the sand around him like the dead on a battlefield. A woman and man looked them over while Joe waited. The woman held the hand of a little girl and boy. Twins, Joe guessed. *Couldn't be much more than seven*, he thought. He remembered when that would have meant something to him, before Cath died, before . . .

The little girl tugged on the mother's hand. "They all look so sad, Mommy." The mother hushed the child while the father haggled with Joe over the price. The day had been slow, so Joe agreed to do both kids for the price of one.

Joe started sketching. His hand leapt over the paper, and the images of the children grew around the emptiness where their mouths should have been. A tear ran down his cheek, but he kept drawing.

He had to. He was hungry.

An afterword for this one, due to the spoilers. The story's structure is simple: a single point-of-view told in four sequential scenes, each introduced by a line of the poem that opens the story. The structure is also circular, with the closing scene mirroring the opening, with two important changes. First, Joe has replaced Cath as the possessed artist. Second, whereas Joe stopped Cath from sketching a child at the start, as the story closes, he's about to sketch not just one child, but two. Joe has fallen even lower than Cath.

I wanted the reader to move from fearing Cath to realizing that she was really the strong and noble one: she fought the thing longer than Joe, she took her life rather than kill Joe, and in the same situation, she resisted what Joe is about to succumb to in the end.

I never explain exactly what the thing inside is. I think it's scarier that way. The less you know, the more you fill in the blanks yourself. Think of it as a supernatural entity, or as a metaphor for the internal personal demons we all fight. I wanted the focus of the story to be the human part—the different choices that Cath and Joe each make when they face the thing.

This is the earliest story in this book—it was my second sale and my first to a major market (InterZone). The story revolves around the so-called Y2K bug, which was hyped to hysteria levels in the years and months and days running up to January 1, 2000. This is the only story I've written that draws heavily from my career experiences in the tech industry, and probably will be the only one. I write for pleasure, not to spend more time in my day job. The story was a finalist for the 1999 Aurora Award. And yes, I'm a fan of Casablanca. It's Bogey who states the theme for this one: "The important stuff in life is black and white, kid."

NEW YEAR'S EVE

971219: Friday, December 19, 1997

Bogey pushed his black queen's pawn forward to meet John's then leaned back. "Rick's Café Américain" throbbed white neon at John through a haze of cigarette smoke. Wobbling overhead, fans swirled the smoke in lazy eddies among crowded tables.

"Another closed defence," John muttered.

"You're a closed kinda guy," Bogey replied, immaculate in a white jacket and linen shirt, black bow tie and slacks. The beginning strains of "As Time Goes By" wafted from a piano somewhere off-display. He glared over his shoulder, motioning to a plump white-haired waiter in a black tuxedo. "Carl, get me a whiskey, and tell Sam to stop playing that damn song."

"Yes, monsieur, and for you, sir?"

"Mr. Dunne doesn't drink, Carl," Bogey said. "He hasn't figured that part out yet."

Carl waddled away, and John reached for his king's knight.

"Predictable," Bogey muttered.

John scowled at him, but a trilling sound cut off his reply. A telephone appeared, hovering above the table. Bogey lit another cigarette. "Still bothers me when it does that."

"And your smoking still bugs me," John said.

"Then you shoulda left smell out of the equation, kid. Answer the damn thing, will ya?"

The call display on the phone showed an internal PCWare extension and the name 'G. Hong.' John spoke. "Hi, George."

The ringing stopped, replaced by a disembodied voice. "J.D., my man, you still gonna walk me through it Monday?"

"Um, sure, yeah, I guess. Nine okay? Down here?"

"Be there. Have a good weekend. Ciao." Dial tone.

The phone vanished. "Um, I gotta go now," John muttered.

Shrugging, the man in the white jacket tipped over John's ivory king. "Well, you woulda lost anyway. Again."

John's jaw clenched. "Why do you try to irritate me?"

Bogey blew a cloud of smoke at him. "You tell me, kid. You're the programmer." He waved his hand around. "Probably revenge for what you did to my place."

"What do you mean? It's digitized right from the film."

"Yeah, but you *colourized* it!" Bogey glared at him, poking a finger at John's chest. "The important stuff in life is black and white, kid. Good guys, bad guys. Winners, losers. Us, them. Ones and zeroes. Everything else is just shades of grey. You'll be happier when you learn that."

"So what am I?"

"A good guy mostly. A loser always. One of them. A zero. Going back to her now?" He smiled. "Sure you are. At least in here, she's there when you get home."

"Shut up!" John snapped, manipulating his finger controls to move through the crowded bar. The chuckle behind him faded.

971220: Saturday, December 20, 1997
Washington Post: "Millennium Nightmare?—As we enter a new millennium, will our computers rerun the old one? For years, computer systems stored dates with only the last two digits of the year. The software simply stuck '19' in front when needed for display or calculations. Why? Well, it saved two bytes for each date in the system. Storage was expensive and smaller records meant faster I/O. Such systems would store today's date as 971220 (year-month-day for sorting). However, on January 1, 2000, a system with six-digit dates will merrily inform you the date is January 1, 1900, based on its stored date value of 000101. Analysts estimate 'Year2000' code fixes will cost $600 billion worldwide, and predict over 90% of current systems will fail on January 1, 2000."

971221: Sunday, December 21, 1997
At a bare white table in his small apartment, Ed Lochs nursed a beer as he dialled into the PCWare LAN from his home machine.

Suspecting all was not well with his job at PCWare, Ed had used his role as a support tech to install a program on the company's internal network. The program scanned e-mail traffic for message text containing his name, encrypting a copy of any such message to a file in Ed's private directory.

Now at home, he downloaded that file and entered a decrypt string. Messages for the week rolled in black and white across his monochrome screen. On the third one, he stopped. *Shit.*

TO: Sanjit Mohammed-taki, HR Director
FROM: Donald Masatoshi, VP New Products
DATE: 12/19/97
TOPIC: Employee Termination Notice needed

Sanj, as discussed, please prepare an ETN for Edward B. Lochs, effective January 6, 1998, based on three consecutive performance ratings below 4.0. Thx, Maz.

Asshole. Taking a swallow of beer, he switched screen windows and ran a program prepared weeks before. It finished and a grin creased his pale unshaven face. Connecting to the network again, he copied the program to a Project VR directory of modules which interfaced to date routines in PCWare's Portals 7.0 operating system. He entered his password as a VR team member to replace the existing program and signed off.

Have to wait a while, two years and a bit, but it'll be worth it. Swallowing the last of his beer, he raised the bottle in a mock toast. "Happy New Year!"

971222: Monday, December 22, 1997
After losing again to Bogey, John stepped from the bar onto New York's 5th Avenue, the Santa Claus parade underway. A huge penguin loomed from a passing iceberg float. Crowds watched in a light snow,

the air crisp with car fumes and people smells.

Hey, cool! I love parades.

The voice made John jump. "Jesus, George! You scared me."

Sorry, compadre. I said hello, but you didn't answer so I just grabbed the other VR unit. So where are we?

"New York, 1946, December morning."

Man, it looks real! A lot better than version zero.

"We use full multimedia links with WorldSource—TV, movies, news, songs, documentaries, encyclopaedias, almanacs . . ."

And everything else our fearless leader bought rights to.

The clip-clop of passing Clydesdales cut through George's words, moving gradually from John's left to right ear.

Hey! You've got directional sound.

"We track head movement relative to the sound source in the scene, adjusting the volume in each ear accordingly."

Holy shit! Literally. I smell the horses, popcorn . . .

"We code scenes with aroma keys. A special hardware unit holds a platter imbedded with over 5,000 highly compressed aroma pellets. The platter spins to the aroma key location and a laser-burst heats that spot on the disk. The unit captures the vapours and shoots them through a tube to the helmet."

Smell-o-vision finally arrives. Yuck.

"Laporte calls it VapourWare. It adds a third sense to the sight and sound of VR. Smell's mostly ignored but it's a powerful sense, you know. Taste depends heavily on smell."

Touch is high on my list, like with that blonde over there.

John squirmed. "Touch is left to the imagination."

Which, in my case, is pretty scary. So, how about a tour?

"Um, okay. I'll empty the street first so it'll be easier moving around. Computer, clear scene." With the words, the crowds and parade blinked off, like a B-movie special effect.

Kinda spooky. So how's it work?

"Okay, each building contains a different VR scene. This street is the main menu. Stroll along and enter buildings, or call up a map image and jump directly. The place on the right is the games room, set for chess in the café from *Casablanca*."

I thought this was New York, 1946?

"Each room can be different. The VR interface creates a room scene based on four characteristics defined by the user: City, time of day, month, year. You can change any parameter in any room. I've played around a bit to test the links."

City and year for location and era. Why month and time?

"Attention to detail. The month for correct weather and flora. Time defines the position of the sun, or moon. But year's the real key. We use it to retrieve multimedia clips from WorldSource to recreate the world you see. So where to?"

Better go over the controls.

John began to explain how to manoeuvre with glove controls and head motions. Then his voice trailed off, as the tall, slim figure of a woman stepped out of a building in the VR background and strolled toward them, each step accomplished with a languid roll of her hips.

Whoa! The scenery just improved. Who's this?

John's stomach knotted. He swallowed. "Uh, we use software 'agents' to execute certain tasks. We gave some human form, like this one. She acts as a guide, help desk . . ."

She stopped near foreground, flipping long black hair over the shoulder of a white pant suit. "Hello." Her voice was husky but feminine. "You're not Johnny. What's your name?"

Uh, George Hong, Team Leader, Millennium Project.

"Voice print validation in progress." Pause. "George Li Hong. Employee: 5053. Status: active. Project VR clearance: invalid." She smiled. "Sorry, Georgie. You're not cleared to be in here. I'm shutting you down. Too bad," she added, with a little pout, "you're kinda cute." The world went white.

She appears to act like a security guard as well.

"Uh, yeah. I'll restart, give you clearance, and switch control to you. I'll turn her off."

I'd rather turn her on. She looked familiar.

John didn't answer. They spent the next hour touring the VR city. Finally, George said he'd had enough. The scene faded to white. John removed a sleek black visor and helmet, blinking at the office lights. Black vines of computer cables hung everywhere, and paper sprouted like white fungus in every corner of the cramped office. He watched George pull off the shiny black VR gloves. "So what did you think?"

Flipping his ponytail over the back of the seat, George tipped his chair back, threatening a precariously balanced pile of manuals. "So it's incredible. I'm blown away. This will grab the small part of the market PCWare doesn't already own. You're a bloody genius." He looked at John. "So why so glum?"

"Maz asked me to demo it to Laporte after New Year's. He wants the VR interface released with version 7.0 of Portals."

"And this is a bad thing? A demo for the man himself?"

John stared at his black VR gloves, his mouth dry. "I'm no good in front of people I don't know. Especially an important person. I'm not good around people period. Don't like bars and parties. That's why Eve and I . . ." He couldn't finish.

"Eve! That's the babe in there! I knew she was familiar. With her hair pulled back, I didn't . . ." George halted abruptly, as John felt his face grow hot. "Uh, sorry, J.D."

"It's okay," John mumbled, embarrassed. "I mean, it's been a year since she . . . we decided to split up."

George gave a small smile. "Yeah, right." He rearranged the VR gloves. "So why'd you pick Eve for the VR guide?"

John fidgeted. "Um, well, we can't use professional models till Legal checks on royalties and stuff. But we wanted someone beautiful. And Eve is beautiful, isn't she?"

"Yeah, J.D., Eve is beautiful," George said softly.

"So I used our home movies, and the multimedia link, to create her as an agent," John said smiling. He felt good talking about her as his creation.

"And Eve said it's okay?"

John hesitated. "Um, sure. I mean, it's not like we don't talk. She calls me, oh, a couple times a week. Just to talk."

George looked away. "Good. Glad you're still friends."

John squirmed in his chair as George went on. "She seemed to really carry on a conversation. How'd you manage that?"

Relieved to talk about something purely technical, John relaxed. "We worked with psych departments, formal language groups, and AI researchers to develop an agent-interface program, an expert system which responds to statements and questions, based on a given Myers-Briggs personality type."

George blinked. "So agents not only carry on intelligent conversation, they have their own personalities, too?"

"Well, I'm not sure how intelligent it is. They respond precisely to system commands, and to a range of questions or statements. However, the longer the chain of questions, or the more obscure, the more their response will seem out of context, or," he added, thinking of Bogey, "like a cryptic platitude."

George played with the black VR helmet absently. "Sight, sound, smell. Access to WorldSource, the largest collection of knowledge on the globe. Now, full interplay with VR humans."

"Not full. No touching." He thought of Eve.

"Or taste," George said with a grin. John grimaced.

980106: Tuesday, January 6, 1998
Ink sketches in ebony frames stood out starkly against eggshell walls in the executive board room. Like some chaotic chess board, white paper pads spotted the obsidian sheen of a huge oval conference table. Black curtains covered each window, in defence against the frosty light and falling snow.

Don Masatoshi, VP New Products, regarded John Dunne, fidgeting in the chair beside him, hands trembling in black VR-gloves under the table. *Damn.* Maz brushed white shag rug hairs from the cuffs of his charcoal slacks and cleared his throat. "John, in the demo, I will do the talking. I know him better than you. You just manipulate the glove controls."

John's shoulders relaxed. "Thanks, Maz-san. I . . ."

"Forget it. We do not pay you to be a salesman. I need your skill with those." He tapped one of John's black gloves.

John smiled weakly then stiffened as the door flew open and Robert Laporte, Chairman, CEO, and majority shareholder of PCWare, exploded into the room. "Let's get this show on the road!" he boomed. Short, balding, and bespectacled, he projected the energy level of a rocket on a launching pad.

A baggy white sweatshirt and black denims flapped loosely on his lean frame, as he strode quickly to where Maz and John sat. "Masatoshi-san, you all set? John, isn't it?"

John rose to shake hands but the VR wires pulled him back. Maz groaned inwardly, but Laporte waved John down, slapping him on the shoulder. "Okay, Maz, so you'll walk me through Project VR, literally. Then we'll talk about whether it's part of 7.0. Which I would hope, since you promised it for 6.0 a year ago."

Maz started to reply, but Laporte chuckled. "I'm ribbing you, Maz. Hell, we weren't sure PCs could handle full VR a year ago. Now the hardware's caught up. The VR gear, too. We've cut unit costs to where I can *give* the gear away with 7.0." Laporte smiled as Maz raised an eyebrow. "Hey, my goal's market penetration, fast acceptance of the VR interface. With each copy, we throw in the helmet and gloves." He grinned. "Assuming you show me a product to sell."

Maz returned the grin. "Certainly." He motioned to John. "John is technical leader for Project VR. I will talk us through the demo, while John manoeuvres us through the scenes, so I do not walk us into a sewer." Maz paused as Laporte chuckled. "Now, please put on your helmet, and we will start."

For two hours, they hid behind the smoky visors and jet gloss of VR helmets, as Maz talked and John worked the gloves to tour the virtual city. Bogey and Casablanca were the hits Maz expected. "It's like the guy's alive," Laporte said.

Bogey shook his head as John declined a chess game. "Like I said, kid, life's black and white. You gotta pick a side and play the game. Is that why she left you? You wouldn't play the game?" He extended his fists, a pawn hidden in each. "Pick one, kid. You might win this time."

What the hell? thought Maz. "Uh, we are running late, and the last room contains just simple office automation. Let's move to questions." They pulled off their helmets.

Laporte shook his head. "Looks fantastic."

"So Release 7.0 will include the VR interface?" Maz asked.

"View-ee," Laporte corrected. "V-U-I. Like in 'gooey' for the soon-to-be forgotten GUI. Virtual Reality User Interface."

"What happened to the 'R'?" asked Maz.

"Verooey was not to Marketing's taste. Plus the VUI gives a new way to 'view' computers. Nice ring to it, too. As in cash registers." Laporte chuckled. "Good work, gentlemen."

Maz grinned, thinking of the vacant post of Executive VP of Operations. *Winners and losers*, he thought, *yin and yang*.

980107: Wednesday, January 7, 1998
Bits and Bytes, PCWare Internal Newsletter: "Yesterday I approved our Virtual Reality User Interface, the VUI (that's View-ee), for Portals 7.0, scheduled for retail March 2, 1998. We'll hold demos for staff over the next month. On a related note, we've promoted John Dunne, Project VR Leader, to Manager, Quality Assurance. Congratulations, John! —Robert Laporte."

980126: Monday, January 26, 1998
Snow opaqued the bottom of the palace windows, splitting each pane into white frost and inky night. Moving among the revellers, John sipped white nectar from an obsidian goblet, which tasted exactly like the milk in his black Batman mug.

He was working late, testing the VUI's date interface with Portals 7.0. A millennium's eve party gave him a fun way to verify the system year would flip to 2000 after December 31, 1999. It also let him be with Eve, alone in the office.

"Eve, set date, 1999-12-31. Set time, 11:30 PM."

She stepped from the crowd in a long black gown. "Another New Year's Eve, Johnny? I would've thought the last one was enough for you." She looked around. "Or have you programmed out the exits, so I can't walk out this time?"

His face grew hot. "Please acknowledge the date change."

She shrugged. "Acknowledged."

John watched as the hands on a nearby grandfather clock whirled to 11:30. He swallowed. "Would you like to dance?"

"Nope. Would you like to come upstairs?"

"What? What do you mean?"

She smiled. "What do you think?" She began a slow climb of the curving staircase. Her long pale legs split the folds of her dark dress with every step. With shaking fingers, John worked the gloves to follow her up winding stairs and through a maze of white carpeted halls until finally she turned into a room ahead of him. Reaching it, he stopped in the doorway.

She stood with one foot up on a bed canopied in black silk, exposing the length of her leg. Reaching under a cascade of dark hair, she undid her gown, letting it fall to her hips. Her breasts were bare, nipples painted black. As she moved her foot from the bed, the gown fell to the floor, sliding over black panties, garter belt and stockings, stark against white skin.

"Eve," he croaked.

Her smile held neither warmth nor invitation. "What's the matter, Johnny? Why don't you come and hold me?" She kicked off black high heels, and flowed onto the white sheets of the bed. Arching her back, she very slowly pulled her panties down to her thighs. Slipping them off, she lay back, legs spread. "Still over there?" she mocked. "You're about as good in a VR bedroom as you were in our real one."

His eyes burned but he couldn't tear them from her.

"Guess I'll just have to do it myself." Smiling, she moved a hand to between her legs. Somewhere a clock chimed midnight.

He continued to watch, until his own orgasm hit him, like in a wet dream. Taken by surprise, his spasms tore the wires from one glove, dropping the link. Ripping off the visor, he sat sobbing in the chair for several minutes, then stumbled to the washroom in the empty office. After, he put his parka on, and headed home in the swirling whiteness of a night storm.

980302: Monday, March 2, 1998

Wall Street Journal: "PCWare Inc. has released version 7.0 of Portals, their popular operating system for personal computers, incorporating the world's first Virtual Reality User Interface, or VUI ('View-ee'). PCWare's founder, Robert Laporte, stated that he expects the VUI to completely replace the GUI point-and-click interface common to most PCs. PCWare's bundling of the VUI and VR gear at no cost into version 7.0 drew charges of unfair competition practices from a group of other software vendors, since only PCWare's VapourWare technology and WorldSource multimedia interface with the VUI."

John leaned back in his chair as he finished reading the article to George. "Think he'll get away with it again?"

George snorted. "Does Mickey Mouse have ears?"

"Pretty soon," mused John, "you won't need a mouse."

George grimaced. "Pretty soon, you won't need a world." Pointing a hand in a black VR glove at John, he made a trigger pulling motion. "Zap! Reality is gone. Virtuality is all. Dial me a year, click me a place, and program me a life."

John thought of Eve, but said nothing.

981130: Monday, November 30, 1998

New York Times: "Early Q4 sales have far exceeded forecasts for PCWare's Portals 7.0. Analysts estimate that 95% of PCs in the world will use 7.0 by Q2 1999. The growth is credited to a rapid and rabid adoption of the VUI and the astute decision by PCWare to provide the requisite VR equipment with Portals 7.0."

981231: Thursday, December 31, 1998
Head bowed, John's tears dropped onto his visor, distorting the image of Eve in a black leather skirt, smoky stockings, and loose white blouse. Through the streaks, her black lipstick smile writhed like an adder across her face. She turned away.

"You can't do this to me again, Eve!" he cried.

"End of the old, start of the new. Time for a change."

"Don't leave. Not on New Year's Eve again. I've changed."

She looked back at him. "No, you haven't, Johnny. You're still the same boring little loser, a zero. You made me so much like the real Eve that I feel the same way about you."

"You are the real Eve," he blubbered. "I love you."

She shook her head. "The choice is always black and white to me, but you always choose wrong." She walked away.

He reached for her, not with the glove controls, but with his arms. Leaning forward in his office chair, he toppled to the floor, ripping wires from the helmet and gloves, cutting the VUI connection. His head cracked against a table leg.

He awoke, George and Maz kneeling over him. George helped him into a chair. "Shit, J.D., what happened? You okay?"

"Eve," he murmured. "She must still be in the building."

"What're you saying? Eve moved to Vancouver a year ago."

"Can't let her leave me again. Black or white. Gotta choose right this time, black or white." He looked up at them.

Maz stared at him for a breath, then turned to George, shaking his head. "Take him home."

George sighed. "Stay put. I'll get your coat."

John stared out the window at pearly flakes falling against the soot of the night sky. "Black or white," he whispered.

990129: Friday, January 29, 1999

Bits and Bytes, PCWare Internal Newsletter: "John Dunne, Project VR team leader, and more recently our QA Manager, is taking a well deserved paid LOA, in recognition of his role in 7.0's success. Thanks John! Enjoy your break! During John's absence, George Hong will act as interim QA Manager."

990920: Monday, September 20, 1999

Los Angeles Times, Fast Forward column: "Industry analysts estimate the world will have 270 million PCs at the turn of the century. With PCWare's Portals 7.0 holding an estimated 95% market share, more than a quarter of a billion people will be plugged into the now ubiquitous VUI by Year 2000."

991217: Friday, December 17, 1999

Maz leaned back into the black leather of the corner booth of Flanagan's dimly lit bar, feeling the warmth from his third scotch. "So what can the new Executive VP of Operations do for his favourite propeller head?"

George Hong sat slumped in the opposite seat, looking like his puppy had died. "Maz-san, you know about Year 2000 date issues, right? Remember a PCWare project called Millennium?"

The older man nodded. "1994. We scanned for year 2000 problems in Portals. Two-digit year fields and calculations. Millennium produced fixes for release 5.2 which hit retail, let's see, November 95. What about it?"

"You remember a PCWare employee named Ed Lochs? Tall, skinny, balding? You turfed him just before the 7.0 release."

Maz frowned. "Yes. Serious performance problems. So?"

The techy sighed. "One of my people was surfing some UK websites. She kept hearing this buzz about a bug in Portals."

Maz felt a tightness in his throat. "And?"

"She traced an e-mail chain back to Ed Lochs. He's on contract for some software apps firm in Dublin. I got worried and checked into what we had him on before he left. His last assignment was Project VR, coding the interface between the VUI and the Millennium date fixes. He added a patch in late '97. I had one of my people look at it."

Maz stared at him. George sighed and continued. "We found a Millennium bug in the VUI date link."

Maz shook his head. "The 5.2 Millennium date routines have been on the market for four years. A 5.2 bug would have shown by now, in calculations projecting past 1999. We never touched 5.2 date code after the fix. When we designed 7.0, we simply called the 5.2 routines, because we knew they were clean."

George nodded. "Yeah, but 7.0 included the VUI. The first thing the VUI does is call a 7.0 module called 'SceneSet' to get the system date. SceneSet then links to WorldSource to set the VR scenario, pulling backgrounds, agent costumes, era detail, etc., *all based on the year in the system date.*"

"Which should be correct from 5.2 fixes," Maz repeated.

George sighed. "Version 5.2 changed the system date to a four-digit year all right, but thanks to Lochs, now SceneSet in 7.0 only picks up the last two digits. Once 2000 hits, the VUI will think it's 1900, and show all rooms as from that era."

"That's it? What about date displays, prints, calcs?"

George shook his head, black ponytail falling down his white T-shirt. "All okay. It's just the VUI scene setter."

Maz snorted. "Big deal. Embarrassing, but the VUI will work. Once the system starts, the user can override to 2000."

"Nope. The scene setter won't accept a future date, since it can't link to WorldSource for a year which it thinks hasn't occurred yet. And the VUI will think it's 1900."

Maz groaned. "So it will be stuck in 1900 forever?"

"Until the real year flips to 2001, when you'll have the much larger choice of 1900 or 1901," George replied. "Plus, most users have by now customized their own VR rooms from different years. Any room later than 1900 will cause an error, defaulting back to 1900 scenes, pissing off a lot of people."

"Only two hundred and fifty million. You sure of this?"

"Shit, yes. I worked through the night on it, then had my staff run through it again today. Sorry, Maz. It's real."

Maz looked at George for a long while. He thought of his promotion, his chalet in the Muskokas, his black Porsche Carrera with the white leather seats.

"Black and white, too," George mused.

"What?" Maz said, startled.

"WorldSource photographs and movie reconstructs for 1900 are black and white. It'll all be black and white."

991230: Thursday, December 30, 1999

New York Times, High Tech page: "PCWare CEO Robert Laporte has terminated the contract of Donald Masatoshi, Executive VP, Operations. Laporte held Masatoshi principally responsible for the 'Millennium' bug in the Portals 7.0 operating system, installed on virtually every personal computer in the world. PCWare also fired a software engineer over the incident."

991231: New Year's Eve, 1999

Maz moved through the kata with the fluidity and grace of a dancer, the sleeves of his white *gi* snapping with each punch and block, his black belt whipping with each hip turn. The doorbell rang as he stepped into the final moves. His shouted "Come" substituted for the *kiai* on the last *shuto*, as he pulled up to the formal ending and bowed to invisible judges.

"Maz-san," a voice said quietly behind him.

Maz turned to face George Hong, standing at the door to the dojo room, black motorcycle jacket over a cream cotton T-shirt. George bowed and entered, tossing a thick white towel to Maz.

Maz wiped his face. "You saw him?"

"Yeah, for all the good it did. Told him Laporte canned him along with you, but I'm not sure he understood." George shook his head. "John's lost it, Maz. Thanked me for dropping in and said he was late for a very important date."

"The white rabbit?"

George didn't smile. "With Eve, in VR. He just turned his back on me, slipped on that damn black helmet, and tuned me out. I kept talking, but he ignored me. I let myself out."

"'The sword and Zen are one'," Maz murmured, stepping through another kata. "Martial arts and Zen agree on many points. Both forbid attachment to things. No matter how many techniques the *karateka* masters, if his mind becomes attached to techniques, he cannot win." Maz finished and looked at George. "The mind must not become fixed. Our John has become fixed, lost by attaching to a memory." He pointed to the white bundle of papers under George's arm. "What do you have there?"

"Another problem."

Maz sighed. "Do you know what the Greeks did to messengers such as you? Come into the sun room." He led George down a black-tiled hall to a glassed room at the back of the sprawling bungalow. They settled into white wicker chairs.

Squinting against the snow outside, George slipped on black Ray Bans. "Been doing some research on the Net. Medical websites, chats with clinics, psychologists, universities."

"About what?"

"*War of the Worlds* broadcast, Nazi propaganda mechanisms. Mass psychoses, large-scale hallucinations." He pulled papers from his pile, plopping them on the table as he spoke. "Mass media campaigns, subliminal advertising, AI. And, new studies on long-term exposure to sophisticated VR, like 7.0."

Maz rubbed his temples, feeling his fatigue. "My friend, I've had better weeks, so if you have a point . . ."

George leaned forward, slipping the sun glasses to the end of his short nose. "Two hundred and fifty million people."

Maz blinked. George went on. "Two hundred and fifty million VR users, thanks to the VUI and WorldSource and VapourWare and Laporte giving away VR sets. All seeing an exact copy of a wrong reality, thanks to the VUI bug. Tomorrow, a quarter of a *billion* VR users will slip on those damned black helmets and into a 1900 world, a world accurate to the minutest detail."

"What are you driving at?"

George tapped the top paper. "Stanford, May 1997: Doctors exposed subjects to a range of everyday scenarios, some in real life, some in VR. As exposure to VR grew, subjects experienced increasing difficulty reconstructing whether events occurred in reality or in VR. The same experiment was repeated with more scenarios and a larger test group at the University of Toronto in '98, and this year at McGill in Montreal." George leaned forward again. "The McGill study had five hundred subjects. Similar effects, but with a kicker: staff controlling the tests experienced the same distorted perception of reality."

"Leading you to believe what?"

George took a breath. "I think that two hundred and fifty million VR users all seeing the same distorted view of reality at once could affect . . . reality. I think that on New Year's Day reality could change to what a quarter of a billion users see in VR."

Maz stared at the programmer, then threw back his head, roaring with laughter as George reddened. "So tomorrow we wake up to 1900 outside? Is that it? We ride in carriages and wear those funny hats? Oh, George, thank you. My problems now seem so small." Maz rose and still chuckling went to a black enamelled cabinet, white dragons on each door. "Scotch?"

George stared at the snow hitting the dark asphalt of Maz's curving driveway. "Yeah, sure." He muttered something else.

Maz handed him a glass. "What did you say?"

"A quarter of a billion people," George said quietly.

000101: New Year's Day
On the first day of the new Millennium, John Dunne rose early, donned his black VR helmet and gloves, and settled down in front of his computer. Shortly before noon, he removed the helmet, placing

it on his lap. He sat for another half hour, black-gloved hand tapping on his white terry robe. Finally he rose, and dressed slowly. Donning a white ski jacket and black toque, he stepped onto the street. The black of city dirt mixed with the white of new snow to cover all with a wet grey smear.

Cabs sped by, ignoring his hail. Buying a paper, he began to walk and read. An article on the new space shuttle program caught his eye, along with a promotion announcement at PCWare.

A clip-clop sound caused him to turn. Still no taxis, but a horse-drawn trolley approached. He hailed it. Patting the glossy black rump of the closest horse, he pulled his Macintosh aside and climbed into the car, placing his top hat on the seat beside him. Turning back to his paper, he read that F.W. Woolworth, projecting revenues of $5 million, had opened his 59th store. He scanned an article on McKinley's "full dinner pail" re-election campaign, and an editorial on the Democratic ticket of William Jennings Bryan and Adlai Stevenson.

The driver signalled his stop, and John stepped down to find her waiting. Mud speckled the ruffle at the foot of her long black dress. She leaned demurely on a white parasol.

"Eve," he said smiling. He pulled her close, thrilling to her body against his, the taste of her lips.

"You're late," she teased, but with warmth.

"Many years late, I fear."

"No matter," she replied. They walked into the park, her white-gloved hand resting lightly on the black of his sleeve.

"I think," he said, "it will be a happy new year."

She smiled but didn't answer.

My favourite SF&F writer is the late Roger Zelazny. I'd like to think that he would have enjoyed this one, another early story. I hope that you will, too.

THE BOYS ARE
BACK IN TOWN

The shrill cry of a harpy sounded as I stepped into our tavern. A pair of them sat slumped in a booth, heads on the table, wings flapping feebly. The Sibyl plopped two drafts between them, and one harpy lifted its head briefly to emit a high-pitched "screeee!" At the bar, an elderly tourist couple and two centaurs stood sipping red liquid from tall glasses. A Tarot spread lay on the bar in front of the ample frame of Dino, my partner, and when the Sibyl returned, she began turning cards. I slipped onto a stool beside her. Dino was scowling.

"Problem?" I asked.

He jerked his head at the harpies as he cleaned a glass. "They keep crapping on the carpet. Stinking spawn of Oceanus."

"Take them out back. They can wait there."

He shook his head. "They don't like being near the gate."

I nodded toward the tourist couple. "Any trouble?"

He shrugged huge shoulders. "Gave them a shot of ambrosia, and they've been fine, 'cept for complaints about the noisy college kids." He glared at the harpies again.

I grinned. We really didn't mind harpies, nor centaurs, fawns, or even an occasional cyclops. The humans were no trouble, either. Better credit risks, too. The real problem in running our establishment was the mix—as in mixing twentieth-century, good-credit humans with creatures that weren't supposed to exist, let alone be buying you drinks in a quiet little tavern.

Keeping it a quiet little tavern—and not a news feature—required some special measures. An illusion spell, activated at the door, convinced humans this was all quite normal. The spell lasted until the ambrosia took hold. After that, lawyers flirted with nymphs, tourists played pinball with satyrs, and professors debated hydras. Tough bet, that last one. Hydras aren't too bright, but just try getting a word in against multiple heads.

The Sibyl turned another Tarot card, white eyes staring straight ahead. "Old friends coming."

"On the ferry?" I asked.

No reply. Conversation wasn't her strong suit but she'd answer questions. Eventually. I was glad she was back on the Tarot. Lately she'd been into goat entrails, and that had really stained the bar.

I glanced at the clock: 7:10 in the evening. The gate would open in forty-five minutes. Then many of our non-human guests would depart the tavern and this world. Forever.

Dino caught my glance. "You weren't in much this week."

I shrugged. "Busy. I miss anything?"

"Last night the gate opened at 7:50."

I laughed. "Come off it. Three centuries, every night, 7:55 on the dot. Never a miss. Why would it suddenly change?"

"Maybe somebody doesn't want to wait."

I chuckled. "You think one of this lot can cycle the gate?"

He didn't smile. "No. Nobody here." The centaurs banged on the bar, calling for wine. "Hoofs off the marble, you two," Dino roared, "or you'll take the ferry out of here, not the gate!"

He left to pour their order while I sat musing. Nobody we knew could cycle the gate except me. Nobody on this side anyway.

The Sibyl turned a card. "Not by the ferry they come."

"Then how?" I asked. No answer. I had a sudden urge to check out back. Sliding off the stool, I walked to a door marked Employees Only and stepped into the grove.

Located on an island in the Toronto harbour, our tavern entirely spanned a tiny finger of land, blocking access to the peninsula's tip. Evergreens lined the shore behind us, broken only by a hidden inlet. We designed the grove to conceal.

I walked a gravel path to stone steps worn smooth over the years by a variety of shapes at the end of a variety of legs: talons and claws, hooves both cloven and uncloven, and the occasional serpentine patron with no feet at all.

I climbed the steps to an octagonal dais ten paces wide and set on mortar and stone eight feet above the grass. Blue flames burned in high recesses of the eight marble pillars that supported the domed roof. Images of gods and demons from scores of ancient religions were carved in each pillar. Carved by my hand. A conceit, but our patrons expected a bit of atmosphere.

We posted no guard. The facility was "Exit Only." At its centre, the platform changed from grey stone to a circular ebon sheen six paces wide. It trembled like the surface of an oily pool. Colours I could never name flickered in its black depths.

The gate.

I bowed. A habit, but I respected anything older than I was. I also respected the last of anything. In those ways, we were alike. Old and alone.

Once these portals pulsed throughout our world. Ages ago, I had defeated its kin, sealing them forever. This one I'd bound, quieting its raging heart to the beat of a sleeping giant. I'd regarded it a million times over not quite so many years.

Now, for the first time in a very long while, I touched it with my mind. Its pulse was slow, unchanged since our ancient struggle, to the best of my telling. I turned to leave. A tingle on the back of my neck, like the hovering of a cold hand, stopped me, and I spun around.

Nothing.

Still uneasy, I descended the steps and walked to the hidden inlet. The Toronto ferry was pulling out from the mainland dock, shuttling tourists and city-dwellers from the downtown heat to the cool of these islands. I scanned the harbour for our own private ferry. There. About a hundred yards out, the air above the water shimmered. Focusing on the spot, I reached with my mind. The shimmer coalesced into a huge, flat barge.

A serpent head reared at the prow, carved from wood as black as the gates of Hades, fist-sized rubies burning in each eye. The wood actually did come from the gates of Hades, but that's another tale. Figures clustered near the front, straining to see the shore. Those would be the travellers, come to use the gate, hoping a better world for their kind lay on the other side. Our regulars, here just to drink with old friends, lazed on the deck.

On a raised platform at the stern, hand on the rudder bar, stood the ferryman. Stood as he had for more centuries than I cared to remember. Charon. His job had changed, yet stayed the same. Even after the fall of Olympus and Asgard, after the exodus of the gods, he still ferried travellers from our world to another. Not death now, but it was still a one-way trip. Or so I thought.

The barge slid onto the beach without a tremor. I watched as the Sibyl led the travellers to our rear entrance. Some were alone, most in groups, many with bundles of belongings. If they could carry it, they could take it. That was our rule.

Then I saw her: flowered sundress, white floppy-brimmed hat, mirrored sunglasses. She was keeping to herself, or the other passengers were taking pains to keep their distance. On a crowded barge, the lady enjoyed a six-foot circle of space. Her figure made the distance of at least the male passengers hard to explain. Then her hat brim moved in the wind. Her hair, too.

Except no wind blew. Not a breeze. I shivered.

The barge emptied before the gorgon moved to leave. I nodded at her. Smiling back, she removed her hat, keeping the sunglasses on. She flowed up to where I leaned against a willow trunk, her hair a writhing frame around a face to die for. Or from.

"You are the proprietor?" she asked, in Latin.

"One of them, my lady," I replied in the same language.

"I wish to use the . . . facilities."

"The washrooms, or the other facilities?"

She laughed. I liked the sound. "The other, if I may."

I nodded. "It'll cycle in about thirty minutes. I'll lead you there when it's time."

"Thank you." She flashed a smile that hit me in the throat, and slithered down my spine. I asked her name. "Euryale," she replied. I gave her my arm, and we went inside.

I introduced Dino and ordered two ambrosias. We moved to my booth. She seemed to be staring at me. The dark glasses made it hard to tell.

"I know you now. You are . . ."

"Paulo," I interrupted. "I go by Paulo now."

"Paulo, then. Paulo and Dino. The gods descended, so to speak." She laughed again. I still liked it.

The Sibyl brought us two snifters of amber fluid. "Almost clear. Old ones come."

I sighed. "Before, you said old friends. Which is it?"

"Were old friends. Not sure now." She turned away. That's the problem with oracles, even your own. Once you've figured out what the hell they mean, it's too late.

I turned back to Euryale. "Your kind didn't follow us once we moved from Olympus to the Norse lands."

"A mistake. Without your protection, we became hunted. We fled to Africa then moved on. Always moving on." She sounded tired. "I have lived everywhere this world has to offer. Now I have a villa in the south of France."

"Doing what?"

"I . . . create. Yes, that is the best word. Sculptures. In stone." She looked away.

I caught a glimpse behind the glasses and shuddered. "Life size? Human figures?" I offered. A nod. I shuddered again.

She laughed. "Please believe me. I am selective in my subjects— murderers, abusers of women and children. I touch those the law cannot."

Shouts from the bar turned both our heads. Two satyrs were arguing, apparently over a wood nymph. One pulled a dagger from his belt. A hush fell on the room. The satyr with the knife lunged, then stopped. A look of serene pleasure washed over him.

Behind the bar stood Dino in full splendour. Sunshine lit the room, and the air filled with birdcalls, lovers' whispers, music, drinking songs. The satyr swayed. A ray of the warmest, cheeriest light flashed from Dino's fingers. The ambrosia beam knocked the creature to the floor, giggling and smiling.

Dino. Dionysus. He can generate an instant party in your head. Followed by a hell of a hangover.

Normal activity in the room resumed. I turned back to a laughing Euryale. "What brings you here?"

Her smile faded. "Immortality and loneliness mix poorly. Sthenno, my sister, killed herself last year."

"I'm sorry." I put my hand on hers. She didn't pull away.

"So now I move on again, to the world on the other side of the gate." She stared at me. "And what has kept you here, Paulo? Your time has passed, too."

I looked around. "Our travellers hope the gate leads to a world where the old gods rule, where they can belong again. But that's not for me. I love this world. Always did, always will."

Euryale started to reply, but the next sound came from the Sibyl. The oracle screamed, a stab of noise that jerked me to my feet. The harpies joined in with long piercing screeches.

"Incoming!" Dino roared, tossing me my walking stick as I sprinted for the back door. I willed energy into the stick. It thickened, shortened, shifted. I burst into the grove, my hammer Mjolnir at my side. A sickly yellow glow etched with strands of black lit the platform. The gate was cycling. I flashed a look at my watch: 7:42. Dino was right. Something *was* wrong.

A mist rose from the black pool, swirling up into a smoky column. As I reached the steps, the column collapsed in light and thunder, throwing me back. Ears ringing, I got up—and blinked. A huge bearded figure stood on the platform, horned helmet on his head, a great spear in one hand. A round, leather shield was strapped to his other arm. Beside him stood a younger warrior, tall and fair, a sword the colour of blood in his hand.

The older one stepped forward, and I looked upon the one who was Odin All-Father, Zeus, Osiris, Brahma—you name it. Pop to me. Grinning, he fixed me with his one good eye, then spoke in a Norse dialect I'd almost forgotten. "Hey, kid! Buy us a drink?"

I hefted my hammer as Dino growled behind me. Pop raised his free hand. "Hold on. We're here to talk, not fight."

"Why should we trust you?" I asked.

He glared at me. "I give you my word."

I snorted, and his glare darkened. The other warrior stepped up. "Thor, Bragi—I give you *my* word."

Frey. One of the few relatives I'd missed. I stared at his sword as he sheathed it. The Red Blade. It could cut a field of carnage at its wielder's command. Unfortunately, it wasn't very discriminating, which is why we gave it to Frey. The god of rain, sunshine, and harvests, his nature was to protect life. He was the only one that we'd all trusted. I realized that I still trusted him.

"All right. But Gungnir stays here," I said, pointing at Pop's deadly spear.

Pop scowled storm clouds but laid it down. "If there's no lightning, there can be no thunder." He glanced at my hammer. I shrugged, shifting Mjolnir back to a walking stick.

They descended the steps, and I gripped forearms with both of them. Dino embraced Frey but just exchanged curt nods with Pop. We'd both had our reasons for staying when the others left. Dino's had been to put some space and time between himself and Pop.

We entered the bar to find the olden folk prostrate on the floor. They never did that for me anymore. Pop bade them rise, while I told the tourist couple that our guests were guitarists with a local band. I declared the gate closed until the next evening. Some travellers left to take Charon's ferry back to their homes, scattered over the globe. But most stayed to drink with the regulars, electing to wait for Charon's late-night run.

Pop and Frey bowed to Euryale. She seemed in awe as I led her away. "Sorry," I said. "Family stuff." She nodded and squeezed my hand. I returned to sit beside Dino.

Pop leered after Euryale. "Nice tits."

"You're still the horniest creature I've ever met," I said.

"Good thing for you," he said. "You might not be around."

The Sibyl thunked four steins of mead down on our table. "Told you. Old friends coming. Not by ferry."

"Yeah, thanks a bunch," I said. "Couldn't have managed without you." She glared at me and left. We clinked steins then sat drinking as the silence grew to an awkward level.

Finally Pop spoke. "You've made some changes."

"Been visiting?" I asked.

"We talk to travellers who come through the gate."

Seeing my look, Frey added quickly. "Nobody gets hurt. They go their way after we talk."

Odin snorted. "Anyway, you two never liked how we handled things. I figured you'd try something different after we left."

"We did," I said.

Pop laughed. "You're running a goddam bar."

"We adopted a hands-off approach," Dino said with a grin.

Pop leaned forward. "Hands-off? Every structure, every religion we set up, centuries of work! You let them die!"

"No," I said. "We killed them."

Pop sat open-mouthed. Frey raised an eyebrow.

I went on. "New religions arose, and we encouraged them. The baser traits of our old pantheons came to be frowned upon. The new gods set high standards. Our family just couldn't cut it."

Pop glowered, but Frey smiled. I continued. "Then we helped science a bit. Hard to believe in Zeus or Odin once you know where thunderbolts really come from. You made a mistake there, Pop, basing our powers in explanations of nature. Discredit the premise, and you discredit the god." Pop didn't return my smile.

"Finally, we introduced economics, ultimately the key move. Tough competing with greed as a god."

Pop slammed down his empty stein. "But we existed! What about all we built, the history of this world?"

"That was trickier. Using the new religions, we suppressed the teaching of history for a few generations. Blasphemy, you know.

Eventually the old gods became myths."

"Myth?" Pop roared. Heads turned. "They think I'm a myth?"

"Afraid so. The hardest part was hiding our old homes as archaeology began to flourish. Olympus, Asgard, Atlantis—all buried."

"You bastard!" he growled.

I shrugged. "Most of your kids were." Frey hid a grin.

Pop's fist shook the table, and the old flames burned in his eyes. "*We ruled this world!* We were gods to these creatures!"

"We played at being gods," said Dino quietly.

"We created life—" Pop snarled.

"And took it," I added.

He ignored it. "We gave protection, magic, wonder. We destroyed any that threatened them—"

"Or us."

"We gave a world to these mortals you coddle!"

"*We* have given them freedom," I said.

"The Old Ones, Saturn and the Titans, Ymir and the Giants, the Demons—" he grabbed me by the shirt "—all fell before us!"

I pulled his hand away. "I know. I was there, remember?"

"We made this world, and we ruled it." He slumped back, glaring at all of us. "If that doesn't make us gods, what does?"

"Have to ask a god, I guess," I said. "Met any lately?"

Pop's eyes narrowed to slits. "What do you mean?"

"You've found something you can't handle."

"What makes you think that?" Pop snapped.

Frey shook his head. "Odin, he knows . . ."

"You were never first through a gate," I said. "You'd send me or Frey first and have us report back."

Pop looked away. "I always knew I could trust you two."

We fell silent. "So how bad is it?" I asked finally.

The centuries came to rest in their eyes. "Bad," Frey said. "A night world, shifting landscapes . . ."

"With creatures that make your lady friend over there look like a kitten," Pop added.

"Our powers didn't work the same," Frey said. "It took time to adjust. We won the early battles, but many died."

I felt a pang of guilt. "Sorry. I didn't ask who's left."

"Figured you didn't care," Pop said, watching me flinch.

"Vidar and Hodur fell in the first battles," Frey said.

I swallowed. My brothers. "You kept our Norse names?"

He nodded. "Ve died the next year. Iduna, too."

An uncle. And Dino's ex-wife. Dino's face was stone.

"We'd lost half the Valkyrior by then," Frey said. "But we were established. Things settled down for centuries. Some skirmishes with local deities, but nothing major." He stopped.

"Then, it seems, we attracted somebody's attention."

"We aren't the only ones who can control gates, kid," Pop said. "This other world has lots, connecting to places that make no sense to us. Higher dimensions, maybe. Gates began opening everywhere." He paused. "Then *they* came through."

"Who?" Dino asked.

He shook his head. "We call them 'the others.' Don't know what they call themselves. They're not big on communicating. Can't even describe them. They're never the same, like they have a dimension we don't. Fast, too. Damn fast."

"They can vanish in front of you, reappear behind you," Frey said. "They caught us in a group one day." His face was grim.

Pop swore. "My brother Vili, Heimdall the Good, Hermod—they fell in the first minute!" I'd never seen fear in his eyes before. "We fought through, Frey leading after Tyr fell."

The god of battles, dead? Tyr the One-Handed. Ares, Mars. Whatever. One tough dude. Frey looked at me. "Freya died, too, Thor."

His sister. A long time ago, I'd loved her. She'd gone by Aphrodite then. I swallowed hard. We sat silent for a while.

"You're missing some names," Dino said finally.

Frey nodded. "He's still alive. Fenrir and Hela, too."

Loki. And his wolf-son and hell-spawn daughter. "Typical that only Loki's family would survive intact," I said.

"He's calling the shots now, Thor," Frey said. "He sent us through first. We're holed up on the other side of this gate. It's the only way out for us." He looked away from Pop.

I could feel Pop's shame burning in him. I waited. When he finally spoke, though, his voice was low and firm. "We're coming back, kid. Nowhere else to go."

"Then what?"

Pop spread his hands, trying to grin. "Then it's business as usual. Just like the old days!" He slapped me on my arm.

"The god business? This world doesn't need us, Pop. These mortals can take care of themselves now."

He snorted. "We've talked to your exodus through the gate, kid. Your precious humans are killing this world."

"They're closer to peace than ever before," I replied.

"Nuclear weapons?" he asked.

"Cities that rival Olympus," I said.

"Environmental destruction?"

"They've reached the moon."

"Can't feed their own people?"

"They've eradicated diseases."

"AIDS?"

I brought my fist down on the table. "All right! They've made mistakes. They'll make more. But at least the mistakes are theirs. They're free, Odin, and they're staying that way!"

"I don't understand you." He shook his head. "We're coming back, kid, whether you want us or not."

"Try it," Dino said, his eyes like slits.

"Two of you, against all of us?" Pop said.

"Doesn't sound like you have many left," I said quietly. "And you can only come through one or two at a time."

"We can use other gates."

I smiled, and Frey's eyes narrowed. "I told you, Odin. He's sealed them. That's why we couldn't find any others."

We sat in silence. Finally Pop sighed. "Guess we'll head back now. We can use the gate?"

I shrugged. "As long as the traffic's outbound."

We all stood. "Sorry it has to be this way," Frey said.

"Me, too." Leaving the Sibyl in charge, I led them past fearful faces. Euryale began to rise, but I shook my head.

Odin and Frey stood on the platform before the black pool of the gate, while Dino and I remained below on the grass. I didn't want to give them a chance to pull me through. If they could get me to their side, they'd win.

"I'll open it," I said.

"Don't trust us?" Odin asked. Frey smiled.

Not answering, I closed my eyes, focusing on the pool. My first warning came as a resistance in the flow, another will pushing back.

"Paulo!" Dino yelled.

I looked up. The inky pillar was already rising. Someone on the other side was cycling the gate. A blue arm stabbed from the blackness.

I knew that arm.

"Behind you!" I cried.

Spinning around, Frey drew the Red Blade and stepped in front of Pop. An azure spear of light flashed from the arm to strike Frey. He screamed and fell back, the sword flying from his hand. The blast knocked Pop from the platform to the grass below.

"Treachery!" Odin yelled as he picked himself up.

I scrambled up the steps. Frey lay frozen, ice-covered limbs and face twisted in agony. His clothes, armour, and flesh reflected the pillar's flames in deep hues of blue.

"The sword!" Dino shouted. The rising black pillar blocked any view of the far side. The Red Blade was nowhere in sight. I moved forward to search just as *she* stepped from the gate.

Her one side pulsed with a cold blue light, ice forming and

reforming on its surface. Her other was human flesh that aged and rotted as I stared. The skin bulged at spots as if something beneath fought to escape. Grey hair fell past a face that kept shifting to a skull. Blood red lips framed black pointed teeth, and her eyes were the white of maggots feeding on a corpse. Sickly, yet tantalizing, as inescapable as death. For Death she was: Hela, daughter of Loki. The mistress of Niflheim, the Underworld. I raised my hammer. An ebon tendril snaked from the gate and expanded to the shape of a shield before her. What in Hades was that? She pointed her blue arm at me.

"Hold, daughter," a voice cooed, all syrup and snake venom. "Leave them to me."

I turned. A slim, black-caped figure stood with a booted foot on Frey. Loki. In his hand was the Red Blade.

Dino moved to the steps. Loki spun, long black hair flying, his free hand drawing a circle. Dino froze.

Loki smiled at me. "Well, well. Hammer boy and the drunkard, still alive. I had hoped your loving family would do my work for me." He hefted the Red Blade. "However, the point is now moot." A high whine sounded, and the Red Blade flew from his hand at an immobile Dino.

"No!" Pop yelled and threw himself in front of my brother. The sword sliced through his breastplate as if it wasn't there. Pop fell, blood spurting from his chest. The Red Blade continued in an arc, returning to Loki.

I don't remember leaping from the platform or covering the ground to where Pop lay, but somehow I was there, cradling his head in my lap, pressing on the wound, trying to stop the flow.

The whine began again. Loki was willing the blade for a second attack. But another sound brought my head up—a groan from the frozen form of Frey at Loki's feet.

The Red Blade shot singing from Loki's hand to bury itself in Hela's breast. She screamed the scream of the damned. Blue light flowed into the sword, and red flames from the blade licked her skin as Death's cold touch battled the sword that drank life.

Frey lived. Centuries as the Blade's keeper had allowed him to wrench control from Loki.

Roaring, Loki kicked out. Frey's body burst into blue shards and scattered over the stone. Dots of fire erupted wherever a shard hit the black pillar.

Released from the spell, Dino fired a beam at Loki. Again an ebon tendril snaked from the gate, expanded to the shape of a hand and intercepted the bolt. How had that happened?

I turned back to Pop, hoping that Dino could keep Loki busy for a while.

Pop shook his head. "No use, kid," he whispered.

Something growled. I looked up to the gate—and into eyes of yellow flame. A huge wolf the size of a horse and black as the gate itself stood on the platform.

Fenrir, Loki's puppy, had come to play.

In ages past, the blind Norns had foretold Ragnarok, the Twilight of the Gods. On the battlefield Vigrid, the story goes, as the world crumbles about us, the gods would destroy each other. I always believed the tale, because it sounded like my family. Fenrir, the Norns said, would slay Odin or me. They were vague on the victim, but the nasty consistency of the victor always bothered me.

I had no time for a throw. But as Fenrir crouched to leap, Hela's battle with the Red Blade ended. Hell maid and sword exploded in a blue blaze, hurling the wolf with a surprised yelp to the grass below. I threw my hammer as he landed thirty feet away, striking him between his flaming eyes. I grinned, but it didn't last. Fenrir shook his massive head, sneezed once, then turned to me, death in his eyes.

Tough puppy.

"Thor!" The voice was a shouted whisper. Pop lay gasping on the grass. In his hand, he held a gossamer loop of light. He released it, and it stayed there, hovering like a halo above him.

Gleipnir.

Softer than air, stronger than a Frost giant. Fashioned for us by mountain spirits eons ago. Fashioned from the noise of a cat's step, the breath of fishes, the senses of a bear, the roots of stones, and the spittle of birds. Fashioned to bind the wolf.

Fenrir leapt. Grabbing Gleipnir, I shoved the silken loop up in front of me, just as the wolf landed on my chest. The stench of battlefields and rotting corpses assailed me. He lunged for my neck—and his head slipped through Gleipnir. His motions slowed. His body shrank, his weight on me lightened. I blinked.

I held a whimpering dog, Gleipnir taut around its neck. Throwing him off, I drove the thread's other end into the ground with Pop's spear. Pop lay very still, but I had no time.

At the steps stood Dino and Loki, a wall of Dino's light dancing between them. Black tentacles from the gate writhed inside that light. Somehow, Loki was manipulating the substance of the gate itself. The tendrils formed into a giant hand and shoved against the wall of light. Dino stumbled, and his shield flickered. Balling into a fist, the black hand came crashing down on him. He didn't rise. The fist reared back again.

"No!" I cried, throwing Mjolnir at Loki. The fist stopped its descent and swooped to ensnare the hammer. Another black tendril coiled around me, lifting me into the air.

Loki strolled over, grinning. "Somehow, I knew it would come down to the two of us. Now, my version of Ragnarok, myself excluded." The fist became an ebon spear, pointed at my chest.

"Good evening." The voice was husky, a sultry stiletto slicing the night. At the entrance to the grove stood Euryale, hands on hips, smile on lips. She again wore both hat and sunglasses. "Man in black," she said, "you have my boyfriend."

Loki gave Euryale a leisurely appraisal, then bowed. "I thank you for the news, maid. Now Thor will watch me enjoy your charms before you both die." He walked to her grinning.

Smiling back, she reached for her glasses. I looked away. Loki screamed.

That scream is a thing I'll always remember, a salve for the memory of Frey and Pop and all the evil Loki had ever done to us.

The grip about me vanished. I fell hard to the ground, but I kept my eyes shut. "Okay," she called. "You can look."

Her glasses were back. Before her stood a stone figure, arms raised as if to ward off a blow. I walked to it. Horror was etched in every line of that face.

Loki hadn't been in Greece with us. This had been his first encounter with a gorgon. And his last. I took her in my arms. The snake heads tickled my neck.

Euryale gasped, and I spun around.

Like the overflow of a putrid bog, a black mist poured over the gate's platform and onto the grass. Black tendrils reached out from it, searching, grasping. The fog quickly rose to the domed roof, hiding the platform structure.

Something cold and alien touched my mind. Something half-forgotten.

Sealer! Tanthol lives!

My jaw tightened.

Do you remember, Sealer?

I remembered.

Pure hate flowed at me. *Come to Tanthol, Sealer. After so many years, it is time.*

The fog parted, revealing the steps.

"Paulo, no!" Euryale grabbed my arm.

I kissed her, then handed her to Dino. "You can't help on this one. Stay here." I turned to the gate. "This ends now."

I climbed the steps to stand before the inky pool. Black flames writhed above it, licking the roof. Behind me, the fog closed in again, pushing me closer as I searched for the place in my mind from where I'd fought this creature so long ago.

Come, Sealer! Feel my fire once more. A dagger of darkness shot at me from the flames. Before me, a disc of light appeared, barely blocking the thrust. I focused. The disc became a white aura around me.

The equivalent of a chuckle formed in my mind. *You have slowed, Sealer. Grown old, weak. You cannot defeat me.*

"Try me," I growled. The fog closed in. I struggled to maintain my aura. "How . . . ?"

Your brethren's attempts to open the way awoke me.

"You helped Loki," I gasped as the fog crushed in on me.

I chose him. The fool believed he controlled me. With each use he made of my essence, I fed on his own until I was restored.

My aura flickered then collapsed. The blackness touched me.

I awoke to nothingness. No light or sound. No smell. No heat or cold. No up or down. Nor was I breathing.

Are you dead, you wonder? Not yet. First I will taste your fear, let you feel this place where you sent me, Sealer.

I tried to focus, to find a weapon. Only blackness came.

I will open the way to those your kin fled. They will suck the juices from your world. I may let you live to watch that.

Only blackness. Centuries ago, my powers as Thor had bound Tanthol, the last of the gates, and destroyed his brethren. Those powers were useless in this void that held nothing to bind, to strike.

Blackness. A tiny hope sparked in my mind.

I'd lived as many beings. Beings this world once called gods. Thor, Set, Techlotl, Yetl. And one other.

Blackness. I reached inside myself to a place unvisited since we stayed behind. It welcomed me, the prodigal son. I was home again. Here lived my true nature.

Hell, I'd even kept the name.

I called upon my power in that place. It filled me as if I were a vacuum. I fanned its flames—and let it burst forth. "Feel my power, demon!" I cried. "Feel the power of Apollo!"

As we said—let there be light.

Radiance broke from my being, consuming the darkness. Its scream exploded in my mind. *No! It burns!*

Then I was falling, stars above, cool air in my lungs. I collapsed on wet grass. A whisper hissed on the night breeze. *Sealer!* Then nothing.

Strong hands lifted me to my feet, and I looked into Dino's worried face. "You okay?" he asked, and I lied with a nod.

"Good. So what in Hades just happened?"

"Paulo!" Euryale knelt with Pop's head in her lap. We rushed to them. Pop's lips moved. I leaned closer.

"Sorry," he whispered. "Didn't want this. Loki used me."

"Don't talk."

He smiled. "All those years—I missed you two." His smile faded, and his head fell against Euryale. Dino was sobbing. I realized I was, too.

The father of the gods was dead.

And on the next day, we rested. Well, sort of. We buried Pop and Frey in the platform where the gate had been, covering it with a marble slab. I carved an inscription in runes. I won't say what it was, but even Dino approved. Two stone figures flanked the steps leading to what was now a family shrine. Loki and Fenrir. Dino christened the spot by pissing on them both.

After, we stood at the lake's edge, my arm around Euryale, watching the sun startle the skyline awake. Dino sat astride Fenrir. Gazing at the city, I remembered Pop's words, about this world, these people of mine. I thought about the wars, the crime, the hunger, the pollution, the suffering. I fingered my stick. "You know, maybe we've been a little *too* hands-off."

Dino grinned.

Euryale squeezed my hand. "Well, we can't leave this world now. So if you need help . . ."

A voice sounded behind us. "The signs are clear." The Sibyl was bent over Hela's remains, knife in one hand, entrails in the other. So much for the Tarot. She looked up. "A change comes," she whispered.

For once, I knew what she meant.

Here's another of my earlier stories and the one that started the clock ticking for my eligibility for the John W. Campbell Award for Best New Writer (I made the final ballot in 2004, but lost to another Smith, the fine U.S. writer, Kristine Smith). It was a finalist for the 2000 Aurora Award and received an honourable mention in The Year's Best Fantasy & Horror. *More on this story later.*

STATE OF DISORDER

And thus the whirligig of time brings in his revenges.
—Shakespeare, Twelfth Night

Tick.

In the banquet hall of a sprawling castle of a house, the woman looks up, startled. The dishes of the night's dinner still litter the long table before her. At the evening's outset, the table had been so clean, its settings so precise. She tries to recall each step in its journey from order to chaos but fails.

Tick.

She jumps again at the sound. A man's wristwatch lies at the table's far end. He has left it, forgotten or unwanted. Or for another reason. The watch is old with a broken strap; the woman young with a broken heart. The watch lies face down, but she knows it is the old-fashioned kind with hands. A date will show in a little window. A date from a time long ago. Two lives ago. It will be today's date. She wonders how she knows that.

Tick.

Rising, she moves toward the watch . . .

"My God, James. Look at this place," Caroline exclaimed.

James Mackaby put down the book he was reading to their young son, David, and looked out the window of their limousine. Their driver was negotiating a street filled with refuse and the abandoned corpses of burnt-out cars. Under a late afternoon sun, men in ragged clothing slept or sprawled on steps before low-rise apartments. The nearest group of men shouted something at the car as they passed around a bottle.

The limousine pulled up to the curb in front of a dirty-grey, three-storied building. Crumbling steps led to a door with a crisscross of planks covering its broken glass. Mackaby surveyed the scene and looked back to his wife. "Looks like Dr. Harnish has fallen lower than I thought."

"Are you sure it's wise to go?" Caroline asked. "He was very uncivil to you when the University dismissed him."

Mackaby felt uneasy at the memory. But for her sake, he forced a smile. "He was treating everyone that way by then."

"Still . . ."

"And he's asking for my help now. Besides, I can't cancel a dinner this late, though I know better ways to spend an evening." He grinned, and she smiled, rubbing her foot against his. He gave David a hug. "Bye-bye, my big man. Be good."

David hugged him back. "Can we read my story later, Daddy?"

"Daddy won't be back until past bedtime, dear. We'll read it tomorrow." He pulled Caroline to him in a long kiss, then stepped from the car into cool fall air, her perfume swirling in his head. He spoke to their driver. "Pick me up at ten o'clock sharp. Apartment 202. If you need to, call me on my cell."

The driver nodded.

Caroline leaned out the back window. "Wait. I have your watch. They fixed it but won't have a strap till next week." She took a man's wristwatch from her purse. Gold hands, black face, broken leather strap. The inscription on the back read, "To James, forever your Caroline."

Caroline stared at the building. "James, do you . . ."

Mackaby kissed her again. "I'll see you before midnight." He put the watch in his pocket and climbed the steps. At the door he stopped to wave to them, but the big Lincoln was already gone. He lowered his hand, his feeling of unease returning.

Tick.

The sound no longer startles her. She walks the length of the table, then stops. She stares down at the watch.

The door to the building squealed open with rusty protests at his tugging. Mackaby stepped into a small vestibule, catching his breath on the stink of urine and sweat. A filthy blanket lay on the floor. Mackaby scanned a row of room buttons, half of which showed neither names nor numbers. Finding one for 210, he counted back to what he hoped was 202. Response was immediate.

"Is that you, Mackaby?"

"Yes, Doctor." He wondered if Harnish had been watching.

A harsh buzz sounded, and the inner door admitted Mackaby to a lobby of stained wallpaper and couches sprouting foam rubber and springs. The elevator was out of order, so he climbed sagging steps to a musty second-floor hall lit by random dim bulbs. He walked along, peering at room numbers. A door opened as he passed but closed quickly when he turned.

Reaching room 202, he knocked. The door opened, and Dr. Roderick Harnish stood before him. Mackaby tried to hide the shock he felt. It had been two years since they had last met. Two years can be a long time, Mackaby realized.

A faded blue robe hung on Harnish's stooped and shrunken frame. Prematurely white hair thrown straight back fell to rounded shoulders. Under his robe he wore a shirt, once white, with a tie knotted off-centre at his neck. Grey slacks with a cuff in need of stitching and dirty brown slippers completed his attire. He thrust out a thin hand that Mackaby fumbled to grip. "Dr. Mackaby! So good of you to come." The older man's voice held a strength that belied his frail aspect. And the eyes in that sallow face burnt as brightly as Mackaby had remembered.

Harnish ushered him into a small living room. A kitchen stood to the right. To the left, a hall led to a bathroom and the closed door of another room. Taking Mackaby's coat, Harnish stroked the material. "A quality garment. How wonderful that you can afford the finer things, eh? For me, well, I must make do with less." He hung the coat in an empty closet. "Please, please, come in and sit. We shall have a drink before dinner."

A few steps brought Mackaby to the centre of the small room's bare floor. The reek of onions now assailed him. He attempted a smile. "Dinner smells wonderful, Doctor."

Harnish motioned him to one of two threadbare armchairs. A small table stood between them, a lamp with a torn shade perched near one corner and a book beside it. "Sit, sit. Ah, yes. Well, dinner will be a simpler fare than that to which you are no doubt accustomed. However, I have learned to hide the quality of the meat with some simple sauces." Harnish chuckled as if this preview of their meal would please his guest. "Now, perhaps a scotch, a sherry? I still allow myself those luxuries."

"A sherry, please." Settling into a chair that groaned in protest, Mackaby surveyed the room. Water stains and peeling paint marked walls unadorned by art or decoration. He peeked at the book that lay on the table. Short stories by Poe, opened to "The Cask of Amontillado."

From a scratched wooden cabinet, Harnish removed a near-empty bottle and two glasses. He walked to the only other piece of furniture in the room, a dining table set for two, and poured the sherry. Handing Mackaby a glass, he settled into the chair beside him, smiling at his guest. "So."

Mackaby felt awkward. "Uh, yes. So. So . . ."

Harnish threw his head back, laughing. "No need for small talk, sir. Neither of us was ever good at it." Leaning forward, he tapped Mackaby's knee with a bony finger. "I will tell you what prompted my invitation, which you were so gracious to accept."

Mackaby tasted his sherry. Dry but of poor quality. "I understood that you wish reinstatement to the faculty and hope that I will plead your case, due to my position on the Board."

Harnish smiled. "I intend for you to play a role in my return to grace, yes." The smile left his face as he spoke. "Do you recall the Amsterdam Conference?"

Mackaby frowned. "I didn't attend. It was, what, five years ago?" Mackaby felt his sense of disquiet return.

"Five years," Harnish said, glancing to where a picture of a woman stood on a small television. Mackaby recalled that Harnish had been married. She had left him after his dismissal. Harnish continued. "You and I were approaching our zeniths. On different courses in related fields but both destined, it seemed, to become part of scientific history." He took a sip. "History. An appropriate topic, considering that conference."

"I don't follow you, Doctor," Mackaby said, letting a touch of the irritation he was feeling creep into his voice.

"Indulge me," Harnish said with a smile. "Do you remember the paper I tabled at that conference?"

Mackaby searched his memory. "I believe that it dealt with Hawking's concept of the thermodynamic arrow of time, the time direction in which disorder or entropy increases."

Harnish nodded. "Hawking argued that entropy also dictates our *psychological* arrow of time, our sense of temporal direction. We remember events in the order in which entropy increases, because we must. This makes the second law of thermodynamics irrelevant. Disorder increases with time because we measure time in the direction of increasing disorder."

Mackaby relaxed a bit, his unease now lost in his intellect. "Yes, I remember. You argued that if one could reverse the state of disorder in a closed system, that is, decrease the entropy, then the system would move backward on the time continuum."

"Backward on the human perception of the time line, yes."

"As I remember, that part of your work was well accepted."

Harnish dismissed this with a wave of his hand. "That was trivial. Obvious. Do you recall the real crux of my paper?"

Knowing where this was leading, Mackaby sighed. "You proposed a closed system in which you could reverse entropy, via antimatter bombardment, I believe. I don't recall the details."

Harnish stared at him unblinking for several breaths. "You don't recall the details," he repeated. "Well, Amsterdam was a long time ago. And as you point out, you did not attend, thus missing the impact your work here had on my own." The smile that twitched at his lips did not reach his eyes.

Mackaby's mouth felt dry. He took a drink. "My work at the time dealt with an obscure offshoot of research into black holes. True, it dealt with entropic boundary issues but—"

"Your research illuminated a flaw in my theory, Mackaby. Boundary definition. Thelbrond of MIT picked up on it in his paper, presented after my own. I proved that my method would reduce the entropy of all matter contained within my shielded system. However, Thelbrond showed that the entropy of the shielding wall containing this matter would increase, offsetting this reduction." His lips quivered. "*Total* entropy within my system would increase, not decrease."

Mackaby said nothing, unable to look away from Harnish's gaze. His hand felt hot and sticky on the sherry glass.

"Thelbrond destroyed my career. Using your work, Mackaby. That, too, is now part of *history*." Harnish spoke as a scientist noting an experimental result, merely reporting an entry in a journal. If the man felt anything, his face did not betray it.

Still, Mackaby felt a chill. "Doctor, I did not realize that Thelbrond had leveraged my early research against you."

Harnish pre-empted him with an upheld hand. "I do not accuse but simply state the facts. After Amsterdam, I faced ridicule at subsequent symposiums and within the faculty. Eventually, I was refused funding." Rising, he walked to the small window. Coarse burlap, strung from uneven rods above, posed as curtains. He stared at the street below. An uneasy silence, as ugly as the window coverings, hung between them. Mackaby was about to end the strange evening when Harnish turned back to him. "Such a lovely neighbourhood. I fear I will forget it." Harnish motioned him to the table. "Please sit. I will serve."

Pondering the odd remark, Mackaby took his place, facing the kitchen. To discreetly monitor the hour, he placed his watch with the broken strap in front of him. A microwave beeped. Harnish returned with two steaming bowls. They ate in silence, the soup a thin potato cream, too salty for Mackaby's taste.

Harnish chuckled, and Mackaby looked up. A crooked smile twisted the man's lip. "Do you know, Mackaby, how I spent my remaining funds after Amsterdam?"

Mackaby shook his head. "You have published no paper since that conference. You fired your assistants—"

"They betrayed me," Harnish interrupted in a low tone. "Telling my secrets to my enemies, stealing my ideas . . ."

He is mad, Mackaby thought. "Yes, well, in any event, you then worked alone. No one knew how you directed your energies."

His host's smile held no warmth. "Then tonight shall bring revelation." Under his breath, almost inaudible, he added, "and much, much more." He stared hard at Mackaby, then around him, as if seeing the room for the first time, a grimace contorting his face. "Enough. It is time," he muttered. Rising, he hobbled to the narrow hall leading to the closed door of the second room.

Mackaby heard a key turn and a door open and close. Then nothing. He waited. Still nothing. His patience exhausted, he rose, intending to leave. Remembering his watch, he turned back to the table. And stopped. The timepiece was nowhere to be seen. He searched the table and floor, but in vain.

The watch was gone.

A low buzz rose above the street noise and climbed quickly to a high-pitched whining. A tingling sensation shot up his spine. Vertigo and weakness flooded him. He slumped back into his chair, knocking the table, spilling his sherry. The stain spread across the tablecloth where his watch had lain.

A noise brought his head up. Splitting diagonally, the wall beside the kitchen door pulled apart. Behind the crack appeared not a view into the tiny kitchen, but an empty whiteness. Mute with terror, Mackaby struggled again to his feet. As he stumbled to the door, the small room stretched away from him. Details thinned, edges blurred, colours faded. With a shriek, the scene shattered like a mirror struck by a hammer. Jagged shards of reality spun into a white void. He heard his son David call "Daddy," heard himself scream, felt himself falling, felt . . .

Nothing.

Tick.

She wonders idly how it can sound so loud, this little watch. Perhaps, she thinks, I only hear it in my mind. This thought does not concern her.

She reaches for the watch . . .

Mackaby wiped his mouth on a fine linen napkin as the final notes of a Vivaldi concerto wafted from the stereo. "Excellent risotto, Doctor. My compliments to your chef."

Harnish picked a thread from his dinner jacket, smiling thinly down the dining room table. "Not my chef, I'm afraid, Mackaby. Such extravagances are yet beyond me. However, I did take the liberty of hiring a caterer."

Harnish had been the perfect host, yet Mackaby still felt uncomfortable. "You shouldn't have gone to such expense, sir."

Harnish's pale lips curled into a one-cornered smile. "I assure you, such items are trifles compared to my other efforts toward this evening." He rang a small silver bell. A uniformed servant appeared through French doors behind him. The man removed the plates, disappearing again into the kitchen.

Mackaby looked over his host again. Short-cropped greying hair on a square head set on a body still ramrod straight as in his youth. "That is the second reference you've made, Doctor, to a singular aspect of this evening. Just what is the occasion?"

"Why, the anniversary of this dinner!" Harnish ignored the puzzled look Mackaby knew he wore. "Mind you, 'anniversary' is not quite correct. A true term does not exist since the event has no precedent. Or rather, as only I know of its occurrence, only I require a word to describe it." He smiled.

Mackaby felt confused. "I do not understand you, Doctor."

Harnish rose and walked to the long wall of floor-to-ceiling windows. Pulling back a lace curtain with a manicured hand, he stared down at the street. Mackaby wondered what could have caught his attention, lovely though the tree-lined boulevard and sculpture garden were.

"You do not remember our first dinner, on this very date, do you?" Harnish asked, his back still to his guest.

Mackaby felt his patience waning. "What do you mean?"

Harnish turned to look at him again. "Pity. It would be so much more satisfying if you remembered it all. I suppose I will have to make do with telling you. Once I am done, that is."

His anger building, Mackaby rose to face the smaller man. "Doctor, I accepted your invitation based on your promise to discuss my reinstatement to the faculty, which you said you could arrange due to your reputation and position. I now find—"

Harnish raised a hand to stop him. "How is your wife, dear boy? Caroline? Lovely girl, that."

Taken aback, Mackaby stammered out, "She is quite well, since you ask. She has had to take a job due to my situation—"

"And your son?"

Mackaby blinked. "We have no children. Neither of us wished to begin a family until I was certain of a steady income." He recovered his composure. "Doctor, I must insist you—"

Again Harnish cut him off with an imperious wave. "Enough. It is time. Again." Without even excusing himself, Harnish departed through the adjacent study. His steps echoed down the tiled hall leading to his private rooms.

Mackaby stood stunned by his host's rude and odd behaviour. Then his anger returned, and he determined to leave at once. As he crossed the dining room threshold, dizziness seized him and a piercing whistle stung his ears. Grasping at a door frame that writhed away from his hand, he pitched forward as the room began to melt, to flow. Colours and shapes swirled into each other like a nightmare soup of reality stirred by a cosmic hand. An image of Caroline, crying, whirled by in the vortex. Her tears became streaks of blood as the maelstrom pulled her image and him down into it, down toward a singularity of pure white nothingness.

Tick.

She holds the watch—and begins to shake. Emotions flow into her or out of her, she isn't sure which. Crying out, she slumps to the floor to lie sobbing, praying for them to end. They cease, but only when she is numbed past resistance. Then the pictures come, and sounds, smells, touches, like waves of forgotten dreams. Of a man she loved. Of a child. Their child.

Tick.

Her hand unclenches. The watch falls to the carpet. She wonders where the man has gone, what has happened to her son.

Having finished the last crumb of his cake, Mackaby put down his fork. Harnish's uniformed butler whisked his plate and cutlery away. Looking up, Mackaby was startled to see Harnish's gaze fixed on him from the end of the long table.

"Hungry, Mackaby?" His eyes seemed to hold a secret joke.

"Roderick! You're embarrassing our guest." Caroline rose from where she sat beside Harnish, smiling at Mackaby. "I'll leave you two alone. Roderick will want his after-dinner cigar, and I have never become used to them."

Mackaby watched her leave, his mind drifting to the ache in his heart like a tongue searching for a missing tooth. Feeling Harnish's eyes on him, Mackaby muttered, "Please excuse me, Doctor. I have not had such a meal in some time."

"Time. Yes. A long time. Five years since I last had the opportunity to host you." The amused expression remained.

Mackaby hesitated, not certain how to respond. "I don't recall another instance when I have been your guest."

Harnish chuckled. "Tonight is the third time we have dined on this very date. Although . . ."—he paused, gesturing around the opulent dining hall—". . . the décor has improved over the first of these feasts." Mackaby stared at him. Grinning, Harnish rose. "Come into the library. Tonight all shall be made clear."

Limping even with his cane, Mackaby followed him out of the dining room. Harnish stopped at the door to the library. "Ah! My apologies. I forgot how your injury has slowed you. I would have thought it healed by now."

Mackaby grimaced, trying to hide the pain he felt. "Arthritis in the knee is the main difficulty now, Doctor."

In the large study, Harnish motioned to a high-backed leather chair. Seating himself beside Mackaby, his feet on an ottoman, the older man pulled a cigar from his jacket. "Terrible thing, that plane crash, though I suppose you count yourself lucky, surviving at all. Fortunate your wife was not with you."

Mackaby looked at a painting over the fireplace. Caroline, in a blue evening dress, sat in a velvet chair. Harnish, in a tuxedo, stood behind her. Mackaby remembered when she had been his. He had planned to ask her to marry him once he became established. Then fate had turned against him. He looked back to his host. "You know I have never married."

Harnish was studying his face intently, amusement flickering behind every twitch. "Ah, yes. Silly of me." Lighting the cigar, Harnish settled into the chair. "Now, for a story. Actually three stories, although you still remember the third, so I will not bore you with that."

"I still remember . . . What do you mean?"

Harnish grinned through his smoke. "Why, your life, Mackaby. Or to be precise, three lives, two of which no longer exist." He put down his cigar and from a pocket removed a man's wristwatch. Holding it, he stroked it like a beloved pet. "Imagine an event which unalterably changes the balance of your life, all that you could have become, all you might have been. You would expect such an event to be memorable, would you not?"

Mackaby felt confused. And something else. He felt the beginning of fear. Irrational. He swallowed but said nothing.

Caressing the watch, Harnish continued. "Your memories of this event could be of either joy or regret, depending on the direction it moved your destiny. You and I, Mackaby, have lived through three such events, all on the very same day, all quite different, except in the aspect of the fortunes each visited upon my future. And misfortunes on yours."

Harnish placed the watch on a table between them. Mackaby fought an urge to pull away. Through a haze of sudden nausea, he realized Harnish was talking again. ". . . say 'future,' like most fools, you extrapolate a continued existence from your present state to a better one, a transformation you effect by dreams and ignorance. I have dealt with my futures. This evening, I am concerned only with our pasts."

Mackaby felt dazed, his limbs weak. A loud ticking filled his head. "What are you talking about?" he whispered.

Harnish chuckled. "After Amsterdam, I invested my remaining funds in researching the role of entropy in other branches of science." He pushed the watch closer, and Mackaby struggled to pull his hand away. Grinning, Harnish continued. "My work led me to communications theory, where signal repetition introduces increasing disorder—entropy—in the signal."

A fire played in Harnish's eyes as the scientist supplanted the man. "I theorized a closed system in which I could generate a wave form of electromagnetic radiation displaying decreased entropy. Such a wave form would move backward with respect to our psychological arrow of time, our perception of time flow. If I could then modulate the wave form, I would have a transmitter. I would, in short, be able to send a message back in time."

Mackaby struggled to form words as the watch's ticking swarmed in his ears. He felt he must shout to be heard, but could only whisper. "Backward to where? Who would be listening?"

"I would, Mackaby. I would also build a receiver and wait in that squalid little apartment after Amsterdam for the Roderick Harnish of years yet to be to send a message. Can you guess the content of that message?" Retrieving the watch again, Harnish dangled it in front of Mackaby. Mackaby sat frozen, terrified he would touch the thing. His mind cried such fear was baseless, but a more primal part knew better.

"No answer? Then I shall tell you." Harnish's face became as stone. "I would direct my younger self into research to bring him accolades, not contempt. I would direct his finances to bring him wealth." Harnish leaned closer. Mackaby could smell his sour breath. "And I would provide young Roderick with knowledge to use against those who had wronged me. Those who had mocked my work, had lied to me and about me." Voice breaking, his jaw tightened. "Those who had ruined my life."

Harnish sat back, the watch swinging like Poe's pendulum blade from his fingers. "Problems arose. I found that I had but certain windows of opportunity to transmit to my earlier self. Using my own new branch of mathematics, I computed the first date when I might transmit. Can you guess that date, Mackaby?"

Mackaby knew but could not speak. Harnish reached out to lay the watch across the arm of Mackaby's chair. Cringing into the far corner of his seat, Mackaby barely dared to breathe. Apparently oblivious, Harnish rose and began pacing the room.

"Today, Mackaby, today. And since you authored my decline, I chose you to share the fruits of my labour. I followed your work and that of your contemporaries. As expected, research emerged four years later refuting your early papers after Amsterdam. Simply the progress of science—we stand on the shoulders of those who went before. But if such results came out earlier, coincident with your own? You would look the fool, an incompetent bungler. And the scientist who published the correct results? His star would be in the ascendant. I was that person, Mackaby. I destroyed you, taking your position and reputation. And much more." He paused before the portrait of Caroline.

"What do you mean?" Mackaby whispered. "I never had a position at the University . . ."

Returning to his chair, Harnish relit his cigar. "Having determined the transmittal date, I invited you to dinner. Early that evening, I left you and entered my machine—my closed system—to send my message back five years. I assumed Harnish-the-sender would vanish the moment I transmitted, since my earlier self would take actions based on my message to prevent my current present from ever occurring. In my new life, I would recall receiving but not sending my message. My current memories would not exist, since I had never lived that life. Such was my belief as I pressed the button to transmit."

Mackaby's eyes flitted between Harnish's grin and the watch that lay so close. The ticking punctuated each word of the tale.

"What happened? Nothing. I felt no change whatsoever. With a bitter heart, I stepped from my machine. And into a new world! I stood in an affluent suburban home. Feeling faint, I looked down. My hands, arms, my very body seemed transparent, insubstantial. I was fading. As this occurred, strange thoughts, conversations, images deluged my brain—new memories, if such a term can be used. A moment of vertigo; then I found myself seated across from you at dinner. I recalled all of my new life after young Harnish had received my message, yet I retained memories of my now-extinct prior life as well. I theorized that the closed system had protected my old memories. On leaving the machine, my old self had merged into my new self."

Harnish plucked the watch from the chair arm. For a moment, Mackaby feared Harnish would touch him with it, and his breath caught in his throat. But the older man just sat back and began speaking again, holding the watch in front of him.

"I had not expected to optimize my life with one try. Now the last five years of my new life filled my head—a source for a second message, to fine tune my past. And yours. For I 'remembered' deciding to re-enact our dinner on the 'anniversary' of when my new life truly began and when I would again have a window to transmit. We had just finished our first course. I stayed for the next, then left again to send my second message. I emerged to this." Harnish swirled his hand and the watch through the air. "Again I melded with my new self, retaining full recall of my now two prior lives. And so, we come to the third instance of this extraordinary dinner."

Mackaby beat down his terror again. "This is ludicrous. You are cruel, Doctor, to lord your success over me like this."

Harnish smiled again. "Your disbelief illustrates the sole flaw in my plan. I lose the sweetness of revenge if you remain unaware or unconvinced. So I formed a theory, now to be tested." He fingered the watch. "At our first dinner, I took this watch from you and into my closed system. It remained there through each transmission, until tonight when I retrieved it."

Mackaby fought for breath against the grip of fear on his throat. Harnish continued. "I hypothesized that if an object of yours from the original time stream was in my system when I transmitted, the object might retain a link to your soon-to-be erased past." Harnish leaned forward to dangle the watch before Mackaby's sweating face. "This is all that remains of that first life you once led. All else was wiped clean by my first message. Do you believe in psychometry, Mackaby? By holding an object, a psychic can read the lives of its prior owners. What might this watch tell you?"

The older man laid the watch again on the arm of Mackaby's chair and leaned forward. "Pick it up." His tone was one of command, but Mackaby didn't move. Not from defiance, but from fear. Harnish's breath rushed out in a sudden hiss. Grabbing Mackaby's nearer hand, he shoved the watch into the open palm and pressed Mackaby's fingers over it.

Stiffening, Mackaby tried to open his fingers, to throw the watch from him. His hand would not open, but his mouth did, to free a sob that ran screaming from his heart. A thousand faces, sounds, smells, conversations stormed his mind. He felt pain; he felt joy. He wept, laughed, lusted, loved. Scene after scene beat upon his numbed soul. And he *knew*. He knew these were his lost lives. One image hovered in front of him. He felt her lips, her skin, smelled her perfume. "Caroline," he cried as she faded. They all faded—the pictures, memories, his lives.

Harnish was talking again. Mackaby looked up at the older man hovering over him and realized he had fallen to the floor.

"Sweet excellence!" Harnish clasped his hands before him. "The missing element is delivered to me. Awareness in my victim." He knelt beside Mackaby. "Caroline was your wife," Harnish whispered. "You had a child named David. You were a giant in your field. Your patents had made you a rich man. I took all that from you, Mackaby. I took it for myself."

Feeling his nausea rise, Mackaby forced himself to his hands and knees just as he threw up on the carpet. When his retching stopped, he wiped his mouth on the sleeve of his threadbare jacket and stood. Trembling with anger and horror, tasting the foulness in his mouth, he faced his foe. But Harnish stared past Mackaby, his face like stone again. Mackaby turned.

Caroline stood in the doorway, a hand on the door frame, eyes wide. "Roderick, I heard my name . . ." she began. Mackaby could not tell if it was a question or an accusation.

Harnish pulled himself up tall. "Caroline, I regret that Doctor Mackaby has had a rather bad reaction to our dinner." He turned to Mackaby. "Or perhaps it was my cigar?"

"Perhaps," whispered Mackaby, feeling his shame, his pain, his nearness to the black abyss of despair. He looked at Caroline, met her eyes for a heartbeat, then turned away.

"James, are you all right?" she asked.

I will tell her, he thought. *I will tell her . . . what?* He turned back to where she stood, the embodiment of all he had ever dreamed of, ever loved. Caroline, David, his life, his lives. He tried to smell her perfume, but it mixed with the stench of his vomit, and he knew Harnish had won. He swallowed. "I'm fine, Mrs. Harnish. I think I should go home now."

Harnish's face relaxed. He shook Mackaby's hand. *A show for Caroline*, thought Mackaby. "A pity," Harnish said. "But I'm glad you could make it, Mackaby. I'll have Wilson show you out." With only a glance at Caroline, Harnish strode from the room.

Mackaby moved to the door but as he passed, Caroline took his hand. "James—oh!" she gasped. He turned. Her eyes were large. Realizing he still held the watch in the hand she grasped, he wrenched it away. "I'm sorry," he cried. Stumbling through the banquet hall, he threw the watch on the table.

As Wilson held the door open, Mackaby looked back. Caroline sat at the dining table staring at him. She mouthed one word. He nodded. Tears streaming down his face, he left the house.

He limped down the long driveway wiping his hand against his coat again and again, the hand that had held the watch, as if to rub the stain of that night from his skin. As he walked, he whispered the word that Caroline had mouthed. A child's name. A child who now had never been. He whispered, "David."

Tick.

Holding the watch, she sits again at the table. Her husband sings upstairs, above the clatter of the servants washing dishes. She should have given the watch to her husband before he walked out the door tonight. But her husband had never been her husband. Her son had never been born.

Tick.

On the table lies a cake. Beside the cake lies a knife, long and sharp. She tries to read the writing in the icing of the cake, but the knife has cut pieces from it. It makes no sense. Her life . . . her lives make no sense. She knows she will never be able to put the pieces back together again, nor recall what they once said.

Tick.

Awakened, she lifts her head from the table. The banquet room is dark, the house silent except for the watch. She wonders why the servants did not rouse her. Perhaps they tried.

Rising, she climbs wide stairs, stands outside the bedroom door, hears the snoring of her husband. She steps inside, closing the door silently behind her. The man in bed is a stranger, yet she knows him. She thinks of James, of David. She thinks of the cake, her life, her lives. All is disorder.

Tick.

In one hand, she holds the watch. In the other, she clenches the knife from beside the cake. She walks to the bed.

Tick.

I spend a lot of time on the structure of a short story, and from that perspective, "State of Disorder" remains one of my favourites. The story is told via two interleaved threads: the first in present tense from the unknown (at the outset) woman's point of view, and the other thread in past tense from Mackaby's point of view. So we're already playing around with time. The Mackaby thread seems to proceed in a normal time flow of an evening dinner: first course, second course, third, etc. But as we learn, each scene represents not just the subsequent course but also a subsequent dinner between Harnish and Mackaby, reflecting the changes Harnish has made to their lives via his time manipulation. These scenes are separated by scenes which are clearly occurring at the end of a dinner party, those in the present tense with the woman. So the structure and tenses play around with time as does the story, but each story line still progresses forward in time until the two time lines converge in the last two scenes. Mackaby's wristwatch provides the linking symbolism between the two story lines, which I thought was fitting for a time travel story. The fact that the watch has a broken strap symbolizes the break in Mackaby's life caused by Harnish. The Poe book in the one scene was a nod to "The Cask of Amontillado" mood I was going for.

This story is appearing here for the first time. Not much to say about it, except that it's short and was an experiment in mood and style.

NOTHING

"It's nothing," he says, not for the first time.

She watches him straighten his tie in the hall mirror. *So he doesn't have to make eye contact*, she thinks.

"I fear nothing?" she says. "Then I must be fearless. I don't feel fearless."

Leaning against the kitchen doorframe, she hugs her faded blue dressing gown around her as if she's holding the universe together. She's staying home. Again.

He shakes his head. He does that a lot lately.

"I mean there's nothing out there to be afraid of." He picks up his briefcase, ready for another day.

But she knows that it's not just another day.

"Nothing out there," she repeats.

"Nothing." He stands by the front door of their little bungalow. "Are you going into work?"

He knows I'm not, she thinks. But not asking would mean he accepts what's happening. And then he'd have to believe it.

"No," she says.

She watches his jaw muscles tighten, enjoying the clarity of predictable stimulus and response.

"Fine," he snaps, and leaves.

She hears the car pull away, feeling no less alone than when he was here. She's sorry he's angry, but he doesn't understand.

He doesn't understand that he's right.

She *is* afraid of nothing.

She makes toast and coffee, taking comfort in the routine. Mundane remnants of the way her world used to be.

At the kitchen table, she savours the smell of the coffee, the heat of the mug in her hand, the sharp edges of the toast in her mouth, the sound of its crunch, the sweetness of the jam. Each of her senses has become a lifeline, snaking out from her, seeking something tangible in a fading reality to anchor herself to.

Later, sitting on the sofa, she holds the phone in her lap and sips her coffee even after it's cold, delaying.

Finally, she dials her parents, punching the area code that is a plane trip away, and then their number as if it were a combination to a lock. Slowly, carefully. She listens, then hangs up.

Yesterday, it rang and rang. Today, it didn't even do that. Silence.

Nothing.

A sense of loss fills her, but it tastes old and stale. She realizes that she lost her parents long ago, when the aura of protection they once gave disappeared. They can't save her. They couldn't even save themselves.

Planning to distract herself by cleaning the house, she turns on the radio for some music, but can't find her favourite station. She picks another and starts to dust. The station fades out to nothing. Not even static.

Three more stations. Same thing. She turns the radio off and stops cleaning.

She thinks of sleeping but decides against it. Even her dreams are empty now. She sits and waits.

He comes home at the usual time, but something has changed.

"What's wrong?" she asks over a dinner of leftovers and silence.

"Nothing," he says. She waits. She knows. Finally, he speaks again. "I visited my client."

She knows the one. On the outskirts of the city.

"Yes?" she asks, knowing what he'll say next.

"They're gone," he says.

"Out of business?" she says, playing the game for his sake. Pretending that the world is still normal.

"Gone. There's nothing there."

"Nothing?"

She looks up when he doesn't answer. He puts down his knife and fork, and she enjoys the solid click-click they make on the kitchen table.

He meets her gaze finally. He opens his mouth, but no words come out. Picking up the knife and fork again, he studies them as if unsure they're real. He shakes his head and goes back to eating.

He's pretending it didn't happen. But she is beyond pretending. She saw his eyes. He knows.

He goes to bed early. She stays up, watching TV, flipping channels as, one by one, the city's stations stop broadcasting.

She keeps flipping. The last station disappears. No test pattern. No static. Just a slow fade to a blank dead screen.

She turns the TV off and sits in the dark. Sleep is not an option. She fears what she will wake to. Or that it will come while she sleeps.

The clock shows that it's morning. She doesn't open the curtains. The grey that creeps around their edges is not sunlight.

He should be awake by now. She listens for his morning sounds. Nothing.

She rises and walks upstairs, feet silent on the worn carpet. Up here, the floor, the ceiling, the walls seem thin, insubstantial. A paleness oozes under their bedroom door, more a rejection of both darkness and light than an actual colour.

Leaving the door unopened, she backs away. It is too late for him. He is gone.

He is nothing.

She goes back downstairs and sits on the sofa. To wait. Alone. Now she is truly alone.

It comes, eating first through the corners of the room, devouring walls and ceiling, crawling across freshly vacuumed carpet toward her. She realizes, as it consumes the very space around her, that she is the centre of a dwindling ball of reality. Or perhaps, she thinks as it draws closer, this world is simply escaping to join with it.

It touches her. And she knows.

He was right all along. About what she feared.

It is nothing.

Nothingness. Void. Nothing exists here. No light, no sound,

no smell, no taste. Nothing to touch or be touched by. Only her thoughts exist here, and even they begin to flee her, not to escape, but to join with the void.

As they leave her, she feels herself joining with it as well. Soon there will be no identity, no separation from it, no *her*.

Her last thought forms, departs.

She . . .

is . . .

. . .

I always enjoy writing stories that deal with other forms of artistic expression and creativity, in this case, music and sculpture. Fans of classical music can try to figure out the inspiration for the names of the three main characters in this story. "Symphony" was a finalist for the Aurora Award in 2000 and won second prize in a contest held by the Canadian literary magazine, Prairie Fire, judged by Robert J. Sawyer, to commemorate Winnipeg native and SF author, A.E. Van Vogt.

SYMPHONY

FAST FORWARD: Third Movement, Danse Macabre (Staccato)

They had named the planet Aurora for the beauty that danced above them in its ever dark skies. At least, it had seemed beautiful at the time. Now Gar Franck wasn't so sure.

Gar huddled on the floor, shielding his two-year-old son, Anton, from the panicked colonists stampeding past them in the newly constructed pod link.

"Damn you, Franck! When will you make it stop?" a man cried from across the corridor. A woman lay in the man's arms, convulsing as her seizure peaked. She was dying, but to Gar's numbed mind her moans harmonized with the screams of the mob into a musical score for his private nightmare.

Anton sat on the floor, a broken comm-unit held before his blank face. The child let it drop to strike the metal surface with a dissonant clang. More people fled by. The child ignored them. With morbid fascination, Gar watched Anton repeat the scene. Pick up the comm-unit, let it drop. Pick it up, drop it. Again. Each clang as it struck the floor was more chilling to Gar than any cry from the dying.

This attack had blown the colony power grid. The only light now came through the crysteel roof. Gar looked up. The aurora blazed and writhed in the night sky, a parody of the chaos below. Greens, reds and purples shimmered strobe-like over the corridor, turning each person's frenzied flight into a macabre dance.

"God no!" the man cried. The woman stiffened then fell limp. "No!" The man pulled her to him, sobbing.

The rainbow lights of the aurora dimmed, and the flickering slowed. The screaming died. Gar stood and looked around, dazed. People were shaking their heads, helping up ones who had fallen, poking at bodies. The man still sat holding the dead woman, his eyes hard on Gar. Other colonists stared at Gar, too.

Gar swallowed. Picking up Anton, he walked past accusing faces toward their dorm pod. Anton squirmed in his arms. The child didn't like to be touched, let alone held.

Someone whispered as he passed. "How will he talk to this *thing* when he can't even talk with his own son." Gar pulled Anton closer, smothering his sobbing in the child's sleeve.

REWIND: First Movement, Prelude (Agitato)

Six months ago. Anton was eighteen months old. Their ship, *The Last Chance*, had just dropped out of the wormhole, leaving a poisoned Earth and the plague behind. Earlier probes through this hole had identified a G2 star with planets within range.

The plague had forced the *Last Chance* to launch before completion of its biosphere. The ship was only partly self-sustaining. They had only a year left to find a new home. It wasn't called the *Last Chance* for nothing.

Gar lay exhausted on the wall bed of the small ship cabin that he, Clara, and Anton shared. Clara's latest holographic sculpture spun suspended before him—shifting geometric shapes in greens, reds and purples. Vivaldi filled the room, wiping words from his head like rain washing graffiti from a wall. Gar lived with words all day. He'd had enough of words.

The jump had flooded MedCon with hyperspace shock cases. Gar was logging eighteen-hour days translating between colonists and doctors. Fluency in ten languages and a name in computerized speech translation had won him his berth as Communications Officer. With over six thousand refugees from all over Earth, both human and automated translators were invaluable.

Gar rubbed his eyes. Overtime was at least an escape from the routine of translating the captain's messages to the crew and passengers. And from the growing tensions of his family life.

He checked the time. Clara worked as a laser and photonics specialist in TechLab. Her shift should be over by now.

Anton sat on the plastek floor, flapping his hands, staring. At what Gar could not say, and a fear grew in him each day that Anton did not know, either. Gar got down in front of the child. "Hey, big guy. What're you doing?" Anton looked right past him.

"He stared like that for twenty minutes today." Gar turned. Clara stood at the door, her lip trembling. "I measured it."

"Clara . . ." Gar felt himself tighten up.

"These spells just seem to blend together now."

"Maybe it's the jump," he said, not believing it himself.

"He was like this *before* the jump, Gar."

"He's just slow developing. How was your shift?"

"Most children are speaking by a year," she said.

"He walked on time, right?" Gar turned up the music a bit, not looking at her. "I just did a translation. They've found the system. We'll be there in four months."

"He never looks up when we speak, Gar."

"We'll have his hearing tested again."

"He won't let me hold him." Her voice broke, and Gar turned back to her. She was leaning against the wall, her arms wrapped around herself, sobbing. "I can't hold my own child, Gar."

Gar swallowed. He walked over and took her in his arms.

Clara pushed away from him. "I want Ky to look at him."

Ky Jasper was MedCon Leader. "He's too busy," Gar mumbled.

"He owes you for all the overtime. Talk to him."

Gar looked at Anton. The child sat with his hands over his ears, rocking back and forth. The Vivaldi, calm and soothing in the background, gave the scene a surreal feeling.

"He's disappearing, Gar. Disappearing into his own world."

Gar closed his eyes to shut out both the scene and his tears. He nodded. "I'll ask him tomorrow."

First Movement, Finale (Largo)

In the ship's darkened MedLab, a hologram of Anton's brain spun glowing and green, areas of red flashing within it. Gar stood stunned beside Ky Jasper and Clara. The imaging unit beeped musical tones as Ky outlined a red area in purple.

". . . repetitive mannerisms and actions. Autistics are neurologically overconnected, as in this area of the cortex that handles hearing. Their senses are so acute they can overload. A touch is painful. Speech scrambles. Soft sounds are like explosions. One overloaded sense can shutdown the other four."

"So he covers his ears. And won't let us hold him." Clara spoke in a monotone, face blank. "Why won't he talk?"

Gar shook his head. This wasn't happening.

Ky sighed. "Autistics are blind to other minds. Anton doesn't know we're fellow beings with thoughts and feelings. To him, we're just things, moving through his world at random."

"Is there a cure?" Gar asked. Clara's sobs and the beeping of the imaging unit played like a discordant sound-track to the scene. Ky turned to him, his face half in darkness, half in green from the hologram. He shook his head.

Second Movement, Main Theme (Accelerando)

They were lucky, the captain had said on reaching the system and finding a habitable planet. Breathable atmosphere, 0.95 Earth gravity. Hotter than Earth, but a polar temperate zone held a suitable land mass. The axial tilt meant they'd be in night for the first 2.4 Earth years, but that was a small issue. Besides, the polar zones offered spectacular auroral activity.

Lucky, the captain had said. Still reeling from the news of Anton, Gar hadn't felt very lucky at the time. Now no one did.

On first seeing the aurora on orbital displays, Gar had felt a dread he couldn't reconcile with its beauty. He had assumed he was subconsciously linking its colours to those of Anton's MedLab hologram. Now he wasn't sure. Now people were dying.

Walking through the main colony dome, Gar noted without surprise that all ceiling panels had been opaqued to block any view of the sky. He cranked up Mozart in his translation headset and tried to relax as he neared the newly built dorm pod.

The construction of the colony on the planet had gone well in the beginning. Gar had made planet-fall with the first group. To translate between engineers and work crews, he had said. Both he and Clara knew he was avoiding the situation with Anton.

Clara had accepted the diagnosis quickly. During the trip to the planet, she had buried herself in researching autism and working with Anton. Gar just couldn't. So he hid in his work.

At their dorm unit, Gar hesitated, then stepped inside. Clara sat with Anton, one of her light sculptures hovering before them. Anton rocked back and forth, eyes on the floor.

"Is that a new sculpture?" he said, forcing a smile.

She looked at him, and his smile died. "Old one. New colours." Gar noted the absence of greens, reds and purples. "Autistics think visually. Words are too abstract," she said. "I hoped the shapes and colours might prompt a reaction."

Gar noticed she wasn't in uniform. "Did your shift change?"

"The captain needs to see you about an announcement. He asked me to brief you." She spoke a command. The hologram disappeared, and a MedLab report appeared on a wall screen.

Clara led a photonics team analyzing the aurora. Gar had no idea how her work had been going. They didn't talk much lately. He scanned the report. ". . . high amplitude gamma waves in the brain, resulting in massive and prolonged epileptic seizures. Most victims are adult females. Attacks match peaks in aurora activity. Shielding attempts have failed."

"So it *is* the aurora," he said, as he finished.

"This thing isn't an aurora." She didn't look at him.

"What do you mean?"

"This planet's magnetosphere is too weak." She stared at Anton. "So are the solar flare levels. Besides, the timing of the attacks doesn't even match the solar wind cycle."

"Then what's causing the aurora? Or whatever it is?"

Clara reached out and stroked Anton's hair. The child began shaking his head violently, and she stopped. "We think we are."

Gar felt a chill. "What?"

"The aurora was stable until our planet-fall. It's grown steadily since. We think our arrival prompted the attacks and our continued presence is causing their escalation."

"Attacks?" He wished she'd look at him.

"It's not a natural phenomenon. The electron flow doesn't even follow the planet's magnetic field. It appears to go where it wants to, and it seems to want to be over our settlement."

"But why?"

Clara finally looked at him. "We believe we're dealing with a sentience, Gar. An alien intelligence. The Captain wants to try to communicate. He's asking you to lead that team."

FAST FORWARD: Fourth Movement, Nocturne (Allegro)

Gar leaned against the wall of the main colony dome, staring at the fire raging above. Out here he was at least alone in his misery. No one else could stand the sight of the sky any more. Gar preferred it to the accusing stares of his fellow colonists.

All their attempts to communicate had failed. His team had used ideas from the ancient SETI project, transmitting universal mathematical concepts. For six Earth weeks, they had broadcast over the full range of EM frequencies detected in the aurora.

If any message had been received, it created no visible effect. The deaths continued. The aurora still burned the heavens, and he could no more tell what message it held than what was in his own son's head. Standing, he started to walk.

He found her sitting slumped against a boulder crying, Anton in front of her. The child had his back to her, rocking gently. Gar sat down and pulled her to him before she realized he was there. She pushed away at first but then collapsed against him. Her sobs stopped, and they held each other for a long while.

"Do you know why I came out here?" she asked finally.

He paused. "You hoped the aurora might reach Anton."

"In a way," she said. Gar had never seen her face so sad.

"Well, it's quite the light sculpture," he said.

"Gar, I came here . . . so this thing would kill our son."

The words ran around his head as he tried to pull some meaning from them. "Clara . . ."

"Practically every victim's been a woman," she said.

"That doesn't . . ." He stopped. He understood.

"What will happen to him then? You won't . . ." She turned away, not finishing. He sat there, his face burning, realizing what she had been living with, and living with alone.

"I'm sorry," he whispered.

"Promise me you'll take care of him, that you'll love him."

"I promise," he said.

They made love then, there on the ground, Anton as oblivious to their passion as he was to the monster rampaging above. After, they lay gazing at the aurora.

"I realize now how Anton must feel," Gar said.

"What do you mean?"

"Blind to other minds. We've been blind to this thing. Now we're shouting, 'Hey look, we're alive,' and it doesn't hear us."

Clara looked at Anton. "Maybe he's shouting, too." She stared at the sky. "Words, mathematical symbols are too concrete, too cerebral for this thing. We need something more abstract. Something with emotion. I can feel it."

"*Music is born of emotion.*"

"That sounds like a quotation."

"Confucius. Music can express ideas, subtleties, and emotions that words can't. The language areas in the brain show activity when we listen to music. Too bad the sky has no ears."

Clara smiled. "You and your music. That's what first attracted me to you, when we met after the launch."

"Really?"

She nodded. "The first crew briefing. You had Bach playing in the room. I remember the colours—all golds and reds."

"Music helps to . . . wait a minute. Colours?"

She looked embarrassed. "I'm a synesthete. Sounds make me see colours. That's why I always have music playing when I work on my light sculptures. Inspiration."

"Synesthesia. You've never told me about this."

"I once worked in a laser lab with another synesthete. With her, light prompted sounds, even tastes and smells. It was so distracting for her that she had to quit her career. So when I applied for a berth on the ship, I kept quiet about it."

"No need to be ashamed. Lots of creative types have been synesthetes. Scriabin even built a 'colour organ' for *Prometheus: Poems of Fire* . . ." He stopped and stared at the sky.

"Too bad my synesthesia isn't like that. I could tell you what kind of music the sky is playing . . ." She stopped, too.

They looked at each other.

"We could use colours for different pitches," he said.

"You mean, correlate the spectrum of EM frequencies displayed by the aurora with sound frequencies of the music."

"That's what I said."

"Rhythm can just stay the same. Brightness for volume."

"What about orchestration? The timbre of each instrument?"

"Holographic images. Different shapes for each instrument."

"Your sculptures! We could adjust sizes, too."

"Small shapes for high notes, larger for the bass range."

"And add more shapes for more volume as well," he said.

"What about harmony? Melody?"

"Tough one. Don't know what colours or shapes go together."

"You'll figure it out." She stood and picked up a wriggling Anton, giving him a hug. "Come on. We've got work to do."

Fourth Movement, Finale (Crescendo)

Gathered under the sea of swirling light, the entire colony seemed to hold its breath as Gar spoke the command. Lasers flared into life, and Schubert's 8th Symphony danced in cubes and stars and dodecahedrons of rainbow colours across the sky. Gar had always thought the Unfinished was music for the end of the world. A fitting epitaph for the colony if they failed.

A computer controlled the shapes, colours, and other aspects of the display, monitoring the aurora and repeating patterns that prompted lower EMR levels. "Audience feedback," Clara called it.

The music of the lights played. The colours and shapes of the music kept changing, and the colony kept waiting. Ten minutes. Fifteen.

The aurora seemed to slow, to drop in intensity. A murmur swept through the crowd, and Gar's heartbeat quickened.

Someone screamed.

Gar spun around. A woman trembled on the ground. Another fell. Then a man. More dropped. Gar's ears buzzed, and his head throbbed. "Gar!" Clara fell to the ground, hands stretched toward him, twitching. Anton still just sat, staring at the sky.

Gar moved to help Clara. Pain flamed in his head, and he fell. The air seemed thicker, misty. Then he understood.

The aurora had dropped from the sky. It enveloped them, a swirling cloud of coloured sparks and flashes. Electric shocks stung his skin. Saliva trickled from Clara's mouth. The comm-unit to control the display lay before him. He forced his hand forward. The screaming grew louder as he clawed the unit to him.

His lips began to form the command to kill the light music when he saw Anton. The child still sat but his eyes . . .

Gar felt a thrill of joy as for the first time Anton's eyes focused on something in this world. Clara's sculptures danced in the sky to Gar's music, and their child followed every pirouette.

Twisting his head, he saw that Clara was watching, too, the happiness in her face shining through the pain.

Whether it was the sculptures or the music or the aurora, Gar neither knew nor cared. He let the comm-unit slip from his fingers. This scene would play itself out.

He reached out to clasp Clara's hand, wondering with a strange calm if they would survive. Together they lay in the dirt of that alien world and watched their son turn to look at them—and smile.

I loved Jack London as a kid. Loved any stories about animals, really, which perhaps explains my fascination with shapeshifter stories. Every society around the world has had (or still has) shapeshifter legends. Were-wolves in France, were-tigers in India, were-lions in Africa. Simply put, wherever there are animals, there are legends of people who can change into them. Which leads to the question: what sort of shapeshifter would live in a modern city?

OUT OF THE LIGHT

The morgue door swung open. Jan Mirocek hesitated at the threshold, clinging to the hallway's bright comfort. Ahead in the dark room, under a lonely cone of light, Detective Garos of the Toronto Metropolitan Police loomed over a shroud-covered corpse. Jan glared up at the single ceiling bulb. *Forty watts max*, he thought. He turned to a clerk slouched at a desk in the hall. "Got any more light?"

The man just shrugged. "Our guests don't do much reading."

Scowling, Jan stepped inside. The door clicked shut behind him, cutting the light even more. He cursed and pulled a small flashlight from a coat pocket, his breathing slowing as the beam brightened his path. *I can do this*, he thought. Trying not to look into the shadows, he walked to Garos.

Morgues didn't bother Jan. He knew death. And corpses.

He just wanted more light.

Garos eyed the flashlight, but the big man didn't comment. "Good to see you in action again, hunter. It's been a while since . . . last time." His beefy hand swallowed Jan's.

Last time. At least, old friend, you have the decency to leave it at that, Jan thought. "I'm retired, Andreas. Why'd you call me?" Ignoring the frown from Garos, he studied the contours of the white shroud. Slim, short, female.

Garos shrugged, then turned to the corpse. "White female, early thirties. Found about 1:00 this morning—just twelve hours ago— on a well-lit, still-busy, street."

Stabbing his beam into dark corners, Jan pulled two extra flashlight batteries from his pocket. He shook them in his hand, calmed by the clicking noise. "So? What do you need me for?"

"You tell me." Garos pulled back the sheet.

Maybe it was the light. Or the darkness. Or perhaps seeing Garos in a professional role again had brought her back, brought it all back. He looked down, and *she* was there. Her face. The way it used to be in the mornings—peaceful—beautiful.

Then the face shifted into someone else—some*thing* else. Jan stared at the desiccated corpse of a stranger, black sunken eye sockets and cheeks, lips pulled back from rotting gums, white hair framing grey translucent skin. The shadows closed in and with them, his terror. He ran from the room.

Ten years old. Lying in bed beside his brother Pyotr, in their house in the woods. His mother's voice rose and fell in her sing-song way of telling stories. But these stories were not of frog princes, or bears and honey pots, or little girls chasing rabbits down holes. These were . . . different.

"To begin his change, the werewolf put on a wolf pelt, then drank water from a wolf's paw-print," their mother whispered. Jan looked at Pyotr. The younger boy was wide-eyed. Jan smiled. *These are stories*, he thought. *Just stories.*

Five minutes after leaving the morgue, Jan sat huddled at a window table of the first bar he had found. The afternoon sun of a Toronto winter did little to remove the chill he felt. A familiar face peered inside. Moments later, Garos eased his bulk into a chair beside him. "You okay?"

Jan lied with a nod. "For a second, I saw . . ." Her name caught in his throat, and he swallowed. "I saw Stasia's face."

Garos frowned, his eyebrows forming a single bushy line. An old woman in Sicily had once told Jan such eyebrows were a sign of the *lupomanari*. She had missed the true signs in her own son. He killed nine people before Jan and Garos had brought him down.

"I shouldn't have called you," Garos said.

"I'm okay!" Jan snapped. Garos looked away. *No, you shouldn't have*, Jan thought, *you of all people.* Jan stared at his hands gripping his beer as if it were a beast about to leap at his throat. He held life that way now, a wild thing to be feared, never trusted to lie quietly at his feet. "Who was she?"

Garos said a name. It meant nothing to Jan. He looked up. "Why *did* you call me, Andreas?"

"Did that look like a fresh corpse to you?" Garos asked.

"The rotting doesn't mean it was done by a shifter."

"Come on, Jan. We saw the same rapid body decay in shifter victims back home."

"Any 'bodies' we saw were in pieces and mostly eaten." *Her* body would've been, too, if he had been able to bring himself to see it. "This one was intact. That's no were-beast."

Looking around, Garos lowered his voice. "We've had other killings, similar to this. We're barely keeping a lid on it."

Jan swallowed. "What's similar about them?"

"Victims killed at night on bright, busy streets. No robbery. Victims in good health. No drugs or sign of sexual assault. No violence except some contusions around the throat, but death wasn't by strangulation, and . . ." Garos leaned forward. ". . . and the corpses rot within hours."

"Any pattern to the killings?"

"None I can see. Both genders, all ages and professions. All over downtown. The only consistency is the body decay and autopsy results, plus the time of night and type of locations."

"Anything else?"

"A witness saw a guy standing over this body. She says she chased him into a dead-end alley. No door, window, fire escape. Nowhere to hide. But also no suspect—the alley was empty."

Jan felt cold. "That still doesn't say shifter."

"Put it with the body decay, it says something weird."

"You believe her story?"

"She gave a description. We're checking it out. And her."

"I'll bet your theory went down well with the brass."

Garos snorted. "I keep my own counsel. They're not from the old country. Don't believe as we do, haven't seen what we have." He stared at Jan. "I need your help."

Jan avoided his eyes. "I came to this country, to a big city, to escape the beasts of the night, Andreas. They don't come to the cities. You don't have a shifter. Even if you did, I can't help you. And you know why."

They sat not speaking, Jan's shame burning him. "Well, I had to try," Garos said as he stood. He looked at Jan. "I know what she was to you. I know you blame yourself. But she knew the risks." He squeezed Jan's shoulder. "It's not your fault, Janoslav. Give yourself a break, for God's sake." He walked to the door, then stopped and looked back. "What if you're wrong?"

Jan stared at him, puzzled. "What do you mean?"

"What if I do have a *kallikantzari*? A beast of the night in your big safe city. What then, hunter?" Not waiting for an answer, Garos turned and left. Jan stayed until the winter sun sank too low. Walking home, he watched the shadows all the way.

Fifteen years old. Returning home from friends, far too late, through winter woods oddly silent. The house dark, even the light in the front room not burning. The door open, tilted at a strange angle. His heart leapt. He ran.

He burst past the ruined entrance to stumble in the dark and fall amongst bloody bodies. His parents. Upstairs, Pyotr's bed empty, room in disarray. Outside again, father's rifle in hand, following prints in the snow. The prints of the beast.

He found it near the quarry. Half-human, yellow eyes looked up from where it fed on his brother. He raised the rifle.

His childhood died. The hunter was born.

After leaving the restaurant, Jan walked home to his apartment over his bookstore on Queen West. His place was small but he'd left most of his possessions behind in the old country. Too many memories tied to them. Besides, he liked this area. Lots of shops and bars that stayed open late. Plenty of neon.

Plenty of light.

Once home, he checked that every light in every room was on.

He read for a while after dinner, then went to bed early as usual. Two flashlights lay on a table beside the bed. He made sure they both worked, then he lay down leaving a lamp on. Maybe tonight he could sleep. Maybe he was tired enough. Closing his eyes, he prayed for escape from dreams.

He awoke screaming her name, sitting bolt upright on sweat-soaked sheets. Sobbing, he fell on his side. There, bathed in light that never touched the night world inside him, he prayed again for deliverance from his darkness.

Twenty-five years old, in a Paris bistro, a stack of papers from around the world beside him. Serial killings got good play. And sometimes the signs were there that spoke to him of shifters. He sat forward. Like this one. Athens paper, one week old. He paid his bill and left, heading for the nearest travel agent.

He had hunted were-bears in Norway and were-tigers in India. He carried a ragged scar on his thigh from a leopard shifter in Kenya. Towns paid a man well to be rid of a beast, a man who knew the signs and was brave—or foolish—enough to follow them.

Jan Mirocek had become such a man.

The morning sun found Jan curled shivering in an armchair in his living room, a flashlight clutched to his chest. Jan thought about the old times and about what he'd become. He realized that he didn't like himself anymore. He realized also, to his surprise, that he had known this for a long time.

Finding his phone, he punched Garos's number, taking vindictive pleasure in waking him. Garos swore, listened, then gave a phone number for the witness and directions to the dead-end alley. Jan swore back when Garos thanked him for the third time. Promising to keep in touch, Jan hung up.

Hell, he thought. *Just like old times.* Grabbing his coat, he checked the pockets for his flashlight and batteries, then stepped out into a cold but bright February morning.

Twenty-five, in an Athens bar. Listening to a young cop named Garos complain. "They won't let me talk to the press."

Jan nodded. "They always hush it up."

"Damn bureaucrats. Well, thanks for the lead."

Jan shrugged. "Thanks for backing me up. I probably wouldn't be alive otherwise. Didn't figure on two of them."

"We worked well together," the big man said.

Jan looked at him. "I'm thinking of taking on a partner."

Garos grinned.

The alley was as Garos had said. Nothing but a few bits of trash. A neon sign over a bricked-up door at the end of the alley advised that "Clancy's Eatery" was now on the next street.

"You the guy who called me?" a voice said from behind him.

Jan turned, startled. She stood at the entrance to the alley. Five-six maybe, short brown hair, long black coat over a slim figure. "Kate Lockridge. You called me, right?"

Jan walked up to her. "Jan Mirocek. Thanks for coming."

"You don't look like a cop."

She had nice eyes, he decided. "Friend of one. Garos."

"Big guy from last night? He was okay." She looked Jan over. "Okay, let's talk. But not here. Gives me the creeps. I know a place nearby. Lousy food but great coffee." She started to move to the street, then stopped, scanning the alley again.

"Something wrong?"

She shrugged. "Place seemed brighter last night. Guess it's coming in here out of the sunlight. And things are always different in the dark, right?" She walked to the street.

Yeah, he thought. *Things are different in the dark.*

Thirty years old, in a little tavern in a little village in Poland, waiting for Garos to get to the point.

Garos coughed. "Mara and I, we're getting married."

Jan had seen this coming. He nodded. "And you want out."

Garos reddened but nodded back.

"I wish the best for you both, Andreas. You know that."

Garos smiled and shook his hand. "Thank you. These have been good years, my friend, but Mara needs a different life."

And I need a new partner, Jan thought.

Late afternoon. The Big Mistake was almost empty. They sat at a sunny window table in the long narrow tavern. A jungle of neon signs, each a visual scream of a beer brand, coloured the dark room in a random rainbow. Kate called to the bartender. "Two coffees, Harry." She turned to Jan. "So what do you want?"

"Garos asked for help on these . . . this killing." He watched a corner of her mouth curl up. "We worked together in Europe."

"How so?"

"I was an advisor on one of his cases." He hurried on before she could probe any further. "So tell me what you saw."

Her story was the same. ". . . I reach the alley and there's no one, nothing. Including no way out. Well, you saw, right?"

Jan nodded and sighed. He asked a few more questions, but it added nothing to the story. "Listen, sorry I wasted your time. Let me buy the coffees." He reached for his wallet.

"So is this body rotting like the others?" she asked. Jan stopped in mid-motion and looked at her. She smiled. "I'm a reporter for the *Toronto Star*, Mr. Mirocek. We need to talk."

Jan sat back again. A reporter, covering the killings. For a moment, despite the sunshine, he felt an old darkness close in.

Thirty-one. Working alone again. He met her in a village in Poland, a reporter up from Warsaw to cover the killings in the town. Her name was Stasia. He trained her. He loved her.

A year later, she was dead.

Harry brought refills while Jan gathered his thoughts. Was it a bluff, trying to see how he'd react? No. She might guess that the separate killings were linked but not about the body decay. "How'd you know about the corpse?" he asked when Harry had left.

"Corpses," she corrected. "Got a source in the Coroner's office who likes to supplement his income." She leaned forward. "That's why Garos called you, isn't it? You know why the bodies are rotting like that, right?" Her voice was eager.

He began to growl a denial but stopped. What could she do? No paper would print it. Besides, he didn't believe it himself. He shrugged. "You're right. I've seen those signs before."

She flicked on a micro-recorder. "What's it mean?"

"It's a sign of a shifter killing," he said, straight-faced.

Her brow furrowed. In a very pretty way, he thought. "Shifter killing? What's that?" she asked.

"Shapeshifters. Garos and I used to hunt them. He thinks you saw one."

Pause. "Shapeshifters?" Her eagerness melted into a dead-pan that hardened into a glare. "Like a were-wolf?"

"Shifters aren't limited to wolves."

She clicked off the recorder and stuffed it back in her purse with a near ferocity. "A were-beast. Right. Thank you for the coffee, Mr. Mirocek." She stood up and grabbed her coat.

To his surprise, he realized that he wanted her to stay. "So how do you explain the rapid decay? How did the Coroner?"

She bit her lower lip. "I can't. Neither could they."

He stood and faced her. "I can." He could smell her perfume, a hint of vanilla.

She stared at him then shook her head and sighed. "Twenty minutes, no more." She sat down, arms folded.

An hour later, Jan sat back, having summarized his life story. He had left out the part about Stasia. Kate looked hard at him. "Jan, I'm certain you believe every word you just said. I also know it can't possibly be true."

"Does it matter? The *Star* wouldn't print it anyway."

She groaned. "Okay, so Garos thinks we have a were-beast in Toronto. Because of this corpse decay, right?"

"Plus the time of the murders. Most shifters assume animal form only at night, to hide in the dark. Out of the light. But actually, beyond that, I don't think it fits with a shifter."

"You mean you don't believe Garos, either? Why not?"

"Shifters live where their animal form is common. Then if seen, they aren't viewed as anything unusual. So were-tigers live in areas with tigers, were-wolves with real wolves."

"So?"

"So what animals are common in downtown Toronto?"

"Dogs and cats, for starters."

"Yeah, but not running free, which they'd need to be."

"How about birds? Maybe it's a were-pigeon," she said.

"Very funny. Too small. So are raccoons from the ravines."

"What's size got to do with it?"

"Mass-energy conservation. It has to be as big as us."

"Sounds like we've run out of animals," she said.

"That's what I think. No such beast."

"So what about the corpse decay?"

Jan frowned. "I don't know. I can't explain that." He looked at her. "It almost sounds as if you believe me now."

Kate shrugged. "I've heard worse. You meet all sorts of weirdos on these streets."

"Thanks, I love being tolerated."

She grinned at him. "You want to stay for dinner?"

He looked outside. The sun had set, and streetlights were winking into life. He should leave. But the area was well lit. Lots of neon. And Kate was smiling at him. "I'd like that," he said. He just wished she didn't remind him so much of Stasia.

Thirty-two years old. Sunday. A small church outside Budapest. Stasia, tall and fair beside him, a hunter for a year now. At the altar in the otherwise empty church stood Father Karman. Their prey.

"His parish suspects," Jan whispered.

Stasia nodded. "But simple tourists like us don't, right?"

The priest turned from the altar and noticed them. He smiled. "Are you here for Mass?" he called.

Jan hesitated. His Catholic upbringing made this hard. A priest in a church. He could at least let the man hold a last mass. They should be safe. Karman needed either time or the taste of blood to shift. Jan nodded. Stasia looked at him, puzzled. "After Mass, outside the church," he whispered.

During the Liturgy of the Word, Jan felt in his jacket for his gun. Stasia's presence at a capture still made him uneasy. As they approached the altar for Communion, Karman stared hard at Jan. He turned his back to pour the wine. The communion began.

After the ceremony, Karman took the cup from them and turned back to the altar. Only then did Jan notice another cup on the altar. The one from which the priest had drunk. Jan's eyes froze on a drop of liquid hanging red and thick on its lip.

Thick as blood.

Jan struggled to his feet, but the room swam. He fell, panic rising in him. The wine. Stasia screamed his name. A face loomed before him, cruel, already bestial, the reek of blood on its foul breath. Jan fumbled for his gun, but the beast struck him hard on the temple. Darkness took him.

As Harry brought Kate and Jan their dinners, Jan noticed an old man sitting in the back, out of the light. He wouldn't have seen him except that the man gestured to Jan with a jerky motion of a stiffened hand. Jan turned to Harry. "Who's that?"

Harry looked over. "Solly? Street person. Comes in sometimes. I'll give him a coffee, sandwich maybe. Don't know how he stays alive. He's usually in the shelter by now. Doesn't like the streets after dark. Last time he stayed late, I had to walk him there after we closed. Only way I could get him out."

Jan stood up. "I'm going to see what he wants."

Solly was a small round man. Round bald pate ringed by grey scraggly hair. Circle of a face under stubble and dirt. Rounded shoulders under a filthy coat, once an actual colour, now unknowable. Round balls of hands, fingers twisted in, peeking surprisingly clean from tattered sleeves, guarding an empty coffee cup. Jan smiled then struggled to maintain it as he caught the smell. Solly waved at a chair across from him.

Jan sat down. "Harry says your name is Solly."

One eye was almost shut. The other pinned Jan, then darted over the room. "Harry's is a good place. Stays the same, you know? S'important, you know? Some places—change. Don't like that. Can't tell if they're just different, or . . ." He fixed Jan with that eye again. "Heard you talking." Jan glanced back to where Kate chatted to Harry. Not a word reached Jan. Solly glared as if he read Jan's mind. "Heard you!" He pounded the table with a crippled hand. "Solly's seen things," he rasped. "Seen things." He looked around again, then lowered his head.

Jan waited, but Solly said no more. Standing, Jan started to walk away when a wheezy whisper stopped him.

". . . out of the light. Gotta know the signs."

Jan turned back to the old man. "What did you say?"

Solly's head was still down. "Remember. S'important." Hunched over his empty cup, he sat muttering to himself.

Kate looked up when Jan returned. "What'd he want?"

Jan shrugged. "You've got me. Buy him a coffee on my tab, will you, Harry?" Harry nodded and left.

They ate and talked. "So if you hunt shifters," Kate said, "and they don't come to the city, why do you live here?"

Jan looked out to where the gathering dark fed on a dying day. "I live here because they don't. I don't hunt them anymore. I got someone killed, Kate. Someone who trusted me."

She bit her lip. "I'm sorry," she said. They sat silent for a moment, then she gave a small smile. "Anybody could understand why you'd want to get away from those things."

He looked back to her. "I wonder if I have."

"What do you mean?"

"Every civilization has had shapeshifter legends. I've always wondered why no such myth exists for our modern cities."

"Why would such creatures live in a city? Why not stay in the wild? Less chance of being seen," she said.

"Also less food. They're predators who prefer human flesh." He shuddered, remembering. "There's more of that in a city."

"Sure, but you eliminated all the animal options."

He stared out at the night. "This is a different jungle. Maybe we've created a new niche, supporting a different predator. Convergent evolution. Its other form may not be animal at all."

"If it's not an animal, what would it be?"

"Don't know, but it's more likely to be seen in a crowded city, so its other shape would need to be downright mundane."

"But *what*?" she repeated.

Jan looked out to where shadows fought pale neon. He wanted to say that it would be a thing as at home with concrete and glass as a wolf was with earth and forest. A thing that breathed ozone like a summer breeze and held metal in its heart and electricity in its veins. A thing that not only lived in this realm of the lonely but fed on it. But he just said, "I don't know."

Kate shook her head then checked the time. "Oops. I've got to go. There was another witness last night—a hooker. She won't talk to the cops but she's meeting me at midnight." She looked at Jan and bit her lip again.

"Why don't I come with you?" he asked.

She broke into a huge smile. "Great!" She put on her coat while Jan wondered what he had just done. Solly shuffled over. "I also told Harry I'd walk Solly to the shelter," she said.

Solly peered outside. "We take Talbot?"

Talbot was little more than an alley, with no lights. Jan shivered. "Let's keep to well-lit streets. We'll use Richmond." As Solly started to argue, Harry called Jan to the phone.

It was Garos. "Janoslav? Did you meet Kate Lockridge?"

"Yeah. I think she's on the level, but she's a reporter. She, uh, knows about the corpse decay and the other victims."

Garos swore. "We checked her description of last night's suspect." He paused. "Jan, it matches a prior victim."

Jan felt a sudden coldness in his gut. "Victim? That doesn't make sense. How could it be a dead guy?"

"Jan, she was at the scene of the most recent killing and described a victim from another. Now you say she has further knowledge of these deaths. We'll be talking to her again. In the meantime, be careful around her." Garos hung up.

Jan stared at the neon signs over the bar, trying to lose himself in their coloured swirls. A hand touched his shoulder. He jumped and turned to find Kate, Solly in tow. Jan's face must have betrayed something. She looked puzzled. "What's wrong?"

Jan shook his head. "Nothing," he lied. "Let's go."

Waving good-bye to Harry, they stepped out onto Richmond and turned east. The snow had stopped, and the sidewalks were slushy. "We take Talbot?" Solly asked again.

"Richmond, Solly, or you go alone," Jan said. Solly glared but fell silent, hanging by the curb and scanning the street as they walked. Jan kept thinking of Garos's call. They reached Jarvis. A young blond woman stepped from a doorway, long white coat over a short red leather skirt, black stockings and boots.

"There's Carla," Kate said and started toward the girl.

A shout made them turn. Solly was backing away, wide-eyed and pointing a shaking hand to something above their heads. "No! Solly knows the signs. You won't get Solly!" Terror on his face, he ran onto the street. Jan spun back. Above the doorway where Carla stood open-mouthed, a neon sign glared "Franny's Tavern." The first word was red, the second blue.

The blue one was moving.

In an eye-blink, the letters slid down the wall to form a glowing pool on the sidewalk. In another blink, a humanoid shape rose radiant white from the pool—female torso, face, hair, the shape of clothing, then colours, facial details.

The face of the murder victim from last night.

"Carla! Behind you!" Kate yelled.

A spear of light stabbed from the creature's hand, striking Kate full in the chest and Jan in the shoulder. Electricity flamed into him. Numbed, he collapsed to watch as the thing grabbed Carla by the throat and lifted her into the air.

Slush seeping into his clothes, choking on ozone, Jan tried to move. A violent tremor shook Carla. Jan's arms twitched. The creature held Carla higher, its glow brightening, colours cycling. Jan could feel his legs again. Carla fell limp, and the thing slapped her down like a wet towel. It turned to Kate.

Gasping, Jan heaved himself to his knees and lunged forward. Somehow he got his hands under Kate's armpits and dragged her just out of reach. "Get up!" he cried.

"Can't . . . move," she gasped. He pulled her to her knees. The thing's colours were fading, its features melting back into a smooth humanoid shape. It shimmered and changed again. And became Carla. The Carla-thing smiled. It stepped toward them.

Inches from its outstretched arms, Jan hauled Kate up, and they lurched into the road. Stumbling but with returning strength, Jan scanned the street. From a dark alley across the road, a small round figure waved, a jerky motion from a stiff arm.

Half dragging Kate, Jan struggled toward Solly. Footsteps sounded behind them. The nape of his neck tingled as if an electrical charge was building at his back. He pushed Kate into the alley as something brushed his coat. Shoving a trash can behind him, he heard a thud and a sound no human throat ever made. The alley was dark, and Jan's eyes still burned from the electrical flash. Ahead, Solly's grey form disappeared to the right. Jan moved along the wall, Kate's hand in his.

"Now that thing looks like Carla!" she panted.

"It takes the form of what it kills," Jan gasped. *That* was why her description of the suspect had matched an earlier victim.

A hand grabbed Jan from the darkness and yanked them both sideways. He could see nothing but he knew the smell. Solly pulled them along. Jan could feel walls to either side. They stopped. Jan reached ahead in the dark and touched another wall.

Solly had led them into a dead end.

"No!" Jan screamed. His nightmare seized him. Trapped in the dark with a monster. And with a woman who trusted him.

Thirty-two. In a church basement outside Budapest. Waiting to die. Total darkness. Lying on damp earth, bound hand and foot. Stale smell of mildew stinging his throat. As he fought to awaken, a scream sliced the black, clearing the flames of pain in his head like a bucket of ice water. Stasia.

He raged against his bonds. She screamed again. "Jan! Oh God, no! No! Help me!" Jan threw himself forward and managed to roll once. Her cries were clearer. But so was another sound.

The sound of something feeding.

Jan threw himself again but something held him fast. He could do nothing but lie in the dark, listening to the beast feed on the still-living Stasia. Praying in the dark for her screams to cease. Praying in the dark for her to die.

An eternity passed. Then only the grunts of the beast remained. The stench of rotting meat grew strong as a huge shape moved closer in the darkness. Jan screamed.

Blinding light suddenly flooded the room, and the roar of the were-wolf echoed in the roar of gunshots. Blood, thick and black and hot, struck Jan's face as Garos shouted his name.

In the dark alley, Jan shoved Solly away and turned to run back. Solly grabbed him, holding on with surprising strength. "No! Stay here. *Out of the light*. Solly knows!"

A glow began at the entrance to the dead-end, but Jan still couldn't see. Kate's hand found his. "Jan?" she said.

Hearing her fear, his panic fled, replaced by a feeling of resolve he had almost forgotten. He squeezed her hand. She would not die. "Solly, talk to me. Tell me what you know!"

Solly's voice quavered. "It don't like the dark. We're safe here. Right?" At this, Kate groaned.

Jan swore, his mind racing. Light was the key. "It must feed off electricity, hiding as part of signs. When you chased it last night, it joined with the sign in the alley."

"That's why the alley was brighter last night," Kate said.

"Sunlight must sustain it in the day, plus electricity. But when night comes . . ." Jan stopped. When night comes, it needed more. It needed its real food: human life force.

The light at the entrance grew, and the glowing form of Carla appeared. "I thought it doesn't like the dark," Kate whispered.

Jan swore. "It must still be hungry and figures we're worth the risk. Solly, how long can it go without light?"

"Five minutes," he whined, "but a lot more if it just ate."

"Wonderful," Kate said.

Twenty paces away now, the thing lit the entire area. Its glow was dimmer, but Jan doubted that would save them. At least now he could see. He looked around, and his heart leapt. The wall behind them and the walls on either side each held a door.

Jan grabbed the door handle behind them. Locked. So was the one to their right. He tried the last one. The handle turned a bit. He leaned on it and heard a click. He threw his weight against the door, and it squealed open with rusty protests.

"Inside!" Kate cried, rushing forward, Solly in hand.

"No!" Jan grabbed her, an idea forming. The thing was ten paces away. Pulling out his flashlight, he stepped into the room and flashed the beam around. The stock room of a store, twenty feet square. Not much space to manoeuvre. Could he do it? Could he finally face his darkness? By walking into it? He turned back. The thing was five paces away. He aimed his light at it.

"No!" Solly cried. "It eats light!"

Jan ignored him. "Kate, take Solly into the corner. After I lead it inside, close the door and don't open it." Kate turned pale but nodded and pulled Solly back. Jan stepped up, playing his beam over the creature. It turned to him. Keeping his light on it, he backed into the room. Darkness closed in on him and with it his fear. What had he done?

The thing stepped inside. The door slammed shut behind it.

It stopped and looked back. Its mouth opened, and a sound like fingers tapping fine crystal, filled the room. And somehow, in that sound Jan heard its hunger and its pain. A wave of empathy flooded him. They were alike. Hunters. Hiding their true shape. Fearing the night. The creature reached for him. *I'm sorry*, Jan thought. He turned off his light.

The thing trembled, and its aura dimmed. But then Carla's features and clothing faded, seeming to melt back into its body. A featureless human form remained, glowing blue-white.

It's conserving energy, Jan thought. It no longer needed to pretend to be human. He swallowed. How intelligent was it?

A deadly game of tag began—the thing pursuing with the same plodding step—Jan retreating, avoiding corners, always leaving two paths of escape. With each passing minute, the thing's aura dimmed, fading to blue, then yellow, then red.

Finally it stopped, arms drooping. Jan sighed and relaxed. He noticed too late that the arms weren't just drooping.

They were growing.

Both arms flashed out, three times normal length, easily covering the space between the thing and Jan. Taken by surprise, Jan dove aside, but a hand brushed his thigh. Electricity numbed his leg. He fell. Looming over him, the thing reached down.

And stopped. Its colours cycled the spectrum then faded to grey. A sound like breaking glass fled a suddenly grotesque mouth. Its feet melted into a pool. The arms flowed back into a shrinking torso. Soon only the pool remained, faintly glowing.

Jan walked to it. The pool bulged once toward him, then its last light died, and Jan stood in the dark. He waited before flicking on his light. The pool was a dull grey. He kicked, and it shattered with a crystal cry, imploding into sparkling powder.

He opened the door and stepped out into the alley. Solly and Kate both backed away, eyeing him warily. "Is it really you?" Kate asked. "Or that thing?"

"Your name is Kate Lockridge, his is Sully," he said, "and whatever *that* thing was, it wasn't a were-pigeon."

Laughing and with tears in her eyes, Kate threw her arms around him. Back on the street, Solly checked every bit of neon in sight, then fixed Jan with that eye. "Gotta know the signs," he said.

Jan phoned the police about Carla's body and left a message for Garos to call.

"So what now, hunter?" Kate asked.

Solly stared up at Jan. "You gonna get the others, too?"

Jan and Kate turned to him. "Others?" Kate groaned.

Jan shrugged then looked at her. "I could use a partner." She said nothing but took his hand as they walked Solly home.

They took Talbot.

Thirty-five. A midnight street. He waits in the dark, watching the signs. She waits beside him. He knows the ways of the beast; she knows these streets. A town pays well to be rid of its creatures of the night. Creatures that breathe ozone like a summer breeze, wear glass for skin and burn electricity in their veins. Creatures that feed on this realm of the lonely.

Once, he shunned the dark where shadows hide their secrets. Now he stalks the night streets, a shadow himself slipping from alley to alley. Now he keeps to the dark.

And stays out of the light.

T his story represents one of the few times where I returned to a universe from a previous story, in this case, the world of Scream, RIP Force, and the Merged Corporate Entity from "Scream Angel." This story was written in response to an invitation from Andy Cox, the publisher of TTA Press in the U.K. Andy had just acquired the venerable U.K. SF magazine InterZone from David Pringle, and was soliciting stories for his inaugural IZ issue. I'd had the pleasure of selling stories to Andy's Third Alternative, so I was thrilled when he invited me, and even more thrilled when he bought this story. The first issue of IZ under a new editor attracted a lot of review attention. It provided me my first experience of having a highly visible story publication and drove home the lesson that you can't please everyone. Most of the reviewers and readers loved it, but a few absolutely hated it. Personally, I prefer that kind of reaction over a universal agreement that a story is "okay." So here it is, for you to love or hate.

ENLIGHTENMENT

They're dead now, the Be'nans. Ta'klu was the last to die. Her body hangs in my arms, as heavy as my guilt, as my footsteps echo in these empty alien streets. And soon we'll be gone from this world, too. I'm the last human in this bizarre, beautiful city. Fan is still here with me—but she's already dead.

The High Places rise above me: two bone-white curves sweeping hundreds of feet into a morning sky from opposite ends of the city, bending inwards like two impossible fingers yearning to touch. Built by generations of Be'nans and now only a body length apart at their lofty tips, the High Places reach for each other. But they don't meet, don't connect. Not yet.

I'll go to them soon, to try to keep a promise. If I fail, and if Ta'klu was right, then what happened here will happen on another world. And another.

But first I must prepare Ta'klu in the manner of her people. She used to laugh when I called her Ta'klu, a name never meant for a human throat. Little here was meant for humans. We aren't capable of understanding. Beside me, Fan nods in agreement.

My first view of the planet Be'na came just before our attack: from orbit, on the darkened observation deck of the *MCES Anvil*, a Merged Corporate Entity ship, manned by RIP Force soldiers of which I was one. I stood with Colonel Keys, staring at the white-green swirl of the planet on the viewplate that covered the bulkhead wall. Fan sat at my feet, unseen by Keys.

Unseen, for Fan was a ghost. I thought of her as a ghost, anyway. One that only I could see. *My* ghost. My guilt ghost. The alternative was that I was insane, and she existed only in my mind. I had not entirely ruled out that possibility.

The screen lit Keys' profile in hard, cold lines. "Did you know, Captain, that these *ips* once had interstellar capability? Gave it all up over five hundred Earth years ago," he said.

Ips: IPs, Indigenous Peoples. A Ripper slur for aliens. RIP: Relocation of IPs, wherever they interfered with planned Entity operations, in this case mining. Survey teams had pegged Be'na as rich in an isotope of berkelium, a rare trans-uranium element and a key material in the shielding for Ullman-Gilmour interstellar drives. But I'd been with the Force long enough to know that RIP held more truth as a word than as initials. "Relocate" was open to interpretation. Fan's people had been relocated. Fan began appearing to me shortly after that.

I'd heard about Be'nan technology. "Do we know why, sir?"

He shrugged. "Dunno. They've reverted to a very simple lifestyle. But from the terraforming and climate control we've seen, they still have technology available somewhere." Another shrug. "Doesn't matter. They've no military capability."

No way to protect themselves from us, I knew he meant. Just like Fan's people. I called her Fan. I didn't know her name. Her people had lived on Fandor IV. They were dead now. Fan was humanoid, but her red fur and the pointed snout and ears gave her a feral look. She was young, maybe four or five, about three feet tall, and reminded me of a stuffed puppy I had as a kid.

The screen switched to an image of an adult Be'nan of unknown gender. Thin, stick-like. Bony face, lots of angles. No hair. Wide eyes, black on silver. Nostril holes over thin lips. Long purple gown, unadorned, straight lines, silky sheen.

Keys snorted. "Not much to look at. At least they're tall. Big buildings, high ceilings." High enough for reuse by us. And empty after we did what RIP did, so we wouldn't waste time and money making our own shelters. The Entity expected a high return from a project world. "Landing fleet ready?" Keys asked.

Fan's earflaps opened wide. I avoided her eyes. "Yes, sir. You still need to set their dosage levels for Scream, sir."

"Level two for pilots, five for the surface teams," he said.

Level five—full combat hits. I pitied any Be'nan that resisted. I saluted and headed off to CommCon to release the dosages, hoping

Fan would stay behind. No such luck. The elevator shushed open, and she stood staring at me, tears running from those big brown eyes. She remembered what RIP did to her people. What Scream *made* them do. Made *me* do.

Think of human emotions as a sine wave function: valleys of pain, peaks of pleasure. The greater your joy, the higher the peak; the greater your pain, the deeper the valley. Scream took valleys and flipped them, made them peaks, too. Screamers reacted to events based solely on the *intensity* of the resulting emotion. Pain brought pleasure, grief gave joy, horror rendered ecstasy.

On Scream, killing was an emotional orgasm. Some nasty side effects, such as a lack of concern about exactly who you killed, meant we weren't given Scream until after military discipline programming in boot camp. RIP kept senior officers clean, but every Ripper below Major was addicted. Withdrawal was long and painful—and fatal. RIP was our only source, keeping us loyal and obedient.

Screamers burnt out fast on RIP work, so they rotated us off every six months. Or sooner, if we showed unusual stress symptoms—like trying to kill yourself on Fandor IV. In my rehab role as Security Officer, my dosage was just enough to avoid withdrawal, but not enough to let me enjoy my depression.

The elevator opened on CommCon. Returning salutes, I walked to the control board. Fan's eyes burned into me as I punched the commands to administer Scream to the landing fleet via the life support systems in their field suits. I informed Keys, and a moment later he barked the landing order over the intercom.

With Fan sobbing silently beside me, I watched in the viewplate as our ships swarmed from the main bay, descending on Be'na like a plague of black shining locusts.

I enter the Place of Judgement, the *be'tig'lacht*, the sole Be'nan structure I've found without windows. Only the Be'nan judges, the *be'ti*, saw what was done here. The single, vaulted chamber, tall even by Be'nan standards, is thick with the smoke of torches and the sweet fumes of the *do'aran'qua,* the milky liquid used in this ceremony, bubbling in a vat beneath the blackened floor boards. Fan peeks from behind my legs, not wanting but wanting to be in this place.

Ta'klu taught me what was done here. I lay her in the Frame of Judging, the *tig'thar.* I'm not worthy to judge any Be'nan, let alone Ta'klu, but I owe her this. The *ba'aran*, the Book of Forms, lies on a stone table. From it, I choose a *do'aran*, a pose, for her upper body. Her cold flesh makes my hands tremble as I position her arms in the High Form—raised above her in two curves, hands just touching at the fingertips. It represents the completion of the High Places: the form reserved for the most holy. Ta'klu wouldn't approve, but Fan nods her agreement.

I plan to arrange Ta'klu's spindly legs, not in accordance with any form in the Book, but rather to fit her final resting place, her *do'lach*. To the Be'nans, the place and the pose became one, together forming the final judgment of a Be'nan.

Yesterday, in Be'nan tradition, I climbed to the place I've chosen, to make an exact cast of where she'll rest. My clothes are torn from that climb, blood crusting on my knees and arms. I washed the cuts on my hands, but they burn and bleed whenever I use them. Staring at the wounds, I think of crucifixion.

I carry the mould I made from the cast to the frame of judging where Ta'klu hangs. Fan urges me on, but the Be'nan sun climbs halfway up the High Places before I've attached the mould to the frame and positioned Ta'klu's legs properly within it.

I step back, judging how I've judged her. I'm not pleased, for there's no pleasure in this duty, but I'm satisfied that I've met my intent. I remove the mould from the frame and crank open the vat of the do'aran'qua. As I wind the winch that lowers Ta'klu into the vat, her position on the frame reminds me again of crucifixion, of her, of an entire race—with us placed beside and below them as thieves. Fan bows her head in a final good-bye to Ta'klu.

Keys chose the city nearest to the berkelium deposits as our base of operations. As it turned out, that was the main city of the Be'nans—*lach'ma'pen'lache*, the Place of the High Places.

Dropping forces outside the city, we secured the perimeter before landing in the main square. Twenty LAShers—Low-altitude Attack Ships—hovered above for emphasis. Unnecessary emphasis. To say that the Be'nans offered no resistance would be misleading. They seemed completely indifferent to our presence—just as well for them, with every Ripper on full combat dosage.

We moved troops into the buildings forming the main square. I didn't ask Keys what he had done with the original Be'nan occupants. I knew. Fan knew, too. Her eyes accused, condemned.

The next morning, I walked with Keys through the city. Fan stayed well back—she didn't like being close to Keys. Be'nan architecture, at least in this city, had an air of delicacy and openness. Most buildings were two or three stories, often with no walls, simply a domed roof resting on tapering pillars or thin arching supports. Where walls were used, they consisted more of window than wall, in a variety of locations and geometric shapes. The predominant colour was white, accented by purple cone flowers and the blue-green of a vine that seemed to grow as it wished. The air was heavy with the musky fragrance of the flowers.

Above the city, large, grey, balloon-shaped creatures drifted. The project file identified them as mammalian, levitating by abdominal gas sacks. Other Rippers shot down several before the herd floated out of range. Fan cried at each corpse we passed.

But the dominant features of the city were the statues: life-sized Be'nan figures in an endless variety of poses and locations, carved from some smooth, milky material. "Their sculpture arts seem rather limited," I said. Oblivious to us, two tall Be'nans, some of the few remaining in the city, paused before a statue and bent forward to touch their foreheads to it. Looking for Fan, I was surprised to find her crouched before a statue, head bowed.

Keys grunted, then nodded his head at the two huge white arches that loomed over the city. "Had a squad check those out. You know what they're made of?" Not waiting for any guess on my part, he jerked a thumb at a statue. "Those things. Can you believe it? They've built those damn arches from statues. One by one, fit together like a giant jigsaw puzzle." He moved on.

I stared up at the High Places, trying to fathom how many statues would have been needed to build the looming fingers. Hundreds of thousands, maybe millions, each carved to fit with those placed before, slowly rising to the sky, reaching to touch each other. How many generations ago had it begun? And *why*?

Suddenly, that question was important, as if an answer would explain why I felt so apart from RIP, so disconnected. As if the space between those tips was the distance between myself and the world around me. Just then, the sun peeked over the High Places, melting the shadow where I stood. Beside me, Fan stared at the arches, her face as sad as ever, yet peaceful. She nodded.

Removed from the vat, Ta'klu has hardened in the pose I gave her. The liquid has saturated her body, mummifying and encasing her corpse in a super-hard, super-light shell. She stands before me again, but now as a *be'nan'ti*, a Judged One. I polish her white surface with ceremonial rubbing creams until she gleams. Her face is turned to the heavens, eyes hidden behind this shell. Fan backs away. Yes, Fan, now we've truly lost her. Somehow, while her body appeared as in life, she was still here with us. Now, she's become a thing. Only my duty to her remains.

I prepare to transport her to her final resting-place. Although she stood a head above me in life, in this pose she's below me in stature, so that I'll be able to carry her. I smile. Below me in stature? In physical stature only.

After attaching straps to her arms, I turn and reach back to grasp the straps. Hunching forward, I pull on the straps to lift her onto my back. She's heavy. I shrug her weight further up until her feet clear the ground enough to let me walk nearly upright. Moving to the door, bearing her like my cross, I step onto the silent streets where Fan already waits.

Keys and I explored much of the Be'nan city that first day. Fan tagged along behind, keeping her distance from Keys. He was mostly silent. I knew that the Be'nans reaction to our presence, or rather lack of reaction, had unnerved him. He scanned each alcove we passed, as if expecting a belated uprising to begin here. We turned a corner onto a side street.

And stopped.

On this street, sculpted arms rose from the pavement itself, twisting and writhing upwards like frozen serpents. Hands clutched, fingers clawed, as if grasping at something, anything, to tear themselves free of some hidden hell. Upright statues lined this street as we had seen throughout the city, but with their backs turned to this display of pleading arms. Behind us, not daring to enter the street, Fan peeked around a pillar.

Keys and I walked slowly along that strange avenue, weaving a path among the arms. Between each pair, rising just enough out of the pavement to be discernible, lay an upturned sculpted face.

Perhaps it was the silence of that street or the Be'nans indifference to our power—or the expressions on those faces. Whatever the reason, Keys kicked suddenly at an arm. Despite the sculpture's delicate appearance, his attack had no effect, beyond generating a pained look on his face and a mournful bell tone that echoed down the narrow lane. He stood there in silence, his hands clenching and unclenching. Then he drew his Tanzer and fired a thin beam at the arm. The arm glowed blue as I felt the radiated heat. Keys holstered his gun and kicked the arm again.

This time, it broke off with a snap. He picked it up, staring at the broken end. I heard him mutter "My God." Then he waved me over. "Captain, look at this."

He handed me the arm, and I examined the end. Instead of the solid substance I expected, the outer whiteness of the arm appeared to be merely a shell. I stared at the contents inside. Although Be'nan physiology differed from ours in many respects, I'd seen enough dismembered corpses in RIP to know that I was looking at bone and mummified flesh.

I've carried Ta'klu only a small way through the empty city, and already I'm tiring. Lowering her to the pavement, I slump against her, resting a moment between the twisted upraised arms here on one of the *mephi'cou*, a Street of the Low Ones. Fan huddles close to me, sensing the evil in this place.

Elsewhere in the city, Judged Ones appear in a *li'do'aran*, a pose of purity, placed so that passersby must look up to them. Those are the majority—not saints, not devils—just good people. Could humans say that of our own race? Fan shakes her head.

But the Streets of the Low Ones interred those judged to be impure, to have regressed from birth on a path to Enlightenment. They were placed beneath the feet of the people, most of their encased bodies hidden, imbedded into the actual roadway.

Such a judgment was never given lightly. Any Be'nan that gave it would rest here as well after death, lining this street, their back turned to the display, a symbol that the Be'nan people rejected the lives of those interred here.

I know each face, each story. Here lies Ves'wa, who opened the way for the Ones Who Watch, from where Ta'klu's ancestors had banished them eons ago—and to where they were returned after the Battle of the Terrible Silence. There I can see the twisted beauty of Ne'sto, whose passion for lovers was equalled solely by her passion for adornments made from those lovers. Beside her lies Ke'bi, who danced with the Dead Things in the City with No Name.

And there, in a darkened alcove, segregated even from these, is Det'syek, a judge himself, who let a desire for artistic impression override objectivity in the poses he gave.

Fan pleads with me to leave here. Sighing, I rise and take up my burden again. For there's another class of Judged Ones: the Be'nan equivalent of saints or buddhas, those who achieved Enlightenment. The Be'nans reserved a special location for the Enlightened. I raise my eyes to the High Places.

The next day, to the surprise of all, Keys halted the removal of the Be'nans from the city. He called me to the house that we'd appropriated for RIP HQ. News of the true nature of the statues had spread quickly among the Rippers. A wariness now replaced their arrogance, an unease amplified by the ubiquity of its source: the statuary literally surrounded us at every turn. Walking from the officers' quarters, I passed several toppled and smashed statues. Fan paused at each one, touching it, head down.

I found Keys in the Ops room, a central airy dome supported by arching buttresses and speckled with high windows. He paced beside a stone slab that now served as a map table. I noted that someone had removed the two statues that had stood on the slab.

"You stopped the relo," I said, feeling Fan's eyes burn into me. Relocation. Even after all the RIP missions I'd been on, all I had seen and done, I still couldn't call it what it was.

Keys stopped pacing and pinned me with a stare. "I've been talking to a head honcho ip. Some sort of priest caste."

"Talking, sir?" I asked. Fan grew suddenly still beside me.

"Talking. As in what we are doing right now."

I was shocked. With no earlier direct contact with this culture, we had estimated a year to figure out their language. "CommOps has made remarkable progress."

Keys snorted. "Those cretins? They'd still be pointing to holos and building goddam syntax charts." He shook his head. "The ips did it. Yesterday, this Tatoo or Takoo or something, she walks in here—at least I think she's a she—and just starts yapping. Perfect Entity Standard English." He plopped into a chair beside the map table and motioned me to another.

I sat, and Fan curled on the floor. "What did she want?"

"After yesterday, the men started breaking those . . . *things*," he said. I knew he meant the statues. "She wanted us to stop."

"That's their first reaction to anything we've done. What did you tell her, sir?"

"I agreed. I ordered the men to cease and desist."

RIP Colonels neither sought nor took counsel from ips. My face must have shown my surprise. Keys leaned forward. "She doesn't just know our language, Captain—she even knew our slang. Called us Rippers, talked about ips, Tanzers, LAShers."

I hesitated. "That could be a result of how they learned our language. They must be recording our conversations, then applying sophisticated pattern recognition and context AI."

"She knew that we're here for the berkelium."

"The men might have talked about that."

"She used our MCE project code. Only you and I know that."

That stopped me. "Maybe they hacked into our ship systems?"

"There's more. She knew stuff about me that isn't on our systems. Stuff from my childhood. Little things, trivial, not something I ever told anybody in RIP."

Again I felt the isolation and loneliness that had flooded me on first seeing the High Places. I felt suddenly naked, exposed to the alienness of this world. "Telepathy, perhaps?"

He shook his head. "I didn't even remember this stuff until she said it. So I thought it best to agree to her request, until we know more." He looked at me. "Which is where you come in."

"Me, sir?" I replied, as Fan's ears snapped up.

"I want you to be our liaison with these ips, through this one. Find out what you can about them, what else they know about us. And, goddamn it, *how* they know it."

"Why me, sir?"

Keys frowned. "You're my 2IC, and our security officer."

Fan shook her head. He was hiding something. I swallowed. "If I'm to succeed, sir, I need to know everything about this."

Keys glared at me, clenching and unclenching his hands, just like he had done before he shot the arm on that street the day before. "All right, Captain. She asked for you. By name."

The vines now cover these silent streets. They part before us as we walk, showing me the way though my goal hangs clear and bright above me. They know who I carry.

We pass many Judged Ones, toppled by Rippers. They stand once more, resurrected, raised up by the vines, broken limbs held in place by blue-green coils, cracked wounds concealed behind leafy veils. Fan tilts her head as the wind mutters in the rustle of the vines, giving voice to dead Be'nans. I know the words they whisper. All life here knows the deed that was done.

And the price the Be'nans chose to pay, in vain, for us.

Keys led me from the Ops room to a garden inside the HQ house. I was surprised to find the garden, untended for only two days since our occupation, already overgrown. Vines choked the paths, and a pungent scent of flowers hung like an unseen curtain. A tall Be'nan stood between two arching fountains.

A vision of the High Places came unbidden to me. In it, this Be'nan hovered suspended between them, as if those strange great fingers were pointing at her, indicating her. Then she stretched out long thin arms to touch both tips, bridging the narrow gap, finally completing the High Places. Or did she hang crucified on them?

The vision vanished. I turned to ask Keys a question but found him gone. Turning back, I jumped, startled to find the Be'nan now standing beside me.

She touched the fingertips of both her hands together in an arch before her, the Be'nan greeting, then repeated the gesture but facing slightly to my left. I turned. Fan stood there, staring up at the Be'nan, lips pulled back in the smile of her people. I'd never seen Fan smile. This so struck me that it was several seconds before I realized the implication of what just happened. I turned to the Be'nan. "You . . . you can see her?" The Be'nan just smiled a very human smile. I cleared my throat. "My name is Jarrod," I said, not knowing what else to say.

She spoke a sound, her name I supposed. Clicks and bird songs to me. "Ta'klu?" I offered, like a child before a teacher.

She smiled again. "That will do."

So began our friendship. And the end of a world.

My muscles burn and scream, but I refuse to rest here. Fan runs ahead, anxious to leave this place behind. Even the vines avoid this street. Here the killing started. Here the Ta'lonae, the huge gas-bag creatures, were slaughtered. Their corpses drape statues and buildings, and cover the street.

Their flesh doesn't rot in the normal way. It liquefies into a thick grease that drips around me and on me, making the street slick and treacherous with the load I carry. The stench, sickly sweet like some strange spice, is overpowering.

As are my memories. I struggle on to where Fan waits.

I lived with Ta'klu from the day we met, spending all my time with her. I don't know if that had been Keys' expectation, but once we met, it never occurred to me to do otherwise.

Ta'klu never explained why she had asked for me, nor why she gave me what she did—more than just all of her time, I received her complete attention, her focus. She took me everywhere in the city, taught me of their culture, their history, their beliefs.

And of a thing called Enlightenment.

"What is it?" I asked Ta'klu one day as we walked in the city, Fan scampering around each vine-covered pillar we passed.

"Your people will call it omniscience, but it is less than that—and more. It is connecting as one with life around you."

"On Be'na?" I asked, touching a statue as we passed.

"And beyond." She raised a long thin hand as I opened my mouth to protest. "More I cannot tell you, Jarrod. Not yet."

"Is it something that humans can aspire to?"

"Your people will desire it."

"But can we achieve it?"

She looked at me for several breaths. "We do not yet know."

"Then can you give it to us?"

"We can open a way," she said, smiling down at Fan.

"Keys will want it," I said. Fan stopped, suddenly solemn.

"Yes," Ta'klu replied.

"Will you give it to him?"

"Can a broken cup hold an ocean?"

I took that as a "no." But I knew RIP and the lengths to which Keys would go. Fan looked up at me. I thought of her people, wiped out by RIP, and my role in that. And I decided. I resolved to withhold all that I learned of Enlightenment from Keys, though I knew that if he discovered this, I'd be court-martialled. Fan smiled. She smiled a lot lately. I liked it.

In those early weeks, Ta'klu showed me what it meant to be Be'nan. Then Keys showed us what it meant to be human.

I awoke one morning to the sizzle of Tanzer fire. Fan stood at an arched window in the room in Ta'klu's house where I slept, gesturing to me. I rose and walked over. A swarm of Ta'lonae hovered above a nearby street, circled by a ring of LAShers. The shimmering around each ship told me that they had their shields set at a wide dispersal: they were herding the Ta'lonae.

For the slaughter.

Houses blocked my view of the next street, but Tanzer beams flamed upwards. No pattern, just Rippers firing at will. When hit, most Ta'lonae would rupture and float down like a huge leaf. But every so often, one exploded loudly in flames, to a chorus of cheers, as the gas inside the creature's sac ignited. Fan jumped at each explosion, and the herd screeched in mournful whistles.

I felt Ta'klu beside me. "So it begins," she said.

"You expected this?"

Her eyes lifted skyward, the Be'nan equivalent of a nod.

"But why? Keys stopped them doing this before."

"He has learned of Enlightenment."

I swallowed. "Ta'klu, I've told him nothing."

Smiling, she laid a spidery hand on my shoulder. "I know."

I considered that as I watched the killing continue. "How do you know?" I asked. When no answer came, I turned and found myself alone. Below me, Ta'klu and Fan emerged onto the street and headed in the direction of RIP HQ. I rushed to follow them.

Keys stood in the Ops room with three Rippers—two sergeants and a lieutenant—facing Ta'klu. Keys fixed me with a look I didn't much like, then returned my salute. The others saluted me only after glancing to Keys. He pointed me to a chair. The other Rippers remained standing, and I knew he'd discovered my duplicity, my failure to inform him of all that I'd learned. I was through. Fan came to stand beside me, as if in support.

Keys turned back to Ta'klu. Even on relo work, I'd never seen his eyes that hungry. "They tell me you're the head ip."

"They?" I asked.

Keys glared at me. "They. All of them. Any of them. You didn't discover that, too? They *all* talk our language now. And every one I ask says the same thing—Ta'klu speaks for Be'na."

Ta'klu bowed. "I have been given this honour."

"Then you have the honour of explaining to me." Keys strode over to her. I think he regretted the move. She overreached him by a good foot, forcing him to look up to her. "Tell me how you manage food production, terraforming, weather control—entire planetary environmental management—all with zero technology."

She did not reply. Fan crept closer to me.

"Or how you can give us exact locations of berkelium, more precisely than we can manage with our instruments—drill depths, yield percentages—again without the use of any technology?"

No reply. Fan looked up at me, as if urging me to act.

"Or how you know as much about Earth and Earth history as we do? Or how you can be in one location, then be reported in another spot, hundreds of miles away, only minutes later?"

I felt that I had to do something, that it was my duty to protect her, as hopeless as it was. "You said yourself that they look the same. And their technology could be hidden—"

"Jarrod." It was Ta'klu. She shook her head, and I stopped. She turned to Keys. "It is called Enlightenment."

Keys smiled, no doubt thinking he had won. "What is it?"

"You will call it omniscience. It is not."

Keys' smile broadened. "Whatever. I want it."

"No," she replied, like a parent to a petulant child.

Keys walked back to the Ops table and sat on the edge. "Oh, I don't think you want to tell me that." He fingered the StAB rod at his belt. Fan hid behind me.

Ta'klu ignored him. "I believe your people have a saying—"

"We have lots," he snapped. "Like 'Don't piss into the wind.' We're the wind, ip, and we'll goddamn blow you away."

"I was thinking 'Beware of what you wish—it may come true'."

Keys snorted. "Are you saying your knowledge is dangerous? That we couldn't handle it?" Snickers ran through the Rippers in the room. "Well, sister, knowledge is power, and we deal with power every day. We carry it with us. We hold it in our hands, and we wield it as a terrible swift sword. You can't scare us."

"Some knowledge can kill," she said, a chill in her words.

Keys stood again. His hands were making and unmaking fists at his sides. "So can I, ip." His voice was low, calm and cold. "You'll give me the secret . . . or I'll kill every last one of you."

A terrible silence descended on that room, like a beast waiting to devour the next sound. Ta'klu stood in that silence, her head down. I wanted to scream at her. *Tell him! You don't know what they are capable of.*

She looked down at Keys. "No," she said.

I bowed my head. Fan stared at me, her face unreadable.

Of all the places in this tomb of a city, I didn't expect to rest here—
an open-air amphitheatre sunk below the ground, terraced rows
sloping down to a round pool. But the bodies of the Be'nans that
had filled this huge bowl are gone now, removed by the vines. Water
shimmers again below as the vines refill the pool. Fan leans over the
water, staring at her reflection.

I look up to the white arches that dominate this alien sky. Ta'klu's
people believed that when the High Places finally met, all of Be'na
would achieve Enlightenment. Would that such a gift had never
been granted to the humans here.

I was court-martialled. Keys could have killed me but that would
have been too kind. He had a couple of Rippers beat me up while he
watched. They dumped me on the street, and he knelt down beside
me grinning, while I spat out teeth and Fan cried.

"Maybe the ips won't talk, but you, Jarrod, you're going to need
a hit soon. Then you'll tell me what you know." He kicked me, then
walked away laughing.

Panic seized me. RIP was my only source of Scream. Withdrawal
meant weeks of agony, without the filter of Scream, then death. Fan
shook her head as if to say "No, don't worry." *Fine for you, little one*, I
thought. *You're already dead.*

In the first week after his ultimatum, Keys killed one hundred
Be'nans. Chosen at random, each was taken to stand in front of
Ta'klu's house. Shot with Tanzer, touched by StAB rod, knifed,
hung, bludgeoned, burnt alive—Keys told his men to use a variety
of methods to see if one particularly unnerved the "ips."

Ta'klu simply stood at her window and bowed to each victim,
making the sign of the High Places with her hands. They would
return the bow. Then they would die, some quickly, some slowly. Fan
stood quietly beside her each time, strangely calm.

I pleaded with Ta'klu. "Why do you let them die? Why don't they resist? Why doesn't someone give in, tell the secret?"

"Some do not know and so have nothing to give. Those of us who do know, know also that the secret would kill your people."

The implication of her words hit me like a charged StAB rod. "You die to protect us? Your killers?"

She smiled. "One day, Jarrod, perhaps you will understand."

That was not my only surprise in that first week. I experienced no withdrawal symptoms from Scream. When I mentioned this to Ta'klu, she just smiled. "A gift to my student," she replied. Fan bared her teeth at me in an I-told-you-so grin.

Keys killed a thousand the second week. Still they bowed and died. Stranger still, I perceived no change in the attitude of those Be'nans that I passed in the ever more empty streets. No panic ensued, no resistance, no flight.

By the third week, the RIP bio-weapons team had engineered a Be'nan plague virus with a short air-borne vector. Keys must have been desperate. RIP used bio-weapons sparingly. You could never be sure of the propagation rate. Too high a rate, and bodies piled up faster than you could get rid of them. Plus they raised the risk of impact on humans and the rest of the planetary ecosystem. I explained all this to Ta'klu as Fan cried.

Keys threatened its release. Ta'klu still refused him the secret. Keys ordered it dropped on a city on the far side of the planet. A week later, a survey team to the city reported one hundred percent kill rate. The Entity had added another nasty little bug to its product list. And Keys added a second city the next week and a third the week after that.

Still Ta'klu refused to cooperate. Still the Be'nans appeared indifferent to their own slaughter.

Then Keys must have recalled our sole earlier act that had finally prompted a reaction by the Be'nans to our presence: the destruction of the statues. But he was smart enough not to waste time toppling figures around the city.

I was awakened one morning by Ta'klu, her usual air of tranquility gone. Her head moved from side to side, a sign of agitation. "He will destroy the *ma'pen'lache*, the High Places," she said. Fan scurried about her in frantic circles.

I struggled to wake. "Keys? What . . . how do you know this?"

"He is attaching mechanisms to the base of each. Explosive devices that can be detonated remotely." Ta'klu bowed her head. "He has won." Fan stared at me, as if willing me to some action.

I shook my head. "He slaughters your living, and you do nothing. He threatens a monument to your dead, and you cave in."

"They are more than that, Jarrod." She turned and left.

"Ta'klu, wait," I called after her. Rising, I went to the window as she stepped onto the street, Fan running behind her. "What *are* the High Places?" I called, but Ta'klu kept walking. "Why do you protect them but not your people?" No reply.

Again I followed her to RIP HQ. Again I found her and Fan facing Keys and his officers. Keys wore a grin that I wanted to wipe away with a Tanzer. He looked startled to see me, but then the grin returned, and he turned to Ta'klu. "Got your attention, I see," he said. "Your call, ip. What's the decision?"

"You are making a terrible mistake. You—" Ta'klu began.

Keys swore. "Captain, radio your men to stand by to detonate." The Captain saluted and spoke into his PerComm.

"You will die. You will all die," Ta'klu said.

Silence choked the room. The Rippers looked at each other, but Keys laughed. "If you had any power, you'd have used it."

"We are protecting you."

Keys laughed even harder, but few Rippers joined in. This planet, this city, the indifference of the Be'nans to their own genocide— all had taken their toll. "Protecting us! How kind." His smile died. "Last chance, ip." He nodded to the captain who raised his PerComm again, but Ta'klu froze him with a look.

"Very well," she said. "I warned you. Remember that." She looked at me, and suddenly her voice whispered inside my head. I had never experienced that before. *You, Jarrod, I will shield. A role remains for you. To you, I grant the boon of ignorance.*

Raising her hands, she touched them together over her head. *Like the High Places*, I thought, as Fan hid behind me. Every object, every person in the room began to brighten, to glow as with some inner light. "I grant you . . ." Ta'klu cried, ". . . *Enlightenment!*"

We turn onto another Street of the Low Ones—and he's there.

Keys. He lies among the twisted arms and grasping hands, face up, his own arms outspread. He has crucified himself, driving a spike through each of his feet and through his left hand into the ground. A mallet lies beside his right hand. He mutilated himself first, his crotch a bloody mess, and gouged out his eyes.

Fan looks away while I pause long enough to urinate on him.

A while later, we reach the nearer of the High Places.

One month after the plague release and a mere week after the "gifting" of Enlightenment, I walked an empty city searching for food, Fan beside me. The only Terrans we found were corpses, all obvious suicides—hanging from archways by ropes or vines about their necks, lying headless with Tanzers in hand, impaled on the broken arms of statues. Fan wouldn't look at them. I hadn't found Keys yet and wondered if he, too, numbered among the dead.

That night, I sat beside Ta'klu as she lay dying. She hadn't eaten since her gifting to the Rippers, and the plague had finally touched her. Fan stood, head bowed, on her other side.

The east wall of Ta'klu's room was just a series of pillars, through which a cold wind now blew. In that direction, you could see the High Places reaching for each other against a starry sky. With an effort that was painful to watch, she turned to gaze at them. "I die, my people die, with our great work unfinished."

"What *are* the High Places?" I asked. "What is their power?"

Her gaze never left those great arches, but she smiled. "No power beyond what a symbol can hold. You know the power of a symbol, don't you, Jarrod?"

Fan made the sign of the cross, and I nodded.

"The ma'pen'lache represent an entire race and its resolve," Ta'klu whispered. "A people complete, connected in a belief, in a noble goal: to regain awareness of the universal life force, an awareness we hold at birth, but soon forget. In one moment, to be part of all life in all places. To be one with the creator."

"Is that Enlightenment?"

"That is what it would be, once all life has achieved it. What some of us achieved is only what an individual may aspire to, but less than an entire race, and much less than what all of life could do. And as each who had reached Enlightenment died, the ma'pen'lache grew."

"What did you give to Keys and his men?"

"What was mine to give. A universal body exists: a web connecting all living things, across time, across space. Life is not the sum of those living things, but the web itself. We cannot know life until we can see the web, feel the strands that join us to each other, to everything. That is Enlightenment."

I swallowed. "You let them touch the web."

She turned to me then. "Yes."

"And they were given knowledge of the life around them."

"And their place in that web of life, and the knowledge that life had of them," she finished.

I began to say that I didn't understand, then her words connected with a part of me that seemed to be born in that moment. *The knowledge that life had of them.*

She knew my thoughts. "Yes, Jarrod. The most dangerous encounter is with a perfect mirror. A mirror that shows us as the universe sees us. As we truly are."

She collapsed further into the pillows. "Your people saw the place that they had chosen in the web. Saw each life they took, each strand they broke. They saw how life regarded them: a thing apart, disconnected from the universal body, an invading disease." She closed her eyes. "And they saw the cure."

"Why did you protect me?"

A smile lived briefly on her lips. "I know *your* place in the web." Beside her, Fan nodded and looked at me, smiling.

"What do you mean?"

"A task remains. You remain. *The two become one.*"

"Ta'klu, no more riddles. Tell me what to do," I pleaded.

"I cannot. You must find the way. It is part of the task."

"But I'm no less a murderer than the others who were here."

"Who better to lead the way through darkness than one who has lived in the night?"

"I don't have the strength."

Her eyes opened for what was to be the last time, to look at me. "You have more than you know. Promise me you will try."

I swallowed, barely able to speak, feeling Fan's eyes burn into me, waiting for my reply. "I promise," I said to Ta'klu.

She smiled, perhaps recalling when we met. "That will do."

She died with the light of day, never speaking another word. Laying her hands on her chest, I looked up. Fan stood at a pillar, staring at the morning sun rising beneath where the High Places strained to touch, to become one. Become one.

The two become one, Ta'klu had said. I looked down at her body, knowing then what I must do.

My climb with Ta'klu up the High Places has taken hours. The Be'nans bore their honoured Judged Ones by this path for centuries, adding to the structure death by death, but none would have come alone as I have. The initial climb was almost vertical, up steps meant for longer Be'nan legs. I'm cold and exhausted, but each time I stop to rest and drink from my flask, Fan urges me forward again, jumping up and down, pointing ahead.

Now at last I near the tip of this finger. The rise has levelled off, but this final part of my journey is the most dangerous. More than one thousand feet above the ground, the finger narrows and slopes to each side. The light is failing, and my footing is unclear. A rising wind sways the High Places, threatening to rip me from my perch. It moans between the dead beneath me, each moan the voice of a ghost, accusing, condemning.

Another fifty feet remain. The wind's too strong. I set Ta'klu down and crawl forward, pulling her behind me. Thirty feet to go. She catches in the spaces and on other statues, and I must go back again and again to free her. Twenty feet. Ten. I can see her resting-place. I move behind to push her the final few feet.

We reach the tip. Now I must stand again, lifting her by the straps, to position her feet above the exact spot, her arms reaching out toward the other side. Fighting against each gust of wind, I lower her inch by inch toward her do'lach. I strain to see past her, to see if her outstretched hands will bridge the gap. She settles into place, her legs melding exactly with the limbs and torsos of those who went before, entwined like lovers. And her arms reach for the other side as if in prayer.

But they don't touch. The High Places don't meet, don't become one. They stay disconnected. And somehow, so do I.

I sink to my knees. The wind carries my cries away, making my grief as impotent as my effort to complete the High Places. But in the wind I hear words, a voice, Ta'klu's voice. I look up. Fan stands at the tip of the other finger, arms stretched toward me. I consider the distance across the span. No more than an arm's length. Could I touch the other side? If I crawl out, balancing on Ta'klu's arms. If I don't fall. If the wind doesn't pluck me off. If Ta'klu will support me in her arms.

Despite my grief and pain, I smile at this last thought and decide. She wouldn't let me fall. I'll try.

Crawling on my belly, my legs gripping each side of the tip, I begin to inch my way out to the end. I can't say why I'm doing this. It just seems right. A way of bringing closure before . . .

Before what?

Before I leave. I realize then that I'd climbed here not just to lay Ta'klu to rest, but to kill myself. I intended to throw myself from this height, final payment for the crime that we've done here. But somehow I know that my death wouldn't be repayment: it would be an escape—from a debt, a duty. I know now what I must do: return to Earth and make my people aware of what has been done here. Of what is being done on other worlds.

I stretch across the gap. Almost. A little more. The tip sways and lurches. The wind claws at me. And on the wind ride phantom sounds and spectral voices. I hear the crash of statues and the screams of Be'nans. I hear Keys laughing.

But above it, yet softer somehow, I hear Ta'klu. *Try*, she says, and I remember my promise.

I edge farther out still until my waist extends past her fingers, and I must grip her body with my feet. On the far tip, Fan gestures me on, pleading with her eyes. I reach again.

And touch the far side.

Electricity, energy, power, a force I can't describe thrills down my arm as my fingers brush the other tip. A chorus of a million Be'nans deafens me. Visions of generations of Be'nan lives burn my sight from me. Fragrances of a world of flowers and the stench of a mountain of corpses choke the breath from me.

And I fall from heaven.

I slip from Ta'klu's dead, hard, cold hands and from the High Places. I scream as I fall, and the world rushes toward me, and I scream again. Then I am silent. For the world has slowed, and I watch my body fall away from me, falling slowly like a feather sinking in amber.

Ta'klu is suddenly beside me, holding Fan by the hand. Other Be'nans hover with us above the High Places, spread across the heavens in an arc, ephemeral hands linked in the web. Ta'klu reaches out to me, and I to her. We touch.

And I am Enlightened.

I look down. Somewhere below me, directly under the High Places, my body now lies. That seems both strange and correct.

I sense Ta'klu with me, clear to me even among the seemingly infinite lives of which I am now aware. I hear the question that she asks me: *Now do you know your role?*

My people must learn, I reply. *But I've no body.*

A human awaits your coming, waits for you to speak through him. When they strike him down, another will accept you. And each time they strike you down, you will rise again, stronger, carrying more of your people with you. You are the prophet.

I remain silent.

Do you accept your place in the web? she asks.

Suddenly we are in the garden again where we first met, and I smell the flowers and hear the fountain. Vines curl around my feet, and through them I sense the infinite web of life of which I am now part. The vision fades, but I know my answer. *I'll try.*

I feel her smile. *That will do,* she says.

I span star systems in a mind-blink to hover above a blue-brown orb layered in swirls of white. I feel Fan now as part of me, as she always was. I plunge through the white until blue resolves to seas, and brown to endless cities, and I sense the billions that dwell in those cities and under those seas.

I know them all, and soon they will know me. I fly eastwards, toward a coming sunrise, to the one who awaits me.

And I think of resurrection.

I wrote the first draft of this story overnight at a workshop that Kristine Kathryn Rusch and Dean Wesley Smith held in Oregon. Their special guest was Denise Little, Executive Editor with Tekno Books, one of the largest book packagers in North America. Attendees at this workshop had a chance to write stories for a themed anthology that Denise was editing for DAW Books. Denise told us the theme—stories told from the point of view of a female villain in fantasy or legend—and we had until the next morning to turn in a draft. I wrote this story. Not sure why, although the US invasion of Iraq was front-page news at the time, even for Canadians, and that war was very much on our minds. I wrote it, and (to my surprise) Denise bought it, and I had a story in an anthology with my all-time favourite title: Hags, Sirens, and Other Bad Girls of Fantasy.

THE LAST RIDE

On the night her life would change forever, Odin's horn wakened Vaya from a peaceful sleep. The mournful wail, echoing with the screams of the dying, called the Valkyries to ride from Valhalla, as it had done through the ages whenever war raged in the world of mortals.

Vaya disentangled herself from the arms of her still slumbering sisters where they lay in the communal bed of the Valkyrior. Throwing back the warm cover of furs, she stood up, naked and shivering in the chill of the sleeping hall. The central fire had died to embers hours ago, and the rough stone floor was like ice to her bare feet.

Vaya dressed quickly as the other Valkyries rose beside her. Moonbeams stabbing through high windows beneath the hall's vaulted ceiling provided the only illumination, but after so many ages, Vaya did not need light to prepare for a ride. She wrapped her short skirt around her waist and laced up her leather tunic and boots. After strapping on a golden chest plate, she added armoured leggings and armlets. Finally, she donned her winged helmet. Then grabbing her spear, she sprinted with her sisters to the stables.

The stable hands had already hitched her chariot to Sleipnir. The eight legged horse was Odin's own mount, but Vaya was Odin's favourite daughter of all the Valkyrior, and she alone was allowed to use the huge black beast.

When all were assembled, Frela, their leader, gave a cry, and Vaya and her sisters rose into the air on their chariots as one. The Valkyries swept down from Valhalla like a golden cloud to the world of mortals, following the scent of blood and death and war as they had done for centuries, until they hovered unseen in the night sky above the battlefield.

Vaya surveyed the scene below. Several units of marines, supported by a small number of tanks, were advancing through a forest and into the outskirts of a bombed-out town. From her viewpoint, Vaya could see the defending army entrenched behind the remaining walls of the town and waiting in ambush. As the two forces came into contact and the exchange of fire began, Frela raised her spear, indicating that the selection of heroes was to begin.

"There!" cried one of Vaya's sisters, pointing her spear at a blood-covered marine leading his unit in a charge against a mortar position. The marine's left arm hung limp and useless, but he still fired his rifle as he ran. "I choose that one!" the Valkyrie cried.

"And I that one!" another Valkyrie shouted, indicating with her spear a small soldier with the opposing forces who had just overpowered two enemies in hand-to-hand combat.

Each time a Valkyrie aimed her spear, a soft beam of golden light shot from its tip, marking the selected hero with a glowing aura, visible only to the Valkyries. Beneath them, both armies fought on, oblivious to the immortals above.

In wars through the centuries, it had been as it was tonight. The Valkyries would select those warriors whose bravery, valour, and honour on the battlefield marked them as heroes. And when a hero fell, a Valkyrie would land unseen beside the soldier and carry their immortal spirit to live forever in Valhalla.

Vaya had witnessed thousands of such conflicts. But still she felt the old battle thrill growing in her that night, felt it in the pounding of her heart, felt it in the warmth spreading from her guts to her groin.

She joined in the selection. One soldier in particular caught her attention. He fought bravely, but more than that, unless forced, he only wounded or incapacitated his opponent, disarming them and moving on. Vaya admired mercy in a warrior as much as she did bravery. She urged Sleipnir lower to the battlefield, where she could get a closer look at this man.

She caught her breath when she saw him: he was as fair as the harvest god Frey, as strong as Thor the Thunderer, as brave as Tyr the One-Handed. Vaya, like all her sisters, had never known a love beyond the love of battle. But from that moment, the thrill of the fight fell before a new and stronger emotion that gripped her. Her heart beat even faster, and the warmth that had begun in her groin blazed to a fire.

Vaya the Valkyrie was in love.

Many of her sisters had now landed on the battlefield, claiming the spirits of the chosen heroes who had already been killed. *Not this one*, she whispered, praying to Tyr, the God of War. *Do not take this one*, she begged. Even as she prayed, she watched in horror as her beautiful soldier approached a crumbling corner of a bombed building. Behind that corner crouched three of the enemy forces, their rifles trained on the point where he would appear.

A Valkyrie was forbidden to interfere with the course of a battle or with the fate of a warrior. Only the gods themselves were permitted such power. But in that moment, Vaya did not care. Her beautiful soldier was going to die only seconds after she had fallen in love with him.

Screaming at Sleipnir, she swept her chariot low to the ground, leaping from it as her soldier turned the corner into the ambush. She materialized in front of the three enemy soldiers as they opened fire. Deflecting their bullets with her golden armour, Vaya shot a bolt of lightning from her spear. The three attackers fell, stunned and unconscious.

But not before a stray bullet struck her soldier. Clutching his chest, he cried out and slumped to the ground.

Vaya rushed to him, cradling him in her strong arms as she tore open his shirt. Blood spurted from his shattered chest.

A Valkyrie knew the wounds of war too well, and Vaya could tell that his was a mortal injury. She read his dog tag. His name was Edward. Her soldier, her Edward, would die unless she acted. In that moment, knowing that she would pay a price, Vaya decided. She touched the tip of her spear to his chest. Golden light flowed from it over the wound. She withdrew the spear. The wound was gone.

Edward opened his eyes and looked up at her, then at her clothing. "What . . . who are you?"

Vaya smiled down at him and stroked his hair. "My name is Vaya. And my story will seem a strange one—"

"Vaya!"

Her head snapped up. Frela, the leader of the Valkyries, hovered above in her chariot, staring open-mouthed at Vaya and Edward.

"Vaya," she moaned. "What have you done?"

Odin All-Father sat on his throne of blood-red pine on a raised dais in the Great Hall of Valhalla. The glare from the torches blazing on every pillar in the hall paled beside the glare that Odin was directing at Vaya with his one good eye.

"Have you *thought* on what you are asking, what you would be giving up, daughter?" he roared, thumping the floor with the shaft of his spear, Gungnir, the Deliverer of Lightnings.

Vaya stood trembling at the foot of the steps leading to the throne. She wanted to throw herself to the floor and beg forgiveness. But she was a Valkyrie. And she had known the consequences her decision would bring. And she knew also the love that still filled her heart. So she drew herself up tall and forced herself to meet Odin's gaze. "I have, father," she answered.

"You would trade immortality here in Valhalla for life with a *mortal*?"

"Our *love* will be immortal. It will live forever."

Odin snorted. He pushed his great body out of the throne and crossed the dais. Descending the steps, he placed a huge hand gently on her shoulder. "But *you*, Vaya, you will be mortal. *You* will die."

"I will have children, father. I will live on through the life I create."

"Ha! That is not living, girl. That is not immortality."

Vaya's anger overcame her fear. "What do *we* know of life? We have never experienced it. We know only death here. The Valkyrior deal only with the ending of lives. We bring nothing into this world, only take from it."

Odin drew himself up to his full height, and thunder rumbled inside the hall. "Careful, daughter. You are my favourite, but my patience with you has a limit."

She dropped her head, but her resolve remained. "I've had enough of war and death, father. I wish for peace and life. And love." She looked up at him again. "If you truly love me, you will grant me the life I desire."

His one good eye burned into her, and though her fear made her want to drop to her knees before him, she did not falter under his gaze. Finally, his face softened, and he shook his head. "Bah! So be it. You're a fool, daughter. But I prefer your foolishness away from Valhalla before it infects your sisters." Lifting Gungnir, he touched the point of the spear to her breast, aimed at her heart.

Then without warning, he thrust the spear into her.

Vaya screamed and fell backward onto the cold stone floor of the hall. Her body spasmed, impaled at Odin's feet as he stood staring down at her, his face unreadable. After what seemed an eternity of agony to Vaya, she heard him grunt and felt Gungnir wrenched from her.

Vaya gasped as the pain left with the spear. But something else left her also. Drenched in sweat, lying helpless on the stone floor, she watched as a cloud of luminescence rose from her chest, clinging like golden blood to Gungnir.

Her immortality. Her power as a Valkyrie.

Struggling to her feet, she touched a hand to her chest. It came away unbloodied. She could find no injury, yet she knew she had been wounded. Mortally wounded. She was dying, having only a mortal's lifetime left to her.

Odin raised his arm, and two huge black ravens flew to land on it. One was Huginn, whose name meant memory, and the other was

Muninn, whose name meant thought. They were Odin's eyes and ears in the world of mortals, and his emissaries. Odin whispered to them, and the two ravens leapt from his arm and flew out one of the high windows in the hall.

Odin turned to Vaya. "I have sent them to fix the memories of your mortal lover. He will recall you as another soldier, not as a shield maiden of Valhalla."

He fell silent, staring sadly at her. Finally, he spoke. "Goodbye, daughter. May you find happiness with your mortal love." He turned his back and said no more.

Fighting back her tears, Vaya ran from the great hall. Outside, a pale-faced Frela waited beside her chariot. She ran forward and grabbed Vaya's arms. "Sister," she whispered, staring at Vaya wide-eyed. "Your skin."

Vaya looked down at where Frela's hands gripped her arms. Where her sister's skin glowed with immortal golden light, Vaya's own flesh seemed dull, a pale pinkish white.

"Vaya," Frela wept. "You are lost to us. Why did you do this?" She hugged Vaya to her.

Vaya nearly broke down in her sister's arms, but then she remembered Edward, and her love for him flared in her heart again, filling the void of what Odin had ripped out of her. "I have bought life and freedom, sister. For me and for the man I love."

Frela released her and stepped back, tears streaking her cheeks. "Father says that I must—that I must take you from Valhalla."

Vaya nodded, and the two stepped into the chariot.

Vaya didn't look back.

Life. Life as a mortal.

To Vaya, as the years passed and she looked back, the memories of her chosen life seemed to return to her in colours, each scene washed over, painted in a particular hue.

Red. Their passion together, Edward's lips soft but hungry on hers, his manhood in her, the roses he brought her, their hearts beating as one.

Black. The night sky, the dark room, Edward's hair on the pillow as he slept beside her after their lovemaking. The darkness in her heart as she lay awake, thinking on the choice she had made. A darkness that would never leave her.

White. Her wedding dress glowing in the chapel. The confetti shower sparkling in the sun. The blossoms bright in the trees. The sheets cool on their wedding bed. The shutters on their little bungalow in the suburbs.

Green. The grass on which they made love on a summer day, the canopy of leaves overhead, the small shoot of a wild rose poking through the earth beside where they lay afterwards, new life growing there like the new life she felt that had just been conceived in her.

Pink. Her baby. That wrinkled bundle of humanity that was Daniel, her son, as she first held him in the hospital. His tiny fingers wrapped around her own. His lips on her nipple as he fed from her.

Black. The darkness still with her, growing now as she had something else to fear for: the life of her son as well as Edward's.

Red. The blood running from Daniel's nose. The flush on his cheeks as he faced his first bully. The blood on the bully's shirt.

Red. More fights. More blood.

Black. That darkness in her. Her fear forever with her.

They lived in a tough neighbourhood, and Daniel was no coward. At least once a week, he would be in a fight, never starting it, usually not even involved at the outset, but always intervening to defend a weaker friend or even a stranger. The street toughs learned quickly not to tangle with him. Though she was mortal now, Vaya had passed on some of her Valkyrie strength to her son. And, she feared, her love of battle.

Red. More fights. More blood. Her son's blood too often.

Black. Her fear. Always her fear.

Red. Black. Red. Black. Blood and fear.

Vaya had seen enough blood, had seen too many mortals bleeding the last of theirs onto a battlefield. She feared for her son every day. Her own mortality she had grown to accept, but she found the mortality of her own child unbearable.

Unbearable, yet she bore it, as all parents do. And soon she came to accept that Daniel was his father's son and like Edward, he had to be what he was—a hero, perhaps not on a battlefield of war, but on the battlefield of life. Considering his parents, how could he have been anything else?

Vaya learned to trust in Daniel's strength, his judgment, his goodness. The darkness in her heart grew smaller. But it never completely left her. The darkness knew what happened to heroes.

Daniel graduated from high school and went away to university, and she had to learn to live without seeing him each day. Then, one afternoon as Vaya, once Valkyrie, stood at the sink scraping dishes, she heard him call "Mom" from the front hall. She ran from the kitchen to greet him, thrilled at this surprise visit. She froze in the hallway where he stood.

He wore a uniform.

Afterward, Vaya couldn't remember what she had said to Daniel, screamed at him, cried to him before he left to be shipped out. It was as if she had said nothing for all the effect it had made. His country was at war, and Daniel wanted to help, as he had always wanted to help in a fight, to step forward and not back away.

Edward couldn't convince him, either, though she could tell that her husband felt a pride in Daniel's decision she didn't share.

No Valkyrie will protect our son as I protected you, Edward, she thought.

On the night that Daniel shipped out, and for the first time since she had left, Vaya dreamt of Valhalla.

In her dream, she rode with the Valkyrior once more, the night wind cold in her face, her body young and strong again in her armour, and the reins of Sleipnir gripped sure in her hands. Her heart filled with the forgotten exhilaration of the ride, and she raised her voice in song with her sisters as they swept down onto a battlefield.

But the darkness in her rose to choke the song from her throat, as she recognized the uniforms of the soldiers fighting below. And Vaya knew, as only a mother can know, that her son was here, somewhere beneath her in this theatre of death.

Unbidden by her, a mist oozed from the tip of her spear, and coalesced into a grey wraith shape. In her dream, Vaya called to the wraith, to her sisters, pleading for them to stop this scene from playing out. But her words rode away on the wind unheard as the wraith floated down to the battle.

Vaya held her breath as the omen of death searched from soldier to soldier, knowing in her heart the one the wraith sought. And when it found him, found Daniel as he led his men over a crumbled wall toward an unseen ambush, Vaya screamed.

And woke up.

She lay in bed, soaked in sweat and gasping in breaths, her heart pounding like a war drum in her chest. Edward lay asleep and oblivious beside her. The clock showed 3 AM.

Closing her eyes, Vaya calmed herself, reaching out with her mind and her heart. With the small part of her that remained Valkyrie, she knew that her son still lived. Daniel was alive. She could still feel him in this world.

The dream was an omen, a vision of what would be. She still had time to . . .

To do what? She was now just a mortal woman. What could she do to save her son? To save the life she had brought into this world, the one piece of immortality left to her, half of everything she loved.

Vaya rose from the bed, stripped off her soaked nightshirt, shivering more from the memory of the dream than from the chill of her sweaty nakedness. Throwing on jeans, a T-shirt and a sweater, she went quietly downstairs and into their small backyard.

It was fall, and the night air was crisp with the hint of an early winter. She cleared her mind and focused her thoughts. Raising her hands overhead and her face to the sky, she called out.

"Odin All-Father, hear your daughter's cry. Send me your messengers, for Vaya of the Valkyrior must speak with you."

She waited there for nearly an hour, her eyes on the sky, her ears tuned to every sound. She saw an owl pass overhead and once heard the distant wail of a train whistle. But nothing else. Then, just as she began to despair that her call had gone unheard or unheeded, the flutter of wings sounded behind her. Turning, she saw two shadows, darker than the night sky behind them, perched on the gutters of the roof.

She realized that she had been holding her breath and let it out slowly before bowing to the two ravens. "Huginn. Muninn. Thank you for answering my call."

Huginn spoke. "What message have you for our master?"

"I wish to meet with my father."

"Why?" Muninn asked.

"I wish to beseech him to grant me a boon."

Muninn let out a sharp caw. "You are no longer Valkyrior, woman. Odin has no dealings with mortals."

Vaya clenched her fists. Odin was her only hope. These creatures must take her message to him. "Listen to me, crow. I am Vaya, daughter of Odin All-Father, and still his favourite." She prayed that her conceit was true. "You will take my message to your master, or you will feel his wrath."

The ravens both flapped their wings and cawed loudly, no doubt not used to being talked to in this manner by a mortal. But finally, they calmed themselves, and Muninn nodded his beak toward Vaya. "Very well, insolent one. We will tell him of your wish. It matters little. He will not meet with you."

Then with an explosion of wings, both ravens leapt from the eaves and into the sky.

And as Vaya watched the dark shapes grow smaller and smaller, her hopes seemed to shrink with them, and the fear in her heart grew darker than the night.

But Odin did answer her plea for an audience, and sent Frela the next night to fetch her to Valhalla. So while Edward slept in their suburban bungalow, Vaya, once Valkyrie, now mere mortal, stood again before her father where he sat on his blood-red throne in the Great Hall of Valhalla.

It was not going well.

"You let me save a mortal before. You let me save Edward," she said, fighting to keep the anger—and the fear—from her voice as she faced Odin. "Why can't I save my son?"

"You paid the price then, daughter," Odin answered. "You bought his life with your own immortality." He rose with a sigh, and walked to where she stood at the bottom of the steps leading to the throne dais. "A life must be bought with a life." Odin stared down at her from under his bushy eyebrows. "What life will you trade for that of your son?"

Vaya swallowed. "Take another. Take someone else on the battlefield."

Odin shook his head. "No, child. The life you offer must be a life that you own."

Something cold squirmed in her gut and crawled up her spine. No, she wanted to scream. Not that.

Odin took her by the shoulders. "You own Daniel's life because you created him. You own Edward's life because you bought it for him."

"No!" she cried, shaking herself free from him, stepping back. "Don't make me choose between them."

Odin shook his head. "I'm sorry, daughter. The price must be paid."

"Then let *me* be the price," she cried, grabbing the front of his tunic. "I own *my* life, too. Take me. If you need a life, then take mine. I'm a mortal."

Odin's expression softened, and his eyes began to glisten. "No, daughter. That I will not do. I could not send you to Niflheim. I love you too much."

Vaya bit back a sob. "So you love me, do you, father? As I love my son? As I love my husband?"

Odin shook his head. "I'm sorry, daughter. The price must be paid."

Vaya stood sobbing. What more did she have to offer? What was the highest price she could think of paying, worth more to her even than her life?

Yes, she thought, *I would do that, if it would save them.*

"I have one more price I can pay," she whispered. She drew herself up as tall as she could. "I will come back to the Valkyrior. I will forsake my husband. I will forsake my son. If only you will save Daniel and not take Edward."

Odin eyed her narrowly. "Vaya, you will never again be able to contact them. You will be dead to them."

"I know, father," she said, her voice breaking.

Odin stepped back and considered her. "To have my daughter return to me. To have you here again in Valhalla." He pulled her to his chest and stroked her hair gently. "Very well, child. I accept your offer—if you are willing to pay that price."

She stood there, letting him hold her, as the darkness she had lived with all these years spread inside her like a black weed, finally choking out any hope for happiness.

"To save my son and my husband," she whispered, "I would pay any price."

"I will send Huginn to the mortal world," Odin said, "to adjust the memories that Edward holds of his wife, and Daniel of his mother, of what became of you. What should those memories be, child?"

"Let them remember the truth, father," Vaya whispered. "Let them remember that I died of a broken heart."

On quiet nights when the cries of war did not call them to ride, Vaya would rise silently from the bed of the Valkyrior and slip down to the stables. There she would saddle Sleipnir and ride the golden path down from Valhalla to the mortal realm.

Unseen, she would slip inside that small bungalow in the suburbs and sit silently on the side of the bed, watching her lover, her husband, sleep. She'd rise then and walk down the little hallway to where her creation, her son, slept safely returned from the war. After a while, she would kiss them both and leave them sleeping and unknowing, and ride alone again back to Valhalla.

When she returned, her sisters would be awake and waiting for her. She would slip back into bed as they gathered around her, and she would tell them of her visit and of the two mortals that she loved.

They would sit quietly after her story, and Vaya would wait patiently for the question. Eventually, one of them would ask—tentative, timid, but they would always ask.

"Vaya," they would say, "tell us again of this thing called 'love'."

And Vaya would smile and remember and tell them, dreaming of her two loves and of the day when the Valkyries would ride no more.

T his is the only story that I've written that is intended for a younger audience. The wonderful Canadian SF writer, Julie Czerneda, invited me to submit a story for an SF anthology that she was editing aimed at grades seven and eight students in Ontario. All stories in the anthology were to incorporate aspects of the science curriculum from those grades. My topic was plate tectonics in geology. I'd always found continental drift fascinating: continents and pieces of the world's crust moving around, all fitting together like a big planet-sized jigsaw puzzle. Hence, this story. It was a finalist for the Aurora Award in 2005. I may return to the Wormers one day.

J I G S A W

Still in shock, Cassie Morant slumped in the cockpit of the empty hopper, staring at the two viewplates before her.

In one, the planet Griphus, a blue, green, and brown marble wrapped in belts of cloud, grew smaller. Except for the shape of its land masses, it could have been Earth.

But it wasn't. Griphus was an alien world, light-years from Sol System.

A world where nineteen of her shipmates were going to die.

And one of them was Davey.

On the other viewplate, the segmented, tubular hull of the orbiting Earth wormship, the *Johannes Kepler*, grew larger. Cassie tapped a command, and the ship's vector appeared, confirming her fears.

The ship's orbit was still decaying. She opened a comm-link.

"Hopper two to the *Kepler*," she said. "Requesting docking clearance."

Silence. Then a male voice crackled over the speaker, echoing cold and metallic in the empty shuttle. "Acknowledged, Hopper two. You are clear to dock, segment beta four, port nine."

Cassie didn't recognize the voice, but that wasn't surprising. The *Kepler* held the population of a small city, and Cassie was something of a loner. But she had no trouble identifying the gruff rumble she heard next.

"Pilot of hopper, identify yourself. This is Captain Theodor."

Cassie took a breath. "Sir, this is Dr. Cassandra Morant, team geologist."

Pause. "Where's Team Leader Stockard?" Theodor asked.

Davey. "Sir, the rest of the surface team was captured by the indigenous tribe inhabiting the extraction site. The team is . . ." Cassie stopped, her throat constricting.

"Morant?"

She swallowed. "They're to be executed at sunrise."

Another pause.

"Did you get the berkelium?" Theodor finally asked.

Cassie fought her anger. Theodor wasn't being heartless. The team below was secondary to the thousands on the ship.

"Just a core sample, sir," she said. "But it confirms that the deposit's there."

Theodor swore. "Dr. Morant, our orbit decays in under twenty hours. Report immediately after docking to brief the command team." Theodor cut the link.

Cassie stared at the huge wormship, suddenly hating it, hating its strangeness. *Humans would never build something like that*, she thought.

Consisting of hundreds of torus rings strung along a central axis like donuts on a stick, the ship resembled a giant metallic worm. A dozen rings near the middle were slowly rotating, providing the few inhabited sections with an artificial gravity. The thousands of humans on the ship barely filled a fraction of it.

This wasn't meant for us, she thought. *We shouldn't be here.*

Humans had just begun to explore their solar system, when Max Bremer and his crew had found the wormships, three of them, outside the orbit of Pluto.

Abandoned? Lost? Or left to be found?

Found by the ever curious, barely-out-of-the-trees man-apes of Earth. Found with charted wormholes in Sol System. Found with still-only-partly-translated, we-think-this-button-does-this libraries and databases, and we-can't-fix-it-so-it-better-never-break technology. Incredibly ancient yet perfectly functioning Wormer technology.

Wormers. The inevitable name given to Earth's unknown alien benefactors.

Five years later, humanity was here, exploring the stars, riding like toddlers on the shoulders of the Wormers.

But Cassie no longer wanted to be here. She wished she was back on Earth, safely cocooned in her apartment, with Vivaldi playing, lost in one of her jigsaw puzzles.

She shifted uncomfortably in the hopper seat. Like every Wormer chair, like the ship itself, it almost fit a human. But not quite.

It was like forcing a piece to fit in a jigsaw—it was always a cheat, and in the end, the picture was wrong. Humans didn't belong here. They had forced themselves into a place in the universe where they didn't fit. *We cheated*, she thought, *and we've been caught. And now we're being punished.*

They faced a puzzle that threatened the entire ship. She'd had a chance to solve it on the planet.

And she'd failed.

Cassie hugged herself, trying to think. She was good at puzzles, but this one had a piece missing. She thought back over events since they'd arrived through the wormhole four days ago. The answer had to be there . . .

Four days ago, Cassie had sat in her quarters on the *Kepler*, hunched over a jigsaw puzzle covering her desk. The desk, like anything Wormer, favoured unbroken flowing contours, seat sweeping up to chair back, wrapping around to desk surface. Viewplates on the curved walls showed telescopic shots of Griphus. The walls and ceiling glowed softly.

Lieutenant David Stockard, Davey to Cassie, lay on her bunk watching her.

"Don't you get tired of jigsaws?" he asked.

She shrugged. "They relax me. It's my form of meditation. Besides, I'm doing my homework."

Davey rolled off the bunk. She watched him walk over, wondering again what had brought them together. If she could call what they had being "together"—sometimes friendship, sometimes romance, sometimes not-talking-to-each-other.

They seemed a case study in "opposites attract." She was a scientist, and Davey was military. She was dark, short and slim, while he was fair, tall and broad. She preferred spending her time quietly, reading, listening to classical music—and doing jigsaw puzzles. Davey always had to be active.

But the biggest difference lay in their attitudes to the Wormers. Davey fervently believed that the alien ships were meant to be found by humans, that the Universe wanted them to explore the stars.

To Cassie, the Universe wasn't telling them everything it knew. She felt that they didn't understand Wormer technology enough to be risking thousands of lives.

He looked at the puzzle. "Homework?"

"I printed a Mercator projection of topographic scans of Griphus onto plas-per, and the computer cut it into a jigsaw."

The puzzle showed the planet's two major continents, which Dr. Xu, head geologist and Cassie's supervisor, had dubbed Manus and Pugnus. *Hand and fist.* The western continent, Pugnus, resembled a clenched fist and forearm, punching across an ocean at Manus, which resembled an open hand, fingers and thumb curled ready to catch the fist. Coloured dots, each numbered, speckled the map.

"What are the dots?" Davey asked.

"Our shopping list. Deposits of rare minerals. That is, if you believe Wormer archives and Wormer scanners—"

"Cassie, let's not start—" Davey said.

"Davey, these ships are at least ten thousand years old—"

"With self-healing nanotech—" Davey replied.

"That we don't understand—"

"Cassie . . ." Davey sighed.

She glared, then folded her arms. "Fine."

Davey checked the time on his per-comm unit. "Speaking of homework, Trask wants surface team rescue procedures by oh-eight-hundred. Gotta go." He kissed Cassie and left.

Cassie bit back a comment that this was a scientific, not a

military, expedition. The likely need for Trask's "procedures" was low in her opinion.

She would soon change her mind.

An hour later, Cassie was walking along the busy outer corridor of the ring segment assigned to the science team. Suddenly, the ship shuddered, throwing Cassie and others against one curving wall.

The ship lurched again, and the light from the glowing walls blinked out. People screamed. Cassie stumbled and fell. And kept falling, waiting for the impact against the floor that never came, until she realized what had happened.

The ring's stopped rotating, she thought. *We've lost artificial gravity.*

She floated in darkness for maybe thirty minutes, bumping into others, surrounded by whispers, shouts, and sobbing. Suddenly, the lights flicked back on. Cassie felt gravity returning like an invisible hand tugging at her guts, followed by a sudden heaviness in her limbs. Hitting the floor, she rolled, then rose on shaky legs. People stood dazed, looking like scattered pieces in a jigsaw that before had been a coherent picture of normality.

What had happened?

The intercom broke through the rising babble of conversations. "The following personnel report immediately to port six, segment beta four for surface team detail." Twenty names followed. One was Davey's.

One was hers. What was going on?

An hour later, her questions still unanswered, she and nineteen others sat in a hopper as it left the *Kepler*. Hoppers were smaller Wormer craft used for ship-to-surface trips and exploration. With a tubular hull, a spherical cockpit at the head, and six jointed legs allowing them to rest level on any terrain, they resembled grasshoppers.

The team faced each other in two rows of seats in the main cabin. Cassie only knew two others besides Davey. Manfred Mubuto, balding, dark and round, was their xeno-anthropologist. Liz Branson, with features as sharp as her sarcasm, was their linguist. Four were marines. But the rest, over half the team, were mining techs. Why?

Davey addressed them. She'd never seen him so serious.

"The Kepler's power loss resulted from the primary fuel cell being purged. Engineering is working to swap cells, but that requires translating untested Wormer procedures. We may need to replenish the cell, which means extracting berkelium from Griphus for processing."

That's why I'm here, Cassie thought. Berkelium, a rare trans-uranium element, was the favoured Wormer energy source. It had never been found on Earth, only manufactured. Her analysis of Griphus had shown possible deposits.

"Like every planet found via the wormholes," Davey said, "Griphus is incredibly Earth-like: atmosphere, gravity, humanoid populations—"

Liz interrupted. "We purged a fuel cell? Who screwed up?"

Davey reddened. "That's not relevant—"

"Operator error, I hear," Manfred said. "A tech misread Wormer symbols on a panel, punched an incorrect sequence—"

Liz swore. "I knew it! We're like kids trying to fly Daddy's flitter—"

Cassie started to agree, but Davey cut them off.

"We've no time for rumours," he snapped, looking at Cassie, Liz, and Manfred. "Our orbit decays in three days. I remind you that this team's under my command—including science personnel."

Manfred nodded. Liz glared, but said nothing.

Davey tapped the computer pad on his seat. A holo of Griphus appeared. "Dr. Morant, please locate the berkelium."

Cassie almost laughed at being called "Dr. Morant" by Davey, but then she caught his look. She tapped some keys, and two red dots blinked onto the holo, one in the ocean mid-way between Pugnus and Manus, and another offshore of Manus. The second site was circled.

"Wormer sensors show two sites. I've circled my recommendation," Cassie said.

"Why not the other site?" a mining tech asked.

A network of lines appeared, making the planet's surface look like a huge jigsaw puzzle.

"As on Earth," Cassie said, "the lithosphere or planetary crust of Griphus is broken into tectonic plates, irregular sections ranging from maybe fifteen kilometres thick under oceans to a hundred under continents. This shows the plate pattern on Griphus.

"Plates float on the denser, semi-molten asthenosphere, the upper part of the mantle. At 'transform' boundaries, they slide along each other, as in the San Andreas Fault on Earth. At 'convergent' boundaries, they collide, forming mountains such as the Himalayas."

A line splitting the ocean between Pugnus and Manus glowed yellow. The line also ran through the other berkelium site.

"But at 'divergent' boundaries," Cassie continued, "such as this mid-oceanic trench, magma pushes up from the mantle, creating new crust, forcing the plates apart. The other site is deep in the trench, below our sub's crush depth."

Davey nodded. "So we hit the site offshore of Manus. Any indigenous population along that coast?"

"Yes," Manfred said. "From orbital pictures, they appear tribal, agrarian, definitely pre-industrial. Some large stone structures and primitive metallurgy."

"Then defending ourselves shouldn't be a problem." Davey patted the *stinger* on his belt. The Wormer weapon was non-lethal, temporarily disrupting voluntary muscular control.

"Could we try talking before we shoot them?" Liz said.

Davey just smiled. "Which brings us to communication, Dr. Branson."

Liz sighed. "Wormer translator units need a critical mass of vocabulary, syntax, and context samples to learn a language. Given the time we have, I doubt they'll help much."

"With any luck, we won't need them," Davey said. "We'll locate the deposit, send in the mining submersible, and be out before they know we're there."

Looking around her, Cassie guessed that no one felt lucky.

The hopper landed on the coast near the offshore deposit. The team wore light body suits and breathing masks to prevent ingesting anything alien to human immune systems.

Cassie stepped onto a broad beach of grey sand lapped by an ocean too green for Earth, under a sky a touch too blue. The beach ran up to a forest of trees whose black trunks rose twenty metres into the air. Long silver leaves studded each trunk, glinting like sword blades in the sun. She heard a high keening that might have been birds or wind in the strange trees.

Southwards, the beach ran into the distance. But to the north, it ended at a cliff rising up to a low mesa. Cassie walked over to Davey, who was overseeing the marines unloading the submersible and drilling equipment.

"Cool, eh?" he said, looking around them.

She pointed at the mesa. "That's cooler to a rock nut."

He looked up the beach. "Okay. But keep your per-comm on."

She nodded and set out. The cliff was an hour's walk. She didn't mind, enjoying the exercise and strange surroundings. She took pictures of the rock strata and climbed to get samples at different levels. Then she walked back.

They captured Cassie just as she was wondering why the hopper seemed deserted. The natives appeared so quickly and silently, they seemed to rise from the sand. Cassie counted about forty of them, all remarkably human-like, but taller, with larger eyes, longer noses, and greenish skin. All were male, bare-chested, wearing skirts woven from sword-blade tree leaves, and leather sandals.

They led Cassie to stand before two women. One was dressed as the men were, but with a headdress of a coppery metal. The other was older and wore a cape of cloth and feathers. Her head was bare, her hair long and white. Beside them, pale but unharmed, stood Liz Branson, flanked by two warriors.

The older woman spoke to Liz in a sing-song melodic language. Cassie saw that the linguist wore a translator earplug. Liz sat down, motioning Cassie to do the same. The male warriors sat circling them. The two native women remained standing.

Cassie realized she was trembling. "What happened?"

Liz grimaced. "We've stepped in it big time. The Chadorano— our captors—believe a sacred object called 'the third one' lies underwater here. Only a priestess may enter these waters. When our techs launched the sub, the natives ambushed us from the trees with blowguns. They grabbed the techs when they surfaced."

"Where's Davey?" Cassie asked, then added, ". . . and everyone?"

"Taken somewhere. They seemed okay."

"Why not you, too?"

"The tribe's matriarchal," Liz said. "The old woman is Cha-kay, their chief. The younger one, Pre-nah, is their priestess. Because I'm female and knew their language, Cha-kay assumed I was our leader. But I said you were."

"You what?" Cassie cried.

"Cassie, we need someone they'll respect," Liz said, her face grim. "That means a female who didn't defile the site. That means you."

"God, Liz—wait, how can you talk to them?"

Liz frowned. "It's weird. The translator produced understandable versions within minutes, pulling from Wormer archives of other worlds. That implies all those languages share the same roots. The Wormers may have seeded all these worlds."

Cassie didn't care. "What can I do?"

"Convince Cha-kay to let us go."

"How?" Cassie asked.

"She wants to show you something. It's some sort of test."

"And if I fail?"

Liz handed Cassie the translator. "Then they'll kill us."

Cassie swallowed. "I won't let that happen."

They led Cassie to a long boat with a curving prow powered by a dozen rowers. Cha-kay rode in a chair near the stern, Cassie at her feet. Pre-nah and six warriors stood beside them.

They travelled up a winding river through dense jungle. Conversation was sparse, but sufficient to convince Cassie that the translator unit worked. After three hours, they landed at a clearing. Cassie climbed out, happy to move and stretch. She blinked.

Blue cubes, ranging from one to ten metres high, filled the clearing. They were hewn from stone and painted. The party walked past the cubes to a path that switch-backed up a low mountain. They began to climb.

Cassie groaned but said nothing, since the aged Cha-kay didn't seem bothered by the climb. As they went, Cassie noticed smaller cubes beside the path.

Night had fallen when they reached the top and stepped onto a tabletop of rock about eighty metres across. Cassie gasped.

A huge cube, at least fifty metres on each side nearly filled the plateau. It was blue. It was glowing.

And it was hovering a metre off the ground.

Cha-kay led Cassie to it, and Cassie received another shock. On its smooth sides, Cassie saw familiar symbols.

The artefact, whatever its purpose, was Wormer.

Cha-kay prostrated herself, telling Cassie to do the same. As Cassie did so, she peeked underneath the cube. A column of pulsating blue light shone from a crevice to touch the base of the artefact at its centre. Reaching down to her belt, Cassie activated her scanner. She'd check the readings later.

Rising, Cha-kay indicated a large diagram on the artefact. In it, a cube, a sphere, and a tetrahedron formed points of an equilateral triangle.

"It is a map. We are here," Cha-kay said, pointing to the cube. "The gods left three artefacts, but hid one. The third will appear when the gods return and lay their hands on the other two." Then, pointing to the outline of a hand on the artefact, Cha-kay looked at Cassie.

"Touch," she said.

With a sudden chill, Cassie understood. *They think we're the Wormers, finally returning,* she thought.

This was the test—the test on which the lives of her shipmates, of the entire ship, depended.

Reaching out a trembling hand, Cassie felt resistance from some invisible barrier and a warm tingling, then her hand slipped through onto the outline on the artefact.

Nothing happened.

Murmurs grew behind her. Feeling sick, Cassie looked at Cha-kay. To her surprise, the old woman smiled.

"Perhaps," Cha-kay said, "it rises even now."

Cassie understood. Cha-kay hoped to find that the third artefact had emerged from the sea when they returned to the beach. Cassie didn't share her hope.

They spent the night there. Pretending to sleep, Cassie checked her scanner readings. They confirmed her suspicions. The column of light showed berkelium emissions. The artefact was connected to a deposit as an energy source.

The next day, a similar journey brought them to the second artefact, located on another flat mountain peak. The only difference was the artefact itself, a huge glowing red tetrahedron. Cassie again saw a column of light underneath and detected berkelium. She touched the artefact, again with no apparent effect, and the party began the trip back.

Cha-kay seemed to have grown genuinely fond of Cassie. She

told Cassie how her people found the artefacts generations ago, eventually realizing that the drawing was a map. They learned to measure distances and angles, and determined that the third artefact lay in the coastal waters. Priestesses had dived there for centuries but found nothing. Still they believed.

Cassie did some calculations and found the Chadoran estimate remarkably accurate. Still, she wondered why the Wormers would locate two artefacts in identical settings on mountain plateaus, yet place the third underwater. Perhaps the third location had subsided over the years. But her scans showed no sunken mountains off the coast.

Cassie enjoyed Cha-kay's company, but as they neared the coast, her fear grew. Cha-kay fell silent as well. As the boat reached the beach, they stood at the railing, clasping each other's hand, scanning the waters for the third artefact.

Nothing.

Cries arose among the warriors. Pre-nah approached Cha-kay. "The strangers are false gods," the priestess said. "They must die."

Cha-kay stared across the ocean. Finally, she nodded. Cassie's legs grew weak as two warriors moved toward her.

Cha-kay raised her hand. "No. This one goes free. She did not defile the sacred place."

Pre-nah didn't look pleased, but she bowed her head.

They landed, and Cha-kay walked with Cassie to the hopper.

"When?" Cassie asked, her voice breaking.

"At sunrise, child," Cha-kay said. "I am sorry."

Cassie boarded the hopper. She engaged the auto-launch, then slumped in her seat, as the planet and her hopes grew smaller.

After docking, Cassie went immediately to the briefing room, as Captain Theodor had ordered. She quickly took a seat in one of a dozen Wormer chairs around a holo display unit. Dr. Xu gave her a worried smile. Commander Trask glared.

Theodor cleared his throat, a rumble that brought everyone's gaze to his stocky form.

"I'll be brief. Our orbit collapses in nineteen hours. Attempts to swap fuel cells were unsuccessful. The team sent to extract the berkelium has been captured and faces execution. Only Dr. Morant escaped."

Everyone looked at Cassie. All she could think of was how she'd failed.

Theodor continued. "Dr. Morant will summarize events on the planet. Then I need ideas."

Cassie told her story, then answered questions, mostly dealing with the artefacts. Will Epps, their expert on Wormer texts and writing, after analyzing her scans, agreed that the artefacts were Wormer.

The team began reviewing and discarding proposals. Finally, Theodor made his decision. A platoon of marines would drop outside the Chadoran city. Three squads would act as a diversion, drawing warriors from the city, while one squad slipped in for a search and rescue. One hour later, a hopper would drop two mining subs at the berkelium site.

"Sir, the priestess dives there daily," Cassie said. "When they see our subs, they'll kill the team."

"That's why I'm giving the rescue squads an hour head start," Theodor replied. "It's not much, but our priority is to replenish our fuel before our orbit decays. I can't delay the berkelium extraction any longer."

Cassie slumped in her seat. Davey, Liz, the others. They were all going to die.

Trask stood. "If Dr. Morant could provide a topographical display of the area, I'll outline the attack plan."

Cassie tapped some keys, and the planetary view of Griphus appeared, including the pattern of tectonic plates.

Like a jigsaw puzzle, Cassie thought. *Why can't this be that simple?*

"Zoom in to the landing site," Trask said.

Freezing the rotation over Pugnus and Manus, Cassie started to zoom in, then stopped, staring at the display. *No,* she thought, *it's too wild. But maybe . . .* She began tapping furiously, and calculations streamed across the holo.

"What the hell's going on?" Trask asked.

Theodor frowned. "Dr. Morant?"

Cassie looked at her results. *My god, it fits. But the time span . . .*

"Dr. Morant!" Theodor barked.

Cassie's head jerked up. Everyone was staring. *It's wild,* she thought, *but it fits.* And she liked things that fit.

"Captain," Cassie said, "what if we proved to the Chadorans that the deposit site is *not* sacred?"

Theodor frowned. "Discredit their religion? I don't—"

"No," Cassie said. "I mean, prove that it isn't sacred because . . ." She stopped. What if she was wrong? But it was Davey and the team's only chance.

". . . because the third artefact isn't there," she finished.

Trask snorted. "Then why will they kill to protect the site?"

"Because they *think* it's there, based entirely on the diagrams on the artefacts."

"And you think those diagrams are wrong?" Theodor asked, but his voice held none of Trask's derision.

"I think they were correct once," she said. "But not any more."

"So where's the artefact?" Theodor asked.

Cassie's hand trembled as she tapped more keys. Two green lights appeared inland on the western coast of Manus, followed by a red light just off the same coast, forming the triangular pattern diagrammed on the artefacts.

"The two green lights are the known artefacts. The red light is both the supposed underwater location of the third and our targeted berkelium site."

She swallowed. *Here goes,* she thought.

"And this, I believe, is the actual location of the third artefact." A third green light appeared.

Everyone started talking at once. Theodor silenced them with a wave of his hand. He stared at the display.

On the eastern coast of Pugnus, on a separate continent and an entire ocean away from the underwater site, blinked the third green light.

Theodor turned to Cassie. "Explain."

"It involves tectonic plate theory—" she began.

"I know the theory. What's the relevance?"

Cassie tapped a key. The mid-oceanic trench between Pugnus and Manus glowed yellow.

"That trench is a 'divergent' boundary," Cassie said, "where new crust is being formed, pushing Manus and Pugnus farther apart every year. But that also means that sometime in the past, they looked like this." The plates began to shift. The two large continents moved closer until the fist of Pugnus slipped into the open hand of Manus like a piece in a puzzle. Someone gasped, as the third green light on Pugnus aligned itself over the red light offshore of Manus.

Theodor nodded. "You're saying the Wormers originally placed the three artefacts as the diagrams show, but the missing one moved relative to the other two as the continents separated."

Xu shook his head. "Cassie . . ."

Cassie sighed. "I know. The time frame is . . . difficult to believe."

"How old are the artefacts if your theory is true?" Theodor asked.

Xu answered. "At least as old as the core sample from the deposit site, which formed as the trench started to spread. Cassie, what was the isotopic clock dating on the sample?"

Cassie hesitated. "Its age was thirty, uh . . ." She swallowed. ". . . million years."

The eruption of exclamations made Cassie want to slink from

the room. Theodor again waved for silence.

In desperation, Cassie turned to Will Epps. "We know that these ships are at least ten thousand years old. But couldn't they be much older?"

Several people squirmed. Their situation was bad enough without being reminded that they were relying on alien technology at least a hundred centuries old.

Will shrugged. "There's so much self-healing nanotech, we can't estimate their age accurately."

"So any Wormer technology could be much older as well, right?" Cassie asked.

"But thirty million years . . ." Xu shook his head, as did others. Cassie was losing them.

She turned to Theodor.

"Captain, it all fits. It explains why the Chadorans have never found the artefact. Why our sub didn't see it. Why Wormers placed two artefacts on mountains, but supposedly put the third underwater. They didn't. They put it on land, too."

"Can't we scan for the artefact?" Trask said.

"The other two don't show on scanners," Epps said. "They're shielded somehow."

"So the third artefact *could* be where the Chadorans say it is," Trask replied.

Cassie sat back, feeling defeated. Then something struck her.

"Both artefacts I saw are located over berkelium deposits, yet neither site appears on the mineral scans. The artefacts shield the berkelium, too."

"So?" Theodor said.

"We detected berkelium at the underwater site. That means nothing's shielding it. The third artefact isn't there."

Trask started to protest, but Theodor raised a hand. "I agree with Dr. Morant. It fits." He stood up. "Cassie, I'll give you the same lead time. Take a hopper down now."

Cassie was already sprinting for the door.

On a mountain plateau, across an ocean from where they had first landed on Griphus, Cassie and Davey stood, arms around each other's waists.

"So you saved me, the team, the entire ship," Davey said, "and made one of the most important discoveries in history. Not a bad day."

Cassie grinned. "Actually, the toughest part was convincing Cha-kay to fly in the hopper. Now she wants a world tour."

Beside them, happiness lighting her face, Cha-kay gazed at a huge glowing yellow sphere hovering above the ground.

The third artefact.

With one difference. A beam of energy shone from the sphere into the sky. The beam had begun the moment Cassie had touched the sphere.

Cassie's per-comm beeped. It was Theodor. "Dr. Morant, all three artefacts now appear on scanners, all beaming to the same point in space—"

"A new wormhole," Cassie interrupted.

Pause. "How'd you know?" Theodor asked.

Cassie grinned. "I'm good at puzzles, sir."

"Hmm. Anyway, Earth's sending a second wormship. We'll all have the option of returning home or exploring the wormhole. Once again, good work, Morant." Theodor signed off.

"You didn't mention your theory," Davey said.

"That the wormhole leads to the Wormers' home world? Just a hunch."

"Explain it to me, then."

Cassie nodded at the sphere. "I think the artefacts were a puzzle—and the wormhole the prize."

"For us or the Chandorans?"

"For us. Another bread crumb in the trail the Wormers left us." She shrugged and laughed. "It just fits."

Davey nodded. "So what about you? Back to Earth or through the wormhole?"

"Wormhole," she said.

He raised an eyebrow. "Okay, that surprised me."

Cassie grinned. "Hey, if the Wormers liked puzzles, they couldn't have been that bad." She stared at the artefact. "Besides, we solved their puzzle, saved ourselves, became heroes to the Chadorans . . ." Her eyes followed the beam up toward the heavens.

"Maybe we fit out here after all," she said softly.

Roger Zelazny once said that his story ideas usually arrived in one of three ways: a character, an unusual image, or an idea, and that his best stories combined all three. For me, the genesis of this story came from a sudden image of this strange creature, the Dancer, appearing on the rush-hour streets of Toronto, yet unnoticed by the city's scurrying commuters. Then I just had to figure out what her story was. I tried asking her, but as you'll see, the Dancer's answers are rather cryptic. This story resulted from an invitation to Under Cover of Darkness, another Julie Czerneda anthology, this one co-edited by the equally talented Jana Paniccia. Its theme was secret societies, conspiracies, and covert organizations, ala The Da Vinci Code. The story was a finalist for the 2008 Aurora Award and inspired the artwork for the anthology's very cool cover, which unfortunately, I can't show you here.

THE DANCER AT
THE RED DOOR

The city has a song.
Its rhythm, a million broken hearts . . .

Alexander King first met the Dancer on the day the street people began to glow.

He drove to his office in downtown Toronto early that July morning in his newest toy, a vintage Jaguar XKE, dark red with black leather seats—a toy he'd always wanted, and one of which he'd already tired. He pondered this as he parked in his reserved spot beneath the building of blue glass and silvered steel that bore his name. Riding his private elevator to the penthouse executive floor, he felt a strange unease awakening with the day.

He met first with his management team to finalize the acquisition of a competitor. They sat in his office, walls hung with original Tissot drawings he'd once loved. Before signing the takeover papers, he noted both the concessions he'd won and the absence of any pleasure in reaching a goal that had consumed much of his considerable energy for seven months.

He ordered the sale of the one profitable plant in the acquisition, and the closing of the remaining operations. But it didn't bring him the rush that exercising new power normally did. He felt none of the usual thrill of moving the pieces in the game. *His* game.

With a growing disquiet, he focused on his senior staff sitting around the huge teak table. He'd picked his team early in their careers, moulding them into business weapons for his corporate arsenal. It came more as confirmation than surprise that he no longer felt pride in them.

After the meeting, he had his assistant clear his calendar for the morning. She closed his large oak office door as she left. Unfolding his tall, well-exercised frame from his chair, he moved to the window to stare down absently at the busy intersection of Wellington and University thirty floors below.

His toys, his deals, his people. Not a good sign, he mused, when the surest symbols of success in your chosen life bring you no happiness whatsoever.

And with that thought, in that moment, he accepted what a secret part of him had known for some time—that he was totally, utterly tired of his world, the world he had built and in which he ruled.

The only fear King had ever known had been of finding a game he couldn't win. He had never expected to become bored by the game. But it had happened.

Well, then he needed a new game.

No. He needed the *right* game.

His reflection, steel grey eyes under steel grey hair, stared back but offered no answers. Brooding on his dark epiphany, he gazed at the street below, not focusing on any detail, just letting the patterns of people and traffic skitter across his eyes like a kaleidoscope of random intents. He was about to turn away when a flash of light caught his attention.

On the sidewalk across the street, a man sat against the building, a hat set out in front of him. A street person—one of the army of the homeless that posted its soldiers at every corner of the downtown core.

A street person who was on fire.

King rubbed his eyes. No, not on fire, but glowing. Glowing so brightly that he obliterated surrounding details of the building and passersby.

And no one hurrying past paid him the slightest notice.

Seized by a sudden impulse, King grabbed his suit jacket and took the elevator to street level.

The day was already hot and humid, the air sticky and stinking with exhaust fumes, something he hadn't noticed going from the cool comfort of his house to car to office. He loosened his silk tie and undid the top button of his tailored shirt as he crossed the street. Scanning the far side for the glowing man, King found him now standing. No sign of the strange light remained.

King reached the opposite sidewalk and stopped. *This is ridiculous*, he thought. He began to turn away, to return to his air-conditioned office and suddenly unwanted life, when he stopped again.

The man was now staring at him. And smiling.

Taken aback but curious again, King walked over. The man wore tattered clothes of competing colours of dirt and held a short-brimmed cloth hat in surprisingly clean hands. His long hair was pure white, combed and untangled. His face was lined, but as clean as his hands. Black eyes, bright and sharp, stared narrowly from above a hooked nose and under snowy eyebrows. He continued to smile at King.

"Do I know you?" King asked, uncomfortable to be conversing with someone so far beneath his own station.

The man didn't answer. Instead, he raised his left hand in a fist in front of King's face. King stepped back, thinking that the man was threatening him. But the beggar simply stood there, fist poised. The back of his raised hand bore a tattoo—a red rectangle within a black one. The red was deep and bright, so shiny that it looked wet, like a patch of blood.

Staring at the tattoo, King felt a tingle of familiarity, mixed with fear. He swallowed. *Get a grip*, he thought. "I asked you if you know me," he repeated.

Still not answering, the man lowered his hand and turned to stare up University Avenue.

Angered at a street person ignoring him, King started to turn away when a sound made him stop. Notes, a tune, a song. Yes, a song. He scanned the passersby, expecting to find a headset dangling from nearby ears, volume cranked to maximum. To his surprise, the song didn't change in intensity, no matter what direction he turned. He became aware then of a deep bass pounding, a dance-like rhythm slowly rising out of the pavement and trembling up his legs.

A swirl of colour and movement caught his eye. He turned.

And she appeared.

The Dancer.

He called her the Dancer the moment he saw her, and the moment he saw her, he knew that she was mad. Or *he* was. She spun into view around the nearest corner, then froze for a second, en pointe as in ballet, arms raised in two graceful arcs. Then she leapt, landing to waltz through the crowd as if the sidewalk were a ballroom and each scurrying commuter her partner. And with each pirouette, madness whirled around her like dead leaves caught in a forgotten winter wind.

She wore only a diaphanous gown of some strange material that changed colour and shape as she whirled, sometimes concealing, sometimes revealing, sometimes seeming to disappear completely. The body it revealed was slim and lithe, with firm breasts, long arms and legs, hair as red as rusted metal, and skin so fair and pale it seemed to glow.

He realized then that the Dancer *was* glowing, just as the old beggar had been. The glow enveloped her in a cocoon of light. In that cocoon, King caught fractured glimpses of a dark moonlit world that was not the bland sun-bright cityscape in which he now stood.

And as with the old man, no one but King seemed to notice the Dancer. People shuffled by like the undead, blinking at the sun finally rising over the towers, newspapers clutched like amulets, briefcases hanging like manacles, coffee sucked from cups as if it were their lifeblood. At some level, they were aware of her, as they'd move aside for her, always in step somehow, but they paid her no more attention than if she were a puddle to avoid.

Remembering the strange old man, King turned. He was gone. King caught a flash of white hair farther down the street, but then it was lost in the crowd.

And lost in the face of the Dancer as she stopped before King, a face that swept the crowds and traffic and buildings from his eyes and mind, not by its beauty, for he couldn't call her beautiful, but by its strangeness. Skin too pale, hair too red, mouth too wide. And green eyes that wandered over him as if searching for something.

But when she smiled at him with those eyes and that mouth, a hope and a fear reached inside him and twisted in opposite directions. A hope that she was real, that somehow she held the key to a door to a new life. And a fear that she *was* mad, that he was trapped in a life he suddenly hated and could never . . .

". . . escape," he whispered, before realizing it.

She laughed, a thing of cold breezes rustling barren trees on winter nights. "You wish to escape me?" she asked, smiling up at him. "So soon?" Her glow was gone, and she now wore a plain green cotton shift and white low-heeled shoes.

"No . . . no," King stammered. "Not you. My life." Embarrassed, he held out his hand. "My name is Alexander King."

In reply, the Dancer turned and spun back up the street. King stood dazed for a second, then hurried to catch up. He found that he had to almost trot to stay beside her.

"So you wish to escape life?" she asked, spinning as they went, still ignored by everyone but King. "Do you seek death, then?"

"No. I . . . I wish to escape *my* life. My world." Despite the crush of commuters, he felt as if he were alone with this strange woman. They reached the corner of University and King Street.

"Then you seek another world?" she asked, whirling around him as they waited for the traffic light.

He grimaced. "I'm not sure. Yes. Something new. Different."

The light changed. The Dancer crossed, weaving through the crowd, sometimes even hooking the arm of someone she passed and spinning around with them as if in a square dance.

And still no one paid her any notice.

King followed her to the stairs leading down to the subway. She seemed to float down the steps, while King, feeling quite dazed, almost slipped hurrying to catch her. Waltzing up to the ticket booth, she raised her arms, spun twice, then leapt gracefully over the turnstiles. The staffer in the booth paid her no attention. Swearing, King dug into his pocket for change. By the time he'd paid and reached the subway platform, the Dancer was boarding a northbound train. He jumped on just as the doors closed.

Apparently indifferent to whether he had followed, the Dancer weaved through the crowded car, each swaying step melding with the rattling rhythm of the train. Despite the number of people standing, she found an empty seat at the rear.

King jostled his way to the back and sat down beside her. The train's air conditioning was losing the battle against the heat and humidity, and the air was heavy with the stink of commuter sweat and boredom. But here in the closeness, he could smell her scent— delicate, bitter-sweet, reminiscent of a night-blooming flower he couldn't recall. He started to ask her name, but then stopped, suddenly not wanting to know, not wanting something as elemental as this creature to be labelled with the mundane. To him, she would remain The Dancer.

"This city has a song," she said suddenly.

He stared at her. She *was* mad, totally disconnected from reality. He should get off at the next stop and go back.

But back to what? King himself *wanted* to disconnect from his own reality, to find a new one. He wanted the Dancer to be real, so he didn't have to return to his old life.

The train pulled into the next station, Osgoode. He sighed. He stayed.

As the train left Osgoode, he turned back to her. Her smile froze him for a second. God, she *was* beautiful. How could he have thought otherwise before? He felt a tightening in his crotch. Well, another reason to stay.

"Fine, you've dragged me this far," he said. "I'll play a bit longer. What song?"

She raised an eyebrow. "Can't you hear it? It's deafening to me."

Mad. He shook his head in reply.

She stared at the passengers. "A million broken hearts beat its rhythm. Whispered lies, unheeded cries scribble its lyrics on walls, their meaning lost in the babble, in the magnitude of the choir. Melody . . . No." She laughed, a bitter sound. "No. There is no melody."

She watched the dark tunnel walls flashing by the car's window. "And in a minor key." She smiled. "Yes. Definitely a minor key."

The train pulled into the next station, St. Patrick. People shuffled off, jostling with those getting on. The train pulled out again. The Dancer stared at the passengers. So did King. A different crowd now, but with the same air of futility.

"Do you hear it now?" she asked again. "The song?"

Still King didn't reply. He had no answers for this odd creature. He had hoped that she would provide *him* with answers—that, in all her strangeness, *she* was the answer.

Finally, he replied with a question, the only question that seemed to matter.

"Can you help me?" he asked, embarrassed by the desperation in his voice.

In reply, she raised a hand, palm toward her face. King stared at the mark on the back of her hand, the same mark the old man had carried—a blood-red rectangle within a larger black one.

"Find the Red Door," she whispered.

As King stared at the symbol, the words "the Red Door" resonated in some secret chamber in his memory, and a cold dread grew in his gut, dread of the place the words were taking him.

The train slowed. The Dancer rose in one flowing movement, no superfluous motion, her body seemingly freed from gravity and inertia, oblivious to the lurching of the subway. King remained seated, gripped by the sudden terror spawned by the symbol on her hand. Unable even to speak, he watched her walk to the door.

The train stopped.

Finally, King forced a word out. "How?" he rasped.

She turned back, surprise on her face, as if she'd already forgotten him.

"Listen for the song," she said. "At the end of day, follow the song." The doors opened, and with one last look back, she was gone.

Finally shaking free of his fear, King jumped up, but the doors had closed, and the train was moving again. His face pressed to the window, he caught a glimpse of the Dancer alone on a dark empty platform, gazing after him sadly. Then his car entered the tunnel, and he was left with nothing but the memory of her face, her smell, and their strange conversation.

And of the terror of the red symbol that was slowly fading like a nightmare retreating before the dawn, replaced by a fear that he'd never see the Dancer again.

He jumped off at the next stop, Queen's Park, ran across the platform and onto a southbound train that was just leaving. The train seemed to crawl along as he prayed he'd catch the Dancer before she disappeared.

The train pulled into the next station. King jumped off. And froze, staring at the station name on the pale green tiled walls.

St. Patrick.

The Dancer had left him at the stop after St. Patrick. King had got off at the next stop, Queen's Park, and taken a train south one stop to this station.

Two stops northbound, one stop southbound.

He shook his head. Impossible. He must have missed a stop coming south, lost in his thoughts.

King didn't travel the subway much, avoiding mixing with the masses, so perhaps his memory of the stations was wrong. A nearby pillar displayed the subway map. Finding St. Andrew where they had entered, he ran a finger up the University line. St. Andrew, then Osgoode, St. Patrick—and Queen's Park.

King swallowed. The Dancer had left him at a station that didn't exist.

He stood staring at the sign. Trains came and left. People pushed by him. He ignored them. For the second time that day, King felt afraid.

An urge to flee overwhelmed him. A southbound train pulled in. Near panic, he shoved his way inside. He sat down heavily, legs shaking, heart pounding, as the train pulled out.

His pride saved him. What if one of his people saw him? Or a competitor? With the same iron will that had built his empire, King forced calm on himself.

He leaned back, his fear slowly dying with each rattle of the rushing train. By the time he got off at St. Andrew, his terror had faded to a pale ghost that finally vanished completely in the sunlight and commonplace bustle on the street, leaving him with only anger at his display of fear.

And anger at the Dancer. At being toyed with, then abandoned. Rejected.

And King wasn't a man who handled rejection well. He headed back to his office, thinking darkly of the Dancer. As he did, every detail of their short time together, every movement she'd made, every word she'd spoken, every look she'd cast his way, rushed back as if he had just lived them again. In that moment, he desired the Dancer more than he'd ever desired anything in his life. And what King desired, he acquired.

He'd found his new game.

The city has a song.
Its lyrics, whispered lies and unheeded cries,
Their meaning lost, in the babble,
In the magnitude of the choir.

Back in his office, King closed his door. It wasn't simply lust for the Dancer that drove him. She had shown him a secret world, one hiding behind the everyday, a dance step left of reality, a half beat off the rhythm of his now unwanted life. That strange creature was the key to the door to that world.

Sitting at his desk, he removed a cherrywood box from a drawer. Inside were business cards acquired over the years. He began flipping through them. He rarely consulted these anymore, relying on electronic lists. But the red symbol had awakened a memory.

U, V, W. He was nearing the back of the box. X, Y, Z.

King sat back, disappointed. It wasn't there.

Yet he remembered holding the card in his hand. In that memory, torch light reflected off black walls, black ceiling, black floor.

Black.

His eyes returned to the box. At the very back, a small black triangle peeked above the divider behind the 'Z's. With shaking hands, King grasped the corner of the hidden card and removed it.

The card was expensive stock, completely black in a matte finish that gave back no reflection at any angle. He turned it over.

On the same black background, a blood-red rectangle stared at him. No lettering. No name or address. No phone or e-mail. Just the same red symbol that the old man and Dancer bore on the backs of their hands. But unlike the black, the red was shiny, so shiny it looked wet, so shiny that if he . . .

He touched it. Gasping, he dropped the card on the desk.

The red had felt . . . sticky.

He looked at his finger. Nothing. King swallowed. Angry with himself, he picked up the card and ran his finger over the red.

And remembered.

Fragments from an evening not so long ago. King's table at his private club. Dinner with a woman lawyer representing a company King wished to acquire. Negotiations. Success. Sipping a sweet dessert wine. Pleased at closing the deal. And so quickly, so easily.

The lawyer mentioning that her client belonged to an even

more exclusive dinner club. King, stung by the discovery of a club he'd never been invited to join, pressing her for details. The lawyer finally offering to take King there.

Then his memories of that evening got . . . fuzzy . . .

A cavernous room . . . torch light . . . black shiny surfaces everywhere . . . incense mixing with smells of roasting meat . . . a man talking to him . . . a powerful man . . . speaking of mysteries . . . of things King had never imagined existed in this city . . . a strange society . . . a world of power hiding beneath the mundane, alongside the everyday, behind . . .

Behind the Red Door.

His hand shaking, King dropped the card on his desk. He swallowed.

The Red Door was a private club. *Very* private. And he'd been there.

Why couldn't he remember more of that evening? And why were the fragments he could recall tinged with the same fear he'd felt in the subway?

Of course. He nodded to himself.

Power. There was power here. King understood power. He moved with the powerful. He was one of them. He could sense power and knew to fear it, especially one hidden, one *he* didn't hold.

Well, one he didn't hold *yet*. He slipped the card into a pocket. He *would* find the Red Door. He *would* be admitted to this club.

But how?

The Dancer. She was his key. What had she said, just before she'd left the train?

Follow the song. At the end of day.

The song.

It was then that King realized that he couldn't recall a single note from the strange song that had accompanied the Dancer's appearance. He summoned his memories of her, hoping they would recall the song to him. Her face, her mouth, her smell, the curve of her breasts and hips.

As those pieces came together, the first hint of the song returned—the beat he had felt rising up from the sidewalk. He remembered her body swaying to that rhythm. As he did, a few notes returned to him, then more, until finally the entire song pounded in his skull with all its original clarity and force.

Afraid to lose the song again, King played it in his head the rest of the day, even tapping its rhythm during meetings he led with detached interest. Late that evening, he rode the elevator to street level, still humming the song.

Follow the song, at the end of day, she had said.

Standing on the sidewalk and following a hunch, he faced north up University. His eyes settled on the subway entrance. The music flared louder in his head.

Smiling, he headed for the station and boarded a northbound train. At St. Patrick, he stood. The next station would be the phantom stop where the Dancer had left. Confident that the song was leading him to a secret path, he moved toward the doors.

Then he felt it—the fear that had seized him just before the Dancer had disappeared.

Shaking and weak, King grabbed at a pole. He sank into a seat, unable to move.

The train emerged from the tunnel into a dimly lit cavern. As his fear grew in his gut, the song began to fade. The cavern flickered in and out of existence, replaced intermittently by grey tunnel walls.

Anger saved him. He was losing his chance to enter a secret circle of power. Perhaps his only chance. What if he could never recall the song again? All because of some foolish fear.

King focused on the song, pulling it back into his head. As its music grew louder, his fear faded, and the cavern outside the train returned.

The train stopped. King gripped the pole beside his seat and pulled himself up on still-trembling legs. The doors slid open with a venomous hiss.

No other passenger made any move to leave. King seemed to be the only person aware that the train had stopped at a station that wasn't supposed to exist.

The alarm signalling that the doors were about to close sounded, not the normal ding-dong chiming, but rather a deep ominous gong. As the doors began to slide together, King took a deep breath and stepped onto the platform. The doors closed behind him, and before he had time to regret his decision, the train was gone.

He looked around.

This "station" was a huge domed cavern, carved from a stone as black and shiny as obsidian, flickering redly under sputtering torches set in high sconces. It smelled of dampness and smoke. The platform was now a pier of blackened timbers that creaked under his feet. A gurgling sound made him turn.

Where the subway tracks should have lain, a dark river now flowed, thick and murky. Something large passed by just under its surface. King jumped back from the edge.

Seeing no other path, he set out along the pier. Still inside the huge cavern, the pier followed the river for what seemed miles. As he walked, King felt as if downtown Toronto was falling behind him by more than just the length of his strides. Finally, the dank smells of the cavern gave way to fresh sea air, and King stepped out onto a mist-shrouded beach of blue sand bordering an inky lake.

Beneath a full moon glaring crimson in a strange starless sky, a huge pyramid of rough-hewn black stone loomed over the entire scene. It looked to be a mix of Mayan and Incan, and something King couldn't place. Beyond the pyramid lay a dark jungle, lush with huge exotic plants shining black in the moonlight and rustling in a wind unfelt by King.

As King's eyes fell on the pyramid, the song flared louder in his head. Somewhat reassured, he set out for the structure, weaving his way between large blue crystal spheres that lay scattered on the sand, something black and spiny throbbing inside of each.

Broad steps led up to the pyramid's summit. King began to climb. Three hundred steps later, he stood at the top, sweat-soaked. Before him squatted a box-like building, barren of any markings save a single door, set in the centre of the wall facing King.

The Red Door.

Trembling from the climb and expectation, King approached it. The Door shone ruddy and glistening in the moonlight. King hesitated, then raised his hand and knocked.

The sound boomed back at him, startling him with its volume. The echoes continued for several breaths, reverberating from the dark pyramid, until finally fading like the last heartbeats of some great dying beast.

A peephole opened in the Door. Eyes peered out at King, midnight black floating in bloodshot whites.

His hand shaking, King reached into his pocket and held up the black and red card.

The eyes narrowed. The peephole closed.

Then . . . nothing happened.

King stood there, near to panic. Should he run? Should he knock again?

As he was about to flee down the steps, metal screamed against metal and a heavy bolt slid back.

The Red Door opened slowly inwards, revealing only darkness.

King stepped forward into a low-ceilinged corridor slanting downwards and lit by torches. He was alone, yet he saw no place where the doorman could have gone. He set out down the passageway.

A strange script covered the walls. Whenever his gaze fell on it, the song in his head suddenly incorporated tortured cries within its music. After that, he kept his eyes ahead, away from the walls. As he descended deeper into the pyramid, the dripping of water added a dismal back beat to his echoing footsteps.

Finally, he heard voices and laughter ahead of him. And music. Not the song that still played in his head, but a strange discordant melody. The corridor ended, and he stepped out.

He gasped, remembering. He'd been here before.

The city has a song.
Its melody—No. There is no melody.
And in a minor key. Definitely, a minor key.

King stood at the top of a broad carpeted staircase above a huge ballroom. The room was cavernous, fifty yards wide by a hundred long with a vaulted ceiling, carved from the shiny black rock. Torches set in high sconces washed the scene in a bloody glow. A large oval dance floor, capable of holding a hundred people at least, dominated the room.

The dance floor was empty, but at scores of tables surrounding it, men in tuxedos or tails and women in formal evening gowns talked and laughed, ate and drank. All wore masks— some simple eye coverings, others ornate and grotesque. Smoke from the torches mixed with the fumes from incense burners lining the dance floor.

Heavy red curtains covered the wall at the far end. Two attendants dressed as footmen stood at each end of the curtains beside draw ropes.

Although many people glanced up at King, no one paid him any particular attention. Deciding it best to act as if he belonged, he straightened his tie, buttoned his jacket, and descended the steps.

A man separated himself from the crowd and approached. He wore the formal attire of a Victorian gentleman and a boar's head mask. He removed the mask. Long white hair. Black eyes, bright and sharp. A hooked nose under snowy eyebrows.

The street person who had appeared to be on fire.

King swallowed, again shaken by the strangeness of it all.

But the man smiled and extended a hand. "Mr. King! Delighted that you have found us once again. Might I inquire how you managed it?" The man had a cultured English accent.

"The Dancer," King mumbled, looking around in near panic. "The song . . ."

The man's smile broadened. "Ah yes," he said, apparently pleased with this answer. "I recall your affinity with the Song from your first visit. Come. Join me."

Taking King's arm, the man guided him the length of the room to where the tables and the polished hardwood of the dance floor ended twenty yards from the red curtains. The remaining space consisted of a raised dais of rough black stone. A pattern of concentric circles was carved into the dais, with spokes radiating outwards from the innermost circle. Below the dais where each spoke ended, a golden goblet stood.

King's host motioned him to a table in front of the dais. They sat. A woman dressed only in a loincloth and a leopard-head mask brought red wine and a steaming roast with a large carving knife. King's host offered him a cigar, lit one himself, and leaned back.

"My name is Beroald," he said, with the same air that King used when giving his own name. This was a powerful man. But a street person?

"You know me?" King asked.

Beroald puffed on his cigar. "We met on your first visit."

King nodded. He *had* been here before. "What is this place? A private club?"

Beroald laughed, a dry throaty sound. King tried to guess his age but failed. "We consider ourselves more of a society. The Society of the Red Door. But like a private club, a society with its privileges."

King's fear of this strange place disappeared. This was what he had come for. He leaned forward. "Such as?"

Beroald smiled. "Watch." He clapped his hands.

Four musicians dressed as medieval minstrels wound their way through the tables. With another jolt of surprise, King recognized them as squeegee kids who accosted him for money whenever he stopped at a light near his office. Two carried mandolins, one a saxophone, and the last a set of bongos. Taking chairs just below the dais, they set up to play.

Beroald clapped again.

The curtains drew back, revealing a dark opening in the black stone wall, like the mouth of a cave. In that mouth, King felt, more than saw, something moving, watching.

"And finally . . ." Beroald said, nodding back toward front of the room.

King turned to look. At the top of the carpeted staircase stood a figure.

The Dancer.

She wore the ever-changing diaphanous gown from that morning, a morning from a lifetime ago. As the Dancer descended the stairs, the torches on the walls died, and the flames in the burners surrounding the dance floor leapt higher, casting the tables into shadow. The Dancer spun the length of the floor, past King and Beroald, to stand silently before the dark opening, eyes unfocused.

She raised her hands above her head, and the squeegee band began to play the now familiar song. At the first note, the opening quivered like a black membrane, then vomited a thick fog. Inside the dark mist, a misshapen form skittered into the room.

The Dancer began to dance. And glow. Her glow grew with each spin she made, each leap she took, until it lit the room and, finally, penetrated the dark mist.

And King could see the thing that had emerged from the opening.

The creature moved on six multi-jointed legs set below a body resembling the carapace of a huge beetle, black and shiny. Dark scales protected a short neck and a bulbous head. Long pincers extended from each side of a slit-like mouth writhing in a horrible parody of a human face. The thing measured at least ten feet from its head to the end of a barbed tail.

Red multifaceted eyes took in the diners. Suddenly, it scrambled forward.

King jumped up, ready to flee, but Beroald put a hand on his arm. "Watch," he said.

The Dancer spun closer. The creature turned toward her. It stopped. The music played, and the Dancer danced. As she moved, the thing stood transfixed, swaying, red eyes locked on her, hypnotized by the spell she wove with her body.

The two curtain attendants, each holding long knives, approached the beast. The nearest drew his arm back, poised to strike.

The Dancer slipped.

It was a small thing, a muscle twitch out of rhythm with the song, but King felt it, as if the dance were a living thing and had skipped a heartbeat.

It was enough to free the creature from the Dancer's spell. Wheeling on the nearest knife wielder, the thing severed the man's head with a snap of its pincers, then turned toward the diners. People screamed and jumped up, King and Beroald included.

The Dancer leapt between them, in control of her every movement again. The beast froze, captured by her dancing once more. The second attendant closed on the creature, and with a smooth precise motion, slipped his blade between the scales around the beast's throat. The creature spasmed once, then slumped to the floor.

Thick blood spewed from the wound, a red so dark it seemed black. It flowed along the channels carved in the stone into the goblets set around the dais. When it stopped, the table attendants collected the goblets and began circulating amongst the tables.

As they did, the Dancer ran the length of the room, up the staircase and disappeared through a side archway. Beroald glared after her, then motioned for King to sit again.

King sat, trembling, trying again to control an urge to flee. The leopard-headed woman poured some of the blood into Beroald's and King's glasses. Beroald raised his and took a deep drink.

King stared at him in disgust. Beroald smiled, blood glistening on his lips. He leaned forward. "Do you recall anything of your first visit?"

King shook his head, not trusting himself to speak.

"How you felt afterwards? The state of your health?"

The sweet smell of the blood reached King then. And he remembered. A host of minor ailments disappearing, a burst of energy for the next week. He looked at his glass, then at Beroald.

Beroald smiled. "The secret of the Red Door, Mr. King. The privilege that I spoke of."

King swallowed. "Immortality?" he asked, not believing what he was asking.

Beroald shrugged. "Who knows? A cure for all known ills and a very long life, to that I can attest."

"What I just saw . . ."

"A ritual, but a practical one. The creatures beyond that black portal may be killed solely by a thrust through a solitary and minute gap in their armour, a strike so precise that it can be executed only if the creature is immobile. The Dancer performs that function for us." Beroald paused. "Preferably more reliably than tonight."

A red-faced man with long white sideburns leaned over from an adjacent table. "Three times this month, Beroald. Three times!"

"I'm dealing with it, Shelby," Beroald replied, his voice icy. The other man paled and turned back to his own table.

Smiling again, Beroald raised his glass in a toast. "To our health, Mr. King. Quite literally."

King looked at the glass of blood before him, struggling to assimilate all he'd just witnessed and learned.

"The efficacy of the blood," Beroald continued, "lasts but a short while."

Immortality, King thought. He raised his glass. He drank.

Sweetness. Heat. Then . . .

A dam bursting inside him . . . a hidden lake released . . . his being flooded with rivers of vitality . . . freed from every bodily pain.

King gasped. He felt wonderful. He felt strong. He felt . . .

Powerful.

He laughed, and Beroald joined him. They roared with laughter, slapping each other on the back. At last, King sat back, wiping away tears of laughter, sipping the rest of the blood, revelling in his new-found vigour. Finally, he asked the question that he feared to raise, but for which he now had to have an answer.

"Beroald, will you accept me as a member here?"

Beroald smiled. "As I said, the Society of the Red Door is not a club. None of us may give or deny admittance. We are each here simply because we found a path to the Door, and can find it again whenever we desire."

King's hopes leapt. "Then I can return?"

Beroald's smile disappeared. "I fear not."

King felt a surge of fear and anger. "Why not? I found a path."

Beroald waved a hand in a dismissive gesture. "Ah, but could you find it again? The Song led you tonight. But the Song plays for one soul and one soul only—the Dancer."

"Yet it played for me," King argued.

Beroald frowned. "No doubt your unprecedented exposure to our lady today fooled the Song into accepting you tonight. Indeed, you still reek of her." Beroald wrinkled his nose, and King wondered at this remark. "But, I assure you, it will not play for you again."

King turned to where the Dancer had disappeared. "Why does it play only for her?"

Beroald shrugged again. "Who knows? The Song will pass to another only upon her death, which is happily unlikely, given her access to the elixir." Beroald rose. "Now I must pay my respects to some friends. It has been a pleasure." Shaking King's hand, he moved to another table.

Oblivious to conversations around him, King sat there stunned, imagining his freshly won vitality draining out of him with every heartbeat. To discover immortality and then to lose it . . .

No! He would *not* let this happen. He belonged here, among the elite, the powerful. There must be a way.

In front of him, the carving knife still lay beside the roast. King stared at the knife. He picked it up. The blade was sharp, slicing through the bloody meat easily. When no one was watching, he wiped the knife clean with his napkin then carefully slid it up his sleeve. He sat there trembling for a moment, then he rose.

Walking the length of the room, he climbed the stairs and went through the alcove where the Dancer had disappeared. He found himself on an outdoor terrace, halfway up the pyramid.

Beside a low stone wall at the terrace's edge, staring up at the red moon and the strange starless sky, stood the Dancer. He touched her elbow. She cried out and drew away, staring at him with wild, clouded eyes. Then a look of recognition danced over her face.

"You came," she whispered.

She flew into his arms, kissing him hard, twining her fingers in his hair, forcing his mouth onto hers. She pulled back. "Free me," she whispered.

"What?"

"Take me away from here. Never to return," she pleaded.

King shook his head. "Are you mad? The Red Door offers freedom from death."

She laughed bitterly. "This place offers many things, but freedom is not among them."

King pushed her away. "I wish to return here, not leave."

The Dancer looked at him, her shoulders slumping. "You will not free me?"

He ignored her. "Can you teach me to find the path to this place?"

"I don't know the way," she said, her voice a dead thing. "I know only the Song."

"Then teach me the Song."

She stared silently at the dark jungle below. Then she straightened, as if reaching a decision. She turned back to him. "I cannot teach it, but I can give it to you."

"How?"

She stroked the outline of the knife under his sleeve. He stiffened. Drawing out the knife, she pushed its grip into his now shaking hand, its tip resting beneath her sternum.

"Free me, as you planned," she said, looking up into his eyes.

The Song will pass to another only upon her death.

"Freedom for me. Immortality for you," she said softly, pressing closer to him until the tip of the knife cut through her thin gown and into her pale flesh.

"Free me," she said again. A patch of blood blossomed around the wound.

Immortality. Only upon her death.

"Free me!" she cried.

Immortality.

With a sob, King stepped forward, thrusting the blade up and into the Dancer. She spasmed, and her head jerked backward. Blood gushed from her chest, soaking her once beautiful gown and King's hands and shirt. Crying out, he pushed her from him, and she slumped to the cold stone, no longer something elemental, just a dead thing.

What had he done? King stumbled backward from her in horror.

And the Song exploded in him.

Before, it had often been so faint he could barely hear it. Now it pounded in his skull, filled his entire being. His very heartbeat seemed to match its rhythm. Beneath the music, he heard a chanting, whispers born in hidden places, words strange and sinister, rasped in cruel guttural tones from throats not human. A paralyzing cold crept into King's limbs. They felt numb, no longer under his control. His legs twitched. His arms jerked.

He began to dance.

He twirled around the terrace, leaping over the corpse of the Dancer, his toes drawing patterns in her blood. He kept dancing, unable to stop, even when Beroald entered.

Beroald looked down at the body of the Dancer. He smiled. He spoke:

"These are fools that wish to die!
Is 't not fine to dance and sing
When the bells of death do ring?"

He turned to King and laughed. "She had become . . . unreliable, as you saw tonight. She would have killed herself, but the Song would not allow it. Any of us would have killed her, but again, there was the Song. On the death of a Dancer, it inhabits the *nearest* person. And none of us wish to know the Song that intimately." He looked at King who was still spinning around the terrace. "That is, none of us who know its true nature."

Inside, the band began to play again, the same music that now pounded incessantly in his head, the Song that King, to his horror, knew would never stop playing for him.

"Mr. King," Beroald said with a smile, "I believe they're playing your song."

King felt himself pulled by invisible hands as strange strings strummed the night air. He began a tarantella, his steps matching the rhythm of tambourines and castanets from the band. Glowing as if on fire, he spun down the great staircase, across the dance floor, and onto the stone dais.

Alexander King danced that night, danced for the patrons of that strange society, danced for the things behind the black portal, danced and danced.

As he would every night until his death, puppet to the Song, Dancer at the Red Door.

For the city has a song, and it plays in a minor key.

oing Harvey in the Big House" (still one of my fave titles) was a finalist for the Aurora Award in 2006. More on this one later.

GOING HARVEY IN THE BIG HOUSE

Big G's first thought each wake time was how much he missed his drawer in his old sector of the House. His new cube was too big.

Rubbing his eyes with a beefy hand, he sat up on his sleep shelf, ducking his head needlessly from habit born of years of waking in a drawer. Triggered by his movement, the ceiling tiles glowed to full brightness.

Big G looked around his cube. Dull green walls. A floor covered with a grey coarse carpet. His private in-chute and dis chute in the opposite wall, with a hidden compartment big enough to make his few personal items seem lonely lying inside. He shook his head. All of this luxury still made him uneasy.

But what bothered him most was the size of the cube. Six and a half feet long, and five feet wide, with a ceiling so far overhead that he had to stand to touch it.

He sighed. Too much space. It wasn't right.

Sometimes now, he'd wake in sleep time, reach out, and feel nothing. He'd panic then, flinging out his arms and legs, snapping his neck back, only to thump his head and crack his knuckles on the walls beside him.

Falling reflex. That's what Tapper, his partner, called it. From when our ancestors built the House generations ago to shelter us from the poisons of the Outside. The Builders would fall sometimes, Tapper said, and they'd throw out their arms and legs, trying to catch a girder or a beam to save themselves.

Tapper used to work in Archives, so he had lots of stories of Outside and the Builders and the House. Big G didn't know about those things. He just knew his new cube made him nervous.

But the Inners had made him a Smoother, and the Inners were the direct descendants of the Builders. *The House protects the People, and the Inners protect the House.* And Smoothers were the arms and legs of that protection. Smoothers needed to be respected and feared, so the Inners gave them cubes. Big cubes.

His ID chip pulsed in his head, signalling an incoming call. Grabbing his specs from where they hung above his sleep shelf, he slipped them over his eyes. The word "Dispatch" flashed in red on the left lens. He touched a finger—the one with his Smoother chip imbedded in the tip—to a stud on the temple of the specs.

"Yeah?" he answered, sounding groggy even to himself.

"What 'yeah'?" snapped the voice in his ear. It was Marker. Marker was an asshole, even for Dispatch.

Big G bit back a retort, glad that ID chips could only transmit basic biometrics, and not thoughts. Still, it wouldn't do for his readings to show him getting angry. He swallowed hard. "I mean, Smoother on shift, sir."

"Better be. Got a Harvey for you and Tapper. Here're the cords." The coordinates for the Harvey's location in the House flashed on his lens as they stored themselves in his specs: Sector E7-S8, Block D32-W26-S33, Cube U19-N7-W28.

The com light winked out as Marker ended the call without another word. Big G sighed. He'd pissed off a Dispatcher. "Got off on the wrong floor with 'im," Tapper would say. Plus he'd been stuck with a Harvey. Great start to the shift.

Beside his sleep shelf stood the flush. Despite protests from his bladder, he just stared at the facility with distaste. His own flush. Before, he'd shared one with his whole block, lining up to use it or to dump his bag. He even missed the smell. Now he only had to bag up for time outside his cube.

Tossing the specs back onto their hook, Big G got up to use the flush. The sleep shelf folded up into the wall, making the room seem even larger.

A soft "hiss-plop" signalled his tube of glop arriving in his in-chute, prompted by his use of the flush. He squeezed the glop into his mouth, enjoying its familiar chalky taste. After his promotion, he'd tried other flavours available to Smoothers, but had quickly gone back to the standard citizen issue.

Glop should taste like glop, he'd told Tapper. Tapper had laughed. "Think it's standard issue? The citizens get No-aggra in *their* glop. We don't. The Inners *want* us aggressive," he'd said. "And happy," he'd added, making a gesture at his crotch.

Big G finished his tube and dropped it into the dis-chute, reminding himself to request a conjugal visit for his next off-shift. Another benefit of being a Smoother.

After wiping depil cream on and off his face and head, he took a quick buzz bath, passing the electrostatic wand over himself. He bagged up and shrugged into his red one-piece. Yeah, his cube was too big, but he still grinned when he put on his reds. Red said Smoother. Red said, "Don't mess with me."

He retrieved his specs and stepped onto the flow disk in front of his door. Calling up the Harvey's cords on his specs, he spoke the "Go" command. As the disk received the destination from the specs, the door to his cube "shooshed" open, and the smells and sounds of the House assailed him.

A rhythmic pulse on her chip awakened Laryn. One slow, two fast. She sat up on her sleep shelf, fully alert. Her illegal trojan programs were warning her of a status change for one of her people. Brushing long dark hair out of her eyes with thin fingers, Laryn donned her specs and spoke the display command.

And swore. Another recent recruit for the Movement had gone Harvey. A Smoother team was already on its way.

After ensuring that her trojans had given the call to the right team, she flagged the file for tracking. She would watch the progress of this one until she went on-shift in an hour.

Laryn sat back, biting her lip, no longer able to ignore the pattern. This Harvey pushed the regression rate in new recruits to over thirty percent. *Has humanity lost so much*, she thought? *Is it already too late for us?*

Or were the Movement's selection criteria flawed? Laryn herself had programmed the trojan that searched for recruits. The trojan constantly scanned the terabytes of data on citizens flowing through the House, searching for a specific mix of intellect, initiative, and motivation, expressed via complex psychological patterning algorithms. She'd based her trojan on software her fellow Inners used to find their own new initiates.

And she was living proof of the flaws in *that* process.

The citizens believed the Inners to be direct descendants of the Builders themselves, believing it because the Inners told them to. But the family social structure that could have supported that myth had died soon after the birth of the House.

In reality, the Inners *chose* who would enter their circle, selecting candidates at a young age after careful screening and then subjecting them to intensive indoctrination.

Not for the first time, Laryn wondered how she'd slipped through. How *she* had become an Inner. *If the Inners can choose so badly, then so can we*, she thought. *Are we doomed already?*

To restore her resolve, she opened a hidden compartment and removed the object that had become her touchstone. She sat back on her sleep shelf, telling herself yet again that she held in her hand the power to free the people.

The object she held was simple enough: an image of a thing, a thing her fellow Inners told the people no longer existed.

In her hand, she held the *truth*.

Staring at the image, Laryn realized that perhaps the Inners had *not* erred in choosing her those twenty years ago.

They'd chosen her to be a leader.

And a leader she would be.

She imagined again that she could see it all happen. In her mind, cracks appeared in the walls, in all the thousands, millions, billions of walls of the House. Next, the ceilings began to sag under the weight of the truth they hid, struggling not to fall, straining not to reveal the thing waiting above.

But she knew they would fall. They would all fall. The House would fall.

As the people rose up.

In the hall outside Big G's open door, a river of humanity flowed by him in both directions at a steady twenty miles per hour. Each person stood on their own flow disk, each disk moving over the magnetic flow fields below, programmed for a wake or sleep time destination.

Big G's cube sat on the east-flow side of an EW-hall. The hall, like most in the House, was twelve feet across with two main central flows running in opposite directions. On each side, short merge paths led from the cube doors lining the hall to the central flow for that side.

Before he was a Smoother, Big G had been in Flow, assigned to Block U7-W23-N14, Sector W3-S8. He'd been in Flow since being certified Clean—no retro traits—at nine calendars of age. But Big G had grown, into his name and out of a job. He could no longer squeeze his bulk through the access doors in the floors and along the maintenance tunnels that ran two feet high below the flow tracks that moved the citizens through the House.

As Big G's flow disk accelerated smoothly forward from his doorway into the merge path, he weight-shifted by habit, not even holding the balance bar that formed a half-circle at waist height. The east-flow adjusted, creating a space between two white-garbed Techs into which Big G's disk slipped with no noticeable change in speed for the other east-side travellers. Big G thought of his years in Flow and felt a stab of pride at his small part in how the House worked, how the Flow kept flowing, moving the people to where they had to be.

The ever-present buzz-hum of the Flow that was the song of

the House washed over him. He breathed in the people smells he missed in his new cube, thick and pungent, and tinged here with a sting of ozone. He watched the travellers passing in the west-flow, mostly white Techs and blue Makers in this sector, some grey Crats, a black Recycler. Each person looked away, avoiding eye contact with a Smoother. He had their respect, their fear.

After ten minutes, his disk entered the flow circle in the intersection with a NS-hall. It orbited, queuing for the down-side of the UD-tube at the circle centre. He checked the Harvey's cords. Down sixty-two levels. *Flush it*, he thought. He hated big drops.

His turn came, and his disk slid onto the next empty slot on the down-side of the tube. Big G swallowed and forced his face to relax as the slot clamps stabilized his disk. Not good to let the people see a Smoother sweat over something as common as a drop. But he still counted every level as they flashed by.

He knew that Tapper would be on his way to the same cords. Tapper was his partner, and Dispatch always sent two Smoothers to a Harvey. Never knew how bad these calls would be. He hoped the Harvey would already be dead. That happened a lot.

He'd asked Tapper once why they called them Harveys. Tapper had said that it came from an *alcool* drink the Builders had made— Harvey Wallbanger, they'd called it. *Wallbanger*, get it? Then he'd laughed. Even Tapper didn't believe that one.

Well, Harveys did generally start with banging the walls of their drawers. Frowning, he checked the Harvey's cords again. This one was in a cube. Harveys were usually in drawers.

His disk reached the Harvey's level and slid out of the down-tube into another traffic circle. It looped around to the north-flow, rode that for ten blocks, then demerged and slipped into the small, dimly lit access lane for the cubes on the inside of that block. Six cubes along, it slowed and stopped.

Tapper was waiting, his small thin frame leaning on the wall, bony fingers drumming a rhythm on his thigh like a mech-claw in a loop. That's how he got his name. But the Inners didn't name him. Inners knew you by your ID and called you by your job. People you worked with, they gave you your name.

"Took ya enough," Tapper said with a sharp-featured grin. "Whadya do? Try to find a route with no drop?" The grin disappeared as he dodged a cuff from Big G.

"So why didn't you clean it up yourself, shorty, you in so much of a hurry?" Big G growled.

Tapper sniffed, faking all serious. "Against the regs. Going solo on a Harvey."

Big G laughed. "When'd you ever stick to regs?"

Tapper's grin returned. "When I'm first at a Harvey call."

Snorting, Big G touched his Smoother finger to a small indentation beside the door of the Harvey's cube. The snoop spot irised open, and he bent down to peer in. He moved his head back and forth, and then straightened. "Can't see a thing."

"Dispatch thinks he covered the lens with glop."

"That's a new one."

"Guess he got sick of that one flavour you like so much."

Big G chuckled, relaxing a bit when he heard that it wasn't a woman. Female Harveys were the worst, at least for him. He didn't like having to hurt them.

"You activate his camera?" Big G asked.

All cubes, except for Inners, contained cameras, as did all intersections, supposedly capturing each citizen's every action. As a Smoother, Big G now knew that it would be impossible to monitor such displays or even store an hour's activity in the House. The ID chips were far more efficient, tracking movements and restricting access to areas as needed. But cameras *could* be activated for a specified ID chip at the request of a Smoother.

Tapper shook his head. "Covered that lens, too."

"So how do we know he's in there?"

Tapper touched a stud on his specs. "Central says his chip's inside. So unless he's carved it out of his head—"

"Been done before."

"In which case, he's bleeding to death somewhere else."

"At least that wouldn't be our call," Big G muttered.

Tapper's face went all smooth, calm. He reached up and squeezed Big G's shoulder. "S'okay. Just our job. Harveys, well, they're already gone once they get to this stage. Nothin' we can do. Nothin' anybody can do. Just gotta finish the job."

"Just our job," Big G repeated, trying to believe it.

"That's right."

"Nothing else to do."

"Nothin'."

Big G sighed and glanced at Tapper. "Ready?"

Nodding, Tapper moved to the door, taser in hand. Big G didn't use a taser, preferring his size and strength in Harvey calls. Besides, Tapper said a taser in Big G's hand was like a warning sign on a hallway riot cannon. Redundant, he called it.

Big G touched his Smoother finger to the cube's door lock. The door slid open, and Tapper dove inside first, Big G shouldering through behind him.

The stench of the room hit him almost as hard as the Harvey. He had just enough time to see Tapper slump to the floor before a naked whirlwind of flesh slammed Big G into the wall beside the door. Something metallic bright, metallic sharp glinted in the hand that flashed up at his throat.

Big G shot out his left arm, blocking the thrust, and drove the heel of his right palm up and hard into the Harvey's nose. He felt the bone give under the blow. The man's head snapped back, long dirty hair flying, and he crumpled to the floor. A foot-long piece of jagged plasteel, which Big G recognized as part of a sleep shelf support, dropped from the man's hand.

Big G hauled Tapper to his feet with one hand and started checking for blood. Tapper slapped his hands away.

"I'm okay. I blocked him with my taser arm," he muttered.

Big G felt relieved. Partners looked out for each other. It wouldn't look good to have your partner go down. Besides, Tapper was his only friend.

"So why'd you . . . ?" Big G frowned, and then started to laugh. "You zapped yourself!"

"He knocked my arm," Tapper said reddening, and Big G laughed harder.

"Shaddup," Tapper said, but he was grinning. He knelt to touch the Harvey's neck as they'd been taught. His grin disappeared. He stood, shaking his head. Pressing a stud on his specs, he spoke, "One unit for recycling, these cords."

Big G turned away, wanting to throw up but not from the smell. He'd used a killing blow by reflex, from training. It had been self-defence, but that didn't make him feel any better.

Tapper spoke finally, low and quiet. "Y'okay?"

"Yeah," Big G replied, just as quietly.

Pause. "Nothing else you could do."

"Yeah." Big G wanted to talk about something else. He looked around the room. "Most Harveys are in drawers," he said, cursing the quaver in his voice.

Tapper nodded. "Some're in cubes, but never this big."

"Even bigger than the ones we get."

Tapper grinned, then spread his arms out to each side and spun around, doing a little dance, oblivious now to the body at his feet. "Yeah. Ain't it great? All this space?"

Big G stared at Tapper as if he'd just gone Harvey himself. "You *like* big cubes?"

"Sure do. Ya don't feel like the walls are closin' in." He shivered, but then grinned. "Hey! Maybe *we'll* get one of these if we do good."

Big G just shook his head. He knew that he wouldn't like an even bigger cube. His walls were already too far away. He continued to survey the room.

To avoid looking at the body, he looked up. Glop covered the ceiling as well, except for a clean circle about a foot across with a small square of colour stuck in its centre. He reached up and tugged at the square. It came away easily, leaving behind a dab of dried glop.

The square was a pictab, a piece of plas-per with an image encoded into its surface. Big G blinked, trying to make the image come into focus, to make sense. It seemed to be a mass of white swirls and curls and curves hanging in a blue nothingness. He'd never seen anything like it. It fascinated him.

"What do you think it is?" Big G asked.

Tapper started to shrug, but then his eyes locked on the image. "Dunno. Let's see," he said, reaching for the pictab.

But Big G pulled his hand back to stare at the image again. "Think it had something to do with him going Harvey?"

"It's a flushin' pictab. Toss it in the dis-chute, and let's get out of this stink before I puke," Tapper snapped.

But Big G continued to study the image, struggling to make sense of it. Tapper sighed. "Okay, tell you what. Give it to me, and I'll check with Archives to see if they know what it is." He held out his hand to take it.

Big G hesitated, reluctant to part with the strange vision. "You'll give it back after?"

"Yeah, sure." Tapper plucked the square from Big G's fingers and slipped it inside his reds. Big G watched it disappear. "Now let's go," Tapper said, stepping out the door.

Big G looked down at the body, then around the cube, and finally up at the ceiling. "Wonder why he put it up there?"

Tapper didn't answer. Tapper was gone.

Still in her cube, Laryn cut her illegal link to Central. Nothing more to discover there. The situation was controlled—the Smoother team had killed her recruit. After sending a coded update to her cell members, she sat back, biting her lip, this time aware of the habit from the pain it caused.

She'd found no trace of interest in her direction, but how long would it take them to see a pattern? To find a connection?

To find her?

She needed to scrub the Harvey's file of any links to her or the Movement. But her spec display was counting down to her work shift. The scrub would have to wait.

That sleep time, Big G didn't dream of falling. Instead, he floated in white swirls and curls and curves hanging in a blue nothingness. The image in the pictab. No straight, sharp, hard lines of floors meeting walls meeting ceilings running on and on and on forever. He felt scared but also excited.

His first call next wake time was a flow break. An easy shift. A sector had lost east-west flow, and he and Tapper had to lead stranded travellers along dim Smoother corridors to the next hall. When he saw Tapper, Big G asked about the pictab.

Tapper looked away as they walked. "Archives had nothin'."

Big G waited for more, but Tapper just kept walking, staring ahead, grumbling about how small the corridors were.

"So where is it?" Big G asked finally.

"Where's what?" Tapper asked.

"The pictab! You said you'd bring it back. It's mine."

Tapper glanced up at Big G, but then quickly looked away again. "They kept it. Gonna add it to the Harvey's file."

Big G stopped walking, and somebody bumped into him. He turned and glared, and the line of faces behind him, Crats mostly, cowered back. He started walking again.

"It's mine," he repeated.

Tapper swallowed and kept glancing up at him, but Big G ignored him. He was thinking of what Tapper had said, about the Harvey having a file.

Things were not going well for Laryn. She'd drawn a double shift, delaying her scrub of the Harvey's file. Now back in her cube, she sat at her secure link and called up the file. Her breath caught as the status flag flashed on her specs.

Someone else was accessing the same file.

Forcing calm on herself, she quickly spoke the command to start the scrub, praying that she wasn't too late.

Off-shift, Big G sat in his cube searching the Harvey's file on his specs. New to being a Smoother and the power it brought, he'd expected an "access denied" message. But after a delay of a heartbeat, the data began to scroll down his lens.

The Harvey had been a mid-level Crat, with a clean work record, no flags anywhere on his file. Big G kept scanning, not even sure what he was looking for.

Until he found it: a repeat visitor, irregular but at least once per seven-shift for the past cycle. A woman. Conjugal visits? But the Recycling autopsy showed that he'd been taking his No-aggra, so it hadn't been sex. Work relationship maybe.

He spoke the command to link the woman's ID to her file. The screen flashed "Link Error." He scrolled back through the Harvey's file to pick up the ID code and enter it directly. No luck. He did a search command then scrolled from beginning to end and back again before he accepted what had happened.

All evidence of the woman's visits had disappeared.

Big G never thought he might have imagined it—he didn't credit himself with having imagination. Shrugging mentally, he spoke the cords of the woman's cube that he'd seen on the file: Sector E8-S8, Block D13-W25-S30, Cube U6-N2-W23/24. Few people could have recalled one of the cords, let alone all eight, but Big G had worked in Flow for fifteen years before Smoothing. Both jobs meant memorizing cords several times a shift.

Storing the cords, he scheduled a visit to the woman for his next shift. An official visit as a Smoother investigating a Harvey, he thought. But then an image of white on blue swirled behind his eyes, and he knew he was lying to himself.

Laryn sighed in relief as the scrub completed. But her respite was short-lived. The in-com light flashed on her specs. She swore as she read the message. A Smoother was requesting a meeting. An unknown Smoother, not the one she expected.

She cross-linked the Smoother's ID to the recent Harvey call. And got a match. No coincidence then.

Fighting down the panic that tried to rise in her, she sat back, frowning. If her fellow Inners had discovered her role in the Movement, they'd move immediately with no warning. But this Smoother was simply requesting a meeting, a full shift away. No sign of urgency. So there was no need for any rash action. No need for what had first flashed through her mind.

To run.

In a way, she felt disappointed. For a heartbeat, her fear of capture had overwhelmed another, much older fear.

A fear of the only place to which she *could* run. A place of legends, legends from childhood and childhood's nightmares.

Laryn sighed. No need for escape yet. Or to wonder how she would lead the people to a place she still feared herself.

Before his visit, Big G tried to discover more about the woman. To no avail. The system refused to provide any details concerning the occupant of the cords he'd memorized.

What the cords themselves told him did not sink in until the time for his visit arrived. Standing on his flow disk, he called them up on his specs. And froze. He stepped off his disk and sat heavily on his sleep shelf.

The woman's cube was U6-N2-W23/24. He stared at the last portion. W23/24. Not just W23 or W24. She had a double cube.

She was an Inner.

Big G sat thinking, already over the shock. Things didn't throw him for long—one of the reasons he'd been picked as a Smoother. "If you met a two-headed citizen," Tapper had once said, "first thing you'd do is check if both heads had a chip."

This explained why he had found nothing on her. He ran a big hand over the smooth skin of his head. He probably should cancel. An Inner's business with a Harvey was none of his.

No. He'd better make the call, if only to explain his mistake. He stepped onto his disk and spoke the "Go" command.

Laryn sat watching the big Smoother as he *apologized* rather than accused. He spoke in short nervous sentences, looking around her cube, not meeting her gaze. He'd have been amazed to know how much she'd learned of him since he first contacted her.

She'd run her trojan that profiled possible recruits against Big G, and found him suitable for the movement—not as a leader, but as a follower. He fell below the desired level of intelligence. But he was fiercely loyal to a cause that tied to his belief system—a key trait for the Movement.

Some of his indicators were ambiguous, especially those reflecting his views on personal freedom versus authority. Still, she could only believe that anyone, once they knew the truth of the House, would rank the right to freedom for billions above maintaining the status quo.

Her last concerns gone, her mind focused on the man. He wanted something and was about to tell her what it was. There was opportunity here. She smiled at him. He seemed to like that. She smiled again. Yes, definitely opportunity.

Big G wanted to be anywhere but sitting in front of this beautiful woman in her far too large cube as she played with her long dark hair and smiled at him. Any Inner he'd ever met had been stern and frightening. To his surprise, she had told him to call her by her name, Laryn. She wasn't even wearing her Inner golds, just off-shift stripes like a normal citizen. Her golds hung by the door like any other garment, and somehow the casualness of their display made him even more nervous.

But as he explained his visit, he realized that he'd come here not to apologize, but to learn. Knowing then that all his discomfort would be for nothing unless he found the courage to ask his question, he stumbled on.

". . . since you knew this Harvey, I mean, this man . . . that is . . . see, I found this thing in his room—" Big G stopped.

Laryn had straightened slightly, her smile freezing like a seized servo-lock. "What kind of thing?" she asked.

He swallowed. "A pictab. It was . . . it . . ." He struggled to describe what still haunted him every time he closed his eyes.

But before he could find words, she produced a pictab from somewhere he didn't catch and placed it on the small table between them. "Was it like this?"

He stared down at the image, different but the same. More blue in this one, but still the swirls of white, still the feeling of floating in something, the absence of the straight hard lines of the House. He swallowed. "Yes," he whispered.

"What do you see?" she asked.

"I don't know. Something blue covered by something white. Or the other way around."

She smiled at him. Big G felt his face burning. He'd made her smile. He wanted to do that again.

"White on blue," she said.

Big G nodded, praying she'd say more. She seemed to be studying him, judging whether he was worthy of a great secret. For he was sure the pictab involved a great secret.

Finally she spoke. "Enough for now. But I'd like to meet with you again, here in my cube. Every off-shift for the next two cycles. To *prepare* you to receive the answer you seek."

Big G swallowed. That meant committing his free time for over fifty off-shifts. But he nodded his agreement.

"You will make no further inquiries into the Harvey that you killed . . ." She paused as he flinched, then continued, "or regarding this." Here she pointed at the pictab. "You will do nothing out of the ordinary, nothing to attract attention to yourself. Is that understood?"

He nodded again. And their first fateful meeting ended.

Over the following cycles, Big G complied with Laryn's instructions to the letter, driven to learn the pictab's secret. But soon his compliance owed itself as much to another reason.

As a Smoother, he could request a conjugal partner any off-shift. But this was different. No woman had ever initiated sex with him or made him feel desired. Her interest in him excited him as much as her body. He thought of her even while on-shift. And off-shift, instead of watching a *realee* on his specs, he'd lay there thinking of her, waiting for their next time together.

Strange and new to him, his feelings for her confused him.

But not as much as the true history of the House confused him, as Laryn slowly taught him during their sessions together.

"It was the greatest undertaking in history," Laryn began his first lesson. "To build a safe haven for billions from an environment that had finally lost the war we'd waged on it for centuries. An environment of deadly toxins, depleted ozone, and mutating retro-viruses spread by multiplying parasites."

The House began, Laryn said, as a "military" "project" by the "government" of the "country" that first conceived the idea.

Big G struggled with these strange concepts, especially with people *choosing* their leaders. Laryn said that, before the House, the people used to have freedom to make most decisions in their lives— their jobs, where to live, what to eat, how to dress, how to spend their time. Big G didn't see how such a world could even function. It seemed so disordered.

In a later session, Laryn explained how the environment's death led also to the death of something called the "economy."

"Industries failed. International money markets and trade collapsed. Free market capitalism fell," she said. "Relations between nations died as each fought its own internal battles."

Laryn spent several sessions explaining these ideas. Big G pretended to understand, but all he could really grasp was that more and more people had come to work on the House project, even from other "countries," as their old jobs disappeared.

"The House paid only in shelter, food, and protection," Laryn explained, "but these people had no other options."

What else, Big G thought later, *would you want?*

"When industries necessary for the House failed—food, high tech, steel—the government took them over, absorbing those workers, too, until they controlled all sources of production for the House. The government itself shrank, lopping off branches no longer needed or not essential to the project."

Laryn had paused then, sighing. "And so, a once great country reduced itself to one single purpose: build the House."

Something new was puzzling Big G. In recent sessions, as the strange, disturbing world Laryn had first described grew closer to the one he knew, he had become more excited. Here was the true story of the Builders! Yet Laryn seemed more concerned, even *sad*, over the strangeness that had been lost.

But he forgot about it as he learned more each session.

"Hundreds of millions of people now worked on the House," Laryn explained, "all under a strict project hierarchy, each with a specific role on sub-teams under teams under team leaders under project managers, all reporting up to a small program committee that was the remnant of the once-elected government."

Big G nodded. The words were strange, but it sounded very much like the House today. Tidy, orderly, efficient. Laryn's next comment echoed that thought.

"We had *become* the House," she said.

Again, he sensed her sadness.

"Elections were postponed so as not to disrupt progress. Dissent was minimal—the need to complete the House was too great." She stared at him intently. "Can you guess what happened next? What *had* to happen?"

Big G's heart jumped. Was *this* his test? If he failed, would the secret of the pictab be lost to him? To his relief, Laryn answered herself.

"All talk of elections, of democracy, gradually died away. The very project structure that had given a small group the power to direct millions of people to *build* the House was used by that same group to *keep* that power. To *rule* those millions."

Laryn paused. "Billions now," she whispered, her eyes no longer on him, unfocused, seeing something he could not. Then she seemed to come to herself and fixed him with a stare. "Do you know *who* that small group was? Who they are *still*?"

Big G swallowed. "The Inners?" he said. Laryn nodded, and he relaxed.

"Should a few have the right to direct the lives of billions?" she asked quietly, her eyes not leaving him.

Big G squirmed his bulk on his seat. To even ask that question seemed . . . wrong. But Laryn was an Inner. Surely the Inners were allowed to question themselves. Perhaps that was how the House stayed strong. Still he struggled for an answer.

"*The House protects the People*—" he began to recite.

Laryn sighed. "*And the Inners protect the House*. Yes, yes. But what if the world has *changed*? From when the House was first built? Wouldn't the House need to change, too?"

What did she mean? The House *was* the world. Big G wished this lesson were over. "How would it change?" he asked.

She leaned forward, taking one of his large hands in both of hers. "To a world where people are free again."

The world before the House that she had told him of, he thought. That strange world of chaos and disorder.

Then the pictab flashed in his mind, with its random white and blue soft swirls, its own chaos and disorder contrasting with the clean predictable lines of the House.

For the first time, Big G felt a twinge of fear of the secret he chased.

The end of the two cycles of teaching Big G was nearing, and Laryn was crying.

She cried a lot lately. At first, she had cried because she was using him. But she'd used others in the past and had used sex as a means before. So why did it bother her this time?

Part of it was Big G himself. To her surprise, she'd grown to care for him over their time together. He was a clumsy lover but gentle, simple but honest, with none of the cynicism of the others in the Movement. Trusting and malleable, he was a child, believing what he was told, believing the lies the Inners fed him, just as *she* had believed as a child.

He *was* the people, embodying all that humanity had become.

But soon, he would be ready for the great truth. And that was why she cried. When she told him, that child in him would die, and with it, the last remnant of the child *she* had once been. But it was too late. Whatever he felt for her—and she was still unsure if he felt more than lust—she knew the blue and white vision still burned in him. He would not stop until he found the secret. She had seen this before.

Better, she thought, *to have him with us when he finds out.*

The next session, Big G arrived at Laryn's cube to find her dressed in her Inner golds.

"It's time," she said, once they were safely inside.

Big G's heart jumped. "You're going to tell me the secret?" he asked, his voice barely a whisper.

"Better than that. I'm going to take you to it," she said.

He opened his mouth but then just nodded, afraid to say the wrong thing and prove himself unworthy after all.

"First," Laryn said, "we must ensure that our movements don't attract attention." She handed him a pair of specs. "Put these on. They block the signal in your ID chip, replacing it with one that says you're still right here in my cube. You won't be able to be tracked, and you won't trip any cameras."

After a moment's hesitation, he took the specs from her. It bothered him to glimpse a system inside a system, one designed to hide. Who did Laryn fear? Surely not the Inners? Laryn was an Inner. But then who?

Laryn knelt and popped the cover off his disk. "I must also program your disk, so that it leaves no record of this trip. Notice anything unusual about these cords?" she asked.

Peeking over her shoulder, he watched her punch coordinates directly into his disk. "Only that I've never been that high."

"Right first time," she said. She smiled at him, and his face grew hot. "In fact, you can't go higher. Not in the House." She stood, wiping her hands on her golds as if they were just the whites of a Tech. Motioning him onto his disk, she stepped on hers and spoke the "go" command. The door to Laryn's cube slid open, and their disks slipped into the Flow.

Their route confused Big G. It looped and crossed itself and even dropped levels. But always it rose again, higher each time. They rode in silence, Laryn in front, an Inner with a Smoother escort. As they rode, Big G struggled to make sense of what she had said: *You can't go any higher. Not in the House.* That seemed to mean that you could go higher if . . .

He stopped that thought, shying back from it, from an idea so impossible, so forbidden that it froze him with fear. If . . .

. . . if you went *outside* the House. But the Outside was poisoned.

274

No one could live Outside. That's why the Builders made the House. The Inners said so. But Laryn was an Inner . . .

He had no more time to ponder. They reached the upper level of the cords and began moving along an empty EW corridor. He checked NS halls at every intersection, but never saw another person. He realized then that he heard only the sound of their own disks. The normal background buzz of the Flow was missing.

As if reading his mind, she spoke. "This level is accessible only to Inners. No one lives or works here."

But as they neared the cords, Big G saw a thin, red-clad figure leaning on a wall. A block away, he knew who it was.

"Pull up that chin of yours 'fore ya trip over it," Tapper said as they stopped in front of him. He grinned but kept kicking the floor with a toe. He did that when he was nervous.

Big G looked at Laryn. She nodded. "Tapper's been with us for some time now. That's why it will be so wonderful to have you join us. We'd have a complete Smoother team."

Big G turned to Tapper. "You kept my pictab."

Tapper jerked his head in Laryn's direction. "Orders."

"Sorry," she said. "We don't want that in circulation. Now, are you ready?"

Big G was still trying to understand Tapper being here, and what Laryn meant about "joining" and "a complete Smoother team." He and Tapper *were* a team. But he said nothing and just nodded.

Tapper turned to the wall and touched his Smoother finger to what must have been a hidden security spot. A door slid open to reveal a small closet-sized space with a series of metal rungs attached to the facing wall.

Laryn stepped forward, grabbed a rung, and began to climb. "Let's go," she called. Tapper clambered up behind her.

Big G followed, barely able to squeeze his way up the narrow chute, but finding the closeness comforting after the strange emptiness of the corridors below. He'd never seen that much open space before, and it had frightened him.

His comfort didn't last. The rungs ended near the top of the chute, which was just a square hole cut in the floor above. Tapper scrambled out. Big G grabbed the side of the opening and hauled his bulk over the edge onto the floor.

And gasped.

There were no walls. Slender columns marched in east-west and north-south processions into the dimness of distance, supporting a ceiling covered in crisscrossing jumbles of pipes, ducts, and glow tubes—a ceiling that hung far too high above.

Tapper was jumping up and down, skipping and laughing. "Isn't this great?" he cried. "Lookit all this space. No walls. Nothin' to close you in."

Big G was well aware of the lack of walls. He was still lying on the floor, afraid to get up, ashamed of being afraid, especially in front of Laryn. Groaning, he crawled to the nearest pillar and wrapped an arm around it, clutching its closeness to him as he clamped his eyes shut against the space.

"Big G," Laryn said softly, her voice close to his ear.

He forced his eyes open. Laryn knelt beside him. She was biting her lip. He knew she did that when she was nervous, like Tapper kicking the floor.

"We're almost there," she said, pointing to a pillar with another set of rungs leading up to what appeared to be a trap door in the ceiling, almost hidden by ducts and cables.

"Is it . . . like this?" he gasped.

She bit her lip again. "It's what you saw in the pictab." She knelt beside him. "It's the secret I promised."

Her closeness helped him push the terror of the open space from his mind. Locking his eyes on the nearness of the floor, he stood on shaking legs and let her lead him to the ladder.

The climb seemed endless. Finally, he bumped into Tapper's feet. Above, he heard a screech of metal grating on metal. He hung there, eyes shut, surrounded by more emptiness than he had ever known, gripping a rung, hugging the pillar, until he heard the thud of something heavy falling on the ceiling overhead.

At first, he thought that they'd opened the cube of some gigantic Harvey. A roar, as from a great mouth, erupted above. The air came alive. It clawed at him with cold fingers. It choked him with strange smells, thin and sharp and cutting, none of the thick muskiness of the House. The shock snapped his eyes open, then his fear of the space around him overcame his fear of what lay above, propelling him up and through the opening . . .

And into a light brighter than any he'd ever seen. Eyes scrunched tight again, he crawled from the hole to fall panting on his back. Finally, his eyes adjusted, and he opened them.

He lay under a great bowl of blue in which billows of white swirled above him. The image from the pictab. But the white shapes in the pictab hadn't been alive, hadn't writhed like mouths ready to devour him. The air tore at him as if it had claws and wished to pluck him from the House and feed him to the mouths above. The blueness and its twisting white monsters surrounded him in all directions, dropping finally to meet the distant edges of this strange highest floor of the House, a floor that curved down to disappear at those edges as if they now sat on some impossibly huge ball.

"It's called the sky, and those are clouds," Laryn said, but her voice seemed stripped of its usual power. Up here, it was a tiny thing, swallowed by the vastness engulfing them. She named other things—wind, roof, horizon. "And that is the sun."

He looked to where she pointed. A cloud, chasing others across the blue, glowed as with some hidden light. The glow grew along one edge, and then a ball of indescribable brightness burst forth, burning his eyes with light and his skin with heat.

He cried out like a child and hid his face from the thing. Blinded, panicking, he flailed about for the trap door as the wind kept clawing at him. Grabbing an edge, he hauled himself head-first through the opening, catching the ladder at the last moment. He half-climbed, half-fell, first to the floor below, then down the other ladder to collapse on the empty House floor with its familiar halls, the comforting solidity of a wall at his back and a ceiling above him that didn't move as if alive.

After a time, he felt a touch on his arm. Laryn sat down beside him. "*That* is what the Inners hide from the people," she said. "The old legends of the Outside may have been true once, but no more. There's a *world* out there again—with air we can breathe and water we can drink—a world to which we can finally return. We're not ready yet, but we will be."

She talked on. Big G listened but didn't hear, unable to grasp what he'd seen. Despite all of her teaching, he had never believed until now that there *was* an Outside. The only world he knew was here, in the House. He lay drinking in the comforting closeness of the dimly lit ceiling, tracing where it met each wall in clean, straight, hard lines, feeling his breathing slow, trying to forget what he'd seen, just happy to be home.

Being back in the House was having a different effect on Tapper. The smaller man sat huddled on the floor, shivering, his eyes darting around the corridor. He mumbled something.

"What?" Big G said, grabbing at something else to focus on.

"Get up, Tapper," Laryn said, rising herself.

Tapper got up, but he just stood there hugging himself, shoulders hunched, head tucked down as if the ceiling was too low and he didn't want to bump his head. "Small," he whispered.

"Let's go," Laryn snapped, stepping onto her disk.

"What's wrong, Tap?" Big G asked, putting a hand on Tapper.

Tapper shivered again. "Too small. In here. Too small."

Tapper turned to him. Something familiar but out of place peeked from behind Tapper's eyes. Big G had seen that look before, but he couldn't remember where. Head lowered, Tapper stepped on his disk and moved down the corridor after Laryn.

Big G looked around. It didn't feel too small to him. The walls, the ceiling—especially the ceiling—all felt wonderfully close.

Laryn knew that it hadn't gone well, that she'd pushed Big G too fast. He'd barely slept since the trip to the roof four shifts ago. He lay beside her each sleep time, staring up at the ceiling. He said whenever he closed his eyes, *it* was always there—the *sky*, writhing like a thing alive.

And she worried about Tapper, who was showing much different signs. Different but familiar.

Big G left her to start his shift. Just then, her trojans warned her of activity concerning one of her people.

The news was bad. Very bad.

Feeling ill, she stopped the display, wishing she could stop what would happen next as easily. And she found, to her surprise, that it was for him that she was afraid, not herself.

What had she done to his world?

To start his next on-shift, Big G was ordered to another Harvey call. He rode the Flow, his thoughts still on the sky, aware of, yet oblivious to, the call's familiar cords. Until he arrived. Until he saw another Smoother team outside Tapper's cube, saw the black-garbed Recyclers carrying out his body.

A gold-clad Inner, a small man with eyes as cold as scan cams, turned and locked those eyes on him. The Inner mouthed a command, and Big G knew that he was scanning Big G's ID chip. The man walked over, looking up but making Big G feel like he was looking down on him.

"Your partner's dead," the man said.

Big G blinked, still trying to make sense of the scene, aware of the Inner's eyes on him. "How?" he asked, ashamed at how normal his first words were. As if this was no big deal. As if you lost your best friend every shift.

The Inner shrugged. "He went Harvey. Notice any unusual behaviour recently?" he asked, burning Big G with those eyes.

Big G remembered Tapper huddled inside on the floor after seeing the sky. Guilt swept over him. He'd known something was wrong. Now he recognized the look he'd seen in Tapper's eyes. He should have understood. He should have been able to stop this. He should have done something. Instead, he'd done . . .

"Nothing," he whispered.

Taking that as an answer, the Inner nodded. But those eyes still burned into him. Big G just stood there, more in grief over Tapper than in fear of the Inner, a small voice whispering to him that right now grief was good, that safety lay in grief.

The Inner reached into his golds and withdrew a pictab. "Do you know what this is?" the man asked.

Big G knew what it would be before he looked down at the blue and white swirls. He took the pictab, because he knew he should, even though he wanted nothing more to do with it. He turned it over, and on the back was the remnant of dried glop. He handed it back.

"We found it in a Harvey's cube. Tapper took it."

"But do you know what it is?" the Inner repeated.

Big G looked at the Inner. "No, sir," he said, and that was true. He really didn't know what the thing called *sky* was.

The Inner stared at him, but Big G felt no fear, only an emptiness, as he thought of doing his next shift without Tapper.

"You can return to your shift now, Smoother," the Inner said finally. "You've been assigned a new partner."

Big G asked who it was, but the Inner just shrugged, so Big G stored the cords for his next call and left.

That night, he dreamed again of falling. Not down a drop tube, not as a Builder falling from the still-being-born House, but of falling through a swirling blue and white void that went on and on. He fell and fell, a blue-white, white-blue mist hiding what he fell toward. And then he knew, in the way one knows in dreams, that the House was gone as Laryn had planned, that he was falling toward nothing, that the blue-white, white-blue was all there was, and he would fall through it forever.

He woke up screaming.

When his next shift started, he turned Laryn in.

Laryn waited for him in her cube, waited well past the end of his shift, well into his sleep time when he should have been there with her. She knew then, as she lay awake staring at the ceiling so close above her in the dark. She knew it was over.

She rose, blinking as the lights came up. Taking a pictab of blue and white swirls from its hidden place, she inserted it in a device and spoke the words she wished written on its back.

"I forgive you. Remember me. Remember the sky." She paused, then added, "I love you." Placing the pictab in a mail pellet, she coded a destination and dropped it in her out-chute.

They were outside her cube now. She activated her illegal security measures, knowing that it would only slow them down.

She wondered if he was with them.

When Big G had scanned on-shift that wake time, the call was on the board at Dispatch, a red "X" beside her name. A kill mark. And his name assigned to it, his name beside hers.

But Squat was on Dispatch, so Big G had asked him to give it to another Smoother. If it'd been Marker, he wouldn't have asked. Marker would've made him do it, made him be the one.

Squat had stared at him, and Big G had wondered if his name being there wasn't a random thing, if the Inners wanted him to do it. But then Squat had nodded. Said he was sorry about Tapper. Told Big G to scan off-shift and cube down.

So that's what he'd done. Back to his cube, to walls and floor and ceiling that had once been hard and strong and sure, but now seemed so fragile, ready to be blown away by a thought.

Or by a vision.

A vision on a pictab that appeared in the tray of his in-chute. A vision of white swirls and curls and curves hung in a blue nothingness. No straight, sharp, hard lines of floors meeting walls meeting ceilings running on and on and on.

Big G took the pictab from the tray and held it in his large hands. He read her message on the back. He stared at it for several laboured breaths and then, with great and careful precision, he tore it slowly in half. Covering the face of one half with that of the other so that the image was hidden, he again tore the pieces in two. One final time he tore them.

He did not even need to move to reach the dis-chute. *So efficient a design*, he thought, *so practical and proper.* He opened the chute door gently, as if removing a garment of a lover. Letting the fragments slip from his hand into the blackness, he held the chute open for a moment, listening for the small "poof" that the pieces made as they vaporized.

He closed the chute again and for a time just stood there, running his hand over the wall, stroking it, taking comfort in its coldness, its solidity. He turned finally to his tiny sleep shelf. Lying on his back, he pressed the top of his head against the wall above his pillow, then stretched out his legs until his feet touched the opposite wall. He placed his left hand on the third wall to which the bed attached.

The humming of the block, of the entire House, sang through the skin of his hand, up his arm, into his chest. It filled his skull and echoed in his mind. This was as it should be. Here lay solace from the void, from unending blue emptiness.

He closed his eyes, and for a moment, the thing called sky hung above him once more, impossibly distant, untouchable. Shuddering, he opened his eyes to the closeness of the ceiling before him and slowly, slowly reached out a trembling right hand to feel for the last wall.

I always use my short fiction to try to stretch myself as a writer, trying out new structures, voices, forms, themes, whatever. This story was the first time I'd written from the point of view of a character who was below average in intelligence, representing not so much an individual in this society but the impact of the totalitarian society depicted here on its citizens. Yeah, the ending's a downer, but it is the only one that I think rings true. Change is scary. Choice is scary. Freedom, to those who have only known control, seems like chaos, like the swirling clouds that Big G saw in the thing called sky. And that can be scary, too.

The genesis of this story was both simple and rare: the first three lines came to me out of the blue. I say rare because my stories ideas usually come to me as an image ("The Dancer at the Red Door," "The Red Bird," "Scream Angel," "Enlightenment," "Going Harvey in the big House," "Symphony"), a character ("The Deadman," "Spirit Dance," "Going Down to Lucky Town"), or an idea ("The Boys are Back in Town," "Murphy's Law," "Jigsaw," "State of Disorder," "New Year's Eve," "Bouquet of Flowers"). The only other story I can think of that started with a set of words coming to me is "By Her Hand, She Draws You Down." Both that story and this one share another rarity: I wrote them more or less in sequence, from opening to ending, whereas I tend to write most stories out of order, often writing the last scene first. Maybe there's a connection. Or not. But both "By Her Hand . . ." and this one are among my favourite stories.

A TASTE SWEET
AND SALTY

The man known only as Stranger lived and died in a town with no name.

Each day he lived.

And each night he died.

One morning, Stranger might wake on silk sheets in a fine villa in the town. Rising, he would walk out onto a broad stone patio and look down over cobbled streets twisting between the red-clay buildings below. Out on the Medicean, ship sails billowed like clouds on an inverted sky. Ships he owned. He was rich. He was powerful.

The next morning, he might wake naked and shivering in a dark forest, his skin painted with dew etched by the tracks of insects that had explored him in the night. He had nothing. He was nothing.

Yet another morning, he would find himself before the altar of the town's only church.

Or on a ship. Or in the governor's palace.

A ditch. A general's tent. A brothel.

Sometimes rich, sometimes poor. Sometimes male, sometimes female. Old, young. Strong, weak. Sometimes known to all, and other times as he ever was to himself—a stranger.

But always, he awoke in the town that huddled under the gaze of the mountain shaped like a skull. And always, before the day had passed into the next, he had died at the hands of another.

He could not remember his life before the town. Sometimes, in that space that lay between sleep and a morning's new life, he tasted it. Not a sight or a sound or a touch.

But a taste, sweet and salty, like the memory of a lover's skin on his tongue. Then it slipped away, swallowed as this town swallowed him each night.

On this particular morning, he woke to breakfast smells—fried bacon, baked bread, espresso—as thick as the babble of voices rising through the floor. He lay alone in bed under cotton sheets and a heavy quilt, in a comfortable but not richly furnished room. Lifting the other pillow to his face, he breathed in the body scent and perfume of a woman. He ran a fat hand over his thick body and through thinning hair.

By the time he rose and walked to the mirror on the door, he knew whose image he would see, who he would be today.

He could tell that he was in the Inn of Shining Hope, and he was therefore Jasper Renaldi, the inn's proprietor. Staring at the fat old man before him, Stranger suddenly began to tremble. He slumped into a wooden chair, burying his face in his hands. How much longer must he endure this? With his dying breath each night, he prayed for it to end, for this death to be his last.

But always the next morning, he found himself cursed again with life.

Finally, he stood up. Delay or avoidance was never of use. His end would find him regardless. And living his days as if he could choose his fate was the only way he had found to feed his dying hope.

He washed with a sponge and the water from a white ceramic bowl on the dresser. After putting on heavy linen pants and a shirt woven from shrub-goat hair, dyed blue like his eyes that day, he went downstairs.

The common room of the inn was roughly square, split into quarters by two intersecting rows of support posts. Travellers and town folk crowded at the long bar or sat elbow to elbow at heavy wooden tables.

He stood unseen in the doorway for a moment, drinking in the bubbling soup of a dozen conversations. Then, with the tired air of an actor in a play that has run too long, he stepped into the room, weaving his way between tables toward the kitchen.

And it began.

A hand, callused and sun-darkened, grabbed his arm as he passed. Stranger stopped. He looked down at Thom Fallo, a farmer whose weathered face carried a line for every crop lost over his sixty years.

"You!" Thom cried.

The babble in the room died to a few orphaned whispers, and Stranger felt every eye prick him like a nettle. But Thom's eyes did more than prick; they burned, as they widened with the sudden knowledge that Stranger knew was awakening in Thom.

"You cheated me!" Thom shouted. "You told merchants from Lorinthia that my grain carried a blight. They refused to even bid, and you bought my crop for a song."

Stranger said nothing. Denial or agreement, apology or explanation—no course of action had ever deflected his daily fate. He pulled his arm free and walked on, Thom's curses striking his back like knives.

Fawn Tores, a flame-haired woman, tall and bony, stood up, blocking his path.

"You swore that you loved me. I waited for years. Turned away suitors. Now I know that you lied." Tears flowed from brown eyes where he could still see the young woman she once was. "You stole my youth. I traded a real life for empty hopes—because of you."

He stepped around her and kept walking toward the kitchen. But the epiphanies continued within the minds of those he passed.

"You spread lies about me . . ."

"You cuckolded me . . ."

"I trusted you . . ."

His face calm, his eyes fixed on the kitchen door, he reacted to each accusation flung at him as nothing more than a morning greeting. But his hands were already trembling, and inside, he was screaming.

The gauntlet of recriminations finally ended as he reached the kitchen, and the wooden door swung closed behind him. He stood there, breathing hard with sweat running down his back. A short woman in a white blouse and plain brown skirt that hung to her ankles stood at the central fire, frying a fish in a heavy skillet. Her hair was long and black, and the fire's light caught streaks of grey when she turned to look at him.

Lara. Her name is Lara, whispered Renaldi's memories. *She is my wife.*

Her face was broad but pleasant, and the age lines didn't show until she smiled at him, a smile that suddenly ran away and hid. Her eyes widened in surprise, then narrowed.

"My sister?! With my sister? That shrew!" Her face twisted into a snarl as she hurled first the contents of the skillet and then the skillet at him. He ducked both.

"How could you?" The fire of her anger died as quickly as it had flared, dampened by the tears that began to flow. She slumped to the wooden floor amidst the food scraps and spills, sobbing. "How could you?"

He stared at her, moved but helpless. No action of his could help. Without a word, he walked over to the bowls of food Lara had prepared and served himself a plate of poached turtle eggs and chopped goat steak. He would keep trying to live as if he had a normal life.

He returned to the common room with his food, preferring the many glares of townspeople to the singular intensity of Lara. He took a seat by a window.

The summer sun warmed his skin but did nothing to disperse the chill emanating from those around him. Looking out the window, he saw a young woman in a blue dress staring at him. Tired of accusing faces, he ignored her. Instead, his eyes traced the road out of town as it snaked up the mountainside.

On another morning, very much like this one, soul-tired and heart-weary, he had set out on that road, determined to escape his cycle of doom and rebirth by escaping this town. No one had tried to stop him that day as he had walked out of town past mansions that dwindled to houses that shrank to shacks. He had hiked beside meadows where scrub hares sniffed at him above the coarse scythe-grass. He had climbed through dark forests of blood cypress and devil's pine, the eyes of dread-dogs tickling the nape of his neck. With the sun drowning in the sea behind him, he'd entered the pass crowning the mountain's skull. An hour later, he had crested the mountain and emerged from the pass to look down on what lay on the other side.

Before him in the moonlight, a road had run like a silver snake down through forest and meadow, past shacks and houses and mansions, to where ships lay anchored in harbour.

The town. His prison.

Stranger had stood there in the shadow of the pass for several moments, regarding the scene. Then he had walked back. If his memory served, he'd been hung that night. He couldn't recall whose life he had lived that day or what had prompted his end.

Another time, he'd bought morning passage on a frigate sailing across the Medicean to Lorinthia. He had stood on the deck watching as the pier, then the spires of the church, and finally the skull peak behind the town shrank and sank beneath the watery horizon. Even when every direction was but a line of the sea, still he had stood watching, watching through the day, until the dying sun set fire to a scribble of approaching land.

Land marked by a mountain shaped like a skull.

The frigate had anchored. He had disembarked. Later that night, he had died as always. He had never tried to leave the town again. He could bear the daily replay of rebirth and death, but would not subject his last remnant of hope to that same fate a third time.

He took a few bites of breakfast, chewing and swallowing but barely tasting. No more verbal attacks were being hurled his way, so he chanced a quick survey of the room. Everywhere small knots of people sat huddled in intense conversation, with frequent glares in his direction.

Trying to keep his hand from shaking as he did so, he took a sip of espresso that tasted as bitter as his mood. He might not even get out of this room. It could happen here, now. He shivered. Despite the daily repetition of his death, he had become inured to neither the pain nor the fear.

To take his mind off his inevitable fate, he mulled over the accusations flung at Renaldi, comparing them to the innkeeper's own memories of the same events. As always, he found a mixture of truth and self-deceit.

Renaldi had indeed told Lorinthian merchants of a blight on Thom Fallo's crop. What Thom had omitted was that the blight had been real. Renaldi had later bought the crop, still suitable for cattle feed, giving Thom at least some income for the year. Renaldi had profited himself, but Stranger could not decide whether the man's motivation had been to protect the potential buyers or his own personal gain.

And Fawn Tores, the red-haired woman? Renaldi had once truly loved her and had told her so. But that love had died, poisoned by her jealousy and suspicions, and then he had met Lara. Fawn never accepted that she herself had driven him away, and had always believed that he would come back to her.

Lara's accusation was different. Stranger could feel the shame and guilt in Renaldi. It had been a moment of weakness, drunk after a fight with Lara, and her sister in a similar state during a separation from her husband. Although it had happened before he had married Lara, Renaldi had never told her, first afraid that she wouldn't marry him, and then afraid that he'd waited too long to tell her. So his guilt grew over the years, until his transgression loomed larger to Renaldi than it should, at least in Stranger's eyes.

He took another sip of coffee. Nothing new in today's awakenings. The town had taught him that people chose what truths they saw, and believed what they needed to. Each person had taken their new-found knowledge of Renaldi's trespasses against them and filtered it through their own self-image, using it to justify their failures, disappointments, and shattered dreams.

Many in the common room crowd began to leave, shuffling out with nothing more threatening than some muttered oaths directed his way. From scores of other days, he could sense his moment of danger passing—for now.

Scores of days. How many? He was approaching the end of his third year in the town, so it had to be over a thousand. A thousand deaths and resurrections. Today would be no different.

He finished his espresso and stood up. He toyed with going back to see Lara, but nothing he could say would change a thing now. He elected instead for a walk around town, choosing again to live his life as if he controlled his fate. Besides, he much preferred dying outside. No one stopped him as he crossed the common room, pushed open the inn's heavy wooden door, and stepped onto the street.

Mid-summer was approaching, and the warm morning breeze carried the sticky promise of the day's heat and humidity. The inn sat on the first level stretch of the main road through the town after it had climbed up from the harbour on its way to the mountain pass. He looked down to the sea. Too many people and too many smells. He turned toward the mountain, remembering a small glade nestled in trees overlooking the town and the Medicean. A good place to think and as good as any to die. He began walking.

A thousand deaths and resurrections. A thousand times asking himself when would it stop. A thousand times begging for it to stop.

His jaw tightened as he walked.

No. He had stopped begging a long time ago.

But he had never stopped asking why. In the beginning, due perhaps to the Christolic upbringing of the townspeople whose lives he briefly led each day, he had assumed that he was being punished for some heinous act in his now-forgotten former life. The Christolic faith preached stridently of sin and retribution in all its canons.

Back then, he had reasoned that if he knew what he'd done to deserve this fate, he could find an appropriate act of atonement and win his release. But his past was an unreachable land, hidden behind mountains in his memory as impassable as the strange peaks that enclosed this town.

With no hope of fitting a crime to his sentence, he had come to wonder if this was not punishment, but simply cruel fate, a game played by the gods. He had then searched each day for the precise act required by those imagined deities to end the cycle.

He trudged on. The road was climbing again, and he had passed the last of the poorer houses, mostly mere shacks, on the edge of town. The air here was heavier away from the sea, and Renaldi's fat body was sweating freely. Despite the heat, Stranger felt a chill as he considered not for the first time that perhaps there was no secret act that would end this game.

The road split a meadow and then a wood, and he began to search for the path into the trees that led to the glade. Finding it, he left the road for the welcome cool of forest shade. He walked for another half mile before bright sunshine shone ahead of him again. He stepped into the glade.

And stopped.

A young woman sat at his favourite spot, on a large boulder at the edge of the cliff. From there, Stranger liked to gaze out to the Medicean, imagining himself on a ship sailing away from the town forever. But the woman had her back to that scene and was instead staring directly at him, as if she had been expecting him.

She stood up when she saw him. Tall and shapely, with long black hair and a dress of robin-egg blue, she recalled memories from Renaldi of a younger Lara. Stranger would have called her beautiful but for the sadness in those green eyes that pierced his heart, pinning him to the spot where he stood.

Something familiar about her tickled his mind, and he searched Renaldi's memories. He felt a rare jolt of surprise when he realized the innkeeper did not recall her.

She walked toward him, and that motion seemed to release Stranger from her spell. He crossed the glade to stand in front of her.

"You don't know me, do you, Mr. Renaldi?" she asked.

Her voice was deeper and huskier than he had expected. An old memory of Renaldi's stirred but did not awaken. He shook his head, waiting for the revelation of some past sin of Renaldi to come to her.

"My name is Marie. Five years ago, I worked at the inn," she said, "for the former owner, the widow Varpon, as a scullery maid and tavern hostess. When you and your wife purchased the inn, you claimed some silverware was missing. You told the widow that I was the culprit. I was working for her as her personal maid then. She fired me and spread the tale throughout the town. No one would give me work. I had to turn to selling myself—to all the respectable businessmen who would not hire me but would bed me."

Renaldi's memory of the event finally awoke in Stranger. He stared down at her, into those eyes that seemed so familiar. "I'm sorry," he whispered, knowing it would do no good.

But she surprised him. She shook her head. "I never knew who told the widow, until this morning when I saw you in the window of the inn, and it came to me as in a dream. But I am not here to accuse you. I forgave you long ago, even if I didn't know until now who I forgave."

Again, Stranger felt surprise. He had never been forgiven.

She smiled. "You see, it was true. I *did* steal the silverware. At first, I cursed my unknown judge, but I came to accept my own role in my fate. I saw myself for the greedy, lazy thing I was."

She turned and walked to the boulder. Seating herself, she stared down at the town, his prison, spread out below them. He sat beside her. She smelled of wild candy-berries and sweat.

"I found that I had other skills. I taught myself crafts, learning more each year. I support myself now by selling my weaving and carvings. But the townspeople still treat me as a whore. They can't see me for who I truly am."

Stranger swallowed, staring at her. "Why are you telling me this?"

She looked at him, and he again felt a memory stir then slip away. "I thought that you would understand," she said, "because they can't see who you truly are either."

As he wondered what she meant, the sound of breaking branches made them both turn to the forest. Angry voices were approaching. Moments later, a crowd of townspeople, maybe thirty strong, entered and nearly filled the glade.

No. Not a crowd—a mob. Stranger knew all about mobs. They all carried sticks or poles, rocks or bricks. Things to hit with. Things to throw. He sighed and stood up. They always knew where to find him. His fate had come early today.

Father Piecrosy, the town's priest, stood at the front of the mob. He raised a bony finger and thrust it like a dagger. "There she is!" he cried.

The mob surged forward as Stranger stood stunned. Then, without thinking, he stepped in front of Marie, facing the mob.

"Stop!" he cried, raising his arms.

The crowd halted, perhaps as surprised by his action as he was.

He addressed the priest. "Father, what is this about?"

The priest scowled at him, and then pointed at Marie again, now huddling behind Stranger. "The whore stole from the church's collection box. Over fifty talons of silver she has taken."

Stranger looked back at Marie. Pale and trembling, she shook her head in denial.

"How do you know?" he asked the priest.

Father Piecrosy straightened himself. "I saw her myself sneaking from the church in the middle of the night. I found the box sundered, the silver gone." As he spoke, the priest addressed the crowd more than Stranger.

Stranger knew two things immediately, as clearly and surely as he knew he was standing there. First, the priest was lying. Piecrosy had stolen the silver himself. In a vision similar to what the townspeople must experience each day as they met Stranger, he saw the priest entering the church in the night and breaking open the box.

The first truth was obvious. Stranger had guessed it even before the vision. Living so many lives, he had grown to be an excellent judge of character.

The second truth, however, was something that he feared to believe in case it proved false—that his chance to escape his cycle of death and rebirth had finally come. For whatever reason, this mob had forgotten Renaldi's sins and was venting its rage today on Marie. Perhaps experiencing the vision of the priest meant that the curse had somehow passed from Stranger to another. Whatever the reason, he was finally free.

The muttering of the mob grew as it came alive again. Yet Stranger stood stunned and unmoving, still afraid to believe he was free. Taking his inaction as acceptance of the priest's story, the mob pushed by him to grab Marie.

She screamed as they dragged her to the cliff. Shouting her innocence, she begged them for mercy. But Piecrosy was a holy man, and Marie was an outcast. The mob would never believe her. Or Stranger.

Stranger turned, watching in horror but torn between intervening and fleeing to his sudden new freedom. Was this not what he'd prayed for each day? Freedom? But freedom to do what?

He sighed. Freedom to choose his fate.

He looked at Marie, and their eyes met. He felt her terror and again that phantom memory. And he made his choice.

"Stop!" he shouted.

The mob turned, Marie held by a pair of them at the cliff edge.

Piecrosy stepped forward, glaring. "Now what do you want?"

Stranger pointed at Marie. "The girl is innocent. Release her." He stopped, his mouth so dry he could barely swallow. Then he spoke again. "*I* stole the silver."

Silence fell. No one moved.

He felt a thrill of a new idea—that at last he had found the secret act the gods demanded to free him from his fate. That his willing self-sacrifice for another had both saved Marie and beaten the game.

But then the first stone struck him on the cheek. He fell to a knee, and a brick smashed into the side of his head. Then they were on him, striking, punching, kicking, and all the while shouting curses against Renaldi for his sins against them all, as Marie cried for him, ignored by the mob, her crime forgotten.

And he knew that nothing had changed.

Except, he thought, as they flung him from the cliff, and the waves and jagged rocks below rushed up to greet him, that he had lost his one and only chance for escape.

In that space that lay between sleep and the morning's new life, Stranger tasted it again, that memory from his forgotten life.

Not a sight or a sound or a touch.

But a taste, sweet and salty, like the memory of a lover's skin on his tongue.

Then it slipped away, replaced by the reek of wet earth and worms that choked him awake. He lay on his back with his arms folded on his chest. Birds were singing nearby. He opened his eyes. A rectangle of blue sky hung six feet above him. He sat up.

He lay in an open coffin at the bottom of an unfilled grave.

After a struggle, he managed to stand. Grabbing the sod at the edge of the grave mouth and using the open coffin lid as a step, he hauled himself out of the hole.

He brushed himself off and took stock. Today, he seemed to be well dressed, young, and fit, but he had no knowledge of his new identity. Then the events of yesterday and his short-lived freedom rushed back at him like the waves that had dashed him against the rocks. He sank to the wet grass, burying his face in his hands. What had he thrown away?

After a while, he rose. It didn't matter. The cycle would repeat forever. He might as well get this day and his next death over with. The cemetery lay about a mile outside of town. He got his bearings and headed toward town.

As he walked, it occurred to him that he had never awakened in any place suggesting of death. And what person could he be who had ended yesterday in a coffin? He pondered this for some time but could make nothing out of it, so he turned his thoughts to Marie. He assumed that she had survived but realized then with a sinking feeling that the mob could easily have turned its rage back on her after they had dealt with him.

So his sacrifice had probably been pointless. That thought extinguished his last spark of hope, and he entered the town aching for death and the brief release it brought.

Intent on a quick demise, he headed for the town square where the crowds would be thick and the accusations would come quickly. As he walked, he bumped into people he passed, trying to prompt their revelations and anger.

But no one he met showed any signs of awakening knowledge of past sins committed by whoever he was today. No one stopped him or accosted him. Indeed, all seemed determined not to notice him at all.

By the time he reached the square, he was grabbing people in the crowd and pulling them around to face him.

"Do you know me, man?" he cried in the face of a very much alive Jasper Renaldi, who had Lara at his elbow.

Both Renaldi and Lara just stared at him, and then turned away, as if the encounter had never happened. Stranger was left standing alone in the middle of the square as people moved by him, apparently oblivious to his existence.

He found her sitting on the side of the stone fountain at the end of the square, her skirt pulled up to her knees, her feet over the side, kicking in the water.

Marie.

Scarcely able to believe his eyes, he ran to her. She turned and looked up at him, staring with no sign of recognition. His heart fell. Of course, why would she know him? He wore a new body, and no one yet today had paid him any attention at all. Why would she be any different?

But then a smile broke across her face, like the sun from behind a cloud. She stood and hugged him, and he smelled again the sweet scent of wild candy-berries.

"My hero," she whispered.

"You . . . know me?" Stranger asked.

She smiled again. "How could I not?"

He didn't know how to begin to answer that, so instead he waved a hand at the crowd. "They don't notice me. It's as if I'm here, but not here."

She nodded. "Nor me." A thought seemed to come to her. "It's as I told you yesterday. They can't see who we truly are."

He looked at her. "Can you? Can you see who I truly am?"

For an answer, she took his hand, and they walked through the town.

They spent that day together, going where they chose, eating where they wished, doing as they pleased. All of the townsfolk they met would acknowledge their presence if confronted, but then appeared to immediately forget them both. After a thousand days of provoking the hatred of everyone he met, Stranger found his new anonymity unsettling at first and then exhilarating.

Evening found them again, as if by an unspoken agreement, in the glade overlooking the town and the Medicean. Lying together on the grass, they watched the sun hide in the sea and then made love while the sky blackened itself around a half-moon and a myriad of stars.

As night deepened, Marie fell asleep in his arms. But he would not let himself sleep. He removed his pocket watch and stared at it in the moonlight. Midnight was approaching. This day was dying.

But he was not.

With Marie beside him and the heavens spinning slowly above, he began to weep softly, accepting that he had truly won his release, if not his memory. He lay there awake, relishing every sight and smell and sound, until finally sometime before dawn, sleep pulled its shade over him.

They awoke to sunlight, birds singing, and a cool breeze off the sea. Hand in hand, they walked into town, wondering how they would be met today. None of their speculations prepared them for what they found.

The town still sat under the gaze of the mountain shaped like a skull. But it sat empty. No person walked any street. No other living soul could they find in any house or store or building. All was freshly swept and clean and ready for a new day, but no one was there to begin that day. Neither was there any trace of bodies. Nor of a mass exodus. Horses whinnied in the stables, wagons and buggies stood waiting, ships lay empty in the harbour.

Stranger and Marie released what animals they found, and then returned to the main square one more time. They did not speak, just stood there holding hands, listening to the silent city and its last unspoken question. Then without a word, they turned and headed up the long road out of town.

The sun was low as they entered the pass that led through the skull peak. Stranger felt a shiver of fear but this time the pass did not lead him back to the town.

Instead, a broad vista of green valleys and little villages lay before them. The road dipped down into a valley, and following it, they soon came to a crossroad. One road ran to the south, another to the north.

Stranger looked to the south and felt the pull of some forgotten familiarity. Without knowing how, he was certain that his lost past lay in that direction. Marie tugged on his arm. He turned.

"I am going this way," she said, and pointed in the other direction, along the road to the north.

He swallowed. "Marie, my past . . ." He looked back along the southern road.

She nodded. "I know." She took his hand. "Perhaps, when you have found the thing you are searching for . . ."

Leaving the rest unspoken, she kissed him hard and long on his mouth, and Stranger breathed in again her scent of wild candy-berries and sweat. Then she turned, and without another word or glance back at him, she headed off toward the north.

Watching her go, he licked his lips, tasting her.

A taste of berries and sweat.

A taste sweet and salty, like the memory of a lover's skin on his tongue.

Stranger smiled. He started to laugh. His laughter built until he finally threw back his head and roared at the heavens. Then, turning his back on the southern road, he ran to catch her.

As I've mentioned, I use my short stories to try to stretch myself as a writer and to try out new structures and approaches to storytelling that I haven't tried before, to add more tools to my writing tool box. In this one, I wanted to write a story where the main character was not the point of view character. I plan to write a novel about the Dead Man, and I wanted to first explore the character as other characters saw him. The story opens with a question, and I wanted the reader to answer that question for themselves just as Mary struggled to answer it for herself.

MEMORIES OF
THE DEAD MAN

You are done for—a living dead man—not when you stop
loving but stop hating. Hatred preserves: in it, in its chemistry,
resides the mystery of life.
—E.M. Cioran, *The New Gods*

You ask me of the Dead Man. What kind of man was he?

Good question. But not the right one.

Some call him a murderer, a cold-blooded killer—or worse. Some call him a hero. Jase and I made it through those days only by his hand in our lives, so you'd think I'd know where I stand on that one.

But even after thirty years, I'm still not sure.

I had dreams once, beyond living another day, but they'd died when I was twenty, died with my husband and daughter in the Plague. For ten years after that, I did what I had to, to feed Jase and me, to survive. That meant taking what we needed and staying in motion, one step ahead and not looking back. Not getting involved. Not trusting.

I made an exception with him, with the Dead Man. No—not that name. You call him that. They call him that. I won't. To us, to Jase and me, he was Bishop. He said his other name was John, but we just called him Bishop.

Yeah, I made an exception with Bishop. But then he was an exception to a lot of rules, even before the Merged Corporate Entity rebuilt Earth under its own rules.

It began in a shantytown, squalid and squatting on the edge of the Alberta Badlands. Began at 4 AM on a chill May night, under a moon as bright and cold and pockmarked as the chrome on the old Buick I'd just hot-wired.

Jase and I left some pissed-off locals in the dust, including Lizard, the skinny boss-man who'd proposed a business deal earlier that I hadn't wanted to consummate. They ran after us down the broken asphalt right to the crumbling ramp onto the old highway until we faded into the night. I'd trashed the alternators on the two other cars in town, so I wasn't worried about pursuit. I planned to drive all night and hide out in the hills come first light.

Jase slept in the back as the road climbed into foothills lying like rumpled sheets on the bed of night. The town fell two hours behind, and an eastern light began to wash away the holes that stars had poked in heaven's black canopy. I began to relax, humming an old lullaby I used to sing to Sally and Jase when Sally was still alive and Jase didn't think he was too old for lullabies. Some of the words even came back to me just before the Buick coughed once, twice. Then it stopped coughing and just stopped period.

It sounded like we were out of gas, but the gauge showed three-quarters of a tank. I popped the hood, as a suspicion grew along with a cold lump in my gut.

They'd rigged the gauge to move no lower than three-quarters. At least I had the two hours head start, and they had no wheels. That hope died as I looked back to the flatlands below. Two pairs of headlights bobbed along the broken highway.

It looked like they kept spare alternators.

My earlier bravado blew away with the cold night wind. I could take whatever they did to me—I'd been ready to die a long time ago—all except for Jase. He was what kept me going on. And these people wouldn't limit their retribution to me. Even if they spared Jase, what would happen to him if I were dead?

I looked around for a place to hide, but we were a good mile from any cover the still-distant hills might provide. Trying to convince myself that maybe we could make it, I checked the headlights below again. The highway started weaving about where they were as the terrain got rougher. I was just figuring we had maybe ten minutes when a black shape following the two cars turned off the highway and cut across the rocky desert, straight for us. A third car, running dark. And the lack of a road didn't seem to be slowing it down much.

Straight for us. Shit. Too late I remembered that I still had the Buick's lights on. "Why don't you just send up a fucking flare, bitch?" I swore at myself.

I ran back to the Buick. Jase was awake and sitting up in the back. He always knew somehow. "Mom?"

"Out of gas, and we got company." Yanking open the driver's door, I killed the lights as Jase jumped out. He threw my bag to me then ripped his open and began pawing through it. I pulled my gun from my belt and thumbed off the safety.

"How close?" he asked, standing again, his own gun in hand.

"Two minutes tops," I said, looking at him. Small for his eleven years, calm and sure, thin sandy hair blowing in the night wind as he scanned the terrain for a place to hide. Ready to fight. *Are you ready to die, Jase? Do you know that's what this is about? Do you blame me for this life?*

I pointed at some rocks about a hundred yards east. Jase nodded, and we ran. We were about halfway when the growl of an engine leapt over the rise behind us. I turned to see a black shadow launch itself over the ridge of the hill we'd climbed in the Buick. Airborne for a full breath, it landed far more smoothly than any car should, then immediately spun toward us.

I stopped, putting myself between the car and Jase. Jase ran for another twenty yards before he noticed. "Mom!" he cried.

"Keep going!" I yelled, but he stayed put, gun out, one eye on the car. I raised my own gun as the car swerved around me and slid sideways to stop between us. It had an oversized Caddy body but this was no Caddy. Tinted windows hid the inside.

The night held its breath. All I could hear was the dying rattle of rocks the car had kicked up and my own hard breathing, louder than the engine in this thing. Both back doors *shooshed* opened. I tensed and sighted along my gun, but no one emerged.

"Get in!" An amplified voice, metallic and cold, boomed from the car. Jase looked at me. I shook my head. The driver's door opened with another *shoosh*. A man stepped out. Dark hair, slim, six foot. Long coat covered in black chain mail, probably crysteel loops, light and strong. Grey T-shirt and faded jeans. Black, finger-less gloves, and a short heavy chain around his neck with metal balls hanging from it. Smaller metal balls decorated the chain mail and the back of the gloves.

Arms raised, he stepped away from the car. I could see a knife sheath strapped to each of his forearms. His movements seemed casual, but he kept his weight low, knees slightly bent. The gravel barely crunched when he moved. He looked from Jase to me, both our guns on him, and he grinned. "Two minutes, and your friends from your car rental will be here for payment." His voice was calm, bantering.

"Why would we trust you?" I said, aiming my gun at his chest.

He shrugged. "Me or them."

I bit my lip. I could hear other engines climbing the rise. "We could shoot you. Take your car."

He nodded. "You could try."

I sighted along my gun at him. His grin faded, and he opened his hands, still held above his head. Two shiny balls like the ones decorating his coat and gloves seemed to hover above each palm. I heard a metallic clicking. What the fuck?

"Mom!" Jase called. I could see him out of the corner of an eye, but I didn't want to take my eyes off the stranger.

"What?" I snapped.

"Mom, he's okay." The approaching cars, now much closer, almost drowned out Jase's voice. "Mom, look at me!"

I hesitated, then shot a look at my son. Jase was smiling at me, running toward the man. "It's okay, Mom. He's okay."

Back then, in the Fall that followed the Plague, before the Entity and its empire, the world consisted of those who survived and those who died. Survivors learned fast what their skills were. Me, I could fix anything on wheels. Jase, he knew people. Just knew them. Could size them up just by looking at them. Got a feeling, he would say. I'd learned to avoid people that made him nervous and to trust the ones he said were okay.

The man dropped his hands and waved us to the car. Jase scrambled into the back seat before I could yell at him to stop. Cursing but committed now to trusting the stranger, I ran to the other side and climbed in as two cars crested the rise and pulled to a stop fifty feet away from us. I squinted out the back window into their headlights.

Two men unfolded themselves from each car, all four carrying short-stock M18 rifles.

The stranger still stood beside our car. Unarmed—I thought. Pointing his arms at the men, he opened his hands. The spheres he held blurred then disappeared. A whistling shriek cut the night. The gunmen jerked as if shot, then crumpled to lie motionless. More men piled cursing from the cars. The stranger reached toward his necklace. One of the larger metal balls leapt loose from the claw that held it and into his hand.

Again he held the ball in his palm, and again it seemed to blur. I'd figured out that somehow he could launch these spheres like projectiles. But now he held only one, albeit larger, against four opponents. Thinking he needed help, I clambered out of the car, gun in hand—just as the night exploded, and I went blind then deaf. A blast of heated air punched me in the chest, and I fell. I blinked my vision back as pieces of dirt, flaming car, and body parts rained down around me.

At least I knew why he only needed one sphere the second time. C-4 with an impact fuse, I guessed. Strong hands pulled me up and into the front seat. The stranger slid behind the wheel while I checked on Jase in the back, his face lit through the back window by the flames of the destroyed cars. "Holy shit!" Jase exclaimed. "How'd you do that?"

"Telekinesis." The man put the car into gear. "Got what you need?" he asked.

"Our bags and us. That's it," I said, still shaking from the explosion. The stranger nodded as if he approved.

"What's tele . . . keesis?" Jase asked as we drove away.

He smiled. "Telekinesis. I can move things with my mind."

"Oh," Jase said.

I couldn't think of anything intelligent to add so I just stared at the road, struggling to make sense of what had happened. It took a moment for the weird lighting of the scene ahead to register. The windshield was an infrared viewer. I checked out the dashboard, which had more instruments than a small plane. I checked them again before I was certain. "Jesus Christ! This is an urban hummer." The man just smiled again.

After the Plague had initiated the first stage of the Fall of Earth, the feds privatized domestic militia and police duties to the Entity. The Entity had introduced a scaled-down version of the military hummers—looked just like a full-size car on the outside. Now I knew how the stranger had arrived ahead of the others—this thing could handle practically any terrain.

"Thanks. I mean, for back there," I said, not knowing what else to say but wanting to break the silence.

"No problem. I pulled into town as they were heading out."

"Why'd you help us?"

"I knew Lizard," he said. "Anyone he'd go after needs help. And usually deserves it. And . . ." Some inner struggle played itself out across his face. "And I had a wife and son once. If they had made it through the Fall instead of me, I'd have wanted someone to help them out."

Jase leaned over the seat. "I'm Jase. This is my mom."

"Mary," I said, holding out my hand.

He took it in a warm, strong grip and held it a little longer than he needed to, giving me a good once over while he drove. "Bishop."

I smiled, feeling no threat from his appraisal, and checked him out as well. He was lean but muscular, with a face of sharp lines and edges around a mouth out of place in all that hardness. Our eyes met, and I caught my breath. Black as old secrets, young-old like a child who has seen things a child should never see. They held me and made me want to hold him, to make those secrets, those things go away.

He looked back to the road. Released from the hold of his eyes, my breath returned, and my gaze fell to a thin chain he wore below the short necklace of metal balls. From it hung a chess piece, a black bishop. But under the traditional bishop's mitre, a skull with two ruby eyes grinned.

I stared at that death head as random figures of rumour, legend and out-right lies jostled and danced themselves into patterns and finally into realization.

"My God," I whispered. "You're the Last Dead Man."

Behind me, Jase fell silent and still. Bishop kept his eyes on the road. "I've had a lot of names, Mary."

A lot of names. A lot of stories. You've heard them. Pick just one and try to settle on it. I tried, as I sat there beside the man who was either the most cold-blooded killer to emerge from the Fall or its greatest hero. But he saved our lives, I told myself, and Jase trusted him.

"Where are we headed?" I asked, just to say something.

Bishop just shrugged. "Why? Someplace you need to be?"

Jase laughed, and I joined in. "Anywhere but here."

"You're in luck. I'm heading there myself," Bishop said.

I thought of the life that Jase and I led. I thought of the past, a husband and daughter long dead. I thought of the future and of Jase, and how this man could protect him better than anyone. And

I made a decision. "Mind if we join you?" I asked.

He looked at me, and I knew then that my life, Jase's life had just taken a new road. "You already have," Bishop said.

The Dead Man wound the hummer through the jumbled terrain as if each dry riverbed was a familiar road and every rock formation a street sign. "You ever heard of the Priests of the Night?" he asked after an hour of silence.

"Sure," I said. "Major bad news. We steer clear of them. Started out as a network of bike gangs before the Fall, I think."

He nodded. "When the Plague broke, the Entity used the Priests as militia in Alberta, a last gasp at keeping control before it all fell apart. They've grown into a small army in the prairies and upper mid-west states." He looked at me. "You run into them lately? Or heard of them around here?"

I shook my head. He looked disappointed. From inside his vest, he produced a photograph, faded and creased in a clear plastic pouch. "Calls himself 'The Pope.' Ever see him?"

I stared down at the picture. Shaved head, lots of skin piercing, and the inverted crucifix tattoo of the Priests on one cheek. Hawk-nose splitting eyes like diamonds, bright and sharp. Nasty grin wrapped around bad teeth. I shook my head. "Nope."

"You're sure?" This time his disappointment was obvious.

"Not a face I'd forget." I showed it to Jase, and he shook his head, too. "Why?"

Bishop just stared at the road ahead. "I'm looking for him," he said, stating the obvious, and I knew that asking again wouldn't prompt any more information.

We drove until sunup, then Bishop pulled into a cave he seemed to know would be there, and we slept. Well, Jase slept. Bishop and I made love, slept, made love, slept. There were no awkward discussions, no bargaining or manoeuvring. Just an unspoken agreement. And in truth, I found him attractive—and a gentle but passionate lover. It had been a long time for me, and the sincerity of my own passion soon caught up to his.

When night fell, he built a fire, and we sat around it eating canned meat cooked on that fire. I couldn't identify the animal, and I'd learned long ago that I generally didn't want to.

"So how do you move things like that?" Jase asked.

Bishop smiled. He seemed to genuinely like Jase. And me, too, but I assumed that was sexual. "Do you tell everyone you meet about that switchblade tucked in your boot?"

Jase's jaw dropped, and he pulled his jeans down to cover the knife. Bishop chuckled.

"Meaning you don't trust us?" I asked. He just shrugged.

"But why didn't you just pull the guns out of those guy's hands, instead of . . ." Jase's voice trailed off, but I knew what he was thinking. Instead of killing them.

"My power has limits, Jase. They were too far away."

I knew he wasn't telling us everything, but it didn't bother me. Survivors learned to keep their secrets to themselves. Trusting was another word for dead.

"What did you do before the Fall?" Jase asked. I cringed. You didn't ask people that—too many memories for survivors, all of them painful. To my surprise, Bishop answered him.

"Worked for the feds. Covert op called the Office."

"Were there others like you?" Jase asked.

He nodded. "Eight in all. We each had a unique . . . ability."

"And the Office called you the Dead Men?" Jase asked.

"No, Jase. That name came later. The Office used the names of chess pieces. I was the Black Bishop." He fingered the piece that hung from his necklace.

"So Bishop's not your real name, either?" I said. He just smiled.

"What did you do for the Office?" Jase asked.

The smile disappeared. He didn't answer right away. "I killed people for them, Jase. We all did."

"Oh," Jase said and looked at me. I swallowed.

Bishop stared into the flames for a long time before he spoke again. "They'd raised us from kids, as a team, trained us as an elite assassination squad. There wasn't a soul on Earth we couldn't get to. At first, we told ourselves we were patriots, that our targets deserved it, that the world was better, safer without them. At first, I think we were right. Then the targets started becoming . . . questionable." The shadows of the flickering fire, or of long buried memories, writhed across his face.

"Then on one target, we said no. We wouldn't do it. They sent another team after him. We took them out. They sent a team after *us*. We took them out, too. Then they sent Father. We called him Father. He'd brought us together. We'd served him all our lives it seemed. He stood before us that day and said 'You're dead men. Each and every one of you—you're all dead men.' I said, 'Good—*you can't kill a dead man.*'"

Bishop threw a log on the fire. "After, we took that name. Not strictly correct—three were women. And one was my wife."

We all fell silent for a while. Then Jase spoke again, his voice low, cautious. "That last target. Why'd you say no?"

"He was just a kid, Jase. Younger than you. A reprisal against his father. They weren't above killing families." Bishop stared at the fire, and I knew he saw more than flames twisting in its depths. "No, they weren't above that at all."

I thought of the wife and son he mentioned, but it would be months before I had the courage to ask that question. "What happened to Father?" Jase asked.

Bishop tossed a last log onto the fire then stood. "I killed him." He walked to where his sleeping bag lay and crawled into it, while I sat wondering what sort of man I had tied us to.

Over the following months, I came to realize that Bishop's claim of having no planned destination was only partly true. Much of the time we indeed just headed for the next known enclave, usually a remnant of a town guarding stockpiles of gas and supplies. But once there, a pattern soon emerged. He would ask anyone he could find two questions: had they news of any Priests in the area, and had they seen the man in the photograph. Any answer in the positive would prompt more questions and determine our next destination.

So our lives changed but stayed the same. A life of wandering still, but with a lover for me, a father figure for Jase, and a protector for us both. A life less lonely. And safer—most of the time.

If we remained too long in any town, Bishop would attract attention. Attention from young bucks looking to carve out a rep by taking down a legend. They would try. And they would die.

Through those incidents, I learned of his ability—and its limits. The closer he was to an object, the more easily he could affect it. It followed the inverse-square law: if he halved the distance, his control increased four-fold. Best was touching something. He said that he transferred some of his power into objects, then used that to animate them, like drawing on the potential energy stored in a battery.

Time offset distance. The longer he could work with something, the more energy he could store in it. He could control an object from across a large room if he'd been in contact with it for a while.

He'd use that as a defence. He'd walk into a place, pick up a glass or ashtray or bottle, hold it a moment, then put it down and wander across the room, repeating the process. Sometimes he'd leave one of his metal balls in some part of the room. He'd do this before he'd take a seat. He wanted objects that he controlled spread around the room, ready for his use from whatever angle he might need.

But not just any object. He couldn't transfer his energy into living matter. Even with a non-living object, the more organic material it contained or was in contact with, the less control he could exert. Metal worked the best. And the greater the mass, the greater the life force required to move it.

That was why he couldn't have taken the guns off our attackers: they were distant objects never touched by him, and in contact with another person. It also explained why he wore the balls and knives: metal, in contact with him, with stored energy from long exposure, giving him instant and total control.

So some of my questions found answers. But with Bishop, questions were like nesting boxes—I opened one only to find another inside. And each box lay in a darkness deeper than the one before, until the one that hid within all the others—the box I would not open, the question I feared to ask—dwelt in a blackness that no light could penetrate.

We'd been together for three months before I found the courage to open that last box. With Jase sleeping in the back of the hummer, Bishop and I made love outside one warm August night. After, lying under him and prairie stars, his body growing heavy on me, his breathing deepening to sleep, I asked him. Asked him of his wife and son, of the Priests, and how his hate was born.

I felt the muscles in his back tense. Then he rolled off me and reached to where his vest lay. From an inside pocket, he pulled a leather pouch, larger than the one in which he kept the photo of the Pope. He sat up and looked at me. I propped myself up on an elbow, held his stare, and waited.

Finally he spoke, his voice soft and low. "Her name was Tess. She was four years younger than me. A lot like you, tough and soft all mixed up together. Our boy's name was Daniel. He was just five when . . ." He stopped and turned away.

After a while, he spoke again. "Tess and I were surprised when they let us marry, said we could have a kid. Looking back, I figured they wanted to know what abilities our offspring would have. Tess could make you see things . . . things that weren't there." He laid the pouch down and ran his finger around and around its edges as he spoke.

"When we rebelled, the Office came after the Dead Men hard. We were easier to find together, so we split up. The rest went their way into deep cover, and Tess and I went ours with Danny.

"I figured we were safest not moving around. Too many probes and cameras in cities and checkpoints. So I bought a secluded cabin near Kananaskis. Paid cash.

"By now, the feds had given the Entity local militia powers, and they'd hired the Priests in Alberta. Finding the Dead Men was a high priority." He swallowed and picked up the pouch.

"And they found us. Or found Tess and Danny. I'd gone into town that day. Tess and I always prearranged an 'all clear' signal. That day it had been the right front window, raised partway. I came home in the evening. The window was down. The Priests were waiting for me, but I'd been warned."

He paused, jaw muscles working as I pictured him descending on the Priests like a hound of hell. "I killed every Priest there, but I was too late. Tess was . . ." He stopped. "Danny died in my arms." Bishop stroked his arm as if smoothing his son's hair. A sad smile lived briefly on lips that suddenly hardened again. "The Pope himself had left before I arrived, but he'd staged the . . . events where our security cameras would catch it all on film. Thoughtful of him—I didn't have to miss a thing. That's where I got his picture. And these souvenirs."

He tossed the pouch in front of me, where it lay untouched— the final box, a container for nightmares—until at last, like Pandora, I reached to open it.

To release the horrors within.

The pictures, arranged it seemed in perfect chronological order, depicted the progress of the bondage, rape, and torture of Tess—the progress from a beautiful frightened woman to a thing in that last picture barely recognizable as human. That last picture—the one I threw from me, that made me cry out, sent me crawling on my hands and knees trying not to puke. That thing of blood and flayed flesh, limbless, a lump that must be a head.

"They tied Danny to a chair," he said. "Made him watch." His words fell like dead leaves, lifeless and brittle, waiting to be blown away.

When I looked back to Bishop, he was carefully putting the pictures back into the pouch. "Got to be careful with these. They're the only pictures I have of my family, the only . . ." He broke down then, sobbing on the ground. My mind clawed at words that skittered away from my mouth, from the memory of that picture. Finally, I said nothing for there was nothing to say—just crawled to him and held him close to me.

"You know what really scares me, Mary?" he asked after a while as we lay there. "I'm starting to forget how Tess really looked." I held him until he slept, no doubt trying to remember how she looked, while I lay awake trying to forget.

We never spoke of it again.

But I still remember that picture.

The pattern of those first months continued unchanged, except that now I knew the demons that drove Bishop. Looking back, the taste of that time lies bittersweet in my memory. In many ways, I have never been happier. Three years we were together, an impromptu family assembled by fate and held together by necessity—and love. Yes, I came to love Bishop—even more than I had loved Jase's father. That love lay like a safe harbour within me, a place I ran to when the horror that strode the Earth like a beast in those days passed too close.

But a different beast dwelt deep within Bishop—a thing of grief and bitterness and hate that lived with him always. And sometimes I didn't know what I feared more: the horrors outside or those inside Bishop.

I was happiest when we had no goal but to reach the next huddling of humanity. Days of ignoring the world, of just being together, the three of us. But as we approached an enclave, my tension rose as if we were climbing to a precipice where mists hid what lay beyond. We'd arrive in the town, and I'd balance on the edge of that precipice while Bishop asked about the Priests. If he heard no news, then the mists and my fears would blow away, and I'd gaze down into a sunny valley of our next days together.

But if he heard of Priests nearby, then that valley became a place of eternal night where dark shapes lurked half-seen in shadows. Dangerous shapes. And one was Bishop.

He never took us to the towns with Priests. He'd leave us behind and come back for us after.

After. I just called it that. *After* he killed whatever Priests he found, and did God knows what else, for he always came back with more information on the Priests. And I don't think they volunteered it to him.

But for three years I pretended I didn't know the things he did. Then one day we were in a mountain village mapping our next destination. Winter was dropping hard and cold out of the high peaks, and a blizzard had closed the pass behind us. We'd be trapped for the winter soon. The only road still open led down the mountain—through a Priest town that Bishop had just visited.

I could see he was uncomfortable about it, but we had no choice but to drive through that town. No choice but to see, for the first time, the corpses he left on his visits. No choice but to notice they weren't only men crumpled in the streets, on steps, against walls. Staring at Jase staring at the bodies, I resolved to finally confront Bishop at the next enclave.

That turned out to be an ugly two-story building crouching in the shadow of the foothills, a refuelling spot and hostel. The lower level was one huge room with a bar to the right of the door, an open kitchen on the left, and rough-hewn wooden tables in the middle. A balcony ran around all four sides upstairs, forming the sleeping quarters. Closed in only by a flimsy railing, it provided just enough room to lay our sleeping bags.

A scrawny, greasy-haired man named Blinder ran the place. Bishop traded him guns taken from the Priests, redundant to Bishop, for gas, supplies and lodging. Blinder wore an eye patch, which I assumed was either payback or motive for his rumoured target in fights. His good eye spent a lot of time leering at me, but narrowed when Bishop mentioned the Priests. Blinder said he hadn't seen any for months. I relaxed a bit but knew that I still had to confront Bishop.

Blinder left as Bishop spread our much-used map on a table. "I don't trust him," Jase said. "He's lying about something."

"He lies by habit," Bishop said, shrugging but frowning, too. He'd learned to trust Jase's feelings. "If he *is* lying about the Priests, they could only be ahead of us, down the mountain."

Because you've already killed the ones behind us, I thought.

"We stick with normal procedure," Bishop said. "I'll check out the next town. You're still safest here." He nodded at an ancient CB rig on the bar. "Call me if you need to. Remember the code phrase." The current code was "Bishop takes Queen". If we *didn't* use the phrase, something was wrong. Jase nodded.

Now's the time, I thought. "Jase," I said quietly, "could you please get me a beer?"

"I thought you said it tasted like—"

"Jase," I interrupted. "Please." Jase shrugged, reminding me of Bishop, and left.

Bishop leaned back, his eyes locked on me. "What?"

I didn't have the courage to look in those eyes. Instead, I stared after Jase. "He was just two when his dad died. He can't remember him."

"I'm sorry."

"He was a doctor. A good man."

"I don't doubt that. What's this about?"

"He saved people." I looked at him. "You kill people."

His jaw tightened. "I've tried to protect you."

"I'm not talking about self-defence. I mean your obsession with the Priests. That last town—Jase saw that."

Bishop said nothing, just looked away.

"He worships you, Bishop."

"Mary—"

"I can't let my son worship a killer." My voice rose, and Blinder and Jase looked over. Bishop reddened and swallowed. I lowered my voice. "You have to choose: the Priests—or Jase and me. Your hate for them—or . . ." I didn't finish, didn't say "your love for us." Bishop had never said he loved us. "Jase loves you. I . . . I love you. But I can't go on like this."

Jase was coming back. Bishop carefully folded the map. "We'll talk about this when I get back."

"We may not be here," I said quietly.

Bishop stood as Jase rejoined us. "I hope you will be, Mary." He bent to kiss me. I turned away. He straightened, then walked out, not looking back.

Jase watched him leave, then glared a mute accusation at me. "I'm going to bed," he said, plopping the beer I didn't want in front of me. You couldn't hide things from Jase. And he sided with Bishop a lot lately. I felt a pang of resentment at that. Jase went upstairs as I heard the hummer drive off—both my men leaving me.

My conversation with Bishop played in my head through the night and the next morning. Then just before noon, I suddenly had other things to worry about.

Jase and I were sitting upstairs on our sleeping bags, reviewing his math lesson for the week, when he brought his head up. "What's that?" I didn't hear it right away, had to wait before I caught a low growl, like a pack of angry dogs approaching. I wasn't far wrong. The growl rose quickly to the thundering roar of motorcycles. A lot of them. We ran around the balcony to the front window.

Priests. At least forty, I figured.

"Downstairs. Out the back. Now!" I rasped under my breath.

"Our bags and—" Jase began.

"Now, Jase!" I snapped, pushing him toward the stairs. Scrambling down to the main floor, we turned to the back door.

And stopped. Blinder stood at the rear exit, pointing a shotgun at us. "Don't think so, folks. Chino's gonna wanna talk t'ya, you bein' friends of the Dead Man an' all."

Bishop had been wrong. The Priests weren't in front of us. They'd been behind us, following us down out of the mountains, following us for weeks. A special hunting pack to take down the Dead Man. Seems like the Pope was getting worried.

Flanked by two Priests, Jase and I stood in the centre of the room before their leader, a small mountain named Chino. He had a big round head, cropped black hair, and a smile that I would have called warm under other circumstances. About twenty Priests lounged around us, with ten more upstairs and the rest outside.

"So you're the Dead Shit's pussy," Chino said to me.

Snarling, Jase lunged at Chino, only to be punched hard in the side of the head by the nearest Priest. Jase fell to one knee, and the Priest grabbed him by the hair, holding him there.

"Stop it!" I snapped, turning to Chino. "What do you want?"

"What do you think? Where's the Dead Man?" Chino asked.

I hesitated. Chino shrugged and nodded to the Priest holding Jase. The man flicked open a switchblade.

"All right!" I said. "He's gone down to the next town."

"Mom!" Jase cried.

Chino smiled and looked at Blinder. "So we hide the bikes and wait till he comes back for these two." Blinder nodded, his head bobbing like a chicken.

I bit my lip. Bishop would die, walking into a trap. Then, of no further use, we'd die, too. "Bishop's not coming back," I lied. Chino spun back to me, and I swallowed. "We had a fight," I said. "All he wanted to do was fuck me. I told him we were through." Jase stared at me wide-eyed.

Chino turned to Blinder, who started shaking. "They had a fight, for sure. Didn't know he wasn't coming back," he mumbled.

Chino picked him up with one hand. "So we sit here, while he gets farther away. And you didn't think I should know that?"

"Couldn't hear," he whined, "Just knew they was fightin'."

Chino tossed Blinder to the floor then turned back to me, his broad face creased in a frown. "Now why would you tell me that? You're worth keeping around only so long as Bishop gave a shit about you. Now . . " He shrugged.

"If he didn't show, we'd be dead anyway," I said.

Chino tilted his head, as if reappraising me. "So what's the deal?"

"I can bring him back," I said quietly, "if you let us go." I could feel Jase's eyes burning me.

Chino's eyes narrowed. "How?"

"He's got a CB radio. I'll call him on Blinder's rig."

"Why would he come back, if you two are through?"

"*I* told *him* we were through. Now I'll say I changed my mind." I put a hand on one hip, trying to look like a woman that a man didn't walk away from easily. It must have worked.

"Blinder," Chino called. "Crank up that rig."

"Not so fast," I said. "Jase and I go free if I do this."

"Once we have Bishop, sure," Chino said.

I knew he was lying, but I had to play along. "Why should I believe you?"

Chino chuckled. "Cuz you got no choice. Cuz you're buying you and the kid a few extra hours. And who knows?" Looking around the room, he raised his voice. "Maybe the famous Dead Man will pull off a miracle and rescue you." That prompted hoots of derisive laughter from the Priests.

Just what I was thinking. "All right," I said. "I'll call him." Jase stared at me as if I'd just pumped a bullet into Bishop. *Jase*, I thought, *this was the only way to warn Bishop, give him time to prepare.* Time was important with Bishop.

And he was our only hope.

"Mary, is everything all right?" Coming over the battered tinny speaker of the CB set, Bishop's voice seemed a small fragile thing, and suddenly so did our hopes.

"Everything's fine," I said. "I just wanted to say I was sorry we argued. That I've changed my mind. I want you to come back to us." I hadn't used the code phrase. I bit my lip and waited. A Priest held a shotgun on Jase.

A silence followed. And grew. "Bishop?" I said.

Then Bishop spoke again. "Who's the head Priest there, Mary?"

Now the silence came from our end, as Chino's face purpled with building rage while I tried to look surprised. Chino grabbed the handset from me, shoving me aside. "The name's Chino, asshole," he snarled.

"Always glad to meet a new Priest, Chino," Bishop replied. "Kind of a hobby of mine. Here's the deal. I walk in. Mary and Jase walk out, unharmed. Me for them."

"You walk in clean. No weapons. Nothing," Chino said.

"I walk in clean. Deal?"

Chino looked like he'd just found a cockroach floating in his beer. A man like him needed to control situations. Bishop had taken over this one, and he'd done it in front of Chino's people. "Deal," Chino said, as if spitting out something he wished he hadn't put in his mouth.

"Bishop . . ." I sobbed.

His voice came soft and low from the set. "Mary, I've been ready to die since Tess and Danny were killed. Been wanting it. This way, I can save you and Jase, something I couldn't do for them. You take care. Give Jase a hug for me."

"Bishop!" I cried, while the Priests hooted behind me.

"Unharmed, Chino. You don't touch them," Bishop said.

Chino flicked the set off and turned to me. "Don't know how, but I know you tipped him." Without warning, he backhanded me across the mouth, knocking me to the floor.

"Mom!" Jase cried. The Priest drove the butt of the shotgun into Jase's belly. He doubled over and fell to his knees. I lay on the floor, head ringing, tasting blood, feeling with my tongue for broken teeth. "You said you wouldn't hurt us," I mumbled.

Chino shrugged. "I lied." He motioned to two Priests. "Strip her and strap her to a table." He grinned down at me, and Bishop's pictures of Tess suddenly seemed superimposed over this scene. Chino raised his hands to the crowd. "Party time!"

Tess's face drifted through the mist of pain and shame of that night, now looming frightened and huge before me, now tiny and distant, now multiplied a thousand times on jagged shards of some shattered cosmic mirror. And through the rape, I kept telling myself that I wouldn't die as she did, that they needed me alive until Bishop arrived.

But they made Jase watch.

Morning. Huddled on floor. They've left me finally. Blanket over me. Jase must have done that. He's beside me, arm around me. Try to move. Pain. Like a fire inside. The smell of them. The taste of them. Shame. Nearby laughter. I feel anger. No. No word for what I feel. Yes. There is.

Hate.

I had never known hate. Fear, yes, after my husband and daughter died. Anger at their dying, but that had been an unfocused, futile, impotent anger, a raging against a world gone mad, a fury with no target. It was hard to hate a plague.

But now I had a target, faces, names. Now I could hate.

Jase felt me stir and helped me rise, wrapping the blanket around me in now pointless modesty, as the Priests ate breakfast and laughed. I walked with him to the crude shower stall in the back, under the watchful eye of a Priest. In the shower, I tried to pee but I was too swollen, and when it finally came, the pain dropped me to my knees. I stared at the water spiralling to the drain, tinged with dirt and urine and blood, wishing that I could wash away last night as easily, wash me clean. Jase helped me dress, and the Priest brought us back to wait for Bishop.

Jase and I sat alone at a table, his arm around me. We didn't speak, and I realized that Jase hadn't spoken all morning. Concern for my son, for what this had done to *him*, pushed through my self-pity. "Jase," I said. He didn't respond. I put a hand on his knee. "Jase," I repeated gently.

"I'll kill them," he said in a voice I barely recognized.

"That won't change anything," I said, not believing it, wanting them dead myself. Wanting to kill them myself.

"I'll kill them," he whispered, his voice a dead thing. I pulled him to me, the victim now the comforter, the mother again.

And in that moment, in Jase's hate, in my own, I began to understand Bishop.

About noon, a cry came from a kid named Fly, younger than Jase, standing at a front window up top. "He's here!"

"Scan him!" Chino called.

Fly nodded and squinted through some sort of scope out the window. A few seconds later, he lowered the device. "He's clean. No guns, no knives."

"None of them metal balls?" Chino asked.

"He's not carryin' nothin'. Except . . ."

"Spit it out!" Chino snapped.

"He's wearing that mail coat. Black, shiny loops all over."

Blinder squinted his one eye. "Tell him to lose the coat?"

Chino snorted. "What's he going to do? Throw it at you?" That brought laughter and a chorus of comments: "Can't protect him . . . Not from all of us . . . I'm going for a head shot anyway . . . Me, too . . .

The *Dead* Man . . . The *dead* Dead Man . . ." More laughter.

Chino held up a hand. Silence fell. "Positions!" he cried, pulling Jase and me to the centre of the room. The Priests fell back to the wall facing the door and the one that held the bar. Made sense. They could shoot from two angles but not be in their own crossfire. Upstairs, more lined all four sides of the railing, aiming down at us.

Forty of them, all with guns, waiting for Bishop. Waiting to kill the man who hunted them.

"Wait till he's with 'em in the middle," Chino shouted. I hugged Jase and lied to him that we'd get out of this. "Fly, open the door," Chino snapped. Fly swung over the railing above and dropped lightly to the floor. Jerking open the door, he scampered back upstairs.

And I could see Bishop.

He walked from the hummer with a slow easy gait toward us, framed by the door, dark and lonely against an empty blue sky, dust devils stirred by a chill wind dancing around him and nipping at his heels like mongrel dogs.

His coat reached almost to the ground, its black covering glinting and glittering as the sun caught each loop of the mail. His head was bare. Our eyes met—and he grinned. God damn him, he grinned. Grinned that grin that always seemed so out of place, even more so now, like a happy face sticker on a corpse.

Time seemed to slow then, and I felt as if my heart was drumming out its final beats, in time with each step of some obscene ballet, with each step that Bishop took toward us.

Step.

He was almost at the door, still grinning, his long coat flowing around him like a black mist.

Step.

Inside, Chino backed away from Jase and me to the side wall as forty guns rose in forty hands. I held Jase tight.

Step.

Bishop came through the door to the sound of the metallic chink of his coat and the clicking of weapons. The room sucked in its breath and all I could hear was the chink, chink, chink of that coat as he walked toward us.

Step.

Bishop began to . . . *blur.* I blinked tears from my eyes but no matter how hard I blinked, the blur remained. Someone shouted. The blur got worse. Bishop seemed to expand outwards, his outline growing more and more indistinct.

Step.

He spread his arms. An opening appeared before us in the blur surrounding him—and I understood.

"Run!" I yelled, pushing Jase ahead. There in the centre of the room, the Dead Man embraced us, while around us a whirlwind rose and spun and screamed, enveloping us like a force field—a whirlwind of tiny loops of crysteel, tiny loops that moments before had covered his coat, not as a network of links but each held there—unconnected and individual—by the power of his mind.

Jase and I pressed ourselves to him. Bishop was shaking and soaked with sweat. The Priests were firing now but the whirling cloud of crysteel shielded us like an impermeable cocoon. The bullets died as bright flashes in the cloud, and the shriek of the tornado about us washed away the sound of the shots. Washed me clean. I felt powerful, invincible, immaculate.

"Hold me," he rasped in my ear. I braced myself against his weight. His body tensed and then spasmed like an orgasm. The cloud of crysteel loops, each harder than diamonds, exploded outwards from us in all directions—and through anything and anyone that got in their way.

And then it was over.

The whirlwind was gone, its shriek gone, the gunshots gone. And the Priests lay dead around us on the floor, slumped over the bar and tables, above us on the balcony, pierced and riddled. Light bulbs destroyed, a thousand pinpricks of sunlight lit the room from holes in the walls and roof—a heaven of stars shining into hell.

Bishop surveyed the room, then walked shakily to the nearest body, stooping to retrieve a handgun. Chino was dead, but some Priests still lived, twitching where they lay. Bishop started turning over bodies, and I knew he was checking for the face that haunted him, a face he wouldn't find. He stopped beside Blinder.

Blinder looked up at Bishop. Blood trickled from a wound on his forehead, and two more red blotches blossomed on his chest. "Help... me," he croaked. "Hurt... bad."

Bishop stared at the gun he held, then at the man lying at his feet. "Mary, take Jase outside," he said quietly.

I stared at his gun, too, and at Bishop. I stared at the dead and dying before me, realizing then that he had not returned just for us. Suddenly I felt as if all the dead of the Plague, of the Fall, were crawling into that room. My Sally, my husband. Tess, Danny. Every Plague victim. Every Priest ever killed by Bishop. Corpse scrambling over corpse, piling themselves higher and higher, choking the light from the room, from my life.

I realized then that still more awaited me—those that I would add to the pile if I took the same path as Bishop. A path that lay before me at that very moment.

In that moment, I chose.

My hate remained, and perhaps, like Bishop, I would never lose that hate, never forgive. But unlike him, I would choose a different path. I'd had enough of death. "Bishop," I said. "Don't. We can help them. The next town—"

"Take Jase outside, Mary," he repeated.

"Hurt... bad," Blinder cried.

"Don't do this, Bishop."

"Mom?" Jase whispered.

"Now, Mary," Bishop said.

"No, Bishop. Don't!"

Bishop shrugged. "Suit yourself." Turning to Blinder, he raised the gun.

"No!" Blinder gasped. "You gotta help me!"

"No problem," Bishop said. And shot Blinder in the head.

Jase stiffened beside me. I grabbed his arm, and we ran to the door as if we were just two more things Bishop had thrown from himself. Another gunshot sounded as that room spit us out into cold sunlight. Still pulling Jase with me, I ran past Priest bikes onto the road. I think I would have just kept running if Jase hadn't twisted free. I stumbled and fell, scraping the skin from my palms on the broken asphalt and landing hard on a knee. I stood, ready to run again. And froze.

Jase was walking back to the building, with slow stiff steps, like an animated corpse.

"Jase!" I cried.

He stopped but didn't turn. "He's doing it for us," he said, his voice a dead thing, flat and lifeless.

A chill rode my spine. "He's doing it for himself, Jase."

"No. For us. Because of what they did to you."

"He doesn't know what they did to me." *He didn't even ask me,* I thought. "He's doing it because he hates them."

"I'm going back." He started walking again.

I can remember that scene so vividly. It lives in me like a thing immortal, never changing, never fading, never dying: Jase walking away from me, that building squatting dark and ugly against a washed-out sky, the dust in my mouth, the wind cold on my face where it dried my tears. And the crack of Bishop's gun, repeated again and again and again.

But one thing I can't remember—what I called to Jase, screamed at him, cried to him before he stepped back inside. Maybe I didn't say anything at all. Maybe I just stood there, waiting. Waiting for the sound that would tell me I'd lost my son after all. The sound that finally came.

The sound of a second gun, joining with Bishop's.

Bishop and I didn't talk that night. We slept apart. In the morning, he was gone. He'd left us the hummer.

We never saw him again.

The Fall bottomed out the next year. The Entity had established some power bases, rebuilding the Earth under its rule, consolidating local warlords into itself or eliminating them. Jase and I were living in a mountain enclave when the Entity hit it. They separated us, put me on reconstruction teams, maintaining vehicles. I heard they sent Jase off-planet.

I never saw him again, either.

You asked me of the Dead Man. And I have told you.

Now, do you want to know the question you should have asked? The question I've asked myself every day since then?

Why did he walk in there that day? Was it to save us, or kill the Priests? What drove him? Love? Or hate?

Both, you say?

Yes, I suppose. But that's not the answer I wanted.

You say he's dead now. You say they finally caught him.

I don't believe you. *You can't kill a dead man.*

So if you see him, tell him . . . tell him I forgive him. For Jase. For everything. Tell him I've learned what hate is. That I finally understand him.

And tell him I still . . .

No. No, damn him. I won't say it.

Just tell him I still think of him.

PUBLICATION HISTORY

"Scream Angel" © 2003 by Douglas Smith. First published in *Low Port* (Meisha Merlin, USA).

"The Red Bird" © 2001 by Douglas Smith. First published in *On Spec* (Canada), Summer 2001.

"By Her Hand, She Draws You Down" © 2001 by Douglas Smith. First published in *The Third Alternative* (TTA Press, UK), Autumn 2001.

"New Year's Eve" © 1998 by Douglas Smith. First published in *InterZone* (UK), February 1998.

"The Boys Are Back in Town" © 2000 by Douglas Smith. First published in *Cicada* (Carus Publishing, USA), Jul/Aug 2000.

"State of Disorder" © 1999 by Douglas Smith. First published in *Amazing Stories* (USA), Winter 1999.

"Nothing" © 2010 by Douglas Smith. Original to this collection.

"Symphony" © 1999 by Douglas Smith. First published in *Prairie Fire* (Canada), February 1999.

"Out of the Light" © 2007 by Douglas Smith. First published in *Dark Wisdom* (USA), July 2007.

"Enlightenment" © 2004 by Douglas Smith. First published in *InterZone* (UK), September 2004.

AWARD HISTORY

"Scream Angel"—2004 Aurora Award Winner
"The Red Bird"—2002 Aurora Award Finalist
"By Her Hand, She Draws You Down"—2002 Aurora Award Finalist
    and *Best New Horror* selection
"New Year's Eve"—1999 Aurora Award Finalist
"State of Disorder"—2000 Aurora Award Finalist
"Symphony"—2000 Aurora Award Finalist
"Enlightenment"—2005 Aurora Award Finalist
"Jigsaw"—2005 Aurora Award Finalist
"The Dancer at the Red Door"—2008 Aurora Award Finalist
"Going Harvey in the Big House"—2006 Aurora Award Finalist

OTHER BOOKS BY DOUGLAS SMITH

Impossibilia (PS Publishing, UK)

By Her Hand, She Draws You Down: Official Movie Companion Book
(Titles on Demand, Canada)

ABOUT THE AUTHOR

Douglas Smith is an award-winning Toronto author of speculative
fiction with over a hundred fiction sales in two dozen languages,
including appearances in *InterZone, Baen's Universe, Amazing Stories,
The Mammoth Book of Best New Horror, Cicada, Postscripts, Weird
Tales, On Spec, The Third Alternative*, and anthologies from Penguin/
Roc, DAW and others. He was a John W. Campbell Award finalist for
best new writer in 2001, and has twice won Canada's Aurora Award.
This is his second collection of short fiction. His first collection,
Impossibilia (PS Publishing, UK), was published in 2008 and garnered
two more Aurora nominations. Doug recently completed his first
novel, an urban fantasy set in Ontario, incorporating shapeshifters,
covert government agencies, and Cree and Ojibwa legends. A film
based on his supernatural horror story, "By Her Hand, She Draws
You Down," is in post-production with TinyCore Pictures in the US.
Doug can be contacted via his web site, www.smithwriter.com.